SOUL SUCKER

SOUL SUCKER

A PARANORMAL ROMANCE

SOUL JUSTICE
BOOK ONE

KATE PEARCE

This book is dedicated to Dianna and Ned for letting Ella lease their basement in Tiburon, and for years of love and friendship. Thank you guys!

Paperback ISBN-13: 978-1-957727-05-9

1

ELLA WALSH CAST ONE LAST LOOK AT THE NAKED MAN SLEEPING in her bed, then frowned down at the note she was trying to write him. What the hell was the guy's name? She'd hooked up with him in one of the tourist traps down by the beach last night and brought him back to her apartment for some hot and dirty sex. The sex had been mediocre, and his name still escaped her.

She settled for writing *Hey, what's up?*—the universal Californian dude greeting—and went on to tell him that breakfast was in the refrigerator, coffee already brewed and to lock up when he left. He'd do what she told him. She'd already implanted the instructions in his mind and he wouldn't be able to deviate from them. During sex, she avoided using her empath abilities to access her hook ups' minds, but making sure they left and forgot what she looked like was essential.

She checked for her weapons and keys and headed for the door. While she fumbled in her pocket for her sunglasses, she screwed up her eyes against the blinding sunlight, barely glancing at her million-dollar view of the Golden Gate Bridge and the city of San Francisco looming in the mist across the bay.

As she headed down the driveway from her basement apartment a screen door rattled above her head and she immediately went for her weapon. She spun around to see her neighbor's eight-year-old grandson waving at her from the balcony of his house. She waved back and he beckoned her urgently. After another quick look around, she turned back.

"What's up, Tom?"

He didn't smile. "That thing? It came back last night."

"The thing under your bed?"

"Yeah. I saw more of it this time. You know in those alien movies when those creatures with the long bony fingers hug your face? It looked like that except more like long fingernails than claws."

"Your gran lets you watch those movies?"

He shrugged off the question. "What should I do?"

"Don't go under the bed."

"Ella, that's stupid. I—"

She put a finger to her lips as his voice rose. "I'm serious. The first night I get a chance, I'll come over and check it out with you."

Tom studied her for a long moment. "You really believe me, don't you?" His face reddened. "No one else does. They all think I'm a wuss."

"I believe you." She hesitated for a second. "Just keep it to yourself from now on, and we'll deal with it together."

"Okay." He took a deep breath. "As long as you let me help you catch it."

She nodded. "I'll definitely need your help. Work permitting, I'll try and come over tonight."

"Thanks, Ella."

She smiled, and then started to walk down the hill toward the oceanfront path that would take her to the Tiburon Ferry terminal. It was only a twenty-five-minute ride into San Francisco. It also gave her the necessary separation between her job and the rest of her life. Not that she had much of a life, but the older she got, the more she needed to distance herself from the craziness of dealing with Otherworld.

The thing under Tom's bed didn't worry her too much. It was unlikely to harm him, but it still needed investigating. If it was bold enough to allow itself to be seen, it might be stupid enough to try and take a bite out of the kid. And, whatever the species, bites were never good. Tom's ability to see the creature so clearly was more disturbing. He obviously had some emerging psychic talent and, as a registered empath, she was required to report in with both governments if she saw the gift in anyone else. Like she'd ever do that.

Some gift.

She inhaled the salty tang of the water and checked ahead to see that the Blue and Gold Line ferry was moored at the end of the dock. The usual line of passengers was already straggling up the gangplank, coffee, laptops and mp3 players in hand. She always preferred to stare out at the water and watch the fog crawl in under the Golden Gate Bridge.

If she reported Tom to the authorities, his life would never be the same again. He'd be taken away to a special school for the "gifted," registered as an empath, and then sent to Otherworld Academy to gain his degree. Having been taken from her parents at the age of five she knew how that went, and she'd hated every minute of it.

She wrapped her long woolen scarf more securely around her neck. It also meant that both governments knew all about you and she hated that even more.

She NODDED to a couple of regulars on the boat and took up her usual spot on the top deck. Despite it being July, it was still freezing and the wind buffeted her face. Maybe Tom's family knew he was different and they were just trying to ignore it. Not many families wanted to acknowledge that one of their own could see monsters. She remembered trying to explain to her mother about the creature that lived in her closet and being laughed at. It wasn't until she'd drawn the thing at school that the authorities had gotten involved and her childhood had ended. She didn't want to do that to Tom. At some point he'd be picked up, that much was certain, but she didn't want it on her conscience.

Decision made, she took a deep breath and slowly let it out. Eventually the restored Clock Tower and the piers like splayed fingers coming off the waterfront of the old San Francisco docks came into view. It was a pleasant way to commute to the city. Traffic now was mainly commuters and tourists as the main working docks were across the bay in the Port of Oakland.

She joined the line disembarking from the ferry at Pier 41, and walked out onto the Embarcadero, along to the main ferry building and then up Market. The offices of the Supernatural Branch of Law Enforcement, the SBLE for short, were housed in an innocuous beige and glass office block that fronted onto Market. Ella slid her passkey through the double entrance door and went into the white marble lobby. The receptionist smiled and she smiled back.

"Good morning, Peach."

"Morning, Ella. Mr. Feehan was looking for you."

"Already? I'm sure he'll find me soon enough." She bypassed the bank of elevators and descended to the lower levels regular office workers were unaware existed. As she stepped out the familiar smell of burned coffee and old carpet hit her and she drew it deep into her lungs. The main office was crowded with cubicles, and had a central area for copying stuff and an alcove where the vending machines pumped out their unpalatable, highly caloric and sometimes unrecognizable wares.

Ella threaded her way through the cubicles to the back of the building where her tiny corner office lay. The door was already open and she could see the unmistakable shape of her new boss sitting at her desk. Mr. Kenneth Feehan was about twenty years her senior but acted more like her grandfather.

"Mr. Feehan." She came through the door and stared pointedly at her chair, which her boss hurriedly vacated. "What's up?"

"I've got an emergency for you. A man was freaked out by something he saw in Golden Gate Park this morning."

"And you're sure he wasn't just smoking weed?"

He didn't crack a smile. "Absolutely sure. He says that one of the giant sunflowers started talking to him and then tried to wrap him up in his leaves and drag him underground."

"Definitely Otherworld then. Where is the guy?"

"He's at San Francisco General in a private room."

"I suppose you want me to go see him?"

"That would be helpful." His gaze swept over her faded jeans, flip flops, purple T-shirt and orange and black baseball jacket. "You do realize the department has a dress policy, don't you?"

"I'm supposed to wear a *dress*?" She widened her eyes at him. "I'll be happy to wear what the hell you like if you're willing to pay for my clothing. Have you any idea how much stuff I ruin chasing Otherworld species?"

"The department can't afford to subsidize clothing." He averted his gaze and studied the fraying beige carpet instead. That was typical of him. Too unsure of himself yet to really piss her off, but compelled to point out every perceived deviation from government code. But he wasn't her problem. He'd work out that this particular branch of the SBLE was different and settle in, or he'd apply for a transfer. It happened all the time.

"If you want me to go home and change, it'll be another couple of hours before I get to the guy in the hospital."

Feehan sighed. "Just do your job."

She met his gaze. "Sure, boss."

THE HOSPITAL WAS huge and always crowded, but Ella had learned to negotiate the hallways and banks of elevators to avoid as much notice as possible. She was well known by the staff because she was usually the first member of the SBLE team called to deal with emergencies like this before they brought in the psychiatrists. The medical profession was one of the few to acknowledge that weird shit did happen and willing to let the SBLE help out as long as they didn't have to know all the details. She nodded at the charge nurse and slipped into the white coat she kept on the back of the door in the staff locker room. For some reason it seemed to convince people she had authority.

"Hey, Jose. Where's Mr. Knight?"

"Room ten, Ella. He should be awake by now."

"Cool. I'll call if I need anyone."

Jose grinned, displaying his dimples. "Knock yourself out. He's babbling like a baby."

She walked down the hall checking the numbers and knocked on the fifth door on the right. There was no answer, so she let herself in.

A man she guessed was in his mid-twenties lay in the bed, the covers pulled up to his chin, his fingers gripping them so tightly that his knuckles blended into the white sheets. He wore the look of complete terror she was accustomed to seeing after an encounter with an Otherworld species.

"Mr. Knight? I'm Ella Walsh from the SBLE. I understand you saw something unusual in Golden Gate Park today."

"Unusual?" His voice rose on each syllable. "A fucking sunflower tried to fucking eat me!"

"So I heard." She grabbed a stool and sat beside his bed, gently wrapping her fingers around his exposed wrist. She immediately both felt his raised pulse and the distinctive buzz of Otherworld energy. "That must have freaked you out."

"Yeah, it did." He focused his gaze on her. "Are you a shrink?"

"Nope." She took a deep breath and concentrated on the stream of energy pulsing through poor Mr. Knight's body. "Think of me as more of a natural healer."

"So you're not going to tell me I'm crazy?"

She looked him right in the eye. "You're not crazy. What you saw was real. I'm going to make sure that the thing you saw is captured and sent back where it belongs."

"You're crazy too, then. Right?"

She smiled at him. "In this job, it sure helps."

His pulse steadied and for the first time he stopped shaking. "I'm not sure if you telling me what I saw was real makes it better or worse. I'm going to be scared to pull up a fucking weed in my yard or buy my girlfriend a bunch of flowers now."

She laughed and he reluctantly smiled back at her. Without fear consuming him he was quite an attractive guy. "Look, can you bear to go through what happened one more time for me?"

His faint color fled. "Do I have to?"

"It would help me pinpoint exactly where I have to go to find this…anomaly."

"Sunflower, you mean."

"Well, it uses the flower as camouflage. It's skilled at hiding in anything."

He held her gaze. "You're serious, aren't you?"

"I sure am. Now would you mind closing your eyes while you tell me what happened? It will help you visualize the scene."

It would also help her identify exactly what had attacked him and then erase it from his memory. One of her class tutors had likened using empath power on the human mind to erasing a song from a cassette tape or an image from a VCR and, even though it was old-school, she kind of liked that idea. It was also why she always told the victim the truth about what they'd seen before she erased the memories. It seemed to help them recover more quickly without leaving a lingering suspicion that they were going nuts.

Mr. Knight sighed and closed his eyes. She closed hers too and concentrated on extracting the images from his head.

"Okay, I was taking a shortcut through the park near the Japanese Tea Gardens when I thought I heard someone call my name. I had my ear buds in, so I took them out and looked around." He swallowed convulsively. "I walked toward one of the flowerbeds and something tapped me on the shoulder. I turned and there was this weird *face* staring out at me from the center of this huge fucking sunflower."

"Did you try to run away?"

"No, I just stood there like an idiot staring at this thing and then it smiled and it had hundreds of tiny pointed teeth like a shark."

She saw the image in his head and drew it into her mind. "Then what happened?"

"I tried to back off, but the thing wrapped its leaves around me and they were getting tighter and the more I struggled, the tighter they got. Then the ground started moving like there was going to be an earthquake and the soil boiled up like lava." He struggled to breathe. "And I just knew that fucking thing was going to try and drag me down there and that if it did, I'd never come up again."

"That's possible."

"So I started to struggle and bite at the leaves and the sunflower just...laughed and dropped me on the ground. It bent over me and hissed something in my face, and that's all I remember."

Ella extracted the last of the images from Mr. Knight's head and stored them carefully in her own mind. She was pretty sure she knew what had happened, but she needed to go over the impressions and make certain that she was correct. She cleared her mind and concentrated on the blank spaces in Mr. Knight's memory until he was relaxed and breathing nicely.

"Mr. Knight, when you wake up you won't remember the sunflower. What you *will* remember is that you fell over a misplaced stone in Golden Gate Park, banged your head, and now you have a concussion." She fed those images into his head like frames of film. "You're still going to be pissed off, and you'll gladly take the large sum of money the city is offering you as compensation for your injury before you sue their asses. Do you understand?"

He nodded, a beatific smile on his face. "Sue their asses. I like that. And you'll take care of that...thing?"

"Yes, I will. I promise."

He sighed. "Okay, then."

She pushed power into his mind, sealing in the new memories and eradicating all traces of the old, and he fell into a more natural sleep. Ella watched him for a while and then rose to her feet and walked quietly toward the door.

Jose looked up as she approached the nurse's station. "How's Mr. Knight doing?"

She took off her white coat. "Much better. He's going to be mad with our great city parks when he wakes up, but no longer babbling about things that aren't there. Concussion does weird things to folks doesn't it?"

"Sure does." Jose handed her a cup of hot chocolate from the vending machine. "Here you go. I know you need your sugar."

"Thanks." He was far more observant than most of his team, and that was something she needed to keep an eye on for her own security. Taking and replacing people's memories was actually quite draining and she really did need energy.

He watched her until she finished the scalding hot drink and threw the cup in the trash. "You free for dinner one night this week?"

She considered his familiar face. He was far too nice to hook

9

up with for just a night and far too dangerous to contemplate having a relationship with. She wouldn't want to lie to him about exactly what she was, and what kind of work she really did. It just wouldn't be fair. Some part of her yearned to say yes and to act like any normal, unattached woman, but it would be both pointless and cruel.

"Sorry, Jose. I wish I could."

He gave an exaggerated sigh. "You've already got a boyfriend, right?"

She laughed. "Well I wouldn't actually say that. But I'm definitely spoken for."

"Shame."

She patted his shoulder. "Much better if we stay friends. We'll always be able to look each other in the eye. I watch the soaps. You know how these workplace romances always end."

"I suppose you're right, but I'm going to keep asking."

"Sure." She winked at him and headed for the exit. "Have a good one."

She called Feehan on her cell, related her conversation with Mr. Knight and got the okay to travel on to Golden Gate Park and confront the miscreant. At the bottom of Mission she spotted one of the tourist buses heading out that way and hopped on board. She sat on the open top deck and let the stream of chatter and excitement of the other passengers wash over her as she focused on what she needed to do next.

It was easy enough to find the spot where Mr. Knight had met his unpleasant sunflower. The grass was trampled and bits of leaves floated around on the breeze. The biggest giveaway for Ella was the hint of Otherworld power she sensed still hanging in the air. She turned around in a slow circle before setting her gaze on a group of sunflowers huddled against a brick wall.

"SBLE. Show yourselves."

Nothing so much as rustled a leaf so she held up her badge.

"SBLE. I know you're there. Come out and we'll settle this right now."

She waited, one hand on her weapon, as the four young Garden Fae disentangled themselves from the plants and slowly revealed their true form. With their yellow eyes and greenish skin and hair they blended far too well with the foliage.

"Which one of you interacted with the human?"

They all just stared blankly at her. Sometimes it was uncanny how much they resembled their human counterparts during adolescence.

She snapped her fingers, letting a little of the Otherworld energy signature she'd taken from Mr. Knight bounce off the sullen Fae. "All I have to do is get close and I'll know exactly which one of you did it. Do you want me to get close?" She focused on the one with the guiltiest face. "Are you really going to let all your buddies take the blame?"

The Fae she'd targeted stepped forward. "It was me. So *makking* what?"

"You have violated the conditions of your visit to the human world. You're only allowed to visit if you don't interfere with anyone."

He shrugged his narrow shoulders. "I was just having a laugh."

"By scaring the shit out of a human?"

He grinned, showing rows of sharp teeth. "I let him live, didn't I?"

"Yeah, but the treaty between our two worlds states that you shouldn't have made yourself known to him in the first place."

"It was just a joke. Humans come to Otherworld all the time and *makk* about with us."

"Bullshit. Most humans who end up in Otherworld have been trapped there by your kind."

"The empath college is full of stupid humans."

"Exactly. Do you think any of us *liked* being stuck there?"

He glanced back at his companions as if looking for support. "You don't need to do anything about this, right?"

She studied them until they began to fidget. "The human ended up in the hospital so there is already a record of this incident in the system. Officially I should bust all your asses, but I'm in a good mood, so I'll let you off if you instantly return to Otherworld." She locked eyes with the tallest Fae. "Deal?"

One of the other Fae nudged him, then muttered something inaudible.

Ella raised her eyebrows. "You have ten seconds to make up your minds before I call in backup."

"All right, we're leaving." The Fae growled. "Humans are pathetic anyway."

"Sure, remember that. It will stand you in good stead in the future."

He stared her down as they started to dissolve into the air, his last words a hiss. "Good riddance, *soul sucker.*"

She gave him the finger and kept smiling. His foul name for her kind didn't bother her, especially when he hadn't even had the balls to say it to her face. And there was some element of truth in the tag. She did steal part of a person's essence when she took their memories, which was why most of Otherworld feared her as much as humans feared them.

With a sigh, she surveyed the now tranquil scene, making sure the young Fae had really gone. They were even more arrogant than human teenagers and far more dangerous because they had magic to add to the usual craziness. She tried to give the young ones a break. With a lifespan of centuries, they had a lot more time to grow up and learn from their mistakes.

The kinder word for what she did was *gatekeeper.* When the human government realized they couldn't stop Otherworld creatures from entering their space, they'd signed a treaty to regulate those visits, using the abilities of their empaths to seek out and police the Otherworld 'guests.'

She contemplated the trek back to her office and the paperwork that awaited her. Human computers didn't work in Otherworld, so she had to type everything up on her laptop, and then print it out to send to the authorities on the other side. Even though she hadn't taken names or officially identified the Fae, she still had to explain what had happened to Mr. Knight, and arrange for his compensation payment from the 'parks' department. The wind picked up and Ella shivered. She wasn't waiting for the bus. The department would just have to pick up the tab for a taxi.

She'd hardly cleared the park before her cell went off and Feehan's name flashed up. Why couldn't the man just let her return to the office before he bothered her again? Despite her reluctance, she took the call.

"Ella? You need to get back here asap."

"I'm already on my way, boss. What's up?" She braced herself for another so-called emergency. Feehan still hadn't worked out that in the SBLE there were emergencies and then there were *catastrophes* that could alter the course of history. She was far more interested in the latter.

"There's been a murder."

She felt her derisive smile fade. "What kind of murder?"

"Possibly an empath."

Shit. She immediately thought about her colleagues. "In San Francisco?"

"Yeah. I'll meet you in the lobby at Market and we'll take it from there."

2

"THE POLICE RECEIVED A DISTURBANCE CALL AT TEN THIS
morning from the neighbors, and went to the apartment to
check it out." Ella nodded as Feehan joined her in the unmarked
SBLE car and filled her in on the details. "After trying the polite
knock-knock route, and failure to locate the building super,
they broke down the door and found the victim lying on her
couch. Luckily, one of the more sensitive cops noticed the bad
psychic atmosphere and also called us."

"She was already dead?"

"Yeah. Music loud enough to shake the whole building,
clothes everywhere, and bottles of alcohol littering the carpet."

Ella nodded, her throat tight as they pulled up outside the
new high-rise apartment block just off one of the entrances to
the Bay Bridge. It must have been a quiet day in the city because
the police and a paramedic crew were already there. Lights
flashing, crime scene tape fluttering in the breeze and several
personnel filling the sidewalk. Feehan opened his window and
they were waved through to park beside the waiting ambulance.
She stared up at the glass building. Something from Otherworld

had been near or in the space; she could sense the dark magic in her bones.

Feehan bumped into her and she jumped. "You okay?"

"I'm good," she managed. "Are we going up?"

"Yes, I've already cleared it with the necessary authorities."

She rode the elevator up to the eleventh floor in silence while Feehan yakked into his cell phone. She didn't like elevators and she didn't like the vibe she was getting at all. There was a sense of immense psychic power laced with a triumphant glee that made her want to puke. Whatever had murdered the woman wasn't quite human. She wasn't surprised that someone had picked up on it and called for help. Despite the government officially failing to recognize the SBLE, most first responders were more than willing to pass the difficult cases over to them.

As usual, the crime scene was busy. Ella stood back and viewed the setting as objectively as she could. The victim was sprawled naked on the couch, arms thrown out, her expression fixed in a grimace that could have been either horror or extreme pleasure. Or both.

One of the cops started talking to Feehan. Apparently, there were no obvious wounds on the body apart from a little blood coming from the woman's ears, nose and mouth. She'd been drinking, and there were no signs of an intruder.

The older female cop lowered her voice. "I'm the one who called you guys." She shivered. "I just got a real bad feeling about this. I've learned to listen to my gut."

Feehan nodded. "Thanks. We appreciate it."

Ella guessed the victim was in her mid-twenties, and tried to think if she recognized her. There weren't that many empaths in the Bay Area, but the face wasn't familiar. She took a hesitant step forward, and shuddered as the residue of the killer's pleasure swept over her.

Feehan appeared beside her again. "We need you to read her

before it's too late. I'm going to get them to clear out and give you some space, okay?"

She nodded. She hated this part of her job. Her kind spent a huge amount of time and energy building shields to protect themselves from the psychic shit they accumulated. Probing another empath's mind, even that of a dead empath, was like trying to pry open a spoiled clam and usually gave her the empath equivalent of food poisoning.

When the noise died down, she picked her way through the debris and knelt beside the brown leather couch. She took her time studying the dead woman's face, carefully opening her senses to anything that still hung around polluting the atmosphere. The victim definitely was an empath. *Shit.* Whatever had killed her had a very distinctive signature, which was both good and bad. It made the murderer easier to track, but indicated a level of power that didn't care about shielding itself. Ella took hold of the victim's cold hand and centered herself on the rapidly disappearing internal psychic signature. Whoever this female was, she hadn't bothered keeping her shields up to the high standards demanded by the SBLE. Despite feeling like she was crawling through barbed wire, Ella was able to get into her mind rather easily.

Rather too easily. There was nothing there, nothing but a confused mass of fear and joy, and—what was that—relief? Was that the only overriding emotion left? And did that mean the empath had been glad to die by the end?

Shaking her head, she sat back on her heels and tried again. She concentrated harder this time, opening herself wider, but now all she sensed were her own signals bouncing back at her like radar.

"Did you get anything?" Feehan crouched down beside her.

Ella released the dead woman's hand and turned to stare at her perspiring boss. "Not really."

His shoulders slumped. "No last image of the killer, no sense that the victim could identify the murderer?"

"It's way worse than that. It's as though all her memories and abilities were sucked out of her head."

Feehan went still. "Seriously?"

Ella rose and glanced at the police officers filling the doorway. "Can we talk about it back at the office? I don't want these guys hearing anything they shouldn't. They already think I'm one of those nutty TV psychics who makes shit up, and they barely tolerate me being here."

"Sure. As long as there's nothing else you need to see."

She kept moving. "They'll send everything over to us, right? We can gather the team together and talk about it then."

Didn't he know that she needed to get out of there? Sometimes she wondered who thought it a good idea to have empaths answering to government employees who didn't understand the immense pressure such encounters put on their staff. When it came down to it, empaths scared the crap out of humans. She saw it every time Feehan looked at her.

Without another word, she pushed through the group of cops and headed for the elevators. The thought of being trapped with Feehan or any other normal human even for two minutes in a tin box made her veer toward the emergency stairs.

"I'll see you by the car," she shouted, opening the heavy fire door and then starting down the brightly lit but barren concrete staircase. Her flip-flops smacked against the steps and echoed in the stairwell. About halfway down, she came to a stop. The murderer had used the stairs. She could smell him, and his triumph. So he hadn't magically shifted in or out of the apartment, which meant it was unlikely he was Fae.

She deliberately opened her senses to his distinctive signature, and shuddered as she met his meticulously constructed mental barriers. He wanted her to see his pleasure at the murder, but nothing more. And the killer was male. She was now sure of that. After checking her own mental shields, she continued down the stairs and out through the lobby into the parking lot.

Feehan waited for her by the car, his expression anxious. The roar of traffic from the Bay Bridge above almost drowned out the police sirens, but not quite. Dirt shimmered and danced on the metal roofs of the vehicles making everything seem out of focus.

"I think the murderer is an Otherworld male and he entered and exited the building using the stairs," she said quietly. "I sensed him there." She scanned the parking lot. "So it's possible he either drove himself here, or used an Otherworld portal."

Feehan nodded. "I'll go tell the police to check out the vehicles in the parking lot, and that we're pretty sure we're looking for a male killer." He hesitated. "They're not convinced it was a murder, by the way."

"Um, what woman commits suicide *naked*? When I go, I'm wearing my best fancy underwear and full makeup."

Feehan stuttered something incoherent.

"They just don't want to be bothered because they hate the paperwork as much as we do." Ella fished out her cell phone. "I'll check the Otherworld app for current portal locations."

Like most things that belonged to that screwed up place, the entrance and exits to Otherworld moved around seemingly on a whim. It had taken years to persuade the Otherworld government to share the latest locations with their human counterparts, and even longer for the Fae nerds to come up with an application that worked with human technology.

She clicked on the app and waited for her phone to recognize where she was. Two red circles flashed on the map, one close to the Bay Bridge and the other by the ballpark at the end of Embarcadero. If the murderer had come from Otherworld, he'd had an easy journey back. And if he was a baseball fan and had chosen the portal farther away, the crowds streaming out of the park would have provided a perfect screen for his murderous activities.

Feehan had left the engine running, so she got in the air-conditioned car and briefly closed her eyes. She'd kill for a soda or something smothered in chocolate. Lately, it seemed to take longer and longer for her to recover from an encounter with Otherworld. But she was about to turn twenty-seven, and everyone knew that was about the limit of an empath's ability to remain sane and do their job properly. It was also probably why Feehan was handling her with kid gloves.

A rush of movement outside the car caught her attention, and she watched as the body was brought out and loaded into the ambulance. They'd eventually take it to the morgue under the SBLE offices, and get as much information as possible to help the team detect the killer. Ella tried to think about the woman and whether she'd seen her before, but she couldn't recall a single memory. Perhaps her mind was so full of psychic shit that her real memories were being erased… She opened her eyes. That was *not* going to happen. She was going to get through this without going nuts or following stupid government procedure.

"You ready to head back, Ella?"

"Sure, boss."

Feehan got into the car beside her. He waited for the ambulance to pull out ahead of them, and then followed along behind, acknowledging the offhand waves of the police officers still gathered around the entrance to the building. She didn't bother. If Feehan thought the way to get promoted was through developing a good relationship with the San Francisco police department, he'd soon learn the error of his ways.

Feehan glanced at her again. "Are you sure you're okay?"

"I'm just thirsty." She opened her eyes wide at him. "What's up? Are you worried I'm losing it?"

To his credit he didn't back down. "You are almost twenty-seven. I understand that can be a difficult time for an empath." He clicked on his turn signal, turned under the Bay Bridge and they were swallowed in the roaring tunnel-like darkness. "Have you received your notification letter from Otherworld yet?"

"No, I haven't."

"Well, it is one solution to your…issues."

"My *issues*?" She glared at him. "A stupid one. I think I'd rather go nuts."

"I doubt that."

"And what would you know about it, boss?"

They emerged from under the bridge into glaring sun and the usual stationary traffic. "Quite a lot, actually," Feehan replied. "My mom was an empath. She died in a home for the mentally unstable at thirty."

Ella swallowed hard. "I'm sorry. That must've been tough for you."

"Tougher for her. She died when I was four." He waited for the secure gate to rise at the SBLE underground parking lot. "It was just before the two governments instigated the new mating policies to keep empaths alive and functioning." He parked and turned off the engine. "So you can see why I'm particularly keen for you to survive. Your work for the SBLE is exceptional, and as a department, we would hate to lose your gifts."

"Is that supposed to make me feel special or something?" She took off her seatbelt and scrambled out of the car. "You can't force me to do anything I don't want to." Gee, now she sounded like a petulant five-year-old. Maybe she should stamp her foot and pout.

Feehan followed suit and stood staring at her. "That's true, but as your superior, I can only offer you the benefit of my advice."

"Well, thanks, I sure appreciate your input." She pushed open the door into the main building and enjoyed the rush of cold air. "Now, shall we focus on catching this killer?"

AN HOUR LATER, fortified by three jelly donuts and two cans of lemonade, Ella sat in the largest of the three conference rooms awaiting her colleagues. She'd taken off her jacket and was busy trying to scrape jelly off her purple kitty T-shirt.

"Hey, Ella." Liz Goddard took the seat next to her and wrinkled her nose. "What the hell is that on your shirt, blood?"

"Nope, just the internal gushings of a donut. I somehow missed my mouth."

Liz shuddered and smoothed out the perfect pleats in her off-white pantsuit. She always looked immaculate. Ella had suffered severe clothes-envy until she'd realized that Liz was part Fae and able to create her own glamor.

"How's Doug?" Ella asked.

"He's good," Liz said, her smile brightening. "He's got a new contract with the government to work on the Fae/Human database, so he's the happiest nerd on the planet."

"Cool. So you'll be able to stay in the city, then?"

"Yeah, which is awesome." She nudged Ella in the ribs. "I need to return the favor and introduce you to some hot dude."

"I don't want a hot dude. I want a nerd like Doug."

"No, you don't. He'd drive you batshit." Liz grinned. "He drives *me* batshit, but somehow that's okay."

"That's because you are a better, kinder person than I will ever be."

"No, it's because when he gets really annoying, I can cast a spell and shut him up."

"I wish I could do that."

Liz gave her a skeptical look. "You can wipe their minds. That's way cooler."

Her smile died. "Not really. Who wants to be the girl no one ever remembers?"

"Ella, are you okay?" Liz reached out and touched her arm.

As Ella opened her mouth to inquire why everyone kept asking her that, Feehan came into the room with the two other guys who made up the SBLE special response team. Ella nodded at Rich and Andrew, and then turned her attention to her boss, who looked almost as tired as she did.

He walked over to the board and stuck up a picture of the apartment building, a shot of the couch with the victim on it, and an enlarged copy of the woman's driving license.

"Okay, you have all the basics here. We have a deceased twenty-seven-year-old female. She was a registered empath named Christa Louise Morehouse. Last known address, according to her driver's license, Humboldt State University."

The name was vaguely familiar even if the face wasn't.

"Then what was she doing in the city?" Liz asked.

"That is unknown at present."

"Do the police think she was living with someone?"

"Apparently not. The apartment was leased in her name."

Liz got to her feet and started pacing. As she walked, a thin stream of silver like a spider's web followed along behind her. The Fae-Web already contained a mesh of words and images connected to the case. Being part Fae, Liz had the ability to perceive problems in different dimensions and was adept at seeing connections that would evade most human investigators.

"What else do we have?" Liz demanded.

"The police are following up with Humboldt State and interviewing her neighbors, so we'll get that information within the next day or two," Feehan said. "I'm surprised you don't remember her, Ella. She was in your class at the Otherworld Academy."

"She was? I vaguely remember the name, but nothing else."

Feehan nodded. "Perhaps it will come back to you."

"I hope so."

"Anything else, Mr. Feehan?" Liz asked.

"Nothing except Ella's take on the victim at the scene." Feehan looked at her. "Do you want to share?"

Ella put her elbows on the table. "It was weird. Most empaths have really strong shields, but hers were paper-thin. I had hardly any problem getting into her head, and when I did, there was almost nothing there."

"What do you mean?" Liz swung around, her expression intent.

"It was as if whatever killed her had ripped out every memory she possessed, both her psychic memories and her personal ones." She shivered. "There was nothing left, apart from a few echoes of her last thoughts."

"And what were those?" Feehan asked.

"Mainly relief."

"The victim was twenty-seven, right?"

Feehan shared a glance with Liz, and Ella stiffened. "So?"

Feehan hesitated. "Is it possible that she did this to herself to avoid going mad?"

Everyone turned to stare at Ella. "Sucked out her own brain? I don't think that's possible."

"The police did say there was no sign of a struggle," Liz murmured as her silver web shimmered with possibilities, none of which Ella liked.

"No. Someone must have done it for her."

"Could she have asked someone?"

"Another empath?" Ella looked down at the table. "I don't think so. We retain all the shit we take in. Taking on another empath's entire psychic burden would probably kill the recipient as well."

"And there was only one victim."

"And it felt like Otherworld," Ella insisted. "I sensed dark magic."

"Fae or shapeshifter or Other?" Feehan asked. "Not Fae or shifter. Definitely Other."

Liz grinned. "Well at least that excludes all of my Fae kin, and Rich and Andrew's shapeshifter families. But then again, 'Other' is fricking scary." She switched her attention back to Feehan. "Didn't you say there was another case like this recently?"

"Not to me, he didn't," Ella said sweetly to Liz.

Feehan avoided Ella's gaze. "I found it when I put the new case details into the database earlier. It flagged another file, and I pulled it." He passed around some paperwork. "I've also emailed you the files, so check them out tonight."

Ella read quickly and frowned. "How come no one at SFPD notified us about this one?"

Feehan shrugged. "Different area of the city, different team. They decided this victim committed suicide."

"It does sound similar," Liz added, as her silver web lit up again and seemed to grow to twice its size. "I wonder whether our killer has developed a habit of doing this? I'll check our international database as well."

"Oh great," Ella groaned. "A potential Otherworld serial killer."

Feehan took the chair next to Ella, his expression sympathetic, and she leaned as far away from him as she could. "Do you feel up to handling this, Ella, or would you like me to draft another empath in? Sam needs more experience."

"Especially if I lose it in the next three months. I don't think he's ready to handle this alone yet. He's just out of college and he's only twenty-one."

"Well, maybe he could act as your assistant."

"Sure, whatever you want. We all have to learn."

It was a pity Sam Nadal already thought he knew everything.

But every empath was cocky when they graduated from the Otherworld college system. It took a few months of working in the field to realize book learning taught you nothing.

Feehan rubbed his hands together. "Great! I'll tell him to talk to you tomorrow."

"I can't wait." Ella smiled and Liz stifled a snort.

"Now, do we have anything else to discuss, or can we call it a day?"

3

"Vadim? There's something showing up on my web that might interest you."

Vadim Morosov turned from his glum contemplation of the Moscow skyline to see Alexei, one of the members of his team—no, strike that—his *former* team standing in the doorway of his darkened office. It was way past clocking-off time, but he'd been putting in some extra hours in a vain attempt to convince his boss that he was sincere and trustworthy.

Not that it was going to work. She was still pissed with him, and worse, he knew he deserved it.

"I don't think you're supposed to be interacting with me, Alexei."

The Fae's already arched eyebrows rose even further. "Says who?"

"Our esteemed boss."

Alexei shrugged. "Oh, her."

"Yeah, the woman who can suspend you just like she did me."

"She can't afford to lose me. I'm too valuable."

"And I'm not?" Vadim asked.

For a second the Fae looked almost serious. "*Makk*, you know I didn't mean it like that. She's just crazy mad at you."

Vadim sat back in his chair. "And rightly so. I killed one of my team members."

Alexei leaned back against the door and folded his arms. "Well, that is debatable. Natasha wasn't exactly the dependable type, was she?"

"She was completely dependable right up until she went nuts and screwed us all over." Vadim shoved a hand through his dark hair. "And until that mess is cleared up, I'm stuck here doing quality control on past cases."

"Not anymore." Alexei smiled.

Vadim stiffened. "What's going on?"

Alexei came in and shut the door. He activated his Fae-Web and Vadim tried to read its shifting images and words.

"There's been a new outbreak of murders."

"What kind?"

Silver images floated across Alexei's skin, circling his head. "Your kind. Serial killer murders."

"Where?" An all-too-familiar mixture of dread and excitement settled in his gut.

"In San Francisco."

Vadim sighed. "*Damn.* She'll never let me go."

"*She* might not have a choice. This is big, Vadim, and you might be the only guy who can help them catch this killer."

ELLA PAID the cashier at the one and only supermarket in Tiburon and then picked up her bag, ready for the walk back to her apartment. On her side of the bay, the sea was shining and lapping gently against the rock-strewn shore. On the other side, the city was barely visible through the encroaching fog and haze of congestion; only the stark parallel lines of the steep streets stood out like a giant tic-tac-toe puzzle.

She nodded friendly greetings to the dozens of joggers and bicyclists who relentlessly made their way up and down the sea path. About five minutes from home, when the path took a definite upward swing, she started to puff. At her age she could do with the exercise, but she'd never been that inspired to actually join a gym or anything proactive. Her crazy lifestyle kept her moving. She glanced up at Tom's house as she passed and saw that the lights were on in the kitchen. Despite her stressful day and the bad feeling the murder had left in her gut, at least she'd be able to keep her promise and go over to help him sort out his little problem.

She dumped her shopping and keys on the countertop and took off her jacket. There was no sign of the guy from last night. He'd even cleaned up after himself and made the bed, which made her very happy.

The bucket of still-warm fried chicken she'd bought at the supermarket called out to her. Did the thing under the bed next door really need it all? Surely she deserved a wing or two. She took a plate from the cabinet over the sink, added a beer from the refrigerator and sat at the granite countertop to eat.

While she ate, she tried to picture Christa Morehouse and place her at the Otherworld Academy. She had a faint recollection of a shy girl who'd spent most of her time hiding behind her long curtain of mousey hair and talking in monosyllables. Even after spending three years with her, Ella couldn't remember what subjects the other woman had excelled in or form any strong opinion about her at all. Christa hadn't been a drinker, or hung out after class, because Ella would have remembered her. So what had changed? Why had the empath ended up drunk and alone in a new apartment with all her memories sucked out?

By the time she'd finished her chicken, the light was beginning to fade, so she headed for the shower and a change of clothes. She knew Dianna, Tom's gran, would be delighted if she stopped by to spend the evening playing video games with her boisterous grandson. In her backpack along with her usual stuff, she put the latest in grandma-approved Pokémon games, and one that was first-person shooter and aimed at teens. That one was definitely not approved, but much more fun, especially for keeping her shooting skills sharp.

She locked up and took the shortcut over the fence to the back of Tom's house. She could see Tom and Dianna sitting at the kitchen table, so she tapped lightly on the glass paneled door. When Dianna looked up, Ella waved.

"Hey guys, what's up?" Ella came in and took a seat opposite Tom. She tossed the video game out on the table. "I've come to extract revenge from your grandson." She stared at Tom. "Are you up for it?"

Dianna laughed and hugged her grandson. "She looks like she means business."

Ella patted Tom on the back. "Come on, buddy. I hope your bedroom's clean enough to receive visitors."

"It's okay," Tom said as he shoved his chair away from the table. "Gran makes me clean up way too much."

"I'll bring you up some snacks later," Dianna called.

Ella paused to look back at her. "I brought some chicken. I hope that's okay?"

"Sure, that boy will eat anything." Dianna chuckled. "I'll bring some iced tea up then."

"That would be awesome."

Ella followed Tom up the stairs to his second floor bedroom, which had been converted out of two small attics. Exposed beams painted a soft cream crossed the ceiling and the triangular-shaped windows faced out over the bay and back at the steep hillside behind the house. When she was a kid, Ella would have died for a room like this. She'd had to share a room with three other kids at school where she'd been dumped, kicking and screaming, at the age of five. She'd been allowed to *personalize* her space, but it wasn't the same.

While Tom set up the video game, she glanced around the room. The bed was against the interior wall and faced the door. The windows were on either side along with a double fitted closet. She gauged the distance between the bed and the various escape routes and considered where best to bait her trap.

"Tom, can you think of anything you do that makes the thing under the bed appear?"

"I don't do anything." He hunched a defensive shoulder and refused to look at her.

"I meant is there a particular time when the thing turns up?"

"When I get into bed."

"Have you usually turned the lights out at that point?"

"I used to, but not anymore."

She hated the vulnerability in his voice and understood it far too well. "So it doesn't wait for it to be dark, then."

"Not anymore."

She hunkered down beside him on the rug. "We'll play some games, wait until your gran checks in on you, and then we'll set a trap, okay?"

He finally turned to look at her, his expression intent. "Do you really think we're going to catch it?"

"Sure I do." She hesitated. "Don't tell anyone, but it's my job to catch stuff like this. That's why I was glad when you told me what was going on, because I knew I could help."

"Your job?"

She had his full attention now and she really didn't want it. "Yeah, I can see the monsters. Because I know where they come from, I can send them back. It's a secret, right? You can't tell anyone, not even your family." If it came down to it, she could wipe the memory from him quite easily, but, considering what he might be, that wouldn't be her first choice. If he was an empath, he needed to understand his world and start to protect himself from it. She would help him build his shields without him even realizing it, because if her suspicions were correct, this wouldn't be the last monster the kid saw.

"Okay." Tom nodded. "Let's play."

"MR. MOROSOV. Come in and shut the door."

Vadim walked into Madame Dubinsky's office and took the seat she indicated without a word. As usual, his boss looked impeccable, her dark hair drawn back into a neat ponytail, her tailored blue suit and brooch reminding him of uptight royalty the world over. She didn't smile but he'd hardly expected her to. He was in deep shit and he knew it.

Her office was so heavily warded against magical interference that it always felt as if he was being smothered. He appreciated the fact that nothing could get in—he had family who just loved to interfere with his life—but it made it hard to focus. Although that was probably intentional too.

Madame studied her folded hands for a long moment before finally looking up at him. "We have a situation that requires international cooperation of the highest order."

Vadim still didn't speak but he allowed himself to look faintly interested.

"*Your* cooperation as it happens."

"But I'm suspended."

"I know that, but I've been ordered to send you on this mission. Apparently no one else will do."

The dryness of her tone indicated her skepticism as to that, but he didn't care. "Exactly what is the mission?"

"The U.S. SBLE authorities have contacted us about a situation in the San Francisco Bay Area. They believe they have an *Otherworld* serial killer who is targeting empaths."

Govno. "I hope not."

"Apparently, when the SBLE in San Francisco were researching their supposed killer, they came across some similar traits to the last series of cases you worked on with Natasha. Alexei picked up the connections as well, and reported them to me."

The mention of Natasha surely wasn't a good sign. Due to the worldwide shortage of empaths, anyone who was involved in the death of an empath was viewed with extreme suspicion, whatever side of the law they were supposed to be on.

Madame looked him right in the eye. "They want you, and despite my reservations, I have been ordered to send you to aid their investigation. You will not fuck this up. You will represent your country and me, and do a good job or die trying. Do you understand me?"

"Yes, Madame." He inclined his head a respectful inch. "When do you want me to leave?"

"Tomorrow morning and take Alexei with you. His knowledge should help add to the overall picture."

He wanted to ask why the SBLE team in San Francisco didn't have Fae resources, but decided against it. Alexei was a pain in the ass, but at least he was company, and Vadim knew enough about the Fae not to trust his companion. Alexei would be reporting back to Madame about Vadim's conduct—he'd bet his life on that. Madame passed a folder of papers across to him. "Read the intel and destroy the file. Alexei has already integrated the information into his Fae-Web, so you'll have that to work with when you get there, in case you forget anything."

Vadim stood up. "I won't forget."

She fixed him with her cool stare and the feeling of suffocation intensified. Her shields were so good that he had no idea what powers Madame did or didn't have, but she scared the shit out of him anyway. He wanted to get out of that room more than he wanted to breathe.

"I expect regular reports on your progress, and if you put a foot wrong, or I hear any complaints about you, I'm bringing you back here and firing you. Is that clear?"

"Yes, Madame."

"Then I wish you a successful trip."

He managed to smile and stroll casually toward the door as all his instincts screamed at him to run. Something about Madame set all his shapeshifter genes on alert. She was a dangerous woman to cross, and would live up to her promise to fire him if he fucked up again. And then what would he do with himself? Crawl back to Otherworld? He shook his head. It had taken him years to escape from his family, and many scars, not all of them visible. Even if he had to work with an empath again, he'd do it. He reached his office and started gathering up his stuff, a pulse of excitement beating in his heart. He'd rather die than go back. That sounded overdramatic but, in the present circumstances, it might just happen anyway.

BY THE TIME it was completely dark, Tom was yawning and Ella turned off most of the lights, leaving the room bathed in the glow from the TV screen and a nightlight that illuminated the door. She put her backpack on the bed, and pulled out the remains of the bucket of chicken and various other things, the most important of them being her gun.

Tom's fingers headed straight for her weapon and Ella smacked them away. "Don't touch that. It's loaded."

"I knew you were going to say that, but I had to try."

"Look, if you want to help me, you have to do what I say. No independent thinking allowed here."

"You sound like my teacher at school."

She sat cross-legged on the bed with him so that she had his full attention. "We want to coax the creature out, so we're going

34

to use the chicken as bait. If it is what I think it is, it loves eating chicken almost as much as small children."

"You're kidding, right?"

"Not really." Ella gazed down at her open-mouthed helper. "In the old days this creature often took small children and babies because they were easy prey. Nowadays, because food is so plentiful here, they tend to go for the easy option, which is take-out from the trash bins."

"Oh, like the seagulls and the pigeons in the park."

"Exactly." Ella placed the chicken on the floor beneath the bed. "So, you're going to lie down and pretend you've fallen asleep."

"And what are you going to do?"

"I'm going to hide under the bed behind the chicken."

"Are you kidding me?"

"No. If it looks like it is getting away from me, I want you to smack it on the head with something heavy."

"Like my baseball bat?" Tom scrambled off the bed and returned with the sturdy bat in his hand.

"That's perfect. You can hide it under your covers. But remember, only hit the thing, and not me, okay?"

"Okay." Tom settled himself back beside her on the bed. "What if I kill it?"

"They have very hard heads, so that's unlikely, but if the creature hasn't listened to my warnings it deserves anything you can throw at it." She patted Tom's scabbed knee. "Are you ready, then?"

"I suppose so."

She smiled at him encouragingly. "It will be fine. These things aren't very brave really, that's why they pick weaker prey."

"Then why do they want me?"

She hesitated. He didn't really need to know that it was probably his emerging empath powers that made him irresistible to Otherworld creatures. She settled on a lesser version of the truth. "You bring a lot of food up here, don't you? Once the thing has gotten used to an easy source of food, he'll stick around."

Tom shivered. "I won't do it anymore."

"After tonight, you won't have to worry about that. You'll be able to eat whatever you like, whenever you like." She gave him a quick hug. "Now you settle down for the night, and I'll turn off the TV and then get under the bed."

While Tom stretched out, she settled herself under the bed and positioned the bucket of chicken temptingly in front of her. Outside, the trees rustled and sighed to the hypnotic rhythm of the ocean breeze. She waited for the first telltale hint of magic to reach her and gripped her gun and flashlight more tightly. A rustling sound from the closet drew her attention, and she peered through the darkness at the shape moving toward her and the chicken.

Tom sighed and the thing paused, giving her a clearer view of coal black eyes and a piglike nose. It sniffed the air and crawled closer, one long bony arm outstretched to hook around the bucket of chicken. As its clawed fingers curved around the container, she moved forward and grabbed hold of its hairy wrist.

"SBLE. Stay where you are."

The thing gave a startled shriek and tried to scrabble backward, but Ella held on to it and allowed herself to be pulled along as well. She locked one arm around the creature's throat and held on despite its thrashing, ignoring the scratch of claws on her jeans and bare arms. When she pressed the barrel of her gun to its big shaggy head, it went still.

"That's better." She tightened her grip. "You know you're not allowed to frighten kids. What the hell are you doing here?"

In a sudden flurry of bedclothes, Tom sat up and swung his

baseball bat dangerously near her head. "What is it, Ella? Can I see it?"

"Sure, get my flashlight."

Tom bent to pick up her discarded flashlight and turned it on full beam making Ella blink hard.

"Ew, it sure is gross," Tom said. "All hairy. It's kind of like a cross between a monkey and a spider."

"Yeah, it is." Ella didn't loosen her grip as Tom stared in fascination at the creature. "You'll probably know it better as a troll."

"Like the internet ones or the one under the bridge with the goats?"

"The goat one. They've been around for a long time. As a species, they are usually quite harmless, unless they feast on human flesh and get a taste for it."

The troll hissed. Tom jumped and picked up his baseball bat again.

"I want the chicken, not the child." The words were issued in a sibilant whisper that she understood more at a basic empath level rather than as speech.

"You sure about that?" She forced herself to delve into the troll's mind. She couldn't allow him to hang around Tom if he ate humans. He'd consider a young empath a true delicacy.

"Stop, soul sucker," the troll squealed. "I don't want the child!"

Ella twisted around so that she could stare into the troll's ageless black eyes. "Do you swear it on the lives of your brood?"

"I swear it! If you get your filthy hands off me, I will leave this place and never return."

"Or tell anyone else about what you found here."

The troll blinked slowly at her, his gaze deadly. "Or tell my brood about the tasty little empath."

She nodded, then removed her gun from his head. "You know I can force the memory from your head."

"We all know that, soul sucker," the troll said. "That's why we hate you. I'll not return."

"Good." Ella looked up at Tom. She wasn't sure how much of the conversation he'd understood. "If he comes back, you'll tell me, won't you, Tom?"

"Sure."

She reached for the bucket of chicken. "Shall we let him have this as a going-away present?"

"Sounds good to me."

She thrust the chicken into his bony hands. "Here you go. Now get out and don't ever come back, because if you do, I'll suck out your every thought and then I'll kill you."

The troll nodded and scuttled back into the darkness and out of the window. After a long moment the scraping sounds of his descent ceased, and Ella let out her breath. "I don't think he'll be back."

"I hope not." Tom was regarding her curiously. "Why was he so scared of you?"

She shrugged. "Because I held a gun to his head?"

"It wasn't just that. He was even more scared when you said you'd suck out his brains." He hesitated. "Is that why he called you a soul sucker?"

"I have no idea." She stood up and stretched out her legs. "I have to get some sleep. I'll see you soon, okay?" He opened his mouth to ask another question, but she forestalled it by kissing the top of his head and walking to the door. "Sleep tight, and give my love to your gran."

"Thanks, Ella. You're awesome. I will."

4

Two days later, Ella licked the remnants of frozen yogurt from her spoon and headed for the vending machines in the center of the office. She'd finished the paperwork on Mr. Knight for Otherworld and started reviewing the case notes on Christa Morehouse. According to the police interviews, until the last night of her life Ms. Morehouse had been a quiet tenant whom no one had either gotten to know or cared about. Of course, that was pretty typical of big city living, and meant nothing.

The reports coming back from Humboldt showed a diligent professor of English respected by her students and her fellow staff members, none of whom could remember her ever drinking or partying to excess. She frowned as she approached the water cooler. Why exactly had Christa rented the apartment in the city? Had she wanted somewhere to let her hair down? Somewhere to meet men and misbehave before she went back to her exemplary life in Humboldt?

Speaking of misbehaving... Ella's gaze came to rest on the broad shoulders of an unknown black-haired man who was studying the vending machines with deep suspicion. He wore a nice dark suit, white shirt and tie, which meant he was either a regular government employee, or some religious groupie that had inadvertently slipped through security. Male was probably a more appropriate word than man, because Ella could already tell there was something not quite human about him. As Ella approached, he turned more fully toward her, and she got her first good look at him. She sighed. He was way out of her league. With his pretty face, height and distinctive cheekbones he could have graced the cover on any magazine. Her appreciative gaze dropped to his broad chest—imagining him, preferably without his shirt on. She'd just bet he worked out.

"What's up?" she asked as he continued to study her. He looked even more confused.

"I beg your pardon?" His Russian accent was as divine as his cheekbones, and she actually wanted to squeal a little. She gestured at the five-dollar bill in his hand and spoke very slowly. "Are you having trouble with the vending machine? Don't they have those in your country?"

His sapphire-blue eyes narrowed. "Yes, they do, and you don't need to worry about whether I can understand you. I spent four years at Harvard, so I speak American."

"You do?" She flashed him her best smile. "Then I'll leave you to it."

His shoulders slumped. "Do I need change for the machine?"

Ella fished out a crumpled dollar bill from the pocket of her ripped jeans and put it in his hand. "Here you go. This one's on me. Don't ask me to recommend what's good. They all taste like shit."

He smiled and her hormones started singing the 'Hallelujah Chorus.'

"Thanks. That's very nice of you." He spoke as though he was still feeling his way with the language. She had to wonder just how long it was since he'd last graced her country's fair shores.

"I don't do nice. I'm just trying to keep you moving along so that I can get some hot chocolate."

"Then I'll get out of your way."

Ella waited while he punched some buttons, slid the dollar into the slot and bent to retrieve his plastic cup of hot watery goodness. His ass was nice too...

He straightened, then nodded to her. "Thanks again."

"Your shields are very good." In fact, they were exceptional, but he didn't need to know that. "What branch of the SBLE are you in?"

He leaned one hip against the countertop and looked down at her. "Are you always this inquisitive?"

"Yeah, I find it cuts out the need for small talk. I'm not good at that."

"I noticed. I'm glad you approve of my shields. I've been working hard on improving them."

"Why's that?" She got her hot chocolate and blew on the scummy brown surface. "Did they fail you?"

The irritated look he gave her was quite impressive. "That's none of your business."

"True." She smiled sweetly at him. "If you want to make them even better, I'd focus on the center. You're still a little thin there. I can see your anger building up and that's never a good idea." She turned back toward her office. "*Nice* to meet you, and good luck with whatever it is you're doing here."

VADIM GLARED at the female as she sashayed away from him. How dare she criticize his shields? At first he'd taken her for some sort of junior intern. Her long blond braid, fresh face and unkempt clothes screamed college kid, but she had way too much confidence for that. In fact, she'd had way too much confidence period. She'd also caught him at a disadvantage, as he fumbled to remember how to speak English after five years back in Russia.

American teens tended to be more brash and confident than their European peers, but he had to assume she wasn't a kid. Her quick assessment of the capability and weakness of his shields had been rude but dead on and hinted at hidden talents. If her magic was strong, it might explain why she was here despite her harmless exterior.

"Mr. Morosov?"

He turned to find the head of SBLE beckoning him from a doorway and, with a last glance over his shoulder, Vadim strolled toward him. Alexei was already sitting at the conference table, his long silver hair tied back at the nape of his neck, his interested gaze fixed on the whiteboard at the front of the room. Vadim took the seat beside him and focused his attention on Feehan. Unfortunately, due to the lack of real evidence, it didn't take long to bring both him and Alexei up to speed.

Feehan sat down and looked hopefully at Vadim. "So, what do you think?"

"I think you have the makings of a serial killer here. However, we need to make absolutely certain he's not human. Sometimes it can be hard to tell."

"My empath is convinced the killer is from Otherworld."

"But empaths can be wrong. We all know that. Especially empaths that are nearing their sell-by date."

Feehan blanched. "I don't think you should say that directly to Ella Walsh's face."

"Why not? She's part of the team, isn't she? She's not infallible."

"Well…"

He recognized the faint sheen of apprehension on Feehan's face all too well. For some reason, empaths seemed to inspire fear in both human and Otherworld species. Due to his recent experiences, he couldn't say that he was very keen on them himself. But he refused to show any fear. Empaths loved that. They fed off emotion after all.

"Where is your empath?" Vadim looked toward the door. "I'm quite happy to speak to her and get her opinion on the matter."

Feehan fumbled with the papers on his desk. "I'm not sure if she is available. I intended to gather the whole team together tomorrow morning after you and your associate had settled in."

What Feehan didn't need to say was that he hadn't expected Vadim and Alexei to step off the plane, and come straight into the office. His surprise at their appearance had been all too obvious.

"We're happy to wait until tomorrow, aren't we, Vadim?" Alexei looked across at Vadim, his pointed gaze telling him to shut up and play nice. "Perhaps you could have someone take us to our hotel, Mr. Feehan."

"Sure." Feehan jumped up. "I'll get Sam to take you. He's just started here as an assistant empath and he doesn't have a heavy workload yet."

"Miss Walsh doesn't share well with others, then?"

Feehan halted in his tracks. "Mr. Morosov, Ms. Walsh is an exceptionally talented individual who works well within her capabilities. Of course, due to her age, we are grooming Sam as her replacement just in case anything untoward happens."

"You mean if she suddenly implodes."

"I hope to God that doesn't happen, but I have to be prepared for it. Now let me find Sam and get you settled in your hotel. It's only a block or two away from here, so you'll be able to walk back over here in the morning." Vadim stood and so did Alexei, and Feehan headed out into the open office. Idly, Vadim wondered if the small blond went by the name of Sam, but Feehan had said "he." She had an empath's arrogance, and obviously had time to spare to wander about the office picking on defenseless newbies. Not that he was defenseless. If she caught him on another day when he wasn't suffering from culture shock and jetlag, she might find that out to her cost.

"Do you really think this killer is human?" Alexei asked.

"No, but I'll be damned if I'll take the word of an empath."

Alexei shook his head. "Careful now, Vadim. Your prejudices are showing."

"Then it's lucky I have you here to show me the error of my ways in your Fae-Web."

"I didn't help you much last time, did I?" For a moment Alexei looked almost stricken.

"But you will this time. You know what happened with Natasha, and you can factor in that data to offset the obvious influence of the empath on this case."

"Sure I *can*, but whether I should is another matter."

"What do you mean?"

"It's like using loaded dice. Sometimes if you try and influence the outcome the results are too predictable and that's not what the Fae-Web is all about."

Vadim pushed in his chair and went to study the two photographs on the whiteboard. "Just do your best for me, okay? That's all I ask."

A young man bounded into the conference room and grinned at them both. "Hey, what's up? I'm Sam."

What the hell were you supposed to say to the greeting "What's up?"

Vadim's interest died, replaced by a wave of exhaustion. Definitely not the feisty blond he'd been dreading. Maybe she was just an unimportant intern after all.

ELLA TUCKED the phone between her chin and shoulder and continued investigating the contents of her freezer while she talked to Laney.

"Yeah, I know! Imagine that, a good-looking guy in my office." She peered at a cloudy zip lock bag and brought it out to the countertop for closer inspection. "Not that he was interested in me, especially after I told him he needed to work on his shields."

"You didn't. Oh Ella…"

Ella laughed right back at her. They'd been dumped into the same empath training program at the age of five and had been buddies ever since.

"So, have you heard anything from Otherworld recently?" Laney asked.

"I'm always hearing from them, you know what that's like."

"And you know what I mean. I got a letter today, and our birthdays are only a few weeks apart."

Ella breathed on the bag and tried to read the faded print. It looked like the remains of a lasagna her mother had made for her. She had no idea how long it had been in there. Nuking it in the microwave was the only way to determine whether it was edible or not.

"Ella? Are you listening to me?"

"Yes, hon, I'm just trying to work out what to eat tonight. What did you say?"

"I said, I got a letter about my upcoming twenty-seventh birthday."

"Really."

"It was hilarious."

"Well, they're a bit out of touch over there and their command of English seems stuck at about 1950." Ella grimaced at the stack of mail on her countertop that she hadn't yet opened. "You're not seriously taking any notice of those idiots are you?"

There was a long enough silence on the phone for her to think they'd been disconnected. "Laney, are you still there?"

"I've decided I'm going to meet the male they offer me as a mate."

"*Laney*, what the fuck?" Ella sat down abruptly on the nearest stool. "We always said we'd never do that. What's changed?"

"I've changed. I'm scared, Ella. I can't keep it together anymore."

Ella gripped the phone. She'd never heard Laney sound so afraid. Her friend had always been the more outgoing and optimistic one.

"It's okay to be scared, but can't we work this out together? We've always been there for each other in the past."

"And I know you'll always be there for me, but it's not enough anymore. I'm drowning in all this psychic shit in my head. I can't sleep, I can't concentrate, and I'm messing up at work..."

Laney worked for the SBLE down in San Jose. Ella shivered as she saw her own future and took a deep breath.

"Are you sure about this?"

"I think I am. I don't want to be alone anymore."

"Then you've got to do what you've got to do. I just hope the male they find for you is hot, well-paid and fucks like a god."

Laney gave a watery chuckle. "I sure hope so. I deserve some kind of god, don't I?"

Ella hung up the phone and tossed the plastic bag in the microwave. The fragrant smells of cheese and meat filled her apartment and her stomach grumbled. Laney's defection hurt more than she had expected. Who was she going to share a padded cell with now? She'd always imagined them going down together. But who was wrong? Laney for wanting to live, or Ella for preferring to die without being beholden to Otherworld for a crummy mate. While she waited she flipped through her mail and right at the bottom she found one of the characteristic brown windowed envelopes from Otherworld.

She opened it and found a typed sheet of paper and a blue

tri-fold brochure. The letter looked as if it had been copied many times.

Dear Empath,

Congratulations on almost reaching your twenty-seventh birthday.

Enclosed is some further information as to what to expect in the coming months, and how you might avoid your inevitable descent into madness.

Yours sincerely,

Otherworld Community Outreach Services (OCOS)

ELLA PICKED up the enclosed blue leaflet and started to read.

ARE YOU AN EMPATH?

Are you worried about your future?

There were no glossy pictures, just the same blurred print, and a pen and ink drawing of some poor person, presumably an empath, with his or her head in their hands. She opened up the first fold.

FACT: 95% of empaths will experience some form of deterioration in their mental health by the end of their twenty-seventh year.

"No shit." She hadn't told anyone, but she'd already felt the first warning signs herself. Recovering from the extraction of a memory was becoming exhausting, leaving her with a terrible headache and the urge to curl up and sleep forever.

FACT: 95% of empaths will be unable to function as gatekeepers to Otherworld or replace memories by the end of their twenty-seventh year.

And that was what really scared the authorities on both sides of the divide, the prospect of losing their gatekeepers. Discovering that empaths could detect those who weren't quite human on a psychic level had both frightened and intrigued the human government. That empaths could take away the memory of a human/Otherworld interaction had been an incredible bonus. Even Otherworld liked that, as it enabled them to control the wilder elements of their society and know when they had transgressed in the human world. When it came down to it, no one was concerned about her at all, just what she could do for them.

FACT: 50% of empaths will attempt suicide before the end of their twenty-seventh year.

She whistled. Wow, that one was a kicker. She hadn't realized the rate was so high. She turned to the center page.

WHAT CAN YOU DO ABOUT THIS?

"Fuck all."

99% of empaths who enter the Otherworld FAM (Find a Mate) program go on to live happy and fruitful lives.

Ella stared at that statistic until her vision started to blur. Ninety-nine percent? That was high, but then who believed Otherworld statistics? Only desperate people like her and Laney. She flipped the leaflet over, and saw another drawing of a happy grinning couple with their arms around each other. Wow, just wow. Did they really think she'd fall for that load of crap?

She dropped the envelope and its contents in the trash, and returned to scraping the lasagna out of the bag and onto a paper plate. A bottle of beer and a fork completed her preparations and she took everything through to her small leather couch in front of the TV. She put the local news on and stared at the screen. Ninety-nine percent of empaths who took a mate survived... Was she tough enough not to cave to that promise? Her personal interactions with other humans had taught her not to trust or rely on anyone except herself, so the concept of a mate seemed repugnant. The prospect of having to thank the government for the continuation of her life rankled even more. But if Laney was reconsidering her options, should she be rethinking her own?

5

Ella sipped her coffee and made her way through the cubicles to Feehan's office at the far end of her floor. There was a buzz of interest in the air that resonated through her senses like a toothache. Whatever was going on, she couldn't wait to make it stop. She was hoping it had something to do with the potential serial killer case, but she'd learned not to get too excited. Things changed rapidly at the SBLE and it could be something totally different.

She stopped at the door to Feehan's office and studied the unknown male Fae seated at the table. He had long pale hair that was drawn into a braid at the back of his neck and he wore a dark blue suit. She wasn't that smart before the caffeine kicked in, but she was guessing this gorgeous guy had something to do with the other guy in the suit she'd met at the vending machine. Didn't they always come in pairs?

"Hey." She took the seat opposite the Fae. "I'm Ella."

He rose to his feet and bowed. "Good morning, my name is Alexei."

"And you're from Russia, right?"

"I am."

"I met your colleague yesterday."

"Vadim? He didn't mention it."

"No reason for him to. I just gave him change for the vending machine. What do you do, Alexei?"

"I work for the Moscow branch of the SBLE. I'm a Fae-Web specialist. I believe we've been drafted in to help you with the serial killer."

Ella glanced up to see Feehan entering the office with Liz and the tall pretty Russian. She deliberately raised her voice. "Really? It would've been nice if the boss had mentioned it to us, wouldn't it, Liz?"

It seemed Liz was too busy gawping at the two Russians to do more than mutter something unintelligible and sink into a seat beside Ella. Feehan took the chair at the head of the table, and Tall, Dark and Handsome sat opposite Ella. If one ignored the distinct lack of welcome in his cold blue gaze, he really was hot.

Ella turned to Feehan. "When did you decide to call in the cavalry?"

Alexei cleared his throat. "As soon as Mr. Feehan added the details of the crime into the SBLE worldwide database, I was alerted to the similarities by my superiors."

"You didn't work it out yourself?" Ella asked.

"Unfortunately, I was involved in another case which took all my attention." The Fae looked suitably contrite. "When I became aware of the new data, I was able to incorporate it into my existing cache and confirm their suspicions."

"What percentage of Fae are you?"

Before Alexei could reply, the other Russian spoke. "With all due respect, I don't see what Alexei's parentage has to do with this discussion."

"I don't agree." Ella focused her gaze on the man opposite her. "It's important to know what facilities a Fae can utilize in both of our worlds. I'm also wondering why we need another web specialist when we already have Liz."

"Alexei is exceptional."

"So is Liz," Ella replied swiftly.

"Perhaps your superiors felt they needed a more impartial observer to determine whether or not this killer is from Otherworld."

She narrowed her eyes. "Wow. There are so many things I find objectionable in what you just said that I hardly know where to start. This team is very competent. I assumed the reason *you* were here was because we had already determined that we have an Otherworld serial killer on our hands."

"A suspected Otherworld killer."

Ella flicked a glance at Feehan, but he was listening intently. So she concentrated her attention on the asshole Russian opposite her.

"What exactly is your problem?"

His beautiful mouth quirked up at the corner. "I'm hardly likely to share important information with you when I have no idea who or what you are."

"You haven't exactly introduced yourself either."

Feehan coughed. "I apologize. I should have taken care of the introductions when we came in. Vadim Morosov, this is Ella Walsh."

His expression went blank. "You're the empath?"

"Don't tell me—you've got a thing about empaths. Did you get screwed over?"

He stared at her for a long while. "In a manner of speaking, yes."

"So why are you here?"

"Because I was sent here. Why are you here?"

"Because I'm the one who had to delve into a murdered empath's mind and discover that every thought and memory she possessed had been stripped away."

He sat back. "And that's why I don't like working with empaths."

Ella refused to look away. "I don't follow."

"Because you make everything about emotions."

"It doesn't bother you that someone had their mind stripped bare?"

"Empaths do it to other people all the time." He shrugged. "Why is it so much worse when it happens to one of their own?"

Ella tore her gaze away from Vadim's and stared at Feehan. "Are you okay with him talking to me like that?"

Feehan held his hands wide, and Ella got the impression that he was enjoying himself. "Mr. Morosov is only questioning your interpretation of the evidence."

"Mr. Morosov can go fuck himself." She stood up. "I guess you don't need me then, boss. I'll leave you in our guest's capable hands." She stalked toward the door.

"So you're not interested in finding out who killed the empath?"

Ella slowly turned around to look at the irritating Russian. "I'm very interested, but I'm not going to allow a complete stranger to walk in here and start casting doubts on my ability to do my job just because he has some hang-up about empaths."

"I'll do my job, Ms. Walsh. Don't you worry about that."

"And I'll do mine if you give me a chance."

"Vadim," the Fae spoke quietly. "I've run Ms. Walsh's evidence through my Fae-Web. It appears her suppositions are correct, and match the patterns we have seen in our previous encounters with this serial killer."

She leaned back against the door and smiled at the Fae. "Great. What do you think, Liz?"

"I agree with Alexei," Liz said promptly. "I would also suggest that having two of us with Fae-Web abilities on this team allows for a great deal of balance *and* impartiality." She glanced at Ella. "And I would also like to say that Ella is the most talented empath I have ever worked with. If you don't wish to work with her, Mr. Morosov, I'll step back from this investigation as well."

Feehan stood up and walked toward Ella who suddenly wished looks really could kill. She'd like nothing better than to see his cold lifeless body laid out on the tan coffee-stained carpet, preferably just as a hungry shapeshifter came by...

"Ella, I don't believe Mr. Morosov was suggesting you weren't capable of doing your job."

"Actually, he was."

Vadim gave a cool nod. "I was, but it doesn't mean that I'm not prepared to work with you."

She brought her hand to her heart. "Oh, gosh, that makes me feel so special."

Feehan reached behind Ella and slammed the door shut. "You are going to work with each other because neither of you wants another empath to have her brains sucked out. I don't care if you hate each other. On this team and during this investigation you will behave like professionals. Do I make myself clear?"

Ella noticed that Alexei was glaring at Vadim and that her nemesis was glaring right back. Were they able to communicate telepathically? What would that make Vadim Morosov? Part Fae? That might explain his good looks. Fae were known to be beautiful *and* treacherous.

Vadim rose slowly to his feet and looked at Feehan. "I'd like to apologize to Ms. Walsh. I'm sure we will be able to work together perfectly."

"Okay, but I'm not apologizing to him."

"Ella..." Feehan said.

"I get it. Play nice. Now can we get on with this, please?"

As he sat down, Vadim flicked a side-glance at Alexei. "*Satisfied?*"

"*I'm saving your ass, here, Vadim. If you can't get along with their precious empath, you'll be on the next flight home trying to explain yourself to our boss. Suck it up.*"

Unfortunately, Alexei was right on all counts, but it didn't mean Vadim had to like it. The sweet-faced little empath had a temper and an attitude to match. If he wasn't so terrified that she'd go nuts on him like Natasha, he might be looking forward to the battle of wills ahead.

He turned his attention to Feehan, who was passing out some paperwork.

"We've had an update from the Humboldt police. Apparently they finally interviewed Christa Morehouse's best friend, and she shed some light on why Christa decided to move to the city for the vacation."

"Was she looking for a new job?" Liz asked.

Despite what he'd said to annoy the empath, Vadim already liked the look of Liz. She was just Fae enough to appeal to his Otherworld senses, but not magical enough to irritate him and remind him of the past. Her Fae-Web was constructed differently to Alexei's. He could already sense they were going to complement each other well.

"Not a job, no," Feehan said. "Apparently she was expecting to meet her OCOS assigned mate. As he was coming in cross country from New York, she agreed to meet him in a more accessible place than Humboldt."

"Where is this Humboldt?" Vadim asked.

"It's in the far north of California, almost three hundred miles away."

"So it would make sense for her to meet her male here." Vadim nodded. "Do we have any information about this man?"

"There was nothing about him in her head." The infuriating

Ms. Walsh spoke up for the first time. "Was there anything in her apartment?"

"We have her laptop, perhaps there is something on there," Feehan offered. "I'll set one of the tech guys on it immediately."

"If we're talking about a communication from Otherworld, it won't be on her computer. They don't use that stuff over there. They don't need it. Otherworld communication comes the old fashioned way, through the mail," Vadim added. And he liked it that way. It kept certain people off his back.

"He's right," Ella agreed. "If she was offered a mate, she would've received a letter."

Feehan frowned. "Would we be able to get copies of any correspondence from Otherworld?"

"I don't see why not. They have a big administration department over there at Merton. But that means one of us will have to put in a request, and you know how long that takes."

"I'll do it," Liz offered. "And I'll pop over there if I have to and hurry them along."

"Good luck with that. Although they might be more likely to help you than they are to help me."

"Do we know the name of this male?" All eyes returned to Vadim. "We can put him into the Fae-Web now and see if there is any data floating around about him."

"Sure." Feehan consulted his paperwork. "His name is George Ralston."

Both Liz and Alexei's Fae-Webs lit up. It was fascinating how their combined data was already entangling like vines and taking on a life of its own above their heads.

"Before we end this meeting," Ella said, "I'd like to hear about Alexei and Mr. Morosov's experience with this serial killer."

So, he was Mr. Morosov now, was he? Well, he supposed it was better than being called a jerk. Vadim felt Alexei's stare and forced a smile. "Most of the files are already available for your perusal on the main SBLE site."

"I know that, I've already downloaded them. I was thinking more of your personal impressions of the case, why you think your killer might have moved continents and carried on murdering empaths."

Vadim leaned back in his chair. "The three victims we dealt with were all found with their minds wiped clear. On the last occasion, we came quite close to capturing the killer. I suspect we might have scared him off."

"You think it is a male?"

"Yes, we do."

"And did your empath get the sense that the victims were almost relieved to die?"

"She said something to that effect, yes." He frowned. "Although I'm not sure if she put it in her official report."

"Can we contact her to confirm that? I think it might be important."

"Unfortunately, she is no longer working for the SBLE."

"But can we contact her anyway?"

He shrugged. "She's dead, Ms. Walsh."

Ella shivered and there was an uncomfortable silence until Feehan took off his glasses and rubbed his eyes. "I'm afraid there isn't any more new information to share with you all. I suggest we wait to hear back from the forensic guys and the medical examiner. Their reports are due tomorrow. Hopefully by then we'll have something to work with."

Vadim nodded. "I'd like to talk to Ms. Walsh about her impressions of the killer if I may."

She was already getting up and grabbing her backpack. "Ms. Walsh has a lunch date and then she's off home. She will see if she has time for you tomorrow." He met her gaze and tried to look approachable and contrite. "I'd really appreciate it if you could give me ten minutes before you go."

She sat down again. He waited until everyone else filed out of the conference room and then got up to close the door.

When he returned to his seat she was quick to lock gazes with him.

"Why the privacy?"

"Why are you so defensive, Ms. Walsh?"

"Because you, Mr. Morosov, are behaving like a prick."

"I apologized."

"And did you mean it?"

"No, of course I didn't. You don't need to be an empath to work that out, but that doesn't mean I don't intend to try and get along with you."

She sat back and folded her arms under her breasts, making her pink flowery shirt gape open to reveal a green camisole. "So you said. I'm still not buying it."

"Look, I admit that I overstepped the mark, but…"

"Overstepped it? You sunk yourself up to the neck in shit. You don't waltz into someone's office and start casting doubts over everyone's competence!"

Vadim let out a long slow breath. She had a point, but he wasn't willing to concede even that to her. "Tell me how it felt when you went into the victim's head."

She stared at him for a long moment, her brown eyes haunted. "Okay, there was nothing left. No stray fragments, no memories, no *nothing*. It was as if something had come in with a laser and stripped everything away."

"How hard did you probe?"

"Until my own signal bounced back at me. It was really weird."

"Did you catch anything at all?"

"As I said in my notes, just a sense of relief, but I can kind of understand that."

"Why?"

"Because empaths deal with a lot of extra stuff in their heads, and I can imagine that for a second, losing all of that might be… freeing, before you died of it, that is."

"We don't know what she died of yet, do we?"

"That's true, but if there is nothing left of you, of your soul, of your essence, or whatever you want to call it, how can you continue to exist?"

She looked into his eyes and he felt an unexpected connection that he quickly suppressed. Beneath her arrogance was a female who thought deeply about her place in the world and the effect of her gift on others. She was either an exceptional empath or a superb liar. Of course, being an empath she could be both. In his all-too-recent experience they tended to be incredibly selfish, much like the Fae. Maybe that was why he disliked them so much.

He nodded. "Well, thanks for that. It was very illuminating."

She actually blushed. "It was a load of bullshit. I don't know what I was thinking about and saying it to you of all people."

"I'd like to tell you that I'll keep it to myself, but we both know I'd be lying. It's going to end up in the Fae-Web." He stopped to hold the door open for her. She gave him an odd look as if she wasn't used to men being courteous. "I want to catch this creature as much as you do, Ms. Walsh."

"I get that." She paused to look back at him. "The question is, why?"

"Because I believe in justice for all?"

She was still laughing when she walked away from him. He frowned at her back. She wasn't stupid and like all empaths she was hyper-sensitive. She'd find out what he'd done, and then she'd be back to question him about it, he was sure of that. The only thing he had to decide was how he was going to handle her when she did.

WHEN ELLA GOT HOME, the light was blinking on her phone so she checked her messages while she put off thinking about her stressful day. She'd left the office early, sure that Feehan wouldn't have the balls to face her again. It was strange to be home in the afternoon, but she planned on taking a long nap. There was something about Vadim Morosov that made her tense and she had a terrible headache.

The first message was from her mom inviting her to Sunday lunch. There was a plaintive note in her mom's voice that made Ella squirm with guilt. Moms were good at that. But she hadn't been out to the East Bay to see her parents for three months, so she was well due. Perhaps she'd take Liz along as backup. She stared out her window at the sun as she waited for the second message to click through, and then smiled when she heard Laney's distinctive drawl.

"Hey, call me! I couldn't get your cell. I've been sent the details of Mr. Wonderful and he sounds…interesting."

"Interesting." She deleted the message.

That sounded way too positive. She'd almost hoped that Laney would've been sent details of some complete dud. She'd never quite understood why any sane male would want to hook up with an empath anyway. She put the phone down and stared at it. Was Laney settling for anything OCOS offered her because she was too afraid of losing it? Was she really that scared? Ella sighed. Hell, she was getting scared. She kept having nightmares about the instructional movies shown at her school of empaths incarcerated in some of the country's best insane asylums. She and Laney had laughed and vowed to jump off the Golden Gate Bridge hand in hand rather than go nuts or seek the help of Otherworld to find a psychic anchor. Twenty-seven had seemed ancient then. Now it didn't seem very old at all.

She reached for the phone and then hesitated. Her mother could wait a couple of days, but she wasn't sure if she was in the right frame of mind to talk to Laney over the phone. Some things were better said face to face. She sent Laney a text and got an immediate answer. Decision made, Ella picked up her backpack and headed toward the door. If she ran, she'd be able to catch the ferry before it turned around and headed back to San Francisco and meet Laney at their favorite hotel bar for a drink.

———

"So WHERE DOES everyone go to enjoy themselves in this town?" Alexei asked Vadim as they walked back to their hotel. Despite the patches of blue sky above the tall buildings, at street level it was dark and rather cold. "It's deserted at nine in the evening, and there are no taxis anywhere."

"I have no idea. I'm exhausted and I don't have your juvenile need to go out and get laid every night."

"I'm not that young, actually." Alexei smiled at a tall African-American woman who smiled right back at him. Vadim grabbed his arm and kept him moving. "And you never know, Vadim. With your bloodline, you might live longer than most humans."

"I hope not." Vadim didn't even want to contemplate that horrific thought.

"Just because you want to be one hundred percent human doesn't make you one."

"I get that, Dr. Phil." Vadim looked right and then left before he crossed the complex traffic junction and avoided one of the local trams.

"Who is Dr. Phil?"

"Forget I said it." Vadim saw the entrance to their hotel and quickened his pace. It was amazing how quickly he was reconnecting with American culture, or lack of culture, depending on how you rated self-help TV shows. "I don't even know if he's still around."

Alexei followed him into the hotel and Vadim felt for his key card.

"I suppose I could ask Liz where she hangs out," Alexei mused.

"Liz wears a wedding ring. I don't think her husband will be too keen on her hanging out with you anywhere." Vadim punched the floor number into the keypad. Jetlag was a bitch. All he wanted was a glass of wine, his bed and oblivion. When had he turned into a cranky old man?

Alexei's smile grew salacious. "You never know. If her husband is Fae, he might be interested in sharing the love."

"I forget, you Fae will fuck anything that moves, won't you?"

"We're a bit more selective than that, but needs must, you know."

"Oh yes, I know." Vadim stepped out onto the brightly colored carpet and turned left. "Whatever you decide to do, leave me out of it."

Alexei snorted. "As if I'd ask you to go anywhere with me."

Vadim reached his door and leaned against the frame. "Just make sure you're ready to go back to work bright and early tomorrow morning, and that you haven't brought the wrath of Liz's husband down on you."

"Sure, boss." Alexei blew him a kiss. "I'll meet you in the lobby at eight."

As soon as he closed the door and locked it, Vadim stripped off his jacket and tie and unbuttoned his shirt. There was no point in getting dressed again as he didn't intend to remain vertical for long. He poured himself a glass of exceptional Napa Valley chardonnay and turned on the shower.

As he sipped his wine and shed the rest of his clothes, he wondered what Ella Walsh was up to. He pictured her in some cheap bedsit in the city with a gaggle of interchangeable room-mates who came and went depending on the current state of their relationships. She still didn't look to be anywhere near the dangerous age of twenty-seven, but appearances could be deceptive. He finished the chardonnay and headed for the shower. He should've told Alexei to call the empath. He had no doubt they both liked to party.

Despite her arrogance, Ella appealed to him at some visceral level he didn't really want to contemplate at this point. He imagined her waiting in bed for him to come out of the shower, of how soft her body would feel against his hardness, how she'd probably make him laugh...

When he came out of the shower, his cell was lit up and he paused to read the text from Alexei. "Guess who I found in the bar? Our favorite empath and one of her buddies. Come down and say hi."

"What was that about me cramping his style?" he asked his reflection. He rubbed his wet hair with a towel, and then carefully folded the towel and placed it on a chair. He was too tired to pretend to be charming to anyone, let alone an empath. He'd have to shield all his thoughts and that took energy he just didn't have. He stalked into the steamy bathroom, put the bath mat away, and scrubbed at the steam on the mirror. Damn, he looked like shit. That settled it. There was no way he was going anywhere near that bar or that damned empath.

"HE SOUNDS OKAY, doesn't he? His name is Peter."

Ella read the letter from OCOS and then glanced up at Laney. Her redheaded friend was sitting bolt upright on the bar stool, her long legs twined around the central pole. She wore a flowery dress and red shoes with four-inch heels that Ella seriously coveted. They were seated in the recently restored Gold Rush Hotel bar which was awash with crimson, gold and stained glass fixtures and fittings that somehow suited Laney to a T. The bar was getting busy and it was hard to hear above the congenial roar.

"Yeah, he sounds great." Ella wasn't lying. The guy chosen for

Laney was college educated, had a full time job, coached junior soccer in his spare time and liked a lot of the things Laney liked. His heritage was the minimum requirement for the mating program of one-sixteenth Otherworld, which meant he'd be pretty normal by human standards. "He plays the guitar and loves modern art."

"I know," breathed Laney. "He sounds adorable."

"Are you going to meet up with him then?"

"He lives in Chicago, so we're going to try and hook up over the internet and take it from there."

"That's great."

Laney grabbed her hand. "You really mean it?"

"If this is what you want, then you should go for it."

Laney let out her breath, picked up her cocktail glass and toasted Ella. "I'm so glad you approve."

"You don't need my approval, hon."

Laney's blue eyes filled with tears. "I know but we've always done everything together, and we always said we'd go out in a blaze of glory over the side of the Golden Gate Bridge."

"Things change, Laney. We have to do what we have to do."

Laney put her glass back down on the bar and fixed her gaze on Ella. "So how about you?"

"I'm not sure yet. I still have some time to think about it."

"About three and a half weeks by my math. My birthday is less than a month before yours."

"Okay, then a few weeks." Ella fidgeted with her coaster. "I don't know, Laney. I'm not sure I want to keep doing this anyway."

"So you'd rather go quietly mad?"

Ella finished her cocktail and looked longingly for the bartender. "Don't push me, hon. I'm happy for you, but let me make my own choice on this, okay?"

"Okay, sweetness, but you know where I am." Laney turned

toward the bar and the bartender appeared instantly. "Two more chocolate martinis please."

"Coming right up."

Sometimes she suspected that Laney had Fae in her ancestry. She had the ability to command the attention of bar staff, find parking spots and helpful shop assistants with a mere blink of the eye. It was a skill Ella definitely lacked. She still got asked to show ID to prove she was old enough to drink.

A flash of motion in the mirror behind the bar made her turn in her seat. She nudged Laney. "Are you up for a little company?"

"Sure. Who is it?"

"My favorite Russian."

"The new guy you mentioned from work?"

"No, his partner, who is far *far* nicer. And, as you are already spoken for, you can let me try my talents on him, deal?" Ella waved at Alexei and his face brightened. He started to walk through the packed table toward them, drawing more than a few admiring glances from both sexes. Like most Fae he projected an effortless glamor that made him seem to glow from within.

He bowed and Laney sucked in an appreciative breath.

"Ella. What a nice surprise!"

Ella gestured at Laney. "Alexei, this is my best friend, Laney Phillips. She works for the SBLE down in San Jose."

"A pleasure to meet you, Laney." Alexei brought Laney's hand to his lips and kissed it. Laney made an *ooh* face at Ella over his bent head. "This is my first visit to San Francisco in a long while. I'm still trying to get my bearings."

"Oh, when were you last here?" Ella asked, as Alexei pulled up a barstool and perched himself on top of it. His hair hung loose down the back of his dark blue open-necked shirt and he wore a faded pair of jeans. He frowned. "In the sixties, I think. I came to see the Beatles at Candlestick Park."

"I suppose you're waiting for me to say you don't look old enough," Ella said.

His smile was charming. "Well, if you want to flatter me, I'm not going to object. I was quite young then, of course."

"Scarcely more than a baby, I bet," Laney agreed. "So are you here to help Ella on this case?"

"Yes I am." Alexei raised an eyebrow at one of the female bar staff and she practically ran down the length of the bar to serve him. Ella pretended not to notice. All she knew was as long as she stuck with Laney and Alexei, she would never run out of alcohol.

Laney shivered. "It's terrible to see empaths being targeted like this."

"I agree. Hopefully, now that we're pooling our resources, we will put an end to this madness." Alexei held up his bottle of beer, and they all toasted each other. "Did you know Ms. Morehouse, Laney?"

"Ella and I were just talking about her. Despite the fact that she spent three years with us at college, she left very little impression on either of us."

"You were at college with Ella as well?"

Laney wrapped an arm around Ella's shoulders. "Yes, sir. Best friends forever."

Ella frowned as a faint hint of silver glimmered around Alexei's head. "Hey, put that away, this is off the record."

Alexei grinned at her. "Sorry, it wasn't intentional. Sometimes I swear that Fae-Web has a mind of its own. Would you both like another drink?"

Ella checked her cell. "Sure, just one more and then I'll have to run, if I want to catch the last ferry."

"You don't live in the city?"

"No, I live in Tiburon on the other side of the bay. It's a lot quieter there, especially when the tourists all leave."

"And I live in Walnut Creek, so I can get the BART home,"

Laney chimed in. Ella was pleased to see that she looked far more relaxed. "So don't worry about us drinking and driving, unless one of us suddenly decides to highjack the ferry or the train." Laney winked at Ella. "Hell, we are getting close to *that* birthday, we're supposed to do crazy stuff, right?"

Ella was about to reply when she noticed someone coming up behind Alexei. "Oh, look. It's the lovely and charming Mr. Morosov."

Alexei turned to stare at his colleague who was still immaculately attired in his suit. "I thought you were going to bed?"

"Then why did you text me?"

"Because I knew you would enjoy getting to know Ella in more relaxed surroundings." Alexei snapped his fingers and another stool appeared. "What would you like to drink?"

To her annoyance, Vadim sat. "A glass of chilled chardonnay, thanks. Unfortunately, the shower I took woke me up when all I wanted was to crash." He held out his hand to Laney. "How do you do. I'm Vadim Morosov."

Laney, the traitor, shook Morosov's hand and gave him the benefit of her dazzling smile. "I'm Laney, a friend of Ella's. It's nice to meet you. Are you still suffering from jet lag?"

"Yes." Vadim's answering smile made Ella blink. He never leered at her like that. He moved closer to Laney so that he didn't have to shout. "I have no idea why it's so bad this time."

He smelled of some divinely masculine shower products that made Ella want to lean in and inhale him properly. She gripped her glass and finished her entire cocktail in one gulp. He didn't deserve any more female attention than he was already getting. Three quarters of the bar were now staring at them, and she didn't think they were looking at her—Laney maybe.

She checked her cell again and slid down from the high barstool. "I'm sorry, guys, I really need to go or I'll miss the ferry."

Laney jumped down too, then hugged her hard. "Thanks,

sweetie. I'll call you as soon as I get my first impression of the guy."

"Sure." Ella hugged her back. "Take care, hon." She realized the Russians were both standing as well and she smiled at them. "Have a good evening."

She turned for the door only to find Morosov following her out. She thought about pretending she hadn't noticed him, but he was damn hard to ignore. He held the outer door open for her and glanced down at the top of her head.

"Do you mind if I walk with you? A bit of fresh air might help me sleep."

She couldn't think of a polite way to say no. "But you didn't get your drink."

"I'm sure it will be there when I get back, or more likely Alexei will drink it for me. He has an incredibly high tolerance for alcohol."

Sometimes his English still sounded rather formal, but Ella was getting used to it. She set a fast pace down Market and kept her eyes on the Ferry building.

"I thought you would live in the city, Ms. Walsh."

"Why's that?"

He shrugged. "Because you seem the type."

She kept her eyes on the sidewalk as if she was intent on avoiding the cracks. "Then you don't know my type. Most empaths need their space, so we tend to choose quieter places to live."

"Not all empaths."

"I thought you didn't like empaths, but you were all over Laney."

"She's charming and I don't have to work with her."

Ella stopped walking and faced him. "Look, are you programmed to disagree with everything I say, or are you just totally obnoxious?"

"Probably a little of both."

69

"Then get over it. I'm already tired of having to argue with you all day."

"You could try agreeing with me for a change."

She started walking again. "*Right.* Like that's going to happen. We're obviously not meant to be best buddies, okay? So let's do what Feehan said and try to get along at least on a professional level."

"You prefer to keep things professional?"

"Of course."

"You don't date your colleagues?"

"Why, are you trying to summon up the courage to ask me out?"

He laughed, displaying a dimple near his chin. His blue eyes crinkled at the corners and he looked so damn sexy Ella almost wanted to smile back. "For the record, Morosov, I don't date."

"Why not?"

"Because…" She glared at him. "I don't owe you an explanation, do I?"

"Not yet."

"Wow, you really are over-confident."

"Not at all. As your colleague, I'm just concerned about your well-being."

"I *have* men, I don't date them."

He nodded. "So you're afraid of commitment."

"My life will probably end at twenty-seven." She looked up at him. "Would you subject someone you loved to *that*?"

Ella regretted the words the moment she said them.

She didn't want him feeling sorry for her.

He let out his breath. "Probably not." He reached out and took her hand. "I apologize."

She flinched as his magic shot through her. "I knew you weren't quite human."

He shrugged and released her hand. "I'm many things."

She gave into *her* instincts, and began walking again, turning left along the Embarcadero. She started to puff. To her annoyance, he easily kept up with her.

"I think the question you should be asking yourself, Ms. Walsh, is why you feel so threatened by me."

She screeched to a halt again. "Threatened, by you?"

"Yes. I think you've got used to getting your own way in that office, and you don't like anyone else coming in and questioning anything you say."

"And I think you're talking out of your ass."

"I don't like incompetence, Ms. Walsh, and I don't like working with empaths on the brink of a breakdown. I'll work with you because I have no choice, but I'll be questioning everything that comes out of your mouth, double and triple checking it and, if necessary, taking my concerns to the very top to make sure I'm heard so I don't get left holding the can when everything goes to shit."

She stared into his eyes and for the first time in her life seriously contemplated drawing her weapon and shooting a fellow professional. But he'd probably like it if she did that, and she still had no way of knowing if he could actually be killed.

Instead, she gave him her best professional smile. "I'm glad you shared your concerns with me, Morosov. I appreciate your input and will consider each and every one of your points very carefully."

He continued to stare at her and she continued to smile. His shields really were good. She had no idea what he was thinking, although she might hazard a guess that his thoughts weren't currently full of love for her.

He nodded. "I'm glad we understand each other then. Good night, Ms. Walsh."

"Good night, Mr. Morosov." Ella walked away and this time he didn't follow her. She wanted to look back, but she had a horrible sense that he would still be standing there watching her, and she didn't want to encounter his death glare again. She headed toward Pier 41 and the reassuring sight of the Tiburon ferry. He was wrong about her. Totally wrong about everything. How dare he suggest she was some kind of workplace bully? He'd only been there half a day. He knew nothing!

Ella stomped up the gangplank and found a seat on the upper deck. Why was he so paranoid anyway? She thought about the SBLE serial killer files she'd downloaded to her laptop. What had gone wrong to screw up an investigation and cause a suspect to flee the country? She smiled out at the choppy waters of the bay. She just knew it had to have something to do with Vadim Morosov and she was damn well going to find out what he'd done and exactly why he hated empaths so much. And *then* they'd see who was really paranoid.

6

ELLA SLUMPED DOWN INTO HER SEAT BEHIND THE CONFERENCE table and tried to conceal her yawns as Vadim Morosov wrote on the whiteboard. He turned to look at her, pen in his hand, a pained expression on his face.

"Am I boring you, Ms. Walsh?"

He underlined Christa Morehouse's name with a ferocious screech of the pen that made her cringe.

"Nope, carry on." She smiled at him. "It's fascinating." While Vadim outlined the cases he and Alexei had dealt with in Russia, Ella worried about Laney and the files from the SBLE database about the serial killer. Guiltily, she brought her full attention back to Vadim who was just summing up the evidence for the third murder.

"At that point we deduced that the victims were all female, and obviously, all empaths."

She sat up. "And how did your empath feel about that?"

He turned toward her, his expression neutral. "She felt much as you did. Shocked that nothing seemed to remain in the victim's head, and puzzled as to why any murderer would want to do that to his prey."

"Was she worried about her own safety?"

"I can't say that I noticed." Vadim shrugged. "She seemed okay about it."

"So at that point you would say she was still behaving in a professional manner?"

"Yes." Vadim stared at her and then glanced across at Feehan. "Is there a point to these questions?"

"I'm just interested as to when you started to believe your empath had lost touch with the case and become a liability."

Vadim's face became a mask and Alexei cleared his throat. "We all noticed something was wrong on her twenty-seventh birthday. No one was prepared for her to implode so completely."

"Why didn't you take her off the case?" Feehan asked.

Vadim put the pen down with a definite click. "Because we were so caught up in the matter we couldn't afford the time to bring another empath up to speed. We needed her input and right up until the last moment, she seemed perfectly fine."

"Even though you all thought there was something wrong with her on her birthday? You just assumed that was normal for an empath?" Her question was general, but her gaze remained on Vadim. "Even though you in particular, Morosov, knew her really well?"

"She assured me that everything was okay. I believed her."

Ella thought about the files she'd read the night before. "You sure did."

"What's that supposed to mean?"

She shrugged. "Just that you fucked up."

Feehan frowned at her. "That's an inappropriate remark. Apologize."

"Why should I? Morosov isn't exactly leaping to his own defense, is he?" Ella tapped her laptop. "Didn't you read the files, Mr. Feehan? He fucked up. He didn't double-check the information she fed him about the murderer and almost got himself and his whole team killed." She waited until everyone was looking at her. "So all this shit about the empath letting everyone down? How about looking at who let her down?" She glared at Vadim and Alexei. "Her whole team knew she was under considerable stress, and yet they put their need to get the killer ahead of her."

Vadim made an impatient gesture. "That's not the way it was. If Natasha was under stress, all she had to do was ask for help. She chose not to and her *choice* put the whole team in danger."

"Don't you understand anything about empaths? They don't have many choices at all. Natasha might not even have realized her gift was so depleted." Ella sat back. "She *killed* herself. You have to accept some of the blame for that."

Vadim held her gaze and she saw it then—the emotion behind the cold exterior, the *pain*...

Feehan clapped his hands and stood up. "Let's move on, shall we? Does anyone else have any more questions for Vadim about the older cases?" He nodded at Liz and Alexei. "I'm sure you two will work this information into your webs as soon as possible and let me know anything useful."

"Of course, Mr. Feehan." Alexei nodded, as polite as ever. He looked across at Liz. "Perhaps we might have lunch together?"

"Sure." Liz smiled. "That would be great."

Feehan picked up the pen Vadim had placed on the table and strode back to the board. "Let's recap. Christa Morehouse rented the apartment in the city so that she could spend the summer getting to know her OCOS mate, George Ralston. Mr. Ralston is due to arrive today at the airport, where we will pick him up and bring him here for questioning."

"Does he know about Christa yet?" Liz asked.

"I don't think so," Feehan replied. "We're interested to see how he reacts to the news."

"Well, if he's only just arriving in town, he can't be the murderer."

Ella forced herself to stop staring at Vadim. "I'll confirm that when I meet him. He's only one-sixteenth Fae, but he should give off some kind of vibe that I can read and match to my memory of Christa."

Alexei looked interested. "You can pick up signals like that?"

"Usually, although with Christa's mind being wiped, I'm not so sure."

"I don't think Natasha had that ability," Alexei mused. "It might have helped."

"Maybe it was one of the things she lost. Some empaths lose their facilities really fast the day they turn twenty-seven." It was hard to speak so casually about something that might soon be happening to her. "What time will Ralston be here?"

Feehan consulted his watch. Ella noticed that apart from the two Russians, he was the only one wearing a traditional watch. Everyone she knew used cell phones to check the time.

"He should be here in about two hours." He glanced around the table. "Can you all make sure you're available?"

There was a brisk knock and Sam stuck his head around the door.

"Hey, Dr. Clegg wants to know if you want to go and see the body or wait until he types up his report."

"I'll go down," Feehan replied. "Does anyone want to come with me?"

"I'll come." For some weird reason, she felt like she needed to be there for the dead empath to protect her from everyone else. She simply couldn't believe that there was nothing left. It didn't make any sense.

She followed Feehan out of the room and down to the lower level that housed the small morgue and the underground parking lot. Footsteps behind her meant that someone else had joined them. She assumed it was Vadim, as the Fae had a horror for human death, but she didn't bother to look around and confirm it. Feehan punched in the code to the morgue and held the door open for her. She shivered as the temperature dropped and a blast of disinfected air that failed to cover the undercurrent of death engulfed her.

She closed her mouth and tried to breathe sparingly through her nose. They didn't get many human corpses in the SBLE morgue. They tended to be Otherworld creatures that came to the city to wreak havoc before they died. She had no idea why it was such a popular pastime, like lemmings jumping off cliffs. But it made her job difficult. Creatures at the end of their lives were much harder to scare back to their own side of the divide and much more likely to cause chaos.

BEHIND ELLA, Vadim allowed the heavy door to close and then stood quietly checking out the space. Feehan went down the hallway to talk to someone, leaving them in the main room. The morgue was small and kept scrupulously clean. He almost wished he'd worn sunglasses as the lighting was so bright and the walls were painted something equally shiny. Gutters ran in parallel across the tiled floor ready to sluice away anything unmentionable. He slowly inhaled and tasted the taint of magic, both good and bad, on his tongue.

Ella nudged his arm. "What's up?"

Today she wore jeans, a green flowered shirt that was missing too many buttons and a pink bra that pushed her breasts up in a way that made him want to bend down and bury his face in her cleavage. She smelled like coffee and pizza and bubblegum, which was far more appealing than dead magic.

"Morosov, are you staring at my bra?"

"It's rather hard to miss."

"Laney made me buy it. She said it's like a sheepdog."

More than willing to be distracted, Vadim frowned. "Why?"

"You know—" she cupped her breasts and shoved them upward, "—round them up and pen them in."

"Ah. That's a new one on me."

"I'm sorry about earlier."

Vadim raised his eyebrows. "Which particular part?"

She had the grace to blush. "All of it, I suppose." She fidgeted with her top button. "I just get so pissed off when everyone starts blaming the empath."

Vadim kept his gaze on her rather superlative bosom. He tended to date tall, thin women who weren't so well endowed but looked spectacular on his arm.

"I suppose I should be grateful. You could have said a lot more than you did."

"About you and Natasha?"

"Yes."

"I thought you said you didn't like empaths?"

"I did until I met her."

"She destroyed your faith in us?"

There was a hint of skepticism in her voice that made Vadim wary. "No, she destroyed my faith in true love."

"Yeah, like you believed in that."

He met her derisive gaze. "Actually I did, but unlike most humans, I don't assume it makes the participants happy." God forbid she ever met his parents. She'd see what he meant.

"So you're a reformed romantic."

"Exactly." He lowered his gaze to her chest again. "I like sex, though. Good, uncomplicated, sweaty, uncommitted sex."

"So do I, and stop staring at my boobs."

He manufactured a sigh. "It's a shame you don't fraternize with your workmates."

She stepped away and shot him a dark look. "Stop playing your little games with me."

"What games?"

"Morosov, your shields are very good, but I'm an empath. I know when you're talking shit to distract me."

"From what?"

Out of the corner of his eye he saw Feehan reappear and beckon to them. Ella started to walk away pausing only to shoot her final remark over her shoulder.

"From your guilt about Natasha."

He opened his mouth, then realized she wasn't even waiting for an answer. Did he feel guilty about Natasha, or was he just still angry with her for letting down the team? He'd tried hard not to let his personal devastation leak into his work, but Ella had seen right through him. She seemed to understand him better than anyone except his own mother. That idea made him want to puke his guts up. He glanced surreptitiously around. If he did want to puke this was the place for it. The whole vibe made him uncomfortable.

Feehan was talking to a tall man in a white coat Vadim assumed was Dr. Clegg. Ella joined the group and started to listen as well, her expression intent. Vadim had already noticed how quickly she slipped from lazy inattention to complete alertness.

The three of them moved away and he made himself follow. The good doctor might think that everything in his morgue was dead, but Vadim knew better. Some of the lost souls floating around needed to be dispatched before the atmosphere became even more polluted. Not that "souls" was the right word for what remained here. Most of these creatures had no belief in a Christian god. Dr. Clegg unlocked a door and ushered them inside.

Vadim leaned against the wall and watched as Feehan and Ella approached the corpse as if it might wake up and start talking. There was nothing there. Even he could sense that. No humanity, no magic, no nothing. He focused his attention on Ella, who had paused by the victim's head, her hand on the pillow almost touching skin.

Dr. Clegg glanced down at his notes. "We have a twenty-seven-year-old female empath. Apart from higher than average levels of alcohol in her bloodstream, she was a very healthy woman."

"Were there any signs that she had been tied up or abused?" Feehan asked.

"Nothing to indicate that at all." Dr. Clegg pulled aside the thin cotton sheet that covered the body. "A couple of bruises, but nothing significant—apart from the fact that her brain seems to have been traumatized."

"Yes, I was going to ask you about that. I think Ella mentioned what she'd sensed—or more importantly— what she hadn't sensed, when she tried to get a reading."

Ella shrugged. "I could've been wrong."

Vadim considered her. She sounded almost uncertain. Was she beginning to lose it, too?

"No, you were right, Ella. There's a distinct lack of activity." Dr. Clegg hesitated. "When I did an MRI, I discovered her hippocampus appeared to have been liquefied."

"What exactly is that?" Feehan asked.

"It's a part of the brain located in the medial temporal lobe that we think plays an important role in the consolidation of information from short-term memory to long-term."

Vadim glanced at Ella who looked as shocked as he felt. He didn't recall the pathologist in Russia mentioning the hippocampus. But it made a sick kind of sense. Dr. Clegg continued speaking. "I used conventional scientific methods and Otherworld diagnostics, but I couldn't pick up anything else." He shook his head.

"I've never seen anything like it."

"And I hope you don't have to see it again," Feehan said. "But we're pretty much convinced we're on the trail of an Other-world killer."

"I thought as much." Dr. Clegg wrote something on his clip-board. "Humans have been known to eat each other's brains, but they tend to make rather a lot more mess getting to them."

His gaze traveled over the dead woman. "This was very precise."

Dr. Clegg headed for the door, followed by Feehan. Vadim lingered to watch as Ella wrapped her arms around herself as if she was cold.

"What's wrong?"

She looked around as if she hadn't realized he was still there.

"I was just trying to see if I'd missed anything, if there was something..." Her words trailed away.

"From what I read in your report, at the time you were pretty certain there was nothing left. What's changed?"

She met his gaze. "It's your fault."

He raised his eyebrows. "As is everything, apparently. What did I do?"

"You reminded me about how crazy empaths get around their birthdays."

"You're not twenty-seven yet, are you?"

"Not for a few weeks." She walked up to him and he straightened against the wall. "It's okay, we can go now. I just wanted to make sure I hadn't missed anything."

"And you didn't. She's dead and something liquefied her brain."

She winced as she opened the door. "Thanks for the visual."

He followed her out into the main hallway and almost bumped into her as her steps slowed.

"What's up now?"

She appeared to be listening to something. "This place needs help."

He barely repressed a shiver. "I know."

Her interested gaze swung back to his. "What do you feel?"

"What do you feel? You're the expert," he countered.

"Trapped souls screaming in torment, and magic gone awry."

"Can you fix it?"

"Why, does it bother you?"

He started walking again. "Not particularly."

"Liar. If you feel it, it bothers you."

"I can live with it. The question is, can you?"

She cocked her head to one side and wrinkled her nose. "Nope."

He watched, fascinated as she drew a deep breath and closed her eyes. Time seemed to stop, his heartbeat slowed and he couldn't have moved even if he'd wanted to. She raised her hands and held them palm up as if she was begging.

"*Come to me.*"

Her lips didn't move. He realized the words were resonating through his skull and the hairs on the back of his neck stood to attention. Around her swirled things and emotions he couldn't quite identify and didn't want to. She took another deep breath. The swirling turned into the roar of a tornado, which seemed to coil tighter and tighter and disappeared into her hands.

He felt a visceral tug deep inside his chest and resisted an urge to wrap his arms around himself and curl up into a little ball. No wonder they were called the gatekeepers. He'd never witnessed an empath channeling lost souls back to Otherworld and he wasn't sure he ever wanted to again. When he opened his eyes Ella was on the move, her smile in place. "That's better. Thanks for reminding me. I meant to come down here last week and see to it, but I forgot."

And it was better. The polluted atmosphere he'd sensed had disappeared.

He found he could move again, and hurried after her. Feehan waited for them by the main door still chatting to Dr. Clegg. He didn't look bothered, so the extraordinary incident Vadim had witnessed hadn't taken much time or been noticed by anyone else.

"Excuse me, guys."

Just before she reached Mr. Feehan, Ella veered off course

and headed into the bathroom. She emerged a couple of minutes later, looking even greener than she had before.

Vadim held the outer door open for her. "Are you all right?"

"Sure." Her grin wasn't good enough to fool him.

"Do you need to lie down or something?"

"I'm fine. What I need is half a dozen iced donuts and a chocolate milkshake. I'll be good to go then."

Vadim held open the elevator door. "You'd be better off having some protein and complex carbs."

"You sound like my mother."

"I'm just saying…" Vadim didn't get to finish his sentence as Ella stormed off to take the stairs. He sighed as the doors started to close and her untidy yellow braid disappeared around the corner.

"Don't worry yourself, Vadim. She's like that with everyone these days."

He turned to find Feehan watching him and tried to think of something neutral to say. He didn't want to give the impression that he wasn't a good team player, or he might get sent back to Russia. He decided to focus on the obvious.

"She doesn't eat very healthy stuff."

Feehan snorted. "She lives on the kind of junk food that would send most people to the hospital. I tried to talk to her about her diet when I first arrived here."

"I assume she didn't listen?"

"She informed me that she wasn't planning on living past twenty-seven, so she'd decided to eat whatever she damned well liked." Feehan paused. "I shut up after that."

"She doesn't plan on taking an OCOS mate?"

"She says not. Although, a lot of empaths change their mind as their twenty-seventh birthday approaches."

"So I've heard." Vadim spotted Alexei waving at him. "If you'll excuse me, Mr. Feehan?"

"Sure. I have to go and pick up George Ralston from the

airport. I'll let you know when you can interview him, so stick around."

"I think Alexei got us some lunch so we can eat here while we go over the case notes."

"Great." Feehan nodded and went into his office, closing the door behind him. Vadim went over to where Alexei was waiting in the smaller of the conference rooms that had become their temporary office.

"I got you a ham sandwich, okay?" Alexei handed him a wrapped parcel.

He sat down and realized his hands were trembling. If he still felt the effect of the bad atmosphere in the morgue, how the hell was Ella Walsh feeling? He'd seen the debilitating effect it had on her. Had she done it deliberately to remind him of the strain Natasha had been under? He shook his head. No, she'd just sensed a problem and dealt with it as quickly as possible.

"Are you talking to me?" Alexei asked, his sandwich poised in front of his mouth.

"No, I was just thinking about Ella Walsh."

"She's interesting, isn't she? Powerful too."

Vadim unwrapped his sandwich. "How powerful?"

Alexei shrugged. "Enough to make herself the center of my Fae-Web."

"In what way?"

"I'm not sure yet, but she will have a profound effect on this case." Alexei's silver eyes took on a faraway look.

"Like Natasha?" Suddenly, he didn't feel hungry anymore. Vadim sipped at his can of jasmine iced tea. "She's not going to implode is she?"

"She's not Natasha. She is connected to you, though."

"We're on the same team."

"It's more than that."

"Don't go all mystical on me. I'm not in the mood for it."

Vadim picked up his sandwich and took a big bite. It was surprisingly good. "I thought you were having lunch with Liz."

Alexei pouted. "Her husband called and she decided to go out with him instead. I did get to meet him though. He seems like a nice enough guy."

"With the flexible morals you require?"

"I'm not sure yet. I'll need to get to know him a bit better. Speaking of which, are you free for lunch this Sunday?"

"I'm free every Sunday."

"Liz said something about us all getting together for a barbecue."

"Sounds fine to me. American beef is always excellent." Vadim concentrated on finishing his sandwich. "The report from the morgue is that Christa Morehouse was not assaulted in any way."

"I've already added that information into my web."

Alexei shuddered. "If it is the same guy, he's obviously getting better. The first victim was tied up, the second was choked, and the third only had a couple of bumps and scratches on her wrists."

"Great. Maybe he does feed off their empath power. Maybe it enhances his."

Alexei sat up and his Fae-Web streamed out around him. "That's an interesting possibility. Let me share it with Liz."

7

VADIM CLEARED AWAY THE REMNANTS OF HIS LUNCH AND deposited everything in the trashcan. He came back and tidied up Alexei's space while his coworker spun his magic. He was just dusting off the desktop with his napkin when Ella came through the door, a large pink box in the curve of her arm and a monster cup of some beverage that was leaking bright orange bubbles through the inadequately fitted lid.

He held out a chair for her and grabbed for the box as it slid off her arm.

"Thanks. Is Feehan back yet?" Ella asked.

She looked less fragile than she had in the morgue. He preferred her in full-on belligerent mode, although why he was concerned about her feelings at all was a mystery.

"I think he only just left." He gestured at the box. "Is that your lunch?"

"Yeah, would you like one?"

He stared through the clear plastic lid at the brightly colored glazed donuts. *Only in America.* "No thanks. I don't have much of a sweet tooth."

Ella's gaze wandered over his body. "I bet you work out, don't you?"

"I try to keep in shape."

She smiled and he couldn't look away. "Of course you do." She opened the box, took out a donut covered in white glaze and purple sprinkles and bit into it. "Mmm…"

He watched, fascinated as she licked the frosting off her lip with the tip of her tongue and then slowly chewed.

"May I have one, please?" Alexei asked.

Ella nodded, and kept eating as Alexei pondered his selection. The Fae could eat just about anything and still retain their beauty. Alexei only accompanied Vadim to the gym to look good rather than because he needed to go. Ella started on her second donut, pausing occasionally to slurp at the disgusting orange concoction.

Vadim had to look away, instead concentrating his gaze on the Fae-Web that still hovered over Alexei's head. It took him a while to interpret the Fae symbols and gain entry, but soon he was enmeshed in the beauty of the web. It took on the dimensions of a tunnel he could walk through with information covering every surface, constantly offering new pathways, new analogies with all roads leading to a central rune that glowed blood red.

Death.

Being immortal, the Fae preferred not to deal with the consequences of death. Only those who weren't purebred could cope with the ramifications of the Fae-Web, of its predictions for the future, of a mortal's ultimate fate. Vadim carefully avoided all avenues that addressed himself, concentrating only on the trail of the elusive killer and the far brighter light of Ella Walsh. But Alexei was right. The red stones of death were definitely drawing closer to Ella, and so was his lifeline…

God, no.

"What are you doing?"

Vadim jumped as Ella poked his arm. He was snapped back into reality with a speed that made him want to vomit. He glanced down at the sleeve of his jacket where a large yellow blob of frosting now rested.

"Give him a second, Ella. He was in the Fae-Web," Alexei said.

Vadim swallowed hard and refocused on the offensive frosting.

"You can see into those things, Morosov?"

He got out his handkerchief and tried to decide whether he would make matters worse by trying to rub the stain off. There was really no other option. He'd have to get the hotel to dry clean the jacket for him tonight.

"Morosov?"

He dabbed at the stain, then wet his handkerchief with water to blot out the stickiness.

"What, Ms. Walsh?"

She rested her chin on her hand and studied him. "I was asking if you could see into the Fae-Web. Liz tried to tell me what it was like, but I couldn't really understand."

"It's...different."

She snorted. "That's a lot of help."

"It just is."

Her brown eyes narrowed. "So what percentage of Fae are you exactly?"

"I have no idea."

"If you're more than fifty percent Fae, Morosov, don't you need a permit to live on this side?"

"You should know, gatekeeper. Isn't it your job to police Otherworld creatures?"

"One of my jobs. I can't tell with you. Your shields are too good."

"What a shame." He returned her earlier smile with interest.

She looked across to Alexei, who was still helping himself to the box of donuts. Vadim noticed they'd managed to eat about half-a-dozen between them already. "How much Fae do you have to be to make that thing work?"

"To operate it? At least thirty-three percent. To see it?" Alexei shrugged, his gaze skipping over Vadim. "That depends on your line."

"Your Fae line?"

"Yes. Some families are more powerful than others."

"I've noticed that. Sometimes it's harder to remove one memory than another, although they initially seem the same." She turned back to Vadim. "Can you create one of those things?"

He repressed a shudder. "No."

"I wish I could see into one. I bet things would make a lot more sense on a case."

"It's not quite that straightforward. Fae logic is not the same as human." He glanced at Alexei who looked amused. "In fact a lot of it is both misleading and irrelevant. That's why we need Alexei and Liz to interpret the data for us."

"He's right, Ella. Sometimes even I don't understand what my Fae-Web is trying to tell me."

"Until it's too late," Vadim said. Alexei had the grace to look abashed. Vadim stood and pushed in his chair. He took off his jacket and laid it over his arm. "Will you both excuse me? I need to clean off my sleeve properly."

ELLA WATCHED him leave the room, then turned back to Alexei.

"What did you miss last time?"

He shrugged. "That Natasha was going nuts."

She considered that and found her gaze drawn back to the door through which Vadim had just left. "Morosov's a bit cranky about his clothes, isn't he?"

"That's a bespoke suit from Savile Row in England. I'd be pissed too."

Ella stared at the remnants of her donut. "No wonder he looks so good in it."

"It's his armor."

"Against what?"

Alexei smiled. "Against everything."

"How much does one of those cost?"

"About four or five thousand dollars, but they are made to last a human lifetime."

"Holy shit." She dropped her donut onto her napkin. "Should I offer to have his jacket dry-cleaned or something?"

"Don't worry about it." Alexei helped himself to another donut. "We get enough in our budget to cover cleaning, and Vadim isn't short of money."

Curiosity was vulgar, but she couldn't help herself, and the Fae were terrible gossips. "He's rich, as well as handsome as a god? Why on earth does he work for the government?"

Alexei sat back. "You'll have to ask him yourself." He idly studied his fingernails. "You think he's handsome, do you?"

"Who doesn't? You'd have to be blind not to notice that ass and that face," Ella sighed. "But it's okay, I'll live."

"He likes you."

"He does not."

Alexei grinned. "Sure he does, but he's fighting it. Natasha really did a number on him."

"Were they that close?"

"Hard to tell. She certainly doted on him. I was never quite sure how he felt about her. Vadim's never been one to like a clingy woman, and by the end she was emotionally needy."

"Like all empaths. I'm a bit of an exception apparently." She grimaced. "I've seen a picture of Natasha. She was stunning. Let's just be grateful I know he's way out of my league. Morosov would do better to date Laney."

"But Laney's just about to meet her OCOS match, isn't she?" She stared at him. "You don't miss much do you?"

He shrugged. "She ended up in my Fae-Web, I have no idea why. Naturally, I picked up some information about her."

"*Supernaturally*, you mean."

"Well, that and some deliberate eavesdropping on your conversation last night."

Ella couldn't help laughing at Alexei's cool admission of guilt. "You're definitely more Fae than human, aren't you?"

"I certainly have more adaptable morals." His gaze dropped to her mouth. "Is it just Vadim you won't date, or does that ban extend to me?"

She took her time looking him over. He certainly was a beautiful specimen and most Fae were spectacular in bed...

"Nope, I can't do it." She shook her head. "It just makes everything complicated at work. I need to keep my mind on Otherworld."

"Not a problem." He picked up his empty cup. "Can I get you anything?"

"No thanks, I've got soda."

He rose to his feet and looked down at her, all delicious silver hair and eyes. "If you change your mind, let me know, won't you?"

"Sure."

He nodded, and she watched him walk to the door with his usual grace and then hesitate. "Mr. Feehan's back."

Ella stood too. "Good to know. I'm going to my office. Come and get me if anything exciting happens."

ELLA LEFT FEEHAN'S OFFICE. She'd done her job and established that George Ralston didn't have any obvious connection to the victim, her apartment or the killer. It would be up to Liz and

Alexei to decide if he was of any further interest to the Fae-Web. She found Liz chatting to Alexei, their heads close together, their Fae-Webs enmeshed.

She coughed loudly and they both jumped. Damn, she should have remembered from lunch that interrupting someone when they were deeply in the Fae-Web gave them a shock.

"Sorry, guys. Feehan wants to see you, Liz."

Liz stretched, and the silver lines of her Fae-Web trembled and disappeared. She walked out to Ella in the hallway. "Did you meet Ralston?"

"Yeah, I did. As far as I'm concerned, he's in the clear. Feehan wants you to meet him too, though."

"I'd be happy to." Liz smoothed down her pink skirt and patted the shining curve of her blond bob. "By the way, is it okay if I bring some guests to the barbecue on Sunday?"

"The more the merrier. I can hide from my parents in the crowd." She'd finally succumbed to Mom Guilt and agreed to visit her family in the East Bay for the weekend. Apparently, they were celebrating something she should have known about weeks ago. Something she'd already forgotten the details of—again.

"Do you still need a ride, Liz?"

"No, we'll bring the others. You can take Laney."

"If she wants to come."

"Is she okay?"

"She's fine. She's just all excited about hooking up with her OCOS date."

"*Laney* is?" Liz stopped walking.

Ella forced a smile. "Yeah, she decided to go for it after all."

"Well, good for her." She patted Ella's shoulder. "You should consider it."

"Hmm..."

Liz knocked on Feehan's door and Ella continued on down to her corner office. She passed the open door of the small conference room and saw Vadim writing on the whiteboard. His precious jacket was placed carefully on the back of a chair and his sleeves were rolled up to the elbow.

She paused in the doorway, ostensibly to check out what he was writing, but also to check him out. Just because he thought he was too good for her didn't mean she couldn't admire him from afar. His hair was almost black and his cheekbones rivaled a supermodel. Luckily, that tough mouth of his saved him from being too pretty...

"Did you want something, Ms. Walsh?"

She leaned against the doorframe. "Mr. Ralston's here if you want to see him."

"What did you think of him?"

She came farther into the room and dropped her backpack on the table. "I can't sense any connections between him and the victim. He seems genuinely upset about her loss."

He exhaled and shoved a hand through his dark hair, which immediately fell back into place. "Damn. I suppose it would've made it too easy if he'd been the murderer."

"And unlikely, seeing as he hasn't ever been outside the U.S."

"That we know of. Otherworld doesn't keep the same kind of immigration records as the U.S. He could have gone through a portal."

"Did your guy actually speak Russian?"

Vadim went still. "That's a good question. I'll have to check Natasha's notes, such as they were."

Ella got out her laptop. "I can do that right now." She found the files and opened the one marked with Natasha's name. Vadim came to look over her shoulder. Up close, he smelled of expensive aftershave and warm, vibrant male. Ella shivered.

"What is it?"

She ignored him and concentrated on the file. "This is the translation. Do I have the original as well?"

"Yes." Vadim leaned around her and tapped something on

the keyboard. A second file came up and they both stared at the Russian script.

"Look." Ella touched the screen. "This bit is in English, right?"

Vadim cursed softly, his mouth close to her ear. "Interesting. That's just above Natasha's comments on the killer's voice and thoughts. Sounds like he is an English speaker." He straightened away from her. "What made you think of that?"

"I'm not sure. Maybe I picked it up when I sensed him in the stairwell at the victim's apartment." Vadim frowned and she hastened to add, "It might not be important."

"But I still missed it." He walked away from her. "And I was all ready to blame you for fucking up this case. Maybe I'm the one who needs to worry."

"Shit happens." She couldn't believe she was the one trying to make him feel better.

He swung around to stare at her, his dark blue gaze intent. "This time I can't afford to make a mistake."

"Because you'll be the one held accountable back in Russia?"

"Exactly." He grimaced. "You don't know my boss. When she says if you fail she's going to eat you alive, she means it literally."

"She's a shapeshifter?"

"And the rest." He picked up his jacket and put it back on. The fabric settled around him like a second skin. "I need to talk to Alexei."

"Sure." She shut down her laptop and put it back in her backpack. "Are you doing anything this weekend?"

"I think Alexei's got something planned."

"Then have a good one."

"Thanks." He smiled at her and she had to remember not to drool.

For a moment she'd considered inviting him to her parents' barbecue, but perhaps it was best that he was busy doing other things. If she had a few beers, she might get up the courage to flirt with him, and despite his avowed dislike of empaths, he might just take her up on it. She might not have the courage to call his bluff and walk away.

Ella sighed and checked her cell. Laney had sent her a text about the party saying she didn't need a ride and would come on her own. A second text said she'd be late because she would be chatting online with her OCOS mate, Peter.

She stared at the text and tried to think how to answer it. For the first time ever, she was aware of feeling a little jealous. None of Laney's other conquests had ever bothered her, but Peter did because—because what? Because he represented Laney's survival, something Ella couldn't do for her best friend? Something she was afraid of doing for herself?

She sat down on the nearest chair. She'd had another letter from Otherworld today, repeating their offer of finding her a mate and reiterating all the benefits. The letter was still stuffed in her backpack. She slowly took it out and studied it, squinting to read the small blurred print she'd earlier ignored. In two weeks they'd be sending her details of her mate anyway. Her only choice was to either agree to meet the guy, or ignore the information. What kind of a man had they found, and who in the hell would ever want to put up with her?

"Ella, are you coming for a beer?" Liz appeared at the door of the conference room. "I said I'd meet Doug at the bar across the street."

"Sure." Ella smiled at her friend. "As long as I make the last ferry."

She stuffed the letter into the pocket of her backpack. Soon, she would be that much closer to madness and know the name of this mythical male who would supposedly make everything right for her. Would she leave off making her decision until it was too late like Natasha had? She slung her backpack over her shoulder and snorted. What a fucking awful set of choices.

8

She parked her VW Golf at the end of the street and walked past the long line of cars that led up to the side of her parents' yard. The ranch house sat on a corner lot surrounded by oak trees and bordered by a small creek that backed onto the parched yellow hills. The back gate was open and she could already smell burning hot dogs, fried onions and warm beer. Her mouth watered. She loved it when other people cooked.

Outside of San Francisco and the bay, the temperature always shot up and today was no exception. Heat shimmered off the parked cars and off the roofs of the houses. As she'd driven over the Dumbarton Bridge heading for Walnut Creek, she'd wished she'd fixed the air-conditioning in her old car and had to crank down all the windows instead.

For some reason, her parents had hired an inflatable for the yard, and festooned the place with pink balloons. Ella frowned as she considered the invitation again. From what she could see, the usual crowd was all here. Was there something specific she should have remembered? She'd left a message to tell her mother she was definitely coming, but hadn't heard back.

Fixing a smile on her face, she walked through the back gate and into the crowd of people milling around the patio. She spotted her two older brothers and younger sister but didn't call out to them. Her father was behind the barbecue, prodding at something with a worried expression on his face. The French windows that led into the kitchen and family room were open, so she went inside. If her mother would be anywhere, it would be in the kitchen directing operations. Ella also hoped she'd come to the right place for a beer.

"Ella!" Her mother was making a fresh pitcher of margaritas. "So glad you could make it. And you even put on a dress! Thanks for making the effort, honey. You look sweet."

Darlene was blond, but the resemblance between them ended there. She was tall and slender, her face tightened, her nose remodeled, her hair blonder, less natural, and more styled than Ella's would ever be. She gave Ella an awkward one-armed hug.

"Did you bring Laney with you?"

"I think she's coming later." She looked longingly at the refrigerator. "Do you have any beer in there?"

Darlene pointed at two tubs under the kitchen table filled with ice and the frosty glint of bobbing beer bottles.

"There are a lot of calories in beer, darling. Make sure you choose one of those nice new low-carb ones, and limit yourself to a couple so that you can drive home safely."

Ella helped herself to the first beer she touched. She took an experimental sip.

"Don't you want a glass, dear?"

"No, I'm fine with the bottle. Liz and Doug Goddard are coming with some friends. Is that okay? You did say I could invite anyone I liked."

Darlene's smile faltered. "Sure. I don't think we'll be having a full moon tonight or anything."

Ella took a longer swig of her beer. Darlene had never been quite comfortable with any of Ella's friends who were not quite human. She was probably worried Doug would suddenly go all wolf on them and devour one of her guests.

"It's okay, I'll tell Liz to chain him up in the yard if he doesn't behave himself."

Darlene's cheek flushed. "That wasn't what I meant, Ella. I was just kidding. You're too sensitive about your friends, you know."

She resisted the urge to stick out her lip and mumble "whatever." Somehow her mom always made her feel like an adolescent again. They'd gotten along just fine in those days, though— what with Ella being stuck in year-round boarding school.

"Dad's barbecuing?"

"I told him to let Scott do it, but as it's Scott and Julie's big day, he insisted on doing it himself."

Ella took another beer, then paused. "Scott and Julie got married last year. Did I miss something?"

The doorbell rang, drowning her mother's reply, although the expression on her face was enough to make Ella beat a hasty retreat to the hallway to see who'd decided to go all formal and demand entry through the front door.

She opened it wide and discovered Liz looking super cool and collected in a lemon-yellow halter dress, accompanied by Doug.

"Hey you!" Doug picked Ella up and enveloped her in a bear hug. His T-shirt bore the words, "Meat Eater and Proud of It" accompanied by a picture of a bloody steak. "How's my favorite empath? You know these guys, right?"

He put her down and moved to one side. Behind him stood Alexei and Vadim. They both wore khaki shorts and polo shirts and looked as if they were heading out to play golf somewhere expensive. Vadim removed his aviator sunglasses and nodded.

"Ms. Walsh."

"Morosov. I thought you had other plans."

He half-smiled. "So did I, but I hope I'm still welcome."

More flustered than she wanted to admit, Ella stepped back and allowed them to enter the house. It was much cooler in the hallway and she hurried to shut the door.

"Welcome to my parents' house. They're celebrating…something." She started to move toward the kitchen. "There's beer."

Alexei lightly touched her elbow. "You're okay with us being here?"

"Sure! The more the merrier. If you could do a bit of magic and enchant my mother, I'd be really grateful."

"How grateful?" he murmured.

She grinned back at him and walked into the kitchen. "Mom, Liz and Doug are here and they've brought a couple of other people I work with."

Darlene's bright smile wavered, but she held out her hand to Alexei. "It's always a pleasure to meet Ella's friends. We see her so rarely."

Knowing how Mrs. Walsh felt about them, Liz and Doug waved and said all the right things before checking out the beer and drifting outside to join the party. Alexei glided over, took Darlene's proffered hand and kissed it. "Thank you for your hospitality, Mrs. Walsh. My name is Alexei, and this is Vadim."

Ella moved out of the way as Vadim went past her and also shook Darlene's hand. "A pleasure, Mrs. Walsh."

"And where exactly are you two from?"

"We're currently based in Russia."

Darlene clasped her hands together. "How exciting. You didn't tell me you were working with Russians, Ella."

"I wasn't until a couple of days ago."

Darlene's gaze lingered on Alexei who was smiling endearingly at her. She blushed and patted at her hair. Ella fought back a grin. Perhaps she would have to ask Alexei to dial it down a bit. Fae glamor could be a little overwhelming sometimes. Vadim came to stand beside her and she looked up at him.

"Would you like a beer?"

His gaze moved down from her face to the bust line of her blue flowered maxi dress.

"You look nice."

"Which bit of me?"

His gaze returned to her face. "All of you."

"Don't sound so surprised."

"Nothing you do surprises me."

She snorted. "You poor, cynical, world-weary man. That's such a cliché."

"Is it?" He braced his hand on the refrigerator door behind her head, cutting off her view of the party.

Rather than look into his eyes, she turned to study his long elegant fingers and the gold signet ring shaped like a dragon. "Are you sure you don't want a beer?"

His smile made her knees wobble. "I was wondering if you had any wine in the refrigerator instead."

"Oh!" She hurriedly straightened. "I have no idea. I'll get out of your way."

She stepped around him and busied herself retrieving her beer. She couldn't deal with his party manners at all. Her younger sister came in from the yard and walked straight over. Madison wore a halter top and cut-off shorts so tiny the pocket linings were visible beneath the frayed denim hem.

"Hey, Ella, you look nice for a change. Where did you get that dress, Goodwill?"

Before Ella could answer, Madison's gaze fell on Vadim, who had just shut the refrigerator door and turned around.

"Holy cow, where did you find *him?*"

"This is my coworker, Vadim Morosov."

Madison tossed back her long blond hair, pushed past Ella and stuck out her hand. "Hi, I'm Madison. The not-weird Walsh girl."

Vadim shook her hand and then looked back at Ella. "You are quite alike."

"You're kidding, right?" Madison giggled. "I'm way taller and thinner than her and way smarter. Oh, and I'm not going nuts in a few months either."

"*Madison!*" Darlene's voice cut across whatever Ella had started to say. "Don't talk about your sister like that."

"Why shouldn't I? It's the truth," Madison demanded. "I'm not sure why we all have to pretend nothing's going to happen."

Vadim leaned down until his mouth brushed Ella's ear. "And I thought you were the outspoken member of the family."

"Usually I am. I'm not sure what's got into Madison today. She'll probably insist on telling me later," she replied as Darlene and Madison squared off. "Would you like to come out into the yard and meet my father and brothers? They're much quieter."

"Like most men."

He followed her out of the open doors leaving Madison still arguing with her mom. Alexei had taken a seat at the kitchen table and seemed to be enjoying himself. Ella headed for her dad, who was brandishing a pepper mill over something that looked like a chunk of steak.

"How's it going, Dad?"

His face softened. "Ella. How's my girl?"

He put down the pepper and she walked into his arms. He smelled of the same spicy aftershave brand he'd been using since the 1980's. For some reason, she wanted to stay with her face buried in his shoulder forever.

"I'm doing fine. How about you?"

He made a face. "Trying to survive your mom and your sister's constant bickering."

"That's what golf was invented for, wasn't it?"

"Exactly." He turned to Vadim. "And who's this?"

"This is my colleague, Vadim Morosov."

He shook Vadim's hand. "You can call me Ned or Mr. Walsh, whatever floats your boat. Russian, eh?"

"Yes." Ella grinned when Vadim looked confused by her father's faux-hippy speak.

"Is he one of yours?"

"One of my what, Dad? Men?"

He retreated behind the barbecue again. "You know what I mean."

"No, he isn't an empath." She looked speculatively at Vadim. "I'm not quite sure what he is."

"He looks like a nice young man."

"Well, appearances can be deceptive." She winked at her dad, who winked back. "Is the food ready yet?"

"Does it look ready?"

She studied the various lumps of meat and the half-cooked sausages. "Nope."

"Anyway, your mother wants to make the big announcement first, so I'm waiting on her orders." He pointed the spatula at her. "Go and take a seat and I'll give you a shout when it's time."

She led the way to a couple of empty chairs that sat in the shade of the covered patio. Her brother was sitting at the table nursing a beer.

"Hey."

He nodded at her and Vadim. "What's up?"

"Nothing much. You?"

"Nothing much." Dave scratched at the peeling label of his beer bottle. "I'm going down to San Diego next semester."

"To do what?"

"Continue my studies, duh."

"Dave's studying to be a doctor," Ella told Vadim who had sat beside her, one hand wrapped around his plastic cup of wine.

"That's an excellent career choice. What specialty?" Vadim asked.

Dave concentrated on his bottle. "Supernatural studies."

Ella put down her beer. "Really?"

He shrugged. "It sounded kind of interesting."

"I suppose it might be," Ella said cautiously. "What exactly do you have to do?"

"First response team stuff, for unusual or abnormal medical situations, liaising with SBLE. You know the drill."

"I didn't realize there was anything official like that around here."

Dave looked up at her. "It's a new thing. Hiding all that stuff away is becoming far too difficult, so our government decided to open up some opportunities for those who are interested."

"And you were interested?"

He dropped his gaze. "Well, having a sister who was never there kind of sucked, you know?"

VADIM LOOKED from Ella to her brother and tried to work out exactly what was going on between them. If he lowered his shields, he'd probably get a better sense of the emotions swirling around, but then Ella would know he was snooping and call him out on it. It was interesting watching her interactions with her family. Even just using his human faculties, he could sense there was a ton of unspoken conflict simmering beneath the surface.

"Have I met all your siblings now?"

Ella tore her gaze away from her brother and looked at him instead. Her expression was uncharacteristically solemn.

"I've another brother, Scott. He got married last year to Julie." She waved a vague hand toward the edge of the pool where Vadim now noticed Alexei was chatting to Madison. "They're over there, somewhere. I'll grab him when I see him."

"Your family seems very nice."

Her smile was quick. "I suppose they do."

Beside Ella, Dave sat forward. "What Ella means is she wasn't around that much to appreciate them." Vadim raised his eyebrows encouragingly and Dave continued. "She was five when they took her away to that fricking boarding school."

"That must have been difficult for you all."

She patted her brother's arm. "We all got over it eventually. It was a good place for me to be."

"Sure, that's why you kept running away, and Mom kept insisting on taking you back. Dad would've let you stay, you know that."

"Mom was right to do it. If I'd stayed here I would have attracted some funky creatures from Otherworld into our house. We would all have suffered."

"All I remember is you crying and kicking and pleading not to go back." Dave finished his beer and abruptly got to his feet. "You're way too nice, Ella. I've never forgiven them for sending you away."

Vadim waited, but she made no effort either to contradict Dave or persuade him to sit back down. After a moment, he nodded at Vadim.

"I'm going to get another beer. Do either of you want one?"

"I'm good," Ella said.

Vadim showed Dave his half-empty plastic cup. "I've got wine, thanks."

He waited for Ella to make some smart-ass remark but she remained quiet, her gaze fixed on the swimming pool. Having an interesting family dynamic himself, he decided to divert the conversation into less volatile channels.

"I didn't know the American government was investing in special medical units to liaise with the SBLE."

"Why would you? You don't live here."

Ah, she was back to being prickly. Vadim sipped his mediocre too-warm wine. "It's a good idea."

"You think so?"

"Surely the more people who are aware of the nature of Otherworld, the better it can be contained."

"I've always got the impression that our government was intent on keeping the majority of the population in blissful ignorance. My folks had to know, but most people would rather not."

"Maybe in this insane digital age, they've realized they can no longer do that."

"That's a good point." Ella tucked her hair behind her ear. He liked it down around her shoulders. He liked her soft blue dress too. "Maybe if they keep opening up the boundaries, they won't need empaths anymore."

"I'm sure there'll be plenty for you to do. Not everything that comes out of Otherworld is super-cute and fluffy."

She shuddered. "Ugh. Some of those things still give me nightmares. I don't think most human brains could survive the experience."

"So you'll always be needed."

"Unfortunately, yes." Her cell phone chimed and she glanced down at the green-lit screen. "It's Laney. She's supposed to be coming over." She frowned. "Looks like she's in the middle of changing her mind. I wonder what happened with her OCOS mate? Maybe I should call her."

She was just about to rise when there was a clapping noise from beside the pool. Ella's parents joined hands with another younger couple Vadim could only assume were the aforementioned Scott and Julie.

"Damn," Ella muttered as she sank back down. "I hope this is quick, whatever it is."

Ned cleared his throat. "Firstly, we'd like to thank you all for coming."

"Yeah, yeah." Ella's cell chimed again and she squinted at the screen.

Her father continued. "Secondly, we'd like to offer our congratulations to Scott and Julie who are expecting their first child at the end of the year!"

Everyone started to clap and whistle. Ella's thumbs stopped texting.

A proud looking Scott stepped forward, one arm around his wife. "I'm also pleased to tell you that we will be having a little girl."

More cheers and then Darlene and Madison started handing around trays of something pink and bubbly. Ella stood up.

"Excuse me."

Vadim rose too and followed her direct path toward the house. She was waylaid by her father who put his arm around her waist.

"Honey, aren't you going to wish Scott and Julie well?"

"Sure!" Ella's smile was brief. "That's awesome news, you guys!"

Julie's eyes filled with tears. "That's so sweet of you, considering everything, I mean..." She swallowed hard. "We're even thinking of giving her your name if..."

"If I don't make it?" Ella disengaged herself from her father's arm. "Cool. Thanks."

She kept going. Vadim followed, ignoring the looks of consternation on her father and brother's faces. She walked through the kitchen, down the hallway and took a left turn into what he guessed was a bedroom. He followed her in and shut the door behind them.

ELLA TOOK several deep breaths and tried to unclench her fists. She was aware that Vadim had come in, but somehow she didn't care.

"It's not that I'm angry with them. It's just that sometimes, when I remember I'm not going to be around to see the future, I get angry with myself." She looked at him, but he didn't say anything. "Sometimes I wonder what it would be like if I could have a family, a kid, a—"

The door burst open and her mother appeared. "How could you?" Darlene shrieked. "You upset Scott and Julie on their special day!"

"And you don't think that I might be upset, to have someone tell me they 'might' name their baby after their delusional or preferably dead auntie?"

"It's not all about you, dear. Julie was trying to do something nice."

"It's *never* about me. You spend your whole life trying to pretend I don't exist. And being reminded that I'm probably not going to be around in my present state to see my first niece being born? That sucks." Ella shook her head. "You just don't get it, do you?"

Darlene raised her chin. "I asked you to the party because I wanted you to share in this special moment, not throw back a kindly meant gesture in Julie's face."

"Wait, you *knew* she was going to say that?"

Her mother looked away. "Your father and I thought it was a lovely gesture."

"Why's that, Mom? Because you're relieved you've already found my replacement? Why the hell would you want another Ella? God help the poor kid if she displays any psychic ability. Everyone will start blaming me."

Darlene shot her a furious glance and marched out, slamming the door behind her. Vadim moved to stand against it.

"I can ward the door to keep everyone out, if you like."

Ella drew an unsteady breath. "That would be awesome. I'm sorry you got stuck in the middle of this. That's why I don't come here very often."

He shrugged. "Last time my whole family got together there were two deaths, one disembowelment and twenty-seven activated curses."

She met his gaze, but there wasn't a trace of amusement in his eyes.

"You're not kidding, are you?"

"I wish I was." He sauntered toward her, one hand in his pocket. "Do you want to leave? I'm more than happy to come with you."

"I can't yet. I have to check on Laney, and then I'll have to apologize to everyone."

He was close enough that she had to look up at him. "Why should you have to be the one to apologize?"

"Because I make them uncomfortable and they don't deserve that. It's not their fault I'm the odd one out."

"And what about how they make you feel?"

"You know how it is. I can't expect them to understand." His mouth kicked up at the corner and she found herself staring at it. "Did you really ward the door?"

"Yes."

She concentrated on his mouth. "Would you kiss me?"

In answer, he bent his head until his lips brushed hers. "Like that?"

"No, like you mean it."

"I thought you didn't date your coworkers?"

"I'm not dating you. I just want something else to think about other than my family. You happen to be standing here, and I want you to distract me."

"Ah."

He kissed her again, this time parting her lips with his tongue and possessing her mouth with a tenderness she hadn't expected. She shut her eyes and kissed him back, let her hand curve around the back of his head to keep him near. He drew her even closer, one arm around her hips, the other around her shoulders until he was practically holding her up.

"Mmm…" she murmured against his mouth. "Very nice."

"You're welcome."

Her cell chimed and then again. She forced herself to stop kissing him. "I have to answer it. It's either Laney or Madison wanting to know why she can't get into her own bedroom." It was also another distraction, but she guessed he knew that.

She scowled at the screen. "Laney's not making any sense. I'll try and call her."

Vadim stepped away. "Go ahead."

She touched the screen and Laney picked up instantly.

"Oh my God, Ella, I can't do this anymore, I just can't…"

"Laney, what's up?"

She was crying so hard that Ella could barely understand her. She glanced over at Vadim who could clearly hear as well.

"I can't, Ella. I'm a worthless mess. I don't deserve to live like this, or find happiness. I just don't. I'm sorry. This is the best thing for everyone."

"Laney, just hang on, I'm coming over right now. Just keep it together."

Vadim was already opening the door. "Where is she?"

"Not far from here."

He nodded and they both headed for the front door. Madison appeared in the hallway and shouted something after them, but Ella didn't even stop.

"Got an emergency! I'll call tonight!"

As Madison opened her mouth again, Ella was already through the door and running. Vadim kept pace with her, his sunglasses neatly in place, his breathing easy. She unlocked her car and leaned across to let him in.

"Thanks."

Ella started the engine, praying that it would turn over. "We'll be there in about ten minutes."

"Good."

She grabbed her sunglasses from her purse and backed out of her space. "The air con is broken. If you get too hot, crack open a window."

She concentrated on her driving, aware of a growing anxiety in her chest.

"Do you think she's totally lost it?" Ella blurted out.

"Has she turned twenty-seven?"

"Not yet. Two weeks to go, I think."

"It's unusual for a complete breakdown to occur before an empath's actual birthday." He sounded way too calm for her liking. "Most empaths I've met have been relatively normal up until then."

"Relatively." She took a sharp right and Vadim grabbed onto the back of his seat. "That's not helping."

"Did you say she was meeting her OCOS mate today?"

"Not in person. He was supposed to call her. Maybe he was a complete dick and she's gotten scared about what will happen if she rejects him."

"It's possible."

She slowed down and searched for a parking spot along the side of the tall apartment building Laney lived in downtown.

"Do you want a space close to here?" Vadim asked. She nodded and made a left turn to circle around again. The next moment, a car started to reverse out of a spot right in front of them. Ella braked and stuck on her indicator. She glanced at Vadim but he wasn't even looking her way.

"She's on the third floor."

He got out, locked his door before she even reminded him, and followed her into the lobby of the apartment building. The bank of elevators was protected behind a set of glass doors with keypads. He touched her arm.

"You have the code?"

"Somewhere." She looked for her phone.

"I've got it." He brushed his hand over the keypad and then pushed the first door. It opened immediately. She studied the elevator lights. "Let's use the stairs."

He found the door and held it open for her. "You don't like elevators do you?"

"No." She kept it short. She'd need all her breath to climb. As she went up, her sense of urgency increased as she caught a scent of something…unpleasant.

"*Hurry.*"

As she ran along the hallway, she dove into the bottom of her purse for Laney's spare key, but it was hard to find it amongst all the junk.

"What number is it?"

"3221."

Vadim went ahead and was already pressing the buzzer when she reached him. She finally found the key and pushed it into the lock. As the door swung open, the sickening all-too-familiar stench of Otherworld magic and death engulfed her.

"Laney," she whispered.

Vadim was already moving ahead of her into the apartment, his gun out, his magical senses on high alert. He stopped so suddenly that she cannoned into the back of him. He held her back, one arm outstretched.

"Ella—"

She pushed past him and took another two steps before coming to a halt again. Laney was on her back on the floor, one hand still grasping her cell phone, her eyes open but seeing nothing, her expression frozen in a scream of anguish.

"Oh my God!" Ella dropped to her knees. "*Laney.*" Vadim crouched between them and took hold of Ella's shoulders. "Don't touch her. Don't touch anything."

She struggled to free herself but he held firm. "Morosov, what's fucking *wrong* with you? Let me go! She needs help, she—"

"Ella." He gave her a sharp shake. "She's dead. Now think! Is the killer still around?"

"She's not, she's…" Ella took another look at Laney and

started to shiver uncontrollably. "There's so much psychic shit swirling around in here, I can't get it straight."

Vadim shook her again. "Yes, you can. Do it for Laney." Still holding on to her he punched in a number on his cell phone. "Alexei? Are you getting this? Call Feehan and get him to call the police."

She took a deep breath and then another and Vadim nodded. "That's it. Get a grip. Help her in the only way you can."

"Let me go." He hesitated. "I swear I won't touch her."

He released her arm and moved out of her line of vision exposing her to the full horror of Laney's body. Her friend lay on the floor, her hair spread around her as if she'd fallen back into a pool.

"I can't see any obvious injuries, can you?" Vadim asked.

His calmness helped steady Ella. She tried to pretend it was just another body, just another weird day at the office, just another dead empath...

"No, just a trickle of blood from her ear and her nose. Like Christa Morehouse." She closed her eyes and focused on what her normal human senses couldn't see. "Same malevolent psychic scent too." She took another breath. "No sense of Laney."

Ella jumped as her cell phone beeped, then she took it out of her purse. A new text message flashed up.

"It's from Laney."

He moved toward her, his hand extended. "Don't—"

But she couldn't help but read it. "Sorry, too busy to chat. I'm dancing with the Siren. X"

She looked up at Vadim. "What the fuck? Who the hell is the Siren?"

He took the phone and reread the text. "I assume he's our killer. Nice of him to leave his name."

Footsteps sounded outside the apartment, and someone

knocked on the door. Vadim patted her shoulder. "I'll go and see if that's the police."

She nodded and remained where she was. Nothing else in the apartment appeared to have been affected. She leaned in to touch her best friend's outstretched hand, which was still warm. A frisson of Otherworld power zapped across to her like an electric shock. But there was nothing left of Laney. Ella didn't mind the pain. She deserved it for not even thinking of warning her friend to be on the lookout for a killer.

"I'll get him for you, Laney. I'll get the bastard if it's the last sane thing I ever do."

Vadim returned accompanied by two police officers and a couple of medics. He came over, then helped her stand up.

"Is there anything else you need to do here, Ms. Walsh?"

She glared at him. "I'm not leaving, if that's what you mean."

"Yes, you are." He lowered his voice until only she could hear him. "You are in shock, and far too personally involved in this to help anyone."

"I am perfectly in control of myself. I won't leave unless you knock me out and carry me."

His gaze narrowed. "That could be arranged. If there is nothing else you can add professionally, will you at least wait on the sidelines until Feehan gets here?"

"So he can kick me out?"

"He's the boss. He can do whatever he likes."

"Not if I don't work for the SBLE anymore."

He went still. "You're quitting?"

"I want to catch this sick bastard and when I do catch him, I want to kill him slowly and painfully. The SBLE won't let me."

"So you'll quit on Laney?"

"Of course not. Didn't you hear what I said?"

He gripped her shoulder. "Ella, the best way to get this man is to work within the SBLE."

"You're just saying that because you need to solve this case."

He scowled. "That's not the only reason. What if I promised you that if we catch this guy I'll make sure his punishment is as slow and painful as you could want?"

"How could you do that?"

"I have...contacts in Otherworld who could make it happen."

She stared into his eyes and for a second he allowed her to feel the complex power he hid so well behind his shields.

"I swear on my mother's grave, Ella. You will get your vengeance."

She sank down onto a chair by the wall. "Okay. But don't fuck this up."

9

ELLA PUSHED HER HAIR AWAY FROM HER FACE AND STUDIED THE worn surface of the table at Laney's apartment. They'd found the pine table at a garage sale. It had taken months to remove the old paint and wax the pine, but it had been worth it.

"Here." Vadim sat down beside her and handed her a can of soda. "It's the full sugar version."

She couldn't quite believe how efficient he was being, deflecting questions from the police and medics, liaising with Feehan and the rest of the SBLE team and somehow protecting her at the same time. Laney's body had been taken away and the apartment was silent. She'd also been aware of Alexei and Liz gathering evidence in their own particular way, but even they were no longer around.

"Do you feel up to driving back to the city?" He took a bottle of water out of the refrigerator.

"You said Feehan was coming here."

"I lied."

She couldn't even raise the energy to glare at him. "Do we have to go into work?"

"Briefly, so that we can bring Feehan up to date." Vadim

117

sipped his water. Despite the air conditioning running full blast, it was still warm inside the apartment. "I wanted to make sure there was nothing else you needed to do here."

She looked around the neat kitchen. "I don't think there's anything left to do. Laney's gone. It's as if she never existed."

Vadim briefly touched her hand. "She'll come back to you. You're in shock."

Ella stood up and carefully pushed in her chair. "Really? I had no idea."

Vadim didn't react to her sarcasm, which meant he must have been feeling very sorry for her indeed. Instead, he found her purse and car keys and handed them to her.

"Don't worry about locking this place up. The police and the SBLE will want to come back in to search for more evidence."

"I'm sure they will."

Ella shut the door and went down the hallway, her footsteps muted by the soft beige carpet.

"Can I ask you one thing before we leave?"

She turned to look at Vadim, who had paused by the closed door.

"Sure."

He caught up with her. "Did you get a sense that the killer was actually in the apartment with Laney, or did he just call her?"

"He was there."

"You're sure about that?"

"Yeah, there's something visceral about his power. It kind of infuses the air with his particular blend of magic. Like a signature aftershave or something."

"So you can smell him?"

"It's not really a scent in the human way, more of a psychic feeling." Ella stopped at the stairs. "It's hard to explain."

"And you wouldn't get that through a phone or internet connection?"

"No, definitely not." She glanced up at him. "Why, what's up?"

"I was just wondering if the OCOS male she was speaking to earlier was able to get at her through the phone."

"Peter?"

"That's right." Vadim held the door open for her and studied her carefully. "Do you want to go back to your parents' first? If you're feeling too overwhelmed by all this, I could ask Feehan to hold the meeting tomorrow instead."

She shuddered. "My parents wouldn't be any help. I'd rather go back to work."

He surveyed the parking lot. "I guess Alexei and Liz didn't wait for me. Are you okay if I come with you?"

"I should make you take BART." She went toward her car. "Did Feehan ask you to babysit me or something?"

"No, I decided to do that all by myself." He held up his hand. "And I'm not babysitting you. I just know how it feels to see someone you love murdered."

"Who?"

His mouth twisted. "My brother."

He yanked open the door and disappeared inside the car. Ella followed him in, yelping as the volcanic heat stored in the seats and the steering wheel burned her hands and the back of her knees. She fitted the key into the ignition. The pathetic air conditioning came on and promptly died. *Shit.* With another curse she wound down the window and Vadim did the same.

"I don't suppose you can fix air conditioning?" Ella asked as she released the handbrake, and guided the car out onto the street.

"I wish I could." Vadim wiped his face with a folded hand-kerchief. "It certainly gets hot out here."

"It'll get better when we cross over the bridge. It's always cooler on the other side."

Part of her couldn't believe she was having a conversation

about the weather when all she wanted was to tear her hair out, beat at her breast and scream for Laney. But Vadim was right. It was such a cliché, but Laney was gone, and the best thing Ella could do for her now was find her killer. When she'd done that, maybe she'd have time to grieve. She'd learned quite young that sometimes in order to survive, you just had to make the best of a bad situation. Her mother said she was cold and unfeeling but how else was she supposed to be? She had to compartmentalize to survive.

As it was the weekend, the journey back into San Francisco wasn't too bad and apart from the usual bands of roving tourists the city center was almost deserted. Feehan's car was in the parking garage and she chose a spot well clear of him. Peach wasn't at her station at the reception desk either, but there were always a couple of guys hanging out at the office just in case anything bad happened. With Otherworld there was always something that needed taking care of.

Vadim walked beside her, wrapped in his own thoughts. He'd been pretty quiet on the journey back, only rousing himself to ask the odd question about a landmark or the name of a place they were passing through.

The lights were on in the big conference room so she headed there, her steps slowing as she neared the door. Rich and Andrew were talking quietly to Liz. Only Vadim's hand at the small of her back propelled her forward.

Feehan came toward her. "Ella, I'm so sorry."

She nodded, then avoided him by slipping into the nearest chair. Vadim shook Feehan's hand and then sat beside her. Ella raised her gaze to the whiteboard and immediately saw a picture of Laney. She looked away, but not before she remembered when the picture had been taken. Laney had insisted on having a new picture for her driver's license renewal and had spent the whole day making herself look beautiful for it.

What a fucking waste.

Feehan resumed his seat at the head of the table. "I'm sorry to drag you all in this weekend, but, as I think you all know, we've had another empath murder."

"From our initial observations, and the fast response of Ella and Vadim to the scene, we can almost certainly say that we are dealing with the same killer who murdered Christa Morehouse and the Russian victims." Feehan paused to look around the table. "Obviously we'll wait to have the findings confirmed by the police department and our lab, but we'll move forward with the assumption that we are dealing with the same man."

"He's even given us his name," Vadim said. "He sent a text message from Laney's phone to Ella calling himself 'The Siren'. The caps are his."

"The Siren?" Feehan looked at Liz and Alexei. "Do either of you have any prior knowledge of this individual?"

"Only of the original Greek variety," Alexei said. "The Sirens were dangerous creatures portrayed as femme fatales who lured sailors with their enchanting voices and music to shipwreck their vessels on the rocky coast of their island."

"So what does that have to do with our current-day killer?"

"Well, he lures empaths into letting him into their apartments, and they don't seem to struggle, do they?"

"That's true," Feehan said.

"It might also explain the feeling of relief both Natasha and Ella said they noticed in the empaths' final thoughts."

"Interesting." Feehan wrote something on his notepad. "Good input, Alexei, thank you. Anyone else?"

Ella looked up. "Only that we have to catch this sick bastard and string him up by the balls."

Feehan and Alexei winced.

"We'll certainly do our best, Ella." Feehan smiled encouragingly at her. "Do you have anything more constructive you'd like to add?"

"That's not constructive?" Ella said. "If we've established we have some kind of serial killer, how is he picking his victims? Where is he getting his information from?"

"All good questions and ones we should discuss at length tomorrow when the preliminary reports come in. Do you intend to speak to Laney's parents when they arrive, or do you want the department to handle it?"

"They won't come," Ella said. "They haven't visited her since she left college."

"But—"

She stood up. "They won't come. They'll probably be glad she's dead and that they don't have to deal with her anymore, *okay?*"

Vadim touched her shoulder. "I think Ms. Walsh has had enough. Perhaps we should reconvene tomorrow?"

"Sure." Feehan went out and straight into his office, closing the door behind him. Alexei moved across to talk to Vadim and Liz drew Ella into a hug.

"I'm so sorry, honey. Every way you look at this, it sucks."

"I know."

Liz searched her face. "You're holding up real good. Laney would be proud of you."

"Laney would..." She couldn't even finish that sentence without starting to cry and she would be damned if she'd ever cry on government property again. "Do you want to come and have a drink?"

Liz's face fell. "I'm sorry, I can't. I have to go with Doug to this local pack thing tonight. He's waiting downstairs for me. Will you be okay?" She hesitated. "I can call him and skip it. I'm sure he won't mind."

"Don't worry about it." Ella stepped back from Liz's obvious concern. "I'm a big girl."

She waited until Liz said goodbye to Alexei and Vadim and then picked up her purse and keys.

"I'm going home now, guys. I'll see you both in the morning."

Alexei looked up as she passed, then enfolded her in a brief hug. "I'm sorry for your loss. Laney was an exceptionally nice human being."

"She was."

The tears she'd been holding back threatened to crawl up her throat. Her smile was already tight with them. She ducked her head and kept going, ignoring Vadim's soft question and heading determinedly to the stairs.

The dimly lit parking lot was almost deserted. She stood there for a moment, savoring the sour smell of old oil and burned rubber. What if the killer was watching her now? Would she be lured into his web just as Laney and Christa had been, or was she stronger? What did the Siren offer that made trained empaths let down their guards so easily?

She found her keys and opened her car door, sinking down onto the worn leather seat with a sense of relief. For a moment, she rested her forehead against the steering wheel and then turned the key. Nothing happened and she tried again. The engine coughed to life, rolled over and died again. She glared at the hood.

"Not now, you fucker. Can't you see I'm having a bad day?"

An episode of an ancient British comedy show her dad loved flashed into her mind, featuring an irate car owner giving his broken-down car a good thrashing. She was *so* tempted to imitate him. A shadow moved beside the car. She immediately dug in her open purse for her gun, cursing her lack of attention.

"Do you need a hand?"

Vadim bent down to the open window and hardly blinked as she shoved a gun in his face. She wondered if he'd had anything to do with her car not starting, but he'd claimed not to have the power to interfere with engines. But who was she kidding? She had no idea what he was capable of. Ignoring him, she turned the key again and the engine stuttered and died.

He walked around the car and got in beside her. "We can do

this one of two ways. You can sit here and call for a mechanic and hope he'll be able to get this rust bucket on the road for you."

"Or?"

"I can fix this little problem for you."

"And why would you do that?"

"To gain the opportunity to see you safely home."

"Why?"

He met her gaze. "Because I am concerned about your welfare."

"And you need me in one piece to help solve this situation."

"Exactly. If my boss hears that another empath has withdrawn from a case I'm working on, she's going to get all the wrong ideas."

"So you're not being noble, you're just being selfish?"

"That's correct."

She searched his shields but could sense nothing of his true intent or his feelings. "Okay. At least you're being straight with me. So how are you going to fix this? Are you going to wave your magic wand?"

"I don't have one." He smiled. "I don't need one. Try the key again."

She did and the engine roared into life. She threw him a sideways glance. "What exactly are you, again?"

He pointed at the exit. "I'd keep the engine running and just head out."

As they crawled across the Golden Gate Bridge, Vadim sat back and let the breeze blow through the open window. It was a curious smell, a mixture of the open sea and the briny waters of the bay, and gave off a metallic odor that reminded him of the taste of blood. Unconsciously, Vadim licked his lips and tasted salt and the faintest hint of the candy-flavored lip-gloss Ella wore. Her ability to separate her emotions from her job impressed him. Like him, she'd learned at a young age to conceal her feelings and focus on surviving. Okay, so she might not have faced death on a daily basis as he had, but as a young female torn away from her family and forced to claim a gift she must have hated, she definitely knew how to detach herself.

He'd heard her trying to persuade Liz to go out with her for a drink and had found himself worrying about her being out and alone while a serial killer targeting female empaths was on the loose. She wasn't stupid, but he knew from experience that alcohol had a way of dulling even the most exceptional psychic powers. When Feehan had called him back and asked if he might consider keeping an eye on Ella overnight, he had been more than willing to oblige. After what he'd seen in the Fae-Web, he knew his and Ella's fates were somehow intertwined, and he'd become an expert at self-preservation. Even if it meant consorting with an empath, he'd do whatever it took to stay alive. He was also more than willing to get drunk with her if that's what she needed. He always wished there had been someone with him when his brother had died...

"Here we are."

"You live here?"

Vadim got out of the car and looked up at the quaint Victorian style house perched on the side of the hill. Outside steps to the front door ran up to the second level. The backyard thrust upward from the house like an open fan with small terraces and opportunities to turn and admire the breathtaking views of the Golden Gate Bridge and the city beyond.

"The house was built in the late 1800's for one of the foremen who managed the railway line that ran along the coast road."

"So it's original."

"And pretty damn old for California." She found her keys

and started toward the lower level of the house, which Vadim realized had its own entrance on the other side of the property. "The owners recently restored it and created the basement apartment."

"It's beautiful," Vadim said, his gaze still drawn to the awesome view of the bridge and the city beyond. "You can breathe out here."

Ella glanced back at him over her shoulder. "Yes, you can. Are you coming in?"

"If that's okay."

"I don't really have much of a choice, do I? Unless you're a really good swimmer I reckon you're stuck in Tiburon for the night."

He followed her into the apartment and paused just inside the open door. He wasn't quite sure what he'd been expecting, but this warm, inviting modern space wasn't it. The floors and kitchen cupboards were cherry wood, the countertops granite and the furniture mostly cream. There was a big window at the front that had glimpses of the bay.

"Shut the door, you're letting the bugs in." He came in and watched as Ella dumped her keys and purse on the countertop. "I'm going to change. Do you want a beer?"

"I'll have some water, if that's okay."

"Help yourself. I think there's a bottle in the refrigerator."

She disappeared through an open door. Vadim caught a glimpse of a double bed covered in discarded clothes before she shut the door behind her. He went over to the stainless steel refrigerator and opened it. The white wire shelves contained a six-pack of beer, two water bottles and a carton of eggs.

He took some water and retired to sit on the couch that faced the view. His stomach growled and it occurred to him that he hadn't eaten since breakfast. The refrigerator door slammed and he turned to see Ella retrieving a bottle of beer and coming toward him. She'd changed into baggy shorts and a sleeveless top that looked as if it had come into contact with a bleach bottle.

"You live in a beautiful place."

She sat on the couch beside him, drawing her legs up underneath her.

"I know. Sometimes I have to remind myself of that." His stomach growled again and she looked at him.

"I suppose you're hungry."

"I haven't eaten since this morning."

"I have chicken nuggets in the freezer."

He shuddered. "I don't eat chicken."

"Why not? I thought everyone in the entire world ate chicken nuggets."

"I don't eat any kind of bird."

"So none of my mom's famous turkey meatloaf either." She took a swallow of beer. "There's a pizza place that does takeout. I have them on speed dial."

"If we have to go out to pick up the pizza, we could eat out instead. My treat," Vadim said.

Ella looked away. "I'd rather not. I don't feel like pretending everything is fine."

"Of course not. That was stupid of me." He considered her averted face. "I could cook us something."

"You cook?"

"I'm no expert, but I like to dabble. Is there a supermarket around here?"

"Yes, it's about a five minute drive."

He rose from the couch. "Then I'll get going. There is no need for both of us to come. Is there anything you don't like?"

"I'll eat anything you put in front of me." She stared up at him and he noticed the tired circles under her eyes and the sheen of tears. "Are you sure you want to do this?"

"You're putting up with me for a whole night. It's the least I can do."

She pouted. "I was wondering when you'd get around to asking if you could stay over. But I suppose the food will help."

"Good, then give me directions to the store and I'll be back as quickly as I can."

***

ELLA SAT on one of the stools at the countertop and watched as Vadim sliced up peppers and onions into neat strips. His knife moved in a blur of speed diagonally, then reversed the motion.

"You're good at this."

"I enjoy it." He didn't look up as he transferred the diced vegetables to a frying pan and tossed them in the already melted butter.

"You're very precise."

His back was still turned to her as he shrugged. "The food cooks more evenly if you slice it like that."

But he was meticulous about everything, the position of the bowls, knives and pans, the filleting of the fish that was now under the broiler. Ella licked her lips as the tantalizing smell of garlic and parsley infused the small kitchen. Having grown up eating institutionalized meals, she'd never had the opportunity to sit and watch her mother cook like this. For some reason, it was comforting.

"Do you want some wine yet?" she asked. He'd opened the bottle to pour over the fish and then put it straight back into the refrigerator.

"I'll wait until we eat." He expertly tossed the frying vegetables and stirred the pot of linguine. "It's almost ready."

"Shall I put out some plates?"

"They are already warming in the bottom of the oven."

"How about silverware?" She jumped off her stool and rummaged in the drawer for some knives and forks. "I have napkins somewhere too."

She put everything on the countertop near where Vadim was cooking, but he was busy with a hundred different tasks, draining the pasta, removing the fish from the broiler and plating everything up. Somewhere he'd found two mats and he put them side by side arranging the plates and silverware symmetrically on top.

Ella climbed back onto her seat and reached for the salt and pepper. "This looks awesome."

Vadim took the seat beside her and deftly removed the salt from her hand. "Try it first before you add seasoning. I'll get the wine."

She waited until he returned with two glasses and the frosted bottle of white chardonnay.

"Thank you."

"You're welcome." He poured the wine, making sure they both had exactly the same amount. "I hope you enjoy it. It's been a long day."

"It's been a horrible day." She took a healthy slug of the wine and Vadim winced. "What's wrong?"

"It's not beer. Sip it so that you can appreciate the flavor."

"I should've known you were a wine snob as well as a food snob."

"They do tend to go together." He clinked his glass against hers. "Thanks for letting me stay over."

She studied him over the rim of her glass. "I'm kind of glad you did." She hesitated. "I'm not sure what I would've done if I'd been here by myself. Probably something stupid."

He smiled. "Don't let me stop you."

She finished the wine and poured herself a second glass, forgetting she hadn't eaten all day either. She ate some fish and discovered it was delicious and just perfect for her unsettled stomach.

"I need to be stopped sometimes. I'm too old to go out and

pick up someone to while away a few naked sweaty hours of my life."

"You're not old."

"I'm almost twenty-seven. That's old for an empath."

He sipped his wine. "Not if you agree to take an OCOS mate."

She lowered her glass to glare at him. "And let Otherworld pick him? I'm not that stupid. And, all this 'destined mate' business, what a load of crap. Who wants to be tied to someone like that? It's unnatural."

"It will save your life."

She finished her second glass of wine and felt it settle unhappily in her stomach. "What's to save? A gatekeeper for two governments, or a person? No one cares about me, just about what I can do for them."

Oh God, what was wrong with her? Why was she becoming maudlin in front of Morosov of all people? "Anyway, that's enough about me. What happened to your brother?"

As she'd hoped, his smile faded and his concerned expression turned to ice. "I told you. He died." He got down from his seat. "Would you like some coffee?"

"No dessert?"

"I bought organic dark chocolate. We can have it with our coffee."

"I suppose it's good for me and I bet the coffee is decaffeinated," she grumbled. When she got down, the floorboards seem to slip around like the deck of the ship.

"Whoa." Vadim caught her elbow and she clung to him. "Perhaps you'd better go straight to bed."

She leaned into him and opened her eyes wide. "Only if you come with me."

He set her gently onto her feet, holding her by the elbows. "I don't think that would be a good idea."

"Why not? You obviously want to get in my pants."

"Not when you are drunk."

"It helps to be drunk. I won't remember the details in the morning."

He guided her toward her bedroom. "I thought you said you were beyond hooking up for sex?"

"I am. This is different. I know you. If you like, I could erase your memory afterward."

"You wouldn't want to." He smiled down at her as he opened the door. "When we make love, we'll both remember every screaming, sweaty second of it. I guarantee it."

She focused all her energy on his shields and couldn't find a way through.

"You're so conceited."

He maneuvered her over to the bed and gently sat her down. "Go to sleep, Ella. I'll be outside if you need me."

She clutched at his polo shirt. "I need you now."

"No, you need a good cry and a good sleep. You'd hate yourself in the morning if you fucked me now." He kissed her on the forehead. "Goodnight."

She reluctantly released her grip on his shirt and he dimmed the lights and shut the door behind him. A tear trickled down Ella's cheek and she rolled over onto her stomach and thought about Laney. Even though the only one who might hear her was Vadim, she still cried silently into her pillow, a habit she and Laney had learned together at school. A habit she doubted she would ever get over.

―――――――

"Good morning," Vadim greeted Ella with a slight smile. "What do you want first, coffee or orange juice?" He pointed to a paper bag. "I picked up some croissants on my way back from my morning walk."

"Stop being so cheerful. It's just *wrong*."

Despite her fears, she'd slept the whole night through and had the headache from hell to prove it. To her amazement, Vadim had not only cooked dinner, but also cleared everything away. Her kitchen looked shinier and in better order than it ever had before.

She wrapped her ratty dressing gown more securely around her waist and managed to climb up onto one of the stools by the countertop.

"Here you go." Vadim slid a glass of orange juice and a buttered croissant in front of her. "I'll get the coffee. I hope you don't mind, but while I was cleaning up last night I made a few adjustments to your cupboard space."

"What?"

Vadim opened her pantry. "You don't have much in there, but what you do have I reorganized according to type of product, ease of reach and sell-by date. It should make it easier to find things now."

He carried on talking as she forced down the orange juice and picked bits off the flakey outer shell of the croissant. The coffee smelled good, so she drank some of that too and slowly started to feel human.

"What time is it?"

He glanced at his watch. "About seven-thirty. I checked the ferry schedule. We should be fine if we leave in the next half hour."

She considered him through narrowed eyes. "We're not driving?"

He shrugged. "I didn't guarantee your car would work forever, just that it would get you home."

"Hmph." Ella picked up her coffee. She knew she should be more grateful but she just couldn't muster the energy. And he had turned her down… "I'm going to shower. I'll be ready in ten minutes."

10

"WE'VE CONTACTED PETER JAMESON, THE PROPOSED OCOS mate, and confirmed that he did speak to the victim on Sunday afternoon. He insists that the conversation went really well, and that they were planning to talk again the next day." Feehan paused to write something on the whiteboard. "We've also confirmed that he was at home with his parents and couldn't physically have been in Walnut Creek during the time of the murder."

"Unless he is more than fifty percent Otherworld," Vadim said.

Feehan consulted his notes. "He lives on our side and he's one-sixteenth Otherworld. I doubt he has the necessary powers to get himself through time and space."

"Did you check where the nearest portals were to Walnut Creek?"

"The closest one was about thirty miles away."

"So how did the murderer get to Laney's building?"

He glanced over at Ella, but she had her head propped up with her hand and seemed to be doodling on the yellow pad in front of her. He'd already handed her some painkillers and another bottle of water but she was too quiet for his liking.

"We don't even know how the killer is getting his information about the empaths or how he is picking his targets." Vadim tried to read what Ella was writing, but he couldn't make it out.

Alexei leaned back in his chair, his Fae-Web spiraling around him. "Liz and I have been considering that and we believe there are only a few possibilities." He glanced at Liz, who nodded. "Information about empaths isn't that freely available."

"Otherworld has that information, as do the current world governments," Feehan replied.

"That's a hell of a lot of people," Vadim said. "And most of them are open to corruption."

Feehan stiffened. "Not on our side. We all know that the moral code in Otherworld is very different."

Vadim couldn't disagree. "Let's assume that the leak originates in Otherworld then." He turned to Liz. "Where would such information be held?"

"That's a great question." She frowned. "There's the empath academy, of course, and a central administration department also based in Merton that keeps records of humans who have Otherworld antecedents, or who are empaths."

"Can you contact them through your Fae-Web?" Feehan asked.

Liz sighed. "No, even our technology doesn't work well across the divide. We'll have to go and see them in person."

"Then you'll have to do that, Liz." Feehan wrote it on the board under the word "actions". "Anything else?"

"Do we have any footage from the security cameras at the apartment complex?" Alexei said.

"Not yet. But I've put in a request for them."

"I doubt our man will show up," Vadim commented, his gaze still on Ella's bowed head. "He's got enough power to evade the cameras."

Ella finally looked up. "How do you know?"

Vadim met her gaze. "Because I could sense his magic. Is there anything else you'd like to contribute to this conversation, Ms. Walsh?"

She glanced down at her pad. "There's one thing. I see a pattern here. He's targeting empaths who are approaching their twenty-seventh birthday."

Liz suddenly sat forward, her gold Fae-Web shimmering. "And members of your graduating class, Ella."

"What?" Feehan turned from his contemplation of the board to Liz.

"I just made the connection. All of the victims, including the ones in Russia, graduated from empath college within a year of each other."

"From the same college?"

"Not exactly. There are a few scattered around Otherworld. Offhand, I know of one for Europeans and two for Americans, and probably at least a couple more for everyone else. But the victims are definitely from the same year."

"Great." Ella put down her pen. "It would be good to get a list of all the empaths who graduated with me worldwide, and check up on their well-being. Maybe we've missed a few suspicious deaths along the way." Feehan paused to look at Liz. "Will the central record office at Merton have that information?"

"They should have." Liz made a face. "The problem is finding it."

"It should be a priority," Feehan said. "Ella, would you be willing to go with Liz to visit the college and the records office?"

"If I have to. They don't like me much over there. I kept trying to destroy their portals when I ran away from school." She gave Vadim and Alexei a pointed look. "Won't we need a foreign language specialist to gain access to some of those files?"

Feehan rubbed his hands together. "I'm sure that will help.

Until then, we'll do another check into Peter Jameson's background, review our victim's phone and computer records, and wait for the results of the autopsy."

She winced and Vadim cursed Feehan for his insensitivity. Had he forgotten that Ella had just lost her best friend?

Vadim cleared his throat. "Are you okay with all this, Ms. Walsh?"

"Why wouldn't I be?"

He held her gaze. "Because you've had a severe shock."

"It's okay, I won't go nuts on you just yet."

"That's not what I meant."

"Yeah." She rose to her feet. "Do you have any more of those painkillers?"

He extracted the bottle from his pocket and resisting the urge to pitch it at her head, tossed it over to her. If she didn't want to talk about anything, that suited him fine. He wasn't quite sure why he was even bothering in the first place. Shouldn't she be grateful to him for turning her down last night? He'd behaved like the perfect gentleman and she was still being shitty. Maybe she understood him better than he understood himself. All he had to do was keep her alive, catch this killer and get back to Russia with his reputation intact.

Liz caught up with Ella and wrapped an arm around her as they walked. Alexei glanced over at Vadim.

"Did you really stay over with Ella?"

"Feehan asked me to. He was worried about her safety."

"So how was it?"

He raised his eyebrows. "I cooked her some dinner and then she went to bed."

Alexei just stared at him. "That's it?"

"What else did you expect?"

"Details, my friend, details."

"I cooked snapper with red peppers in a white wine sauce. Do you want the recipe or something?"

"Damn, you're a close-mouthed bastard sometimes, Vadim."
Alexei stretched his arms over his head. "If I'd got to stay with
Ella, I'd be telling you all the juicy details."

"And that's probably why Feehan sent me."

Alexei opened his silver eyes wide. "You can pretend to be
human all you like, Vadim, but at your core, you're no different
than me."

"That's where we'll have to disagree. I've made a choice as to
how I want to live my life and I'm happy with it."

"So you say."

Vadim fixed Alexei with a cool stare. "Shall we just leave it at
that? As a fellow team member, Ms. Walsh needs our support
and nothing else."

"You've changed your mind. You were the one who wanted
her out."

Vadim stood and shoved his chair in. "I want to solve this
case. Messing around with an empath who is already in a highly
emotional state isn't going to help me do that. I refuse to be
responsible for another meltdown."

He wanted to laugh at his own words. Hadn't he already
crossed that line last night by taking care of her rather than
simply fucking her brains out? Wasn't he already emotionally
compromised?

"So you're quite happy to leave Ella to me."

He glared down at the Fae. "Have you listened to a single
word I said?"

"I listened." Alexei tilted his head back so Vadim could see
his face more clearly. "Have you ever wondered if you are the
problem and not the empath?"

"That's ridiculous."

"Are you sure about that? Repressing your true nature
behind all those shields must give any empath who comes near
you a hell of a headache."

Vadim shook his head and walked away but Alexei kept talking. "So you're okay to be the one who goes to Otherworld with Liz and Ella then."

He had to stop. "I don't go there. You know that."

"As I said, Vadim. Are you sure you aren't the problem?"

Vadim started walking again and this time he didn't stop.

LIZ KNOCKED, then poked her head around the door of Ella's office.

"Are you okay, hon?"

Ella manufactured a smile. "I just got off the phone with my mom. She's still going on about my 'behavior' at the party yesterday."

Liz sat on the corner of Ella's desk. "Did you tell her about Laney?"

"She didn't give me a chance." Ella made a face. "And when she does find out she'll be on at me for not telling her. Maybe I'll text her later."

"Your mom isn't the most observant of people, is she?"

"That's a nice way of putting it, but at least she still talks to me. I also spoke to Laney's parents who— guess what?—can't make the time to come to their own daughter's funeral. Apparently their other 'normal' kid is graduating med school or something *important*. They asked me to send a wreath in their name and they'd settle up with me later."

"I hope you told them to go fuck themselves."

Ella looked up at Liz's flushed face. "You don't usually curse."

"I don't usually have to, but the way some human parents deal with their kids just amazes me. In Fae, you'd have to do something far more interesting to get disowned by your family."

"Like killing or maiming a whole bunch of people at a wedding."

Liz made an airy gesture. "That was just a one-off. My family is usually pretty well behaved. I've arranged for us to go and visit the college and the records office in Merton this afternoon. Are you okay to come with me?"

"If I must."

"We'll keep it short."

Ella groaned. "If they'll let us."

Liz slid off the desk. "I'll be back for you in about an hour." She got as far as the door before she turned around. "By the way, how was your evening with the gorgeous Mr. Morosov?"

"He cooked me dinner, I drank too much wine and I went to bed."

"Alone?"

"Of course. What kind of a girl do you think I am?"

Liz sighed. "I know what kind of a girl you are. He didn't even try and hook up with you?"

Ella hastily repressed her memories of exactly who had been propositioning whom. "You know I don't date people I have to make eye contact with ever again."

"But he's going back to Russia."

"That's not far enough and I don't think he's really Russian. He's *totally* Otherworld." Ella lowered her voice. "How much Fae do you think he is?"

"He's obviously got something going on, but what exactly, I'm not sure. His shields are too good. Do you want me to ask Alexei?"

"No! I'm not *that* interested. I just wondered what you'd picked up."

"I know Vadim is important to this case and he has a connection with you."

"Yeah, we're colleagues."

"It's more than that."

"Oh jeez, you've got that faraway look in your eyes again."

Liz shrugged. "I can't help it. The Fae-Web knows stuff I can't yet comprehend. But I can tell you that Vadim Morosov isn't going away anytime soon."

"Great. I'll see you later. I have to call a dude about a giant caterpillar he saw in his yard last night."

When Liz shut the door, Ella finally let her smile slip. She covered her face with her hands and simply sat there in silence. It was all well and good telling herself that she was going to avenge Laney and catch the killer but it didn't make up for the hole left in her life. Normally she would've been calling Laney right now to tell her about her embarrassing evening with Vadim so that they could pick over the details and laugh hysterically. She'd never even got to hear what Laney really thought about Peter Jameson...

Ella slowly inhaled and then let out her breath. She had to get her shit together or the department would be pensioning her off to the empath nuthouse out in Marin County and letting Sam take over the case. That would never do. She had to survive this for Laney, and for all the other empaths that had died so horribly.

She picked up the phone and dialed the number Peach had left on her desk.

"Hey, Mr. Collins? I understand you have a giant bug problem..."

VADIM LOOKED AROUND THE FOYER, but there was no sign of Alexei. He walked by the reception desk for the second time and stopped to talk to the pink-haired administrator who smiled so enthusiastically up at him.

"Can I help you, Mr. Morosov?"

"Have you seen Alexei anywhere?"

"Oh yes!" She fished for something on her desk. "He asked

me to give you a message. He had to go out and assist on a case with Ella and he's not sure when he'll be back."

"They both went out?" He checked his watch. "Is Liz here?"

Peach picked up the phone. "I can check for you."

"Thanks."

While Peach chatted, he paced the lobby, watching the lights on the elevators flash up and down. Ella came in from the street eating an ice cream cone.

"Hey. Are you waiting for me?"

He studied her flushed face and whipped out his handkerchief. "You have ice cream on your nose."

"Thanks." She took the handkerchief from him and patted her face. "Is that better?"

He nodded as Liz came out of the elevator and advanced toward them.

"Where's Alexei?"

Ella finished her ice cream and used Vadim's handkerchief to wipe her fingers before stuffing it in her pocket. "I left him with Mr. Collins."

"The guy who saw the caterpillar?" Liz asked. "Yeah, well *apparently*, Mr. Collins is one-eighth Fae, and he's related to Alexei, who is also related to the young Fae Mr. Collins trapped in his yard."

"The caterpillar, right?"

"Exactly. Apparently it was some kind of legendary Garden Fae family hazing joke, which Mr. Collins didn't know about, being as he doesn't live in Otherworld anymore. Alexei had to explain it."

"So you didn't have to wipe his mind?"

"Not this time. Alexei said he would take care of it for me before he departed. When I left, they were still catching up on ancient family history."

"Alexei is supposed to be here," Vadim interrupted.

Ella and Liz looked at him. "It's no big deal. You can come with us instead, right?"

He stared at them for a long moment. If he refused, would it get back to Feehan and more importantly his Russian boss? His conduct had to be exemplary and Ella needed to be protected. Mentally he strengthened his shields. He could manage a quick trip back to Otherworld. He'd be in and out before anyone or anything picked up a trace of him. At least, he hoped he would.

"Where's the nearest portal?"

Ella took out her phone and clicked on the app. "The one at the end of Embarcadero near the ball park is still open. We can walk there."

If he hadn't have been too busy thinking up gruesome ways to slaughter his extremely hard-to-kill Fae partner, Vadim would have enjoyed the walk more. The sun was shining and despite the brisk breeze blowing in off the bay, the walkways were thronged with a mixture of tourists and office workers seeking a late lunch. Ella led them through a complex route of backstreets that brought them out close to the walls of the ballpark. He stopped to admire the statue of an unknown baseball player. "Who is this?"

Ella gave him a look. "It's Willie McCovey, dude."

"It might surprise you to know that outside America, baseball isn't such a big deal."

"Maybe not in Russia." Ella held up her phone. "Where is this damned portal?"

He pointed at a spot close to the brick wall. "It's there."

Liz gave him a surprised glance. "You can see them?"

"Sometimes when I'm close," Vadim admitted. "Shall we get on with it?" He headed for the portal, his hand outstretched, and felt the wall dissolve at his touch. When Ella and Liz stood beside him in the small circle of light, he closed his eyes and spoke out loud.

"Registry at Merton, please."

Although his body didn't appear to move, he was aware of a strange whooshing sensation in his head. When he opened his eyes, the circle of light had turned green. He touched the nearest solid surface and pushed through it to find himself outside an old-fashioned brick building four stories high with a double fronted black door. There was no one else on the cobbled street and a light rain had begun to fall. A sign on the door told any caller to use the side entrance. In small print at the bottom it also said "at your own risk," but that was a pretty standard disclaimer for Otherworld.

"I haven't been here before," Ella said.

"I have." Liz shuddered. "Prepare to whisk yourself back fifty years in time."

Vadim walked around the side of the building and his magical senses flared to life. He pushed open the side door and a bell jangled somewhere deep within the building. The hallway opened up into a large, dimly lit room that appeared to be empty. A long high countertop made of gleaming oak divided the space neatly in half. Lamps with green shades cast inadequate light into the dark corners where things listened and lingered.

"Where is everyone?" Ella whispered.

Liz headed for the counter. "God knows, but it doesn't matter. It's all done with bits of paper anyway." She took a sheet of the yellow lined paper and a pencil from the pot and started to write. "You have to be very careful how you phrase your request or you end up with something you didn't expect."

"We want a list of my graduating class from six years ago, and if they have it, lists for all the other colleges in the same time period."

"Right, and we also want copies of any correspondence between Otherworld and either of the two victims," Liz added.

As the women discussed what to ask for, Vadim prowled around the space, trying to keep his shields up and yet delicately sense what was going on. A shadow flitted by him, brushing his face, and he almost recoiled. He had the unwelcome sensation that something was already inside his head, delicately peeling back the layers of his defenses until he'd be exposed in his true form.

"How long will this take?" he asked Liz.

She pointed to a clock set on the countertop. "What time's the next pick up?"

He squinted at the cloudy glass clockface. "In about three minutes."

Liz handed him the sheet of paper. "Put it in the basket next to the clock and step away from the counter." Vadim did as she asked and, for good measure, retreated behind Ella. "Do we need to ring the bell or something?"

"God, don't do that." Liz shuddered. "You really don't want to make them angry."

A door opened at the back of the official side of the room. Vadim turned his attention to the young man who approached the desk. He looked quite human, his hair a nondescript brown and his eyes hidden behind a pair of thick glasses.

"Don't acknowledge him," Liz whispered. "Let him get on with his job."

The man took the paper out of the basket, scanned the contents and then reset the clock. He disappeared back through the door without saying a single word.

Vadim waited until the door shut until going back to check the clock.

"He can't be serious. How can it take half an hour to get the information?" Vadim didn't want to stay there for five more minutes, let alone another thirty. Somewhere deep in his mind he could feel his mother stirring, reaching for him...

"Because they can't use the internet here," Liz explained. She gestured at the rows of filing cabinets that lined the walls on both sides of the counter. "Everything has to be typed out on a manual typewriter, photocopied or faxed."

"Don't forget all the illegible handwritten notes, as well." Ella leaned her chair back until it balanced on two legs. "But you must know all this already, Morosov. You're from here, aren't you?"

Vadim refused to rise to the bait and instead took another hasty walk around the office. "Is there anything in these more public files that might help us?"

Liz looked around. "I doubt it, but it would give us something to do while we wait for the information."

"I'm not sure why Ms. Walsh and I have to be here," Vadim said.

"Because the officials like to know who wants the information and decide if they are going to provide it."

"We haven't seen anyone except the desk clerk."

"Oh, they've seen us," Liz assured him. "Can't you feel it?"

Vadim could feel it all too clearly, but he didn't want Liz or Ella to know that. He concentrated on maintaining his shields. "What's in these more public files?"

Liz rose from her seat and walked over to him. "It depends."

"On what?"

"On what you are seeking."

"Typical Otherworld logic," Vadim snapped. He jumped as the filing cabinet closest to him rocked back and forth. He'd better be more careful or he'd be bringing far worse than the custodians of the records room down upon them. "Maybe I'll start by looking up references to the Siren."

He walked along the rows, looking for the relevant drawer and eventually found one that included the letters S—Sl. It opened easily and he considered the neatly labeled alphabetical paper files. He wasn't really surprised to see there wasn't a nice file ready for him telling him all he needed to know about his adversary. That would've been far too easy.

Ella was looking at some files on the other side of the room and Liz was somewhere else. The clock on the countertop ticked loudly and was the only sound apart from the rustling of paper. Vadim shut the drawer, then went across to Ella, who hurriedly put the files she was looking at back and moved away.

He considered the drawer she'd been searching through and pulled it open again. A corner of a file labeled Morosov stuck up above the neat row. He took it out and opened it, but there was nothing inside. Had Ella taken something, or had someone from his family removed all traces of him? If so, why not take the folder as well?

"Did you find something interesting, Ms. Walsh?" He turned to study Ella.

She glanced at him over her shoulder. "Nothing so far. How about you?"

He considered her for a moment and then shut the drawer. "I wonder if there is a file about you?"

"There are probably several. I'm not the most popular human in Otherworld."

"I don't think they like empaths, so I wouldn't take it personally."

"I don't." She opened another drawer. "There's nothing about Alexei here either."

"It seems that the powers-that-be don't want to help us with anything." Vadim looked impatiently back toward the counter. "I wonder if we'll get the information we need?"

Liz surveyed the rows of filing cabinets. "I suppose it depends if they want us to catch this killer."

"As they don't like empaths for opening up their world to humans, they might be quite happy to see the whole lot of us exterminated," Ella said.

"That's also true but we have to ask." Liz sat down at the table again and checked her cell. Ella joined her. "Dammit, I can't even play games on my phone while we wait."

He took the seat next to Ella. For some reason, when he was near her, his sense of danger dissipated. As his anxiety grew, he wasn't averse to taking any help he could get.

He tensed as Ella slid a piece of paper in front of him. "Why is there a photocopy of a blurry bird in your file?"

"Ella, you're not supposed to take things out of there!" Liz whispered. "Go and put it back *immediately* or we might not get our information."

"Fine." She picked up the sheet of paper and walked back to the filing cabinets. "I was just wondering what it was for." She glanced back at Vadim, who had remained in his chair. "Hey, Morosov, are your family connected with Mother Goose or something?"

"Hardly."

She opened the drawer that had contained his file and flicked through them. "Your file's disappeared. Did you take it?"

Liz shot to her feet and rushed over to Ella. "Of course he didn't! You've probably just misplaced it." After going through the entire drawer she looked as puzzled as Ella. "What did you do?"

"I just looked through the file and found this bit of paper. There wasn't anything else to see."

"Oh God," muttered Liz. "Where are we going to put this now?"

Ella opened the next nearest file. "We could shove it in here?"

Liz grabbed her wrist. "Don't do that! We'll just have to put it in on the countertop and hope that nobody sees it until after we've left. What were you doing looking in Vadim's file, anyway?"

She rolled her eyes. "Because he won't tell me exactly what he is, and I can't penetrate his shields. Why else would I be looking?"

"I can hear you, Ms. Walsh. I'm sitting right here." He turned to look at her, one eyebrow raised.

"I know, so what?" Ella put the piece of paper on the countertop and returned to sit next to him at the table. "It's all your fault."

"For not blabbing my entire life history to you?"

"I'm not asking for it all, just the juicy parts." He didn't answer and she sighed. "So what's up with the bird picture, then?"

"I have no idea."

He shifted slightly in his seat and Ella got a sudden image of flying before his shields slammed shut again. Otherworld was certainly doing a number on him. He looked distinctly uncomfortable.

"You don't like it here, do you?"

He finally deigned to look at her. "I like it about as much as you like elevators."

"That bad, huh? What happened?"

"What happened when?"

"Don't prevaricate. Why don't you like being in Otherworld?"

His smile was bitter. "If I told you that, we'd be here all night."

"We have time." She sat forward and held his gaze. "Okay, shoot."

The door at the back of the office opened and Vadim looked away from her. "Here comes the messenger of doom. He's early."

"Luckily for you." Ella put her phone away.

Liz waited until the man deposited something in the box before she stood up, tucked her hair behind her ear and approached the counter. She froze, her hand poised over the message as the man spied the single sheet of paper Ella had put on the counter and picked it up.

"Sorry about that," Liz said "It just fell out of something."

She received no reply and waited smiling bravely until the door shut again. She exhaled with a whoosh and scooped up the sheets of paper.

"Let's get going. Even if this isn't the stuff we need, I don't think we'll be getting any more help today. We'll go and speak to the administrators at the college next. It's just up the street, so we can walk there."

Ella looked up at the brick frontage of her *alma mater* and grimaced. It hadn't changed a bit. She'd spent two and a half years of her life being trained to suck out memories from both humans and Otherworld. Because of the shortness of their potential working lives, the trainee empaths received almost no vacation time to be with their families. It had just been constant work to get them out into the field to do their dangerous job.

Not everyone had made it.

She led the way into the building and turned left into the large administration wing. The two ladies who manned the front desk had been there for as long as anyone could remember. Ella had decided they weren't actually human because they never seemed to age.

"Ella Walsh."

She smiled at the dark-haired one who didn't look terribly pleased to see her. "Yes, it's me, Miss Vera. It's just like old times, isn't it?" She turned to her companions. "I was in here a *lot*."

Liz hid a smile and approached the desk. "I'm Liz Smith. We have an appointment with Mr. Perry."

Miss Vera checked the calendar in front of her. "I'll just call and see if he's available."

"Thank you."

Liz wandered away to look at the pictures on the wall. Unlike most colleges there were no trophy cabinets for sports awards, or outstanding academic brilliance. Instead, there were honor roll calls of empaths who had died for the cause. Ella had sat in the office for so many hours that she practically knew the names by heart. At eighteen, convinced that she had all the time in the world, she had scoffed at the idea of caring whether you died at twenty-seven or earlier.

Miss Vera put down the phone. "You may go in, now.

I'm sure Ella remembers the way."

Ella pointed at the door at the end of the hallway. "Follow me."

She knocked and held the door open for Liz and an uptight Vadim to go in front of her. He hadn't been kidding when he said that he didn't like being in Otherworld. His shields were already struggling to cope with whatever was attacking him— and something was; she could sense it very clearly. It was another good reason to keep this meeting short so they could get the hell out of there.

Mr. Perry's welcoming smile faltered. "Miss Walsh. You're still alive?"

"Yeah." Ella took a seat. "But don't worry, I'm due to go nuts in a couple of weeks, so all your dire predictions about my future will come true."

Liz threw her an exasperated look and Ella shut up. Perry meant nothing to her now. He had no power and she could almost feel sorry for him having to deal with multiple eighteen-year-old idiot empaths like her.

Perry ignored Ella and focused on Liz. "How can I help you, Ms. Smith?"

Ella was impressed with how neatly Liz described what was going on without giving too much away. Perry's expression changed as Liz told him what they thought was happening, and what the college could do to help the SBLE.

"This is appalling." Perry shook his head. "After all the expense to the government of educating these empaths, they end up dead before their time."

"I don't think they die worrying about the expense, Mr. Perry." Ella couldn't help herself. "They die with all their abilities stolen from them and no sense of who they are. Don't you think that's more important?"

"Miss Walsh…"

Liz intervened. "I'm sure Mr. Perry meant no disrespect, Ella. He is obviously concerned about the overall loss of the empaths to the community."

"Yeah, right."

Ella noticed Vadim's hand slowly closing into a fist until his knuckles shone white. A bead of sweat wended its way down from his forehead to his cheek. She didn't have time to goad Mr. Perry. Vadim needed to get away.

Liz took up the conversation again. "We would like a list of all the empaths who graduated in Ella's year from this college and a list of the staff who were here at the same time."

"I'm sure we can provide you with that information, Ms. Smith. It might take a few days, but I'd be more than happy to help." Perry stood up and fixed his gaze on Ella. "Despite everything, the idea that any murderer is targeting empaths makes me angry and I'd like to see it stopped."

Liz shook his proffered hand. "Thanks, Mr. Perry.

We appreciate it."

She didn't bother to offer her hand and neither did Vadim. His desire to bolt was consuming him and infecting both her and Liz. It was debatable which one of them raced back toward the portal fastest, although Vadim made a credible attempt to make it look as if he was deferring to her and Liz. Inside the portal, the light was yellow, which meant they were clear to leave. She waited for Vadim to speak the words, but he seemed distracted. She elbowed him in the side.

"You brought us here. You need to take us back. Just ask for SBLE, Embarcadero. That should do it."

Vadim opened his mouth and then he hesitated, his gaze traveling around the small space.

"What's wrong?"

He exhaled. "I can't say the words."

"Why not?"

"Something doesn't want me to leave."

Ella felt it then, the sense that something big, bad and dangerous was coming right for them.

"We need to leave right now, Morosov."

"I know that!"

She grabbed his hand. "Mouth the words as I say them." His fingers were cold and shaking, the pulse at his wrist jumping around like an animal in shock. "*Morosov.*"

He nodded and she closed her eyes and spoke as loudly as she could above the shrieking in her head. "SBLE Embarcadero, please."

Nothing happened and Vadim gripped her hand even tighter. "Liz, hold his other hand, and let's try this together."

She felt the power of Liz's energy join them and resolutely closed her eyes again. "SBLE Embarcadero. *Please.*"

She gulped as they were swallowed up into a spiral of screaming rage. All she could do was hold on to Vadim's hand with all her might.

Suddenly, the screaming stopped. She touched the side of the portal, depositing all three of them on the ground beside the ballpark in a heap. Liz rolled away and Ella landed right on top of Vadim, their clasped hands sandwiched between them on his chest.

"My hero," she cooed.

He glared up at her. "I didn't do that intentionally. Get off me."

She wiggled a little and had the satisfaction of feeling him go still. "Who wants to keep you in Otherworld?"

"No one you would know."

She leaned as close as she could and kissed him, enjoyed the hitch of his breath and the unexpected jolt of his erection against her stomach. He stared up at her and with a muffled groan, kissed her back, his fingers in her hair, his tongue plundering her mouth.

"Ouch!" Ella looked up at Liz. "What was that kick for?"

Liz spoke through the side of her mouth. "You're attracting a crowd."

"Sorry. I couldn't resist." Ella rolled off Vadim and got to her feet, dusting off her knees and avoiding his eyes. Why had she kept kissing him when she'd only been trying to piss him off? He followed more slowly and half-turned away from her to brush the dirt from his previously immaculate shirt and pants.

She followed Liz back down the street, her legs still trembling and her heart rate all over the place. Vadim made no effort to keep up with them. When she glanced back his expression had returned to normal, but she could sense the heat coming off him and the turmoil within. What would he be like without his carefully constructed defenses, with all that immense control shattered? She swallowed hard. Damned scary.

At the office, Liz called the elevator and waited with Vadim while Ella took the stairs. By the time she came through the door, they were already sitting in the conference room drinking bottled water.

Feehan came in behind her and snapped on the main lights. "What did you get?"

"I'm not sure yet. The college will be sending us something, and I got these from the record office." Liz took out the folded papers and laid them carefully on the table. "We have correspondence between OCOS and both Christa and Laney naming their mates. Sam can check the info against what we already have. The next one looks like a list of Ella's graduating class." Liz paused. "There weren't many of you, were there?"

Ella craned to look as well. "Less than a dozen who made it, I think, and most of us were female."

"Ten," Liz said. "Two of them male, which leaves eight females."

"Two of whom we know are already dead," Feehan added helpfully. "Ella is here, so we only need to check on five. Can we do that using human resources or do we need to go back to Otherworld?"

Ella, Vadim and Liz all shuddered.

"Most empaths live in the human sphere."

"They can live in Otherworld too?" Feehan asked. "I didn't realize that."

"Occasionally someone chooses to stay on and teach at the college, or work for the government. It's not encouraged because we're supposed to be out in the field." Ella unwrapped a piece of candy. "Sometimes a mated couple will go and live there. God knows why."

"Maybe they have family over there," Liz suggested. "I know some of Doug's pack who remain in wolf form prefer it."

"That's right. According to the original treaty, if you can't look like a human, you're not really supposed to be over here, are you?" Feehan nodded. "It makes sense." He cleared his throat. "Now where were we? Ella, can you check on the empaths here?"

"Sure."

"And Liz, can you liaise with Alexei about the others?"

"If Alexei ever turns up." Vadim inspected the sleeve of his suit for damage.

Feehan looked up. "Alexei's here. Were you looking for him?" He jabbed a finger at the next sheet of paper. "What else do we have?"

"This is a list of all the graduates in our requested time period from all the empath colleges in the world." Liz tapped the paper as she counted. "Less than three dozen. We can check up on those guys too."

"Great." Feehan hesitated. "The results of the autopsy are in. It seems that our latest victim died in exactly the same way as Christa Morehouse. Her hippocampus was also liquefied."

Ella looked away. She hadn't needed to be told that all sense of Laney had been removed. Apart from the psychic stench of the Siren, the apartment had felt empty. Sorrow engulfed her, streaming through her senses like an unstoppable tidal wave.

Just as Feehan cleared his throat Alexei strolled into the room and smiled at Vadim, who didn't respond. "Let's call it a day and meet back here tomorrow when we have a clearer picture about the remaining empaths." Liz and Alexei started talking to each other, their Fae-Webs intermingling. Feehan joined them, leaving Ella sitting by herself at the table. "Ms. Walsh?"

She looked up to see that Vadim was watching her closely.

"What?"

"I just realized I must have left my wallet in your car."

"Oh dear."

"My hotel passkey is in there."

"I'm sure they'll give you another one."

"Not without ID. That was in my wallet too."

She raised her chin to meet his smiling, apologetic gaze. "Can't you use your magic to get whatever you want?"

He leaned closer and she smelled his now-familiar citrus scent. "I try not to use magic in the human realm."

"Why's that?"

He sat on the corner of the table, which made him about level with her. "Because it identifies me."

"And you're scared of being caught—by what?"

He shrugged. "Otherworld."

"I noticed that today." She studied his beautiful face. "You're part shapeshifter, aren't you?" His expression didn't even flicker. "What kind? Dragon?"

"Why would you think that?"

"Because of your ring and because of that honking great clue in your Otherworld file."

"Honking, funny." He glanced down at his hand. "The ring was a gift from one of my godparents."

"You have godparents in Otherworld?"

"They are guardians or mentors who are concerned more with your life or death choices rather than your spiritual ones."

"That makes sense. So what kind of bird are you?"

"Would it be possible for me to come back with you on the ferry and retrieve my wallet?" He stood over her, one hand in his pocket, the other clenched on the back of his chair.

"A rooster? A chicken? I know you said you didn't eat birds."

He slowly exhaled and looked heavenward. "I don't even have to speak to you on the ferry, just as long as you can spare five seconds to unlock your car and hand me my wallet when we arrive at your house. I'll turn around and go right back, I swear it."

"Couldn't you just sleep with Alexei?"

He smiled. "Been there, done that, don't want to do it again."

She stared at him. "You've hooked up with Alexei? You're gay?"

Again, that devastating smile. "He's Fae. He'll fuck anything that doesn't run away fast enough."

"And did you run?"

"Not really." His gaze settled on her mouth. "We were young and I like to experience everything both worlds have to offer."

"So you're bi."

"Why do empaths always insist on sticking labels on everything?"

"So we know what we're getting ourselves into." Ella stood up, but Vadim didn't move away and she was far too close. She raised her chin to stare at him. In her experience, attack was always preferable to retreat and it was always amusing to see him having to be polite and conciliatory.

"If you prefer men, why are you still coming on to me?" Ella asked.

"I don't prefer men, and you're the one who was all over me earlier."

"I was amusing myself at your expense."

"I noticed. You're good at that."

"It's a talent of mine." She refused to look away from his beautiful blue eyes. "I have some paperwork to do before I leave. If you want to wait and come back with me that's cool."

"Thanks, I'll do that." He nodded and, to her relief, finally walked away.

11

She glanced sideways as Vadim disembarked from the ferry alongside her. It was still warm and sunlight glinted off the water like shards of glass, making her slide her sunglasses down onto her nose. He took off his jacket and slung it over his shoulder. He looked like something out of a fashion magazine.

"Is this really about your wallet?"

"I can't manage without ID."

She turned right and started up the slight slope toward her home. "Did Feehan ask you to come home with me?"

"He did, but I'd already decided to do that anyway."

Ella stopped walking and faced him. "Why?"

"That's a good question. Sometimes I just have to follow my instincts."

"Your big bird instincts?"

His delicious mouth curved up into a half-smile. "You don't give up, do you?"

"That's right. I'm a tough cookie and I don't need protecting."

"I don't doubt that you are strong, but this particular killer seems to have the ability to disarm the most competent of empaths."

"Did he kill Natasha?"

"I can't prove anything, but I suspect he had something to do with it." He looked out over the sea. "She was certainly acting irrationally."

"All empaths do that when they turn twenty-seven." Ella started walking again. It was too hot to linger. "You know that."

"But they don't tend to betray their colleagues."

"Is that what she did?"

"We'd set up a trap for the killer at one of the empaths' apartments and at the last possible moment, Natasha blew our cover. The Siren escaped with his intended victim and murdered her at a different venue. Natasha left in hysterics and killed herself."

Ella kept walking as she imagined the chaos Natasha had caused. "Did you find her?"

"I found both of them."

Ella waited for him to elaborate, but he just paced alongside her, his dark hair blowing in the soft breeze, his expression unreadable.

"Do you think the Siren wanted you to find them?"

"Seeing as they were both dumped in my apartment, I'd say that he did."

"Oh, shit." Despite the fierce sun Ella shivered. "So Natasha was living with you at the time."

"She was certainly there a lot."

"Is that why you were suspended from duty?"

He looked down at her. "Someone's been doing their research. My boss decided that I was at fault for a) becoming intimate with a team member, and b) for not realizing that said team member was unstable."

How were you supposed to know that Natasha would lose it like that?"

"Apparently, as team leader, I should have known. And she *was* an empath."

Dammit, she was starting to feel sorry for the man and that would never do. Ella dug in her purse for her front door key, opened the door and then handed the bunch of keys to Vadim. "Go check the car for your wallet."

She left the door open and went inside, glad of the instant chill of the newly upgraded air conditioning. The light on her phone was blinking. It would be her mother asking a million questions about Laney that she really didn't want to answer. Her stomach knotted at the thought of another evening on her own.

She jumped as Vadim knocked on the door and held out her keys. "I found my wallet. Where shall I put these?"

"On the countertop is fine."

He placed the keys carefully in the center of the glass bowl and stepped back. "I'll see you tomorrow, then, Ms. Walsh."

He was almost out the door before Ella really believed he was leaving. "Hey, Morosov!"

He looked over his shoulder at her. "What?"

"You can hang out here with me for a while."

"I don't want to miss the ferry."

"Oh for God's sake, don't make me ask nicely. If things go well and we manage to stand each other's company for a few hours, you can always sleep on the couch again."

"Are you sure?"

"If I wasn't, I wouldn't have asked."

"Then I'll stay for a while."

She waited until he came in and shut the door. "You have to cook me dinner though."

"I guessed that. Or we could order in some pizza. I like pizza."

"So do I."

He held up his wallet. "I'll even pay for it."

VADIM CLOSED the lid of the pizza box and secured it tightly.

"That was excellent."

"Yeah, they do a pretty good job." Ella patted at her mouth with one of the red-checked napkins the pizza place had given them, burped discreetly and put her paper plate on top of the pizza box.

Vadim removed it and stood up. "I'll put this in the refrigerator for you."

"Sure and while you're there, can you get me another beer?"

He picked up the pizza box, her empty beer bottle and the two plates. "Where does the recycling go?"

"There's a green container under the sink." She looked back at him over her shoulder. "Don't worry about it now. Come and sit down and belittle this cop show with me."

He ignored her and focused on cleaning up the kitchen, finding two more beers and locating the recycling bin. When he returned to the couch she held out her hand for the beer without taking her gaze away from the TV.

"Thanks." She pointed at the screen. "Look at that guy. He's getting results to a complex DNA issue overnight!"

Vadim cautiously stretched out beside her and sipped at his own beer. It was time to catch the last ferry, or stay and risk ending up in Ella's bed. He couldn't deny that he was tempted. Despite his distrust of empaths, she intrigued and excited him in a way no other woman ever had. She always came right back at him, questioning his judgment, arguing about everything and generally getting in his face. Most empaths were far too sensitive to want to tangle with him. Alexei had been right about Vadim's shields; something about their complexity, the darkness behind them repelled empaths. Even Natasha, who claimed to love him, had been unwilling to trust him one hundred percent.

The fact that Ella didn't seem to be repelled was in itself

enough to send him running for the ferry. He was in no position to take on any commitments other than the preservation of his own life. But he had to stay because he needed her to solve the case. So wasn't he doing what was best for them both? His instincts screamed she was in danger and that he was the only one who could keep her safe. And when it came down to it, he wanted to stay with her. He *liked* her, goddammit.

"Are you okay with me sleeping on the couch again?"

She looked at him. "You can sleep wherever you like."

"The couch will be fine."

"Whatever." The phone rang. She glanced at the caller display and went still. "Damn."

"I'll get it," Vadim offered.

"No, it's my mom and she'll just start asking why you're here, and I don't need that right now." She picked up the receiver and cradled it against her shoulder. "Hey."

Ella's expression gradually changed from relaxed to uptight and haunted.

"Yeah, I know that, Mom. I tried to tell you yesterday, but—"

Her mother was off again.

"I *know*. Fuck it, she was my best friend, don't..." Even though she sounded strong, Vadim was fascinated to see tears falling down Ella's cheeks. He offered her his handkerchief but she refused to relinquish her tight hold on her beer. Leaning close and, ignoring her ferocious frown, he dabbed at the tears himself.

Eventually even Mrs. Walsh ran out of things to say and Ella concluded the call. She dropped the receiver back into its cradle and flung herself down on the couch, one hand over her eyes.

"That woman drives me mad. She's telling me off because Laney was killed."

"She can hardly blame you."

"Apparently I should've taken better care of her. Laney was the only one of my friends my mother ever liked."

Vadim wrapped his fingers around her ankle. "You can't always save people, you know."

"Yeah, I know. I've lost far too many colleagues not to understand that. I think I'll go to bed." Vadim moved out of her way and she stumbled toward the bathroom. "You know where the sheets are, right?"

"Yes." He waited to see if she'd invite him to join her, but she just closed the bathroom door behind her with a snap. He stared at the pine door, not sure whether to be insulted or not. It would be far better if they could solve this case and then get together. Perhaps that was what the Fae-Web predicted, a nice quick heated affair before he left. But by then Ella would either be hooked up with an OCOS mate, or on her way to a madhouse...

When she emerged from the bathroom wearing only her bra and panties, her hair loose around her shoulders, Vadim resolutely kept his gaze on his bedding. "I'll come to Laney's funeral with you, if you like."

She paused. "I thought you'd be there to check out the mourners. You know how the ghouls are sometimes drawn to the scenes of their 'triumphs.'"

"I would've come with you anyway."

"I appreciate that." She headed into her bedroom. "Night, Morosov. Sweet dreams."

ELLA CLOSED her bedroom door and leaned back against it. Not asking Vadim to join her had been easier this time. The more she got to know him, the less she wanted to use him just for sex. How annoying was that? Unfortunately, it went right along with her dating creed. She'd fucked as many men as possible in the vain hope that she could avoid her fate and meet a potential mate, but that hadn't happened and she'd gotten tired of having to erase herself from men's memories. Perhaps she was finally growing up. Approaching death and madness could do that to a person.

"Good evening, Miss Walsh."

She blinked at the naked man who lounged seductively on her bed. His hair was gold, his eyes a celestial silver and every single muscle on his body was toned and buff and yet kind of soft and *feathery*...

"Who the hell are you?"

"Don't you know?" He smiled at her and she felt it in her core. "Am I not familiar in any way?"

She stared at him again and certain things fell into place. She raised her voice.

"Morosov? Can you come in here?"

She just remembered to peel herself away from the door as it opened abruptly behind her. Vadim appeared, his gun at the ready. With a disgusted sound he slammed the door so hard it hit the wall.

"For fuck's sake, Rossa. What are you doing here?"

The naked man didn't even flinch. "I might ask you the same thing. She's hardly your type, is she?"

"She is my colleague. Now sod off back to Otherworld."

"What's wrong? Are you afraid I'll tell on you?" She poked Vadim in the ribs. "He's related to you, isn't he?"

"You might say that."

"He's like a blond version of you, but fifty times sexier."

The blond gave a crack of laughter. "She's certainly amusing. Is that why you keep her around?"

Ella took a step closer to the bed. The man's chest was covered with fine, white, downy feathers she yearned to stroke. "You can shut the fuck up and get out of my bed."

He held her gaze, his gray eyes glowing, daring her to delve into their depths and never come up again. Her shields flexed but held steady, and his confident smile wavered. He glanced at Vadim, who had remained by the door with his weapon raised.

"Not quite what she seems is she?"

"Quit talking about me as if I'm not here," Ella said. "I've asked you nicely to leave. Don't make me have to get nasty."

"What could you do to me, little human?"

"Suck you dry?"

"I'd like that. You on your knees…"

She smiled, then flicked his raised knee with her fingertip. He jerked away.

"Ouch! Don't touch me."

"She's an empath, Rossa. She really can suck you dry," Vadim said.

"Then why in *makking* hell are you hanging around with her?"

Vadim straightened. "As I said. Ms. Walsh is my colleague. We work together."

"*Work?*" Rossa shook his head. "You make me sick, Vadim, or whatever you call yourself these days."

"I don't care what you think. I agree with Ms. Walsh, and I want you to leave."

"All right then, but if anyone asks after you, I'm telling."

With a flash of light, the blond disappeared, leaving Ella gaping at her now empty bed.

"I apologize for that. Rossa can be very immature."

She turned to Vadim, who was disarming his gun. "Is that all you have to say?"

"He's gone. He knows what you are. I doubt he'll be back." He started walking toward the kitchen.

She followed him out. "Hang on a minute. What the hell just happened? Who is he, and what was he doing in my bed?"

Vadim was filling a glass of water from the refrigerator. He'd already taken off his tie. His shirt was open, displaying his muscled chest and rather nice abs.

"I told you. His name is Rossa, and he normally resides in Otherworld. He must have sensed I was over there the other day and come to check up on me."

"Then why didn't he get into *your* bed?"

"He probably did. Alexei would've told him where I was. They are friends." Vadim added three ice cubes. "Rossa won't harm you."

"How do you know?"

"Because if he'd wanted you dead, there would've been nothing you could do about it. Now he knows you're an empath, he'll be more careful. Even Otherworld realizes you have your uses for catching their criminals. No one wants to face the penalties for murdering one of your kind."

"Apart from the Siren." She glared at him. "And how exactly do you know all this?"

"It is a little complicated to explain."

"I don't care. Take your time and tell me."

He took a slow sip of his water, then went across to his immaculately made bed and placed the glass on the coffee table beside his pillow. Ella tapped her foot. "Well?"

He took off his shirt and laid it carefully over the back of the nearest chair. "As Rossa said, we are connected. I can sense his thoughts, so I know what he's likely to do next." He undid his belt and Ella realized she couldn't look away.

"But he was one hundred percent Fae."

"Almost one hundred percent."

Vadim unzipped his pants and then stepped out of them, lining up the seams before laying them next to his shirt. He wore tight cotton knit boxers, which molded far too well to the muscular curves of his spectacular ass. She found it hard to swallow.

"What else?" He turned to look at her and her gaze immediately dropped to the luscious bulge of his cock. "You said that it was complicated."

He shrugged. "It is, but that's all you need to know."

"Says who?"

She forced herself to look away from his boxers and into his face. He smiled at her. Had he done it deliberately? Flaunted his perfect body to distract her? She'd bedded some awesomely fit surfer dudes, but she reckoned there wasn't a single inch of fat on this man. Her fingers twitched and she made her hands into fists. She would not reach out and see if he was as hard as he looked.

"Ms. Walsh, all I'm concerned about is your safety. Rossa has nothing to do with this case. He's just an annoyance, one that I can easily control if I have to."

Ella thought back to the brief moment when she'd touched the Fae and felt his power. Was Vadim suggesting he was more powerful than that? She also knew from past experience that he was unlikely to tell her anything else.

"Fine. I'm going to bed. Alone." She stomped back toward her bedroom.

"Good night, Ms. Walsh."

She made the mistake of looking over her shoulder just in time to see Vadim shed his boxers to reveal his ass before stretching luxuriously. She closed her eyes and repeated to herself, "I do not sleep with coworkers. I do *not* sleep with coworkers." But she wanted to *so* badly... For the first time in her life she actually bolted.

12

"Hey, Sam. How's that empath list coming along?"

Ella paused at her associate's cubicle and concealed a smile as he jumped a foot in the air and hastily clicked away from whatever social media site he'd been on. His thick red hair stood up on end as if he hadn't brushed it for a week, and she was sure he'd been wearing the same T-shirt for three days straight. He made even her look respectable.

"It's going okay. I'll have it for you by the end of the week." He leaned back in his chair and looked at her. "The survival rate for empaths isn't very good, is it?"

"No." She rubbed a small circle on the back of his faded T-shirt. This wasn't something she could make light of with another empath. "But males tend to deal with it better than females."

He didn't smile. "I'm definitely getting a mate when I'm twenty-seven."

"Good for you." Ella straightened and turned away.

"Why haven't you got one?"

She decided not to answer him, and instead headed for her office. She sat down at her desk and rubbed her hands over her face. It had been a horrible week. She'd attended both Christa and Laney's funerals, Vadim and Alexei at her side, but there had been no sign of the Siren. Sam had confirmed that the OCOS correspondence between the empaths and their intended mates had been authentic and that both women were connected with the correct mates. They had also turned up nothing about the two men, who seemed to be just what they were supposed to be.

Everyone was on edge, knowing that another killing was likely unless they made some kind of breakthrough in the case. And yet there was nothing to go on. Nothing at all. The Siren had disappeared as silently as he had emerged.

Her birthday was fast approaching and Feehan was starting to give her concerned looks as her concentration wavered and her temper got shorter. Even Liz and Alexei had started to tread warily around her. The only person who seemed unaffected by her bitchiness was Vadim. In fact, he'd been almost too nice and over-protective of her for the last few days. But then he was convinced she was unstable anyway, and was already expecting the worst.

Ella sighed and peered through her fingers at her backpack. She'd had another letter from Otherworld and she was avoiding opening it. She stood up. Coffee first. The letter second.

When she returned to her desk, she shut the door and took out the now-familiar brown envelope from Otherworld. She placed it in front of her and slowly drank her coffee, hoping the kick of the caffeine would shield her from the contents of the note. She also spared a thought for the poor male who had been picked for her and who was currently oblivious to the fact that his fate hung in the balance. He would only find out about her if she agreed to go ahead with the match.

And she wouldn't do that—would she? Her fingers trembled as she slit open the flap and then shook out the single sheet of typewritten paper.

Dear Empath,

As you approach your most significant birthday, OCOS is delighted to present you with the name and some basic information about your pre-approved mate...

She read it through once and then read it again. "God, no."

If you wish to meet with this male, please reply with all speed to the address at the top of this form.

If you choose not to accept this offer, we wish you well with the remainder of your short and painful existence.

Yours in anticipation,

The OCOS team.

She shot to her feet, then stormed out of her office, straight for the smaller conference room where she could see Alexei and Vadim. They both looked up as she screeched to a halt in front of them.

"May I speak to you, Morosov?" She glared at Alexei. "Alone?"

Alexei disappeared, slamming the door behind him in his haste. She held out the letter to Vadim.

"Did you know about this?" He took the letter from her and read it through before tossing it on the table. "Well?"

He stood up and looked at her, one hand resting on the table, which started to rock. *"Fucking hell."*

"Why would they pick you?"

"I don't know. I swear to God I didn't have anything to do with it."

She took a deep breath and retrieved the letter. "It doesn't have to change anything. I don't have to accept the match. Hang on. Why aren't you as furious as I am?"

"Because I received a letter, too." He opened the drawer of

his desk, drew out a familiar brown envelope and tossed it on the table.

"When the hell did you get that?"

He shrugged. "I can't remember."

"You lying fuck." She snatched the envelope, took out the letter and read it out loud.

"Dear Potential Mate,

Thank you so much for your application for the position of psychic mate and anchor to one of our world's most misunderstood subspecies —the empath. Your sacrifice enables our two great nations to live in harmony, offers you the opportunity to reside in either domain, and significantly impacts your quality of life.

When your potential mate contacts our office to accept you, we will be in touch.

Thank you again, and good luck!

*More details will be provided when your offer is accepted.

The OCOS team."

She scrunched the letter into a ball, then threw it at Vadim, who didn't even flinch.

"When did you know about this?" Her voice shook but there was nothing she could do about it.

"I wasn't one hundred percent sure until I got the letter."

"Okay, so when did you *suspect* something was up?"

"When I went into Alexei's Fae-Web. Our fates seemed far too closely aligned. I assumed it meant we might have an affair, but when I got this, I realized the Fae-Web might be indicating a more permanent arrangement."

"And you didn't think to share that with me?"

"Why the hell would I? Do you think I was happy about it?" he snapped. "The last thing I need is to be trapped into another damaging emotional relationship with an empath."

"And so you said nothing. Didn't it occur to you that if you'd mentioned it earlier, I might've been able to find another mate?"

He retrieved the mangled letter and straightened it out, smoothing the paper with his long fingers, his gaze averted. "Don't be ridiculous. Everyone knows that OCOS mates are the best possible matches for empaths. It's one of the rare things that both governments agree on." He met her gaze and she could still see the cold fury in his blue eyes. He liked to be manipulated about as much as she did.

"Listen, if it stops you from going mad, I'll do it."

"*What?*"

"It might work."

"I couldn't do that to you. I couldn't do that to *anyone.*"

"Look, just think about it, will you?" He retreated behind his desk and pretended to shuffle his papers around.

She studied him closely. "Are you really that desperate not to fuck up this case?"

A muscle flexed in his jaw. "If that's what you want to believe, go ahead. I've made my position clear."

She folded her letter, then stuffed it into her pocket. "And I think I've made mine clear too."

She turned and walked out, back to the sanctity of her office where she sat down and tried to make sense of the horrible, awful mess her life had become. Had she secretly decided to take the match OCOS offered her? Was that why she was so angry when she realized it was Vadim? Shouldn't that make it better? She *knew* him. He was a great cook, had an awesome bod and tolerated her far better than the average person. How the hell had he gotten mixed up in this and why was he willing to go through with it?

Another far more awful thought occurred to her. Had the SBLE connived with OCOS to produce Vadim as her mate? Was her government determined that she stay sane enough to finish investigating this case? Vadim's superiors certainly didn't love him. Was that why he'd been so furious? Even though he hadn't shared his earlier suspicions with her, this was no picnic for him either. Ella let out a shaky breath and considered her options. She could leave early and have everyone wondering whether she'd finally cracked up, or she could tough it out, show everyone—and by everyone she meant Morosov—that she was *totally* in control.

A knock on the door made her sit up straight. "Come in."

Liz put her head around the door. "Are you okay?"

Ella found a smile from somewhere. "I'm good. What's up?"

"Feehan's called a progress meeting." Liz made a face. "I'm not sure why because there isn't any, but it makes him feel better."

"I'll just get some more coffee and I'll be right there." She heaved herself to her feet and joined Liz in the hallway.

"Are you sure you're okay, hon?" Liz asked. "Alexei said you were shouting at Vadim earlier."

"What's new? You know how we are. I definitely need more coffee."

"You can't afford to alienate him, Ella," Liz said quietly. "He's important both to the case and to you."

"So I gather."

She went into the conference room carefully avoiding looking at the whiteboard, which still showed pictures of Christa and Laney. Unfortunately, it meant she found herself looking straight at Vadim, who still reverberated with fury. She put her coffee on the table and got out her cell. She'd play a few rounds of zombie golf while she waited for Feehan to show up.

Eventually Feehan called the meeting to order and asked for updates. Sam raised his hand and Feehan smiled at him.

"What do you have for us?"

"I've tracked down a couple more of the empaths that graduated with Ella." Sam consulted his notes. "Both of them are dead."

Ella winced.

"By what cause?" Alexei asked.

"Jennifer Barton took an overdose and Maria Cordova was in a fatal car accident."

"Do you have any more details?"

Sam looked up. "What else do you want to know?"

"Were there any suspicious circumstances surrounding the deaths? Police reports, autopsies, that kind of thing?" Alexei said patiently.

"I can find out." Sam hesitated. "It does seem weird though, doesn't it? All these empaths dying so young."

"Tell me about it," Ella said and then became aware that everyone was staring at her sympathetically. "But Sam has a point. The death rate for my particular graduating class does seem remarkably high, even for empaths."

"Anything else?" Feehan looked around the table. Everyone shook their heads. "Well, keep looking, Sam. I'm sure we're going to find something soon."

Everyone except Sam and Ella stood up and started to leave. Ella looked over at Sam's glum face. "What's up?"

He heaved an exaggerated sigh. "I wanted to get home early today. It's the weekend."

"You go. Send me the files. I've got nothing much going on."

"Are you serious?" Sam started to smile. "That's awesome. I'll shoot the files over to you right now."

"You're welcome."

Ella watched him practically skip away and found herself trying to remember when she'd last been that happy. She didn't begrudge him a moment of it. In six years' time, he'd be feeling just like she was. But he'd already decided to take a mate, hadn't he? Maybe shadowing her for the past few months had convinced him that it was the only option.

WHEN SHE NEXT CHECKED THE time, it was far later than she'd realized and the office was curiously silent. Even Feehan slipped out early on Fridays to avoid the traffic and get home for the weekend. Her investigations into the other empaths hadn't cheered her up much either. She had a strong suspicion that both Jennifer Barton and Maria Cordova hadn't died by accident. It seemed as if the authorities were so hung up on the idea of empaths choosing to kill themselves that they swept all the deaths under the rug regardless. Whether that was to avoid bad publicity, or to cut down on the paperwork, she didn't have a clue.

She stretched and turned her computer off, aware of a headache beckoning and that she had no plans for the weekend ahead. Since Laney's death, she'd lost interest in going out entirely. She didn't even want to have sex. Well, that wasn't quite true; she wanted to have sex with Vadim Morosov but every woman on the planet probably felt the same way.

But he'd offered to become her mate... Because he hated to lose a case.

Ella picked up her backpack and headed for the door. She'd get some beer and a pizza, pick up some old movies and have a weekend in her jammies. She didn't have many more before she lost it, so she might as well do what she wanted.

In an effort to conserve energy, the main lights had already been dimmed and the office seemed deserted. She got herself some more coffee and checked the time of the next ferry back to Tiburon. If she walked quickly, she'd make it.

As she wandered out toward the bank of elevators, she felt a presence behind her and the sharp, familiar scent of citrus.

"Hey, Morosov."

Vadim came up alongside her. "Hi."

One of Madison's favorite phrases came into Ella's mind. *Awkward.* "You're here late."

"I was checking out some of the foreign empath graduates

for Sam. I speak several European languages and he was struggling with interpreting the data."

"You mean he wanted to get home for his hot and heavy weekend."

He didn't smile. "That too."

"How did your research go?"

"Bad, Ms. Walsh. If you include Natasha, all the Russian empaths are dead."

"And no one noticed?"

"Since the fall of communism, the various governments have been busy dealing with a lot more important issues than the lack of empaths."

"There's no need to be so patronizing. I do know what's going on in the rest of the world."

He didn't reply, his gaze fixed on the call button for the elevator.

She couldn't think of anything else to say, and turned instead to the stairs. "Damn it."

"What?"

She pointed at the yellow and black tape festooned over the entrance to the stairwell. "How did I miss that? The stairs are shut for maintenance."

"The elevators are working."

She shivered. "I hate small spaces."

"It's only one floor up." He pressed the illuminated call button. "You can hold my hand if you like."

"I'm not quite that pathetic." The elevator doors opened and she forced herself to step inside.

"It will only take a minute, Ms. Walsh."

She couldn't even look at him, her attention focused on the doors, and the upward motion of the elevator. A faint ding heralded their arrival and she was finally able to let out her breath.

"See? That wasn't so bad," Vadim said.

Ella didn't deign to answer him, and stepped as close to the doors as she could. As they started to open, she stared fixedly at the narrow slit of white marble in the lobby. A sudden jolt sent her rocking back on her heels. Vadim caught her as the elevator made a terrible screeching sound and started to fall back down the shaft.

"Hold on to me!"

Vadim pulled her into his arms and curled his body around hers, drawing them both down to the floor and using his magic to protect them from the impact. Her scream exploded against his chest as the elevator hit the bottom of the shaft and everything went black.

He opened his eyes into complete darkness. Ella was fighting his hold, her breathing ragged, her nails slashing at his skin.

"Ms. Walsh, get a grip." He grabbed hold of her upper arms and held her as still as he could. *"Ella."*

She shuddered so convulsively he felt it resonate through his own body. "I have to get out of here, *right now*. Don't you get it?"

"Listen to me." He gave her a gentle shake. *"Listen.* We'll get out of here. We only fell a couple of levels."

"I don't care how far we fell, I have to get out!"

"Take some deep breaths and help me think this through." She tried to pull away from him, but he held tight. "Is your cell working?"

He relaxed his grip sufficiently to allow her to forage in her pocket. She pulled out her smart phone and clicked on the screen. Nothing happened and she moaned.

"Try mine. It's in the pocket of my pants."

She retrieved his phone, but there was no response from his network either.

"Oh fuck," Ella breathed. "Oh fuckety-fuck."

"It's probably because this part of the building is magically warded against the outside."

"Not helpful, Morosov." She took a deep trembling breath. "Can't you use your magic to get us out?"

He considered the space around him. "I don't think that's going to work either." He wasn't sure if she sensed it yet, but he was aware of plenty of magical power encircling them already. Unfortunately, he had no idea if the magic was benign or hostile.

"Why not?"

"I'm probably not powerful enough to break through the SBLE shields by myself."

He wasn't sure if that was true, but he didn't want to use up all his power in case there was worse trouble ahead. He also didn't want to mention that to Ella.

"Can you contact Alexei?"

He tried. "No, there is something blocking my thoughts."

"Something from Otherworld?"

"I don't know. It could just as easily be the SBLE."

"Then what are we going to do?" Her breathing fragmented again. "We're going to die down here, and no one will ever find us."

He wrapped an arm around her shoulders. "No, we're not."

"I'm going to die anyway, but it's not fair to you."

He kissed her nose and she made a growling noise. "Don't be so negative. There are other options to explore."

"Like what?"

"There should be an alarm button to push somewhere. We could start with that."

"They usually only ring within the building and I bet everyone has gone home for the weekend."

"Let's find it anyway."

He crawled across to where he thought the doors were, eventually bumping his knee against the steel plated metal. Kneeling up, he felt over the smooth surface until he discovered the control panel. He systematically pressed every button he found, but nothing lit up.

"Morosov?"

"I'm right here."

"I can't hear any alarms going off." Neither could he.

"We're trapped, aren't we?"

He turned back to her. "Just for the moment. There might be a remote alarm that rings straight through to the fire department."

"The air is going to run out and we'll suffocate."

He found her hand. "We won't. This thing isn't sealed. There's plenty of air coming in for just the two of us."

"Stop being so fucking reasonable!"

"It won't help if we both panic, will it?"

"Shut *up*." She squeezed his hand so hard he heard his bones crack. "I just want to get out of here."

"We could try and climb out."

"You're right. There has to be a service hatch. How are we going to reach it?"

"You could stand on my shoulders?"

"Do you really think that would work?"

"I don't see why not." He pulled her to her feet. "Put your backpack and jacket down, take off your shoes and climb up to my shoulders."

She took off her jacket and he caught hold of her around the waist. "Go on."

She scaled him with an ease that reminded him that she had older brothers. He steadied himself as she tentatively knelt on his shoulders.

"I can't see a thing."

"Use your hands. Aim for the center of the space."

"There's something there, but I can't…" He almost staggered as she pushed upward. "I can't make it move."

"Slow down and think it through. Tell me what you can feel of the mechanism."

"There's a square hatch about two foot wide. In the center of it is a wheel-type thing, and at one corner there is some kind of latch."

"Okay, so you probably need to turn the wheel and then somehow use the latch."

"Easy for you to say."

He kept quiet while she obviously fought with the mechanism. "I can't do it. I'm not strong enough." She slithered back down to the ground and he held her in his arms. "I'm sorry. I couldn't move it even an inch." He kept holding her, aware of the frantic beat of her heart against his and the fear shuddering through her.

"And there's another thing."

"What?" he murmured into her sweet-smelling hair.

"There's a shitload of magic swirling around down here. Even if we did get out I'm worried about what we'd encounter next." She swallowed hard. "Do you think the Siren had anything to do with this?"

"I'm not sure, but I don't like the feel of it, either."

She sagged against him. "Then we're stuck. I know I'm not due to go nuts until my birthday, but I think I'll make a start now."

He took a deep breath. "There is one alternative."

"What?"

"You won't like it."

"Tell me."

"You *really* won't like it."

"Tell me!"

"If we were a mated pair, we might double our powers."

"What exactly does 'might' mean?"

"Mated couples take on some of their partners' magic abilities."

181

"But I don't have any."

"You do, but I have a lot more."

"And how would that help us?"

"If we doubled my magic, we might be strong enough to find a way through that escape hatch."

She rested her head against his chest and he closed his eyes. Anger shook through him. He had a terrible sense that they were both being manipulated, but he had no idea by whom.

"Are you just saying this because you want to have sex with me?"

"Yes, that's it, Ms. Walsh. I just want to fuck you before I die. I set this all up to get in your pants." He took a steadying breath. "It's your decision. We can wait it out, and hope someone raises the alarm, or we can mate and try and save ourselves."

"You don't sound very happy about it."

"What do you expect? It's not exactly a great situation is it?"

She touched his cheek, her thumb catching the corner of his mouth. "It's not exactly fair either. If we go ahead, I get all the benefits and you get saddled with a mate for life."

"I already offered to mate with you."

"But what happens when you find a woman you really love and want to marry?"

"Ella, we don't have time to discuss this in depth right now. Either accept me or wait it out. I'm okay with either option."

She rested against him, her body still trembling.

"I don't want to go mad and die, Morosov," she whispered.

"Then live."

ELLA BREATHED in his warm citrus scent and heard the reassuring boom of his heart. Could she do it? It was a momentous step, but at this moment, with her fear driving her, she wanted to clutch at his offer and run with it.

"It would just be about sex, right?"

"If that's what you want."

"We don't have to get all emotional around each other?"

"No, we don't."

He sounded so calm and reassuring that she suspected she was dreaming. She opened her eyes but they were still stuck in the elevator. How long had they been there now? How quickly would someone come and rescue them? Dread crowded her reason and her fingernails dug into Vadim's flesh.

"I can't wait. I need to get out of here."

"Then let's sit on the floor."

He drew her down until his back was against the side of the elevator and she was straddling his lap, facing him.

"What if we're rescued in the middle?"

"We'll hear them coming and we can stop."

Was there a hint of resignation in Vadim's voice or was she imagining it? For the first time in her life since she was five she felt vulnerable and terrified. Her intellect told her it wasn't a good time to be making life-altering decisions, but her instincts screamed at her to take what Vadim offered her and change her destiny.

He cupped the back of her head and brought his mouth close to hers.

"It's okay, Ella. Just kiss me and try and forget everything else."

She almost snorted. The man was so conceited! And then his lips touched hers, and she was kissing him back, both of them igniting, mouths fused together in a deep, passionate kiss she hadn't expected. Imminent death obviously had more of an impact on the libido than she realized. Lust shuddered through her and she rocked against him, felt his already hard cock jerk beneath the fabric of his pants.

His hand was on her ass, pressing her even more closely against him, making her sex ache and throb.

She shoved a hand between them and worked on his belt buckle and the button of his pants, heard his breath hiss out as she stroked his cotton-clad erection.

"Wait." He caught her hand. "You need to get out of those jeans."

"Dammit!" She returned to kissing him even as they both struggled to unzip her jeans and shove them down. Not caring how she looked, Ella managed to wiggle out of one leg, taking her panties with the jeans. While she fought her way out of the denim, Vadim lifted his hips and pulled down his pants and briefs. When she lowered herself over him, the heat and stiffness of his wet cock surged against her.

He kissed her hard as she rocked back and forth over him until he slid inside, making them both moan. His hips arched forward, driving him deeper, and she took him in greedily until she could feel every thick, throbbing inch. One touch of his fingertip against her clit and she was coming around him. With a savage sound he thrust even deeper, his other hand on her hip controlling her movement, keeping him deep.

Another climax threatened. She gasped against his mouth as a succession of psychic sensations threatened to overwhelm her. She could see herself, feel Vadim's satisfaction, his uninhibited sensual enjoyment of her body, of her mind... She'd never felt such perfect symmetry with another sexual being before in her life. It was the most amazing feeling in the world.

"*God...*" she breathed. Felt the word resonate through his mind, and his primitive response. Not human, not human at all. Underneath that beautiful exterior was a complex beast. His magical power swamped her and made her second climax so sharply edged with pleasure that she forgot to breathe. Even as she shuddered around his shaft he kept on drawing her pleasure within himself, her fear, her power, her *everything...*

She collapsed over him as he climaxed, the roar of his emotions so powerful that she almost blacked out. Whatever happened next, she'd just had the most incredible sex of her life —maybe enough to let her die happy. She had no idea how long they stayed like that, neither of them wanting to disengage, neither of them wanting to face the enormity of what they had just done. She opened her eyes. Or maybe it was just her. Had Vadim felt the same? She could hardly ask him. Reluctantly, she sat up. His cock kicked up inside her and then slid free.

"Are you okay?" Vadim asked. He sounded as shaken as she felt. She tried to see his expression but it was impossible in the darkness. "Do you need a handkerchief? I have one in my pocket."

"Thanks."

She moved off his lap, and set about straightening her clothing. She was glad that he couldn't see her properly because she was sure she looked wrecked.

"How do you feel?"

"I'm not sure." She finished zipping her jeans. "How should I feel?"

"I don't know. I've never mated anyone before." He reached out and took her hand. "I felt you in my head, though. Did you feel me?"

"Yes." The touch of his hand made her feel breathless. She wanted him again. Wanted him right now... She pulled away. "This is weird."

"I know." He hesitated. "Suddenly, I don't care about getting out of here."

"Well, I do." She balked at his intimate tone. "It's just sex, remember? Now should we try that service hatch again?"

He cleared his throat. "When you get up there and find the hatch, open your mind and I'll feed some magic through to you, okay?"

Vadim sounded remarkably composed for someone who had just had amazing sex in an elevator. Far too composed, actually.

Ella made sure to almost kick him in the nuts as she scaled him to sit on his shoulders.

"Okay, I've found the wheel."

"Keep still." She felt the strange sensation of magical power flowing through her fingertips and the wheel started to spin until there was a creaking sound.

"Now try the latch."

She reached for it and it sprang free, allowing her to push on the panel and reveal the still, fetid blackness above the elevator. Even though she hadn't been short of air, the sight of the open escape hatch made her breathe more easily.

"What now?" she asked.

"Get down, and we'll make sure the elevator is set in the off position. We don't want it starting up as we're climbing out."

"That would be bad." She climbed down and waited while Vadim searched the control panel once more.

"Got it. I think."

She found herself touching his sleeve. "So how are we both going to get out of there?"

"Do you remember all your jokes about me being a chicken?"

"How could I forget them?"

"Well, we're going to use that flying ability to help us get out of this elevator shaft quickly."

"I can fly now?"

She sensed him smile. "Not quite. We'll start by you climbing out onto the top of the elevator and then wait for me to join you. You'll have a better sense of balance and the ability to jump higher and faster."

"Like a helicopter?"

"Sort of. You'll notice the difference when you have to jump or reach for something."

Ella glanced dubiously up at the hatch and then back at Vadim's broad shoulders. "Will you fit through there?"

"I have no choice." He cupped her cheek, his fingers warm. "I can't let you go by yourself, now, can I?"

"It's okay. If you got stuck, I could probably manage it from here and get help."

He kissed her softly on the lips. "Thank you. Now up you go. I'll bring your backpack and jacket up with me."

She did as he asked and managed to pull herself out of the service hatch without any issues. It really did feel as if she had an extra spring in her step. Whether Vadim's magic was still helping her or not, she didn't care. It took all her resolve to neither look up or down, but to concentrate on the small square of the hatch where she hoped to see Vadim emerge. Magic swirled around in the heated darkness and Ella raised her shields. One minute she was alone and the next Vadim crouched beside her.

"There should be a ladder against one of the walls." Vadim's shoulder brushed hers as he leaned forward. "Ah, here it is. Do you want to go first?"

Before he even finished speaking, she was reaching for the ladder and grabbing the metal rungs. She started climbing and again, found it easier than she had anticipated. Had she gained Vadim's legendary fitness along with his magic? That was something she was more than willing to appropriate.

It seemed to take forever to reach the first set of metal doors that led back into the SBLE offices and the obstructed stairs.

"Should we keep going?"

"It's up to you. We can try and get in here or head up to the lobby level." Vadim's voice echoed from below her. "How do you feel?"

"Not too bad. I think I'd like to keep going."

She suited her actions to her words and kept climbing, her gaze fixed on each rung of the ladder as she took hold of it.

"There's a light up ahead," he called. "I wonder if the lobby elevator doors are open?"

"That would be really cool." She was tiring now, her breath coming out in great big puffs. She kept climbing, though, and saw the light spill over onto the ladder making the metal glint gunmetal gray.

"It's about five meters above you, Ella. Keep going."

"What the hell is a meter?" She kept going, her hands aching from gripping the bars so tightly. Light flooded into the elevator shaft now and she was finally able to place a hand on the cold white marble floor of the lobby and crawl out. There was no one there to see her dramatic entry so she stayed on the floor facedown like a landed fish and just appreciated the space around her.

"Are you all right?"

She rolled over onto her back and stared at Vadim. He looked the same, but different, as if she no longer saw just the outer, beautiful shell. There was something in his eyes that made her feel a soul deep connection to him...

What the crap was she thinking? Survival had obviously turned her brain to mush.

"Thanks." She struggled to stand up, avoiding his proffered hand. "I really should be getting home now." Without another word, she headed for the outer doors. He caught up with her on the sidewalk. It was surprisingly dark outside, the long shadows of the high buildings turning everything a murky brown.

"Ella. Ms. Walsh, I don't think you are in any fit state to go home on the ferry alone." He glanced at his watch. "In fact, you might have missed the last one."

With distant surprise, she realized she was trembling and that the last thing she wanted to do was be alone.

"I have to get home and lie down. I'm a wreck."

He took her hand and she swayed toward him. "Come back to the hotel with me."

"I can't do that."

His grip tightened. "And I can't leave you alone. You are too vulnerable to meet anything from Otherworld tonight."

"Says who?"

He met her gaze. "Me. And before you get mad, I feel the same. We're both vulnerable at the moment." His thumb caressed hers. "Come back to the hotel. You can stay in my room and I'll bunk up with Alexei."

"You can't tell him."

"Tell him what?"

"About us having sex."

"Why not?"

"Because I don't want anyone to know."

"But…"

"Morosov, you should be agreeing with me. If Alexei finds out you're fucking another empath on your team, you'll be hauled back to Russia so fast your ears will bleed."

He studied her for a long moment. "Okay."

"Okay, what?"

"I won't say anything for the moment, but someone is going to notice if you don't go crazy on schedule."

"We'll deal with that when it happens." She pulled out of his grasp. "You never know, maybe we'll have solved the case before that and you'll be gone."

He didn't look convinced. "But you'll come back to the hotel?"

Ella's whole body shook with exhaustion. "Okay." She let him reclaim her hand and walk her through the streets. It wasn't her style, but for once she needed the physical support, *his* support if she was honest. At some point during their fiery sexual encounter she'd felt more connected to him, more *sure* of him than of any other person in her life before. And that incredible sensation of trust still lingered. Dammit, she had no intention of delving into that emotional minefield until she'd slept on the matter—preferably alone.

Vadim ushered her into his hotel room and gave her a passkey.

"I'll be right next door if you need anything."

"Thanks, I'll definitely holler."

"You don't even need to do that." He tapped her forehead. "Just call me."

"How?"

"Think it."

She scowled at him. "Damn it, Morosov, don't get all odd on me. I'm too tired."

He kissed her forehead where he'd tapped it. "Get some sleep."

She closed the door in his face and wandered in to inspect his room. It was incredibly neat and not just because housekeeping had been in. There wasn't a single garment thrown on the floor, an open suitcase or a discarded book. When she got the chance to stay in a hotel she positively enjoyed throwing her stuff everywhere. Ella went into the bathroom and surveyed the ranks of Vadim's cleaning products, his electric razor and his two types of aftershave.

A shower would be good. Her whole body ached. She put on the water and amused herself messing up the order of Vadim's stuff. When she stepped under the water, she sighed and tried to relax. The scent of Vadim's lovemaking curled around her and she thought back on those few frantic, possibly life changing minutes. She'd never think about elevators in the same way again...

VADIM SHUT the door into Alexei's upgraded suite and listened carefully. He suspected his friend was out, but you never knew with Fae and he didn't want to deal with Alexei right now. Fae were far too good at detecting sex. Vadim picked his way through Alexei's discarded belongings and went into the bathroom. A shower would revive him and then he could go and check on Ella.

Ella.

With a sigh, Vadim sat on the edge of the toilet seat and contemplated what he'd done. There had seemed no other option. He had a terrible sense that from the moment he'd walked back into Otherworld he'd been compromised. But why this? Why a human mate? Was it some kind of punishment? He raked his fingers through his hair. There wasn't any point in trying to understand. He of all males knew that the ways of Otherworld were beyond comprehension. If they wanted him to know why, someone would make sure to come and spell it out for him.

With a groan, he stood up. He didn't want to stay with Alexei. He wanted to be in the shower with Ella and then in bed with her. Maybe he'd let her out after a week or two, but it would be close…

"*Shit,*" Vadim muttered. "This is bad."

Mating with her had set off all sorts of instincts that he'd very carefully quashed. If he disappeared, left his job and his painstakingly built identity, what would happen to Ella? Did a mated empath still go mad if they were abandoned or was it now a done deal? He groaned, the sound echoing in the tiled space. But he couldn't disappear completely, could he? Current events had proved that. The Fae-Web had indicated Ella was important to his own survival. He had to stick with her at least until the case was solved. Nobody came to talk to him about the craziness, so he took off his clothes, got into the shower and rather unwillingly washed all traces of Ella Walsh from his body.

13

"ELLA!"

Ella woke up to find someone leaning over her and fought a scream. A familiar hand cupped the side of her face.

"It's me. What's wrong?"

She managed to open one eye and glare at Vadim, who was hovering an inch in front of her. Either she'd left the bedside lamp on, or he'd put it on when he'd come in.

"Get off me." She turned her head and bit his thumb and the hand disappeared.

"Ouch." He sucked his thumb into his mouth. "You were shouting in your sleep."

"Loud enough to wake you next door? This must be a shit hotel." She sat up. "How did you get in?"

"I had another key." He sat beside her on the bed and she realized he only wore his boxers. "I heard you in my head. You woke me up."

She winced. "I'm sorry. I didn't mean to. I must've been having a nightmare."

Without asking he walked around to the other side of the

bed and settled himself beside her as if he belonged there. "It felt like Otherworld to me, so I thought I'd better check up on you."

She stared up at the ceiling. Somehow his belief that she'd be okay with him lying on her bed irritated her. "It's an old favorite dream of mine. I get trapped in an elevator and some handsome dude insists I mate with him."

He sat up. "You had a nightmare about that?"

"Just kidding. The nightmare is the reason why I got scared of elevators and small places in the first place."

"So that phobia was caused by a dream?"

No," she sighed. "Keep up, can't you? The experience triggered the nightmare, and the nightmare is triggered by new experiences, get it?"

"I think so." He rearranged the pillows behind his head as if he was settling in for the night. "So what happened originally?"

She looked sideways at him. "Why do you want to know?"

"Because if you're going to wake me up, I'd like to understand when I need to worry, and when you're just processing an old fear."

"You don't need to worry about me," she said more sharply than she had intended. "I'm quite capable of looking after myself."

He didn't say anything, just looked at her until she leaned back against the pillows. She suddenly realized she was naked under the covers and that all her clothing lay in an untidy heap on the bathroom floor. In movies, the women always managed to gracefully drape a sheet around them before they made their dramatic exit. She'd have to get the sheet out from under Vadim and then untuck it from the sides of the bed and she didn't see that working at all.

"Okay, when I was about five, just before I got sent off to school, I was at home with my siblings playing hide and seek. One of our favorite places to hide was in a big Chinese chest on the upper hall landing. We were told not to get in there because there was no safety catch, but none of us took any notice. So, I was looking for a place to hide and decided to go in there for the first time. The thing was, when I put the lid down, I thought one of my other cousins had already got in there, so I turned toward them and—there was no one there."

Vadim edged closer and put his arm around her shoulders. "What happened then?"

"I looked down and there was something on my leg. At first I thought it was a spider but it was too big." She swallowed. "It was also creeping up from my ankle to my knee and whatever it was had long black nails and hairy skin."

"Troll?" Vadim stroked her skin with his thumb.

Ella nodded. "At that point, I had no idea what it was, just that I had to get away from it. I tried to stand up and push the lid off the chest but it was too heavy for me, and I started to scream."

"Did it bite you?"

"Just as I felt its teeth graze my skin, my oldest brother appeared, opened the box and picked me out of it. I was screeching like a lunatic. He threatened to put me back in there if I didn't shut up, so I stopped. No one believed what I said. They just put it down to an overactive imagination." She managed a shaky laugh. "I didn't know until years later that Otherworld creatures consider young empaths a special delicacy."

"And you've hated small spaces ever since."

"Yeah. Lame, eh?"

"Not at all." He hesitated. "One of the reasons I like things to be in order is because my early years were lived in such chaos."

"Makes sense," she murmured, guiltily aware of the mess she'd made in his bathroom. "Did Alexei come back?"

"Not yet. I think he's out with some Fae kin. He could be hours. They have an amazing tolerance for alcohol and sex."

"Lucky them." She allowed her head to remain on Vadim's shoulder. "Did you get any sleep at all?"

"A little." He glanced at the clock on the bedside table. "It's about two in the morning now."

She considered how safe she felt with him next to her. It freaked her out.

"Do you want me to go?" he asked softly.

"It's your bed."

"Then I'll stay." He rolled onto his side and got up. "I'll just go to the bathroom, okay?"

While he was gone, she pulled down the covers so that he could get in beside her. For the first time in her life she felt like one of those women who needed a man sleeping next to her. Was that what mating had done to her? Made her dependent?

"What the hell did you do to my bathroom?"

She sat up and blinked at Vadim. "What's wrong?"

He pointed behind him. "You trashed it in less than three hours."

"Oh for God's sake, it will clean up fine. I just moved a few things around."

"*Deliberately.*"

"Maybe." She flung herself down on the sheets. "Make up your mind, Morosov. Continue having your hissy fit, or shut up, turn off the light and come to bed."

The light snapped off and she waited in the darkness, not sure if she wanted him to storm off in a huff, or join her. Her breath hissed out as he came down on top of her, his skin warm from the shower, his cock already hard and pressing against her stomach.

"Hissy fit?" He kissed her. "You are…"

She kissed him back and he shut up, his mouth gentling, his body aligning against hers, his already wet shaft pushing between her legs. She wrapped her arms and legs around him, trapping him, but he didn't seem to object, only surged deeper and set up a steady thrusting rhythm that ignited all her senses, both physical and psychic. At some point, she grabbed his hair and pushed him over onto his back and rode him that way. He didn't seem to mind, his mouth busy with her breasts, his clever fingers on her clit, her ass...

This time, when she came, the pleasure was even more powerful and she felt it reciprocated in him. She sank down over him and just lay there until her heartbeat returned to almost normal. His hand threaded into her hair and he lay quietly beneath her.

"Go to sleep, Ella," he murmured, "and no more nightmares."

So, she did.

"I DON'T THINK you should go home."

Vadim's unshaven jaw was set in an obstinate line that made Ella want to punch him. It was late morning and for once the sun was streaming in through the window of the hotel. They'd shared an amicable breakfast, which had swiftly deteriorated when Ella had stated her intention of leaving.

"It's not up to you, is it?"

"As I've already said, we need to stick together." He sat on the side of the bed looking disgustingly attractive despite the fact that he'd just come back from an early-morning run.

"Why? Didn't you have enough sex last night?"

His eyes narrowed. "No. Did you?"

Despite everything her girly bits perked up at the very thought of even more sex. She clamped her lips together before she started whimpering and instead spent a moment retying the sash of Vadim's silk robe around her waist.

"I'll be quite safe at home."

"Like the other empaths?"

Ella scowled at him. "I'm seeing Rich and Andrew on Sunday and I'll hang with my neighbors for the rest of today. Satisfied?"

"Not really."

"I'm going to shower and then I'm going home."

He didn't say anything but she was aware of him staring at her as she shut the bathroom door. If it were up to her lady parts, she'd be straight back in that bed and she'd never get out again. She turned on the shower. What was even more frightening was the thought that Vadim seemed to feel the same. He made love like a god and had the stamina of a full-blooded Fae.

Below the noise of the shower, Ella allowed herself a quiet moan as she thought of Vadim moving over her. She had to go home and think this through. Antagonizing him wasn't going to work, so she'd have to try something else.

When she emerged from the bathroom, Vadim was finishing his breakfast. He looked up as she retrieved her coffee cup.

"I'm sorry, Ms. Walsh. Of course you should go home. I'll walk you to the ferry."

"Seriously?" She eyed him over the rim of her cup. "What brought about this change of heart?"

He sighed. "I was being overbearing."

"What's new?"

"It's the most obvious way of sending you running, though, isn't it?" He met her gaze, his blue eyes serious. "And I don't think we can run away from this one."

"Don't say that." Ella looked distractedly around the room. "I can't find my clothes."

"I hung them up for you in the closet last night."

"You did?"

"Of course I did." He pointed at something on the bed. "I also bought you some panties in the shop downstairs on the way back from my run."

"That was...really nice of you."

"You know me. A neat freak through and through." His smile was devastating.

Why did she want to leave again?

Ella went across to the closet and found her disreputable garments hanging neatly between his snowy white shirts, khakis and dark suits. As she turned with the hangers in her hand, Vadim nodded and went toward the bathroom.

"I'll leave you to it, then. I'll just have a quick shower and we can go."

While she waited she got dressed and finished off the last donut without getting any of it on herself. Part of her wanted to leave while he was in the shower, but she didn't want him to think she was afraid or anything. And she wasn't afraid. She was just...*conflicted.*

Conflicted was a good word.

She had no idea how to process what had happened to her, especially when Vadim was close. All she could think about when she saw him was sex. Just keeping her shields in place was extremely stressful when she sensed that if he chose to, he could blow them away like rice paper. She supposed she could do the same to him, but she didn't want to. All she'd wanted was to get out of the elevator alive. She had no desire to *bond* with him. He was still way out of her league.

"Are you ready?"

His calm voice made her jump and turn away from the window. He was dressed in jeans and a gray T-shirt that stretched over his chest and cuddled his biceps. She just about stopped herself from drooling and throwing herself at him.

Ella grabbed her backpack and jacket. "Let's go."

TWO HOURS LATER, she was huddled on her own couch, biting her nails, her mind racing as she pretended to watch some baseball. She wished Vadim was sitting beside her with all the intensity of a fifteen-year-old girl on her first crush. It was ridiculous. Once again, she longed for Laney. If her best friend had gone ahead and mated, Ella might have had a better idea about what to expect. This *longing* was unexpected and terrifying. They hadn't even kissed when Vadim had left her at the ferry; she'd been too terrified to make any physical contact in case she dragged him back to bed. She didn't think he would've stopped her either.

Ella found her phone and checked through her contact list. Mari Jones had worked at SBLE for a year as Ella's superior before being transferred to Seattle. She was a mated empath and the closest Ella had to someone to talk to about such a very peculiar subject. As she tapped the number, Ella found herself wondering why OCOS harped on about the death angle of not taking a mate, and not on the unforeseen issues that arose when you *did* take a mate.

"Hello?"

"Hey, Mari? It's me, Ella Walsh. Do you have a moment to talk?"

"Sure!" There was the sound of yelling in the background and a door closing, shutting out the noise. "That's better. I've shut the kids in with their dad. That'll give me at least ten minutes before they notice and try and break down the door."

"How are the kids?"

"Dave's driving me mad and I think Nick is psychic but it's early days yet."

Ella frowned. "How old is Nick?"

"Three, but there's definitely something funky going on with him." Mari sighed. "You know how it is."

"Are you okay about that?"

"Not much I can do about it, is there? His dad is one-eighth Otherworld, so it was more likely. And things have changed since we were kids. They don't take them away to special schools at such a young age anymore."

"Thank God for that."

"Anyway, what can I do for you? I'm sure you didn't call to talk about my kids." Mari paused. "By the way, I heard about Laney. What a terrible thing to have happened. Is that why you called?"

Ella swallowed hard. "No, I'm just about dealing with that. I miss her terribly though."

"I'm so sorry, hon, and you have no one to talk to about empath stuff. No wonder you called me. I'm so glad you did."

"You're way too nice. I don't deserve it. I'm a terrible friend."

"We empaths have to stick together. You're at the potential end of your career. I *totally* understand how draining it becomes when you're close to twenty-seven. It's not quite so busy out here. I don't think the Otherworld creatures like all this rain. So, what's up?"

"I'm less than two weeks away from my birthday."

"Have you changed your mind and decided to take an OCOS mate?"

"Well, put it this way, due to unforeseen circumstances my OCOS mate and I happened to already know each other. We accidentally pre-empted the prescribed date for us to contact each other through OCOS, and we hooked up."

"You've already mated? That's awesome!"

"Are you sure about that? It seems a bit weird."

"In what way?"

Ella lowered her voice. "The sex."

"You mean the fact that you can't keep your hands off each other?"

"Yes."

"Oh, that's quite normal."

"Are you sure?"

"Didn't you get the information pack from OCOS?"

"As I said, we didn't actually *mean* to hook up yet. Technically, I haven't even agreed to meet him."

"That's kind of funny."

"No, it's not."

"Oh, hon, it is. If it's too much sex for you, it's definitely funny."

"I didn't say it was too much. I just said it was surprising, seeing as we hadn't exactly hit it off before."

Mari managed to stop laughing. "Listen, it's a gift. Take it and run with it. Sharing your mind with another person can be a pain in the ass sometimes, but there are compensations."

"Like great sex."

"Exactly, and not going mad. That's another good thing. Basically, the sexual act helps you learn to trust your mate and open your mind to him. As you share your thoughts and feelings you gain power and stability from each other."

"I suppose so." Ella sighed. "I still don't understand why anyone would agree to mate an empath."

"Don't be dumb, Ella. Stupendous sex, increased magical powers and the opportunity to legally reside in two different worlds? Most men would jump at the chance."

Not Morosov. He seemed as shaken by the consequences of their actions as she was, and from what she could tell, he already had all the advantages Mari had just listed.

"What happens if we just want to keep it casual?" Ella asked.

"What do you mean?"

"Well, just about the stupendous sex."

"You could try, I suppose, but don't you want someone to share your life with?" Mari's voice gentled. "It really does make a huge difference to everything."

"But what if we don't even want to live in the same place?"

"I think you'd find that very difficult. Mated couples are supposed to be together."

"So I could go mad anyway if he leaves?"

"I don't know, Ella. Why would he want to leave? If he volunteered for the FAM program, he must've known what he was getting into."

"I guess," Ella said.

"I know this has all been something of a shock to you, but it really is a good thing. Your male will be able to help you with the psychic overload from your work *and* provide you with a safe and secure life. I don't know how I managed without Cameron. He's literally been a lifesaver."

There was no doubting Mari's sincerity. Ella smiled. "Thanks. I feel a bit better now."

"Good." Her tone turned businesslike. "Now, you should go ahead and register your consent with OCOS anyway. They can proceed in their own indomitable fashion and send you all the information you'll need about the mating process."

"Even though I've already done it."

"It's not quite as simple as that, Ella. It's a lifelong commitment."

"Oh God, don't say that," Ella groaned. "I was just starting to think about allowing myself to enjoy the sex."

Mari started laughing again. "Start with that, definitely, and call me if you have any more questions. I'm dying to hear how it goes."

"Will do. And Mari? Don't tell anyone, will you?"

"Only Cam, and I swear he'll keep it to himself."

The yelling started up again and Mari groaned. "I'd better go and see what's up with the boys. Take care, Ella, and keep in touch."

Ella put the phone down and stared out the window. So it was okay.

Having stupendous sex was quite normal for mated couples.

And she was quite determined not to see Vadim Morosov until Monday morning at the office.

With the rest of the team. Fully clothed.

She buried her face in the sofa cushion and howled.

14

VADIM LOOKED UP AS ALEXEI JOINED HIM IN THE LARGER OF THE conference rooms. The Fae wore an immaculate charcoal gray suit with a silver tie and white shirt. His long hair was tied back at the nape of his neck and his expression reminded Vadim of a purring cat.

"Where were you all weekend?"

Alexei fluttered his eyelashes. "Having fun. Why?"

"No particular reason." Vadim sat back in his chair and studied his partner. "It would be nice if you'd let me know your plans in future."

"You're not my mother." Alexei took a seat at the table.

"No, but I am your superior on this assignment and I need to be able to get in touch with you."

"If you'd really needed me, I would've heard you."

Vadim thought back to those frantic moments in the elevator. "I'm not so sure about that."

"What's up?" Alexei asked.

"Don't you start saying that," Vadim groaned. "I hate it."

"Okay, let me try again. Why are you in such a bad mood?"

"I'm fine."

"No, you're not." Alexei stared hard at him. "You need to get laid."

Vadim smiled.

"No, seriously, Vadim, you've enough Fae blood in you to make it a necessity."

"I've never liked that Fae excuse for debauchery and I don't intend to use it." Vadim looked up at the door. "Feehan's here and I see Liz and Ms. Walsh just behind her."

What the hell was Ella wearing today? She had a tie-dye shirt on and a pair of baggy denim overalls that were ripped at the knee. Her hair was in two braids on either side of her face. She looked like she'd just come in from raking the hay or something. Despite that, he found himself sitting up and sniffing the air like a bloodhound. She looked in his and Alexei's general direction and muttered something vague but didn't make eye contact. It didn't matter. She couldn't fool him any longer.

After she'd left him to go on the ferry, he'd struggled to know what to do with himself. Feeling conflicted wasn't a new sensation but he still didn't like it. Despite his resolve to protect Ella and see the case through, he disliked not knowing how she felt about him and what conclusions she would draw about their relationship when he wasn't there to interact with her. He'd spent the remainder of the weekend doing tourist stuff, research on empaths from all over the world and taking cold showers. If she smiled at him, he might leap over the table and take her to the floor and...

"Everyone here?" Feehan asked.

Sam burst through the door wearing a pair of dark shades. "Sorry, guys."

"Take a seat."

Everyone waited as Sam settled himself down and took out a tatty folder with a picture of a skateboarder on it.

"Who wants to start?"

Vadim raised his hand. "I checked out the remaining

empaths from outside the U.S. in Ms. Walsh's graduating year. All the Russians are dead, as are the Norwegians, Swedes and Danes." He consulted his notes. "A total of nine in all."

Feehan wrote the details on the board.

Alexei glanced at Liz. "Would the rest of you agree that our killer seems to follow a pattern here? He likes to finish a job. From the dates Vadim gave us, the Siren has gone from country to country systematically murdering empaths."

"Why hasn't anyone noticed before?" Feehan stopped writing and turned around.

"Probably because the numbers in each country were relatively small until he reached Russia."

"I have another suggestion." Sam waved his hand in the air like a school kid. "From what I've seen so far, does he also kill them in alphabetical order?"

"What?" Feehan stared at Sam who opened his folder.

"Well, I spent a bit of time last night looking at all the empaths who had been killed so far in the U.S. I noticed that the ones who are left, all have names that are at the end of the alphabet and the last one to die was Laney Phillips."

Vadim felt Ella's wince in his head and glanced across at her. She immediately looked away.

"And the previous victim was Christa Morehouse," Feehan added. "So who's left?"

"There are four." Liz went over to the whiteboard and started writing.

Jodi Petrello Fay Roberts Ella Walsh Trini Yamada

"And do we know the whereabouts of Ms. Petrello and the rest of them?"

Sam looked up. "I'm still working on it."

"Then work faster. We might need to put a guard on these women."

"I think I'm okay, boss." Ella glanced around the table. "I feel fairly well protected."

Vadim opened his mouth to say something about him being all the protection she would ever need and then realized he couldn't. That galled him far more than he would have expected.

"Anything else?" Feehan asked.

"Have we checked out the two male empaths who graduated with Ella yet?" Alexei said.

Vadim turned to stare at Alexei, who sat at ease in his chair. "Why would we do that?"

"Because the killer is male, and maybe one of these men—who would know all these American woman personally—might have lost it and turned to murder."

"Mike Nichols and Paul Baker," Ella said.

"That's their names?" Alexei nodded to Liz and both of their Fae-Webs shimmered and expanded to meet over the table.

"I can't see either of them having the nerve to be a serial killer, though. Most nights, they were too scared to come out with the girls for a drink." Ella half-smiled.

"Do you keep in touch with them?"

"Not really. I think Mike moved across the east coast. I have no idea where Paul went."

"Who would know?"

"Either SBLE or the Merton office in Otherworld." Feehan wrote the new names up on the board. "I'm unsure of the protocol. Do male empaths get offered mates?"

Ella reached for her coffee. "Yeah, they do."

"Do we know if these guys are already mated?" Alexei asked.

Ella shrugged. "I have no idea. You'd have to check with Otherworld."

"I can do that."

Vadim tensed as Ella stood up. "I'm going to get more coffee. I'll be back in a sec."

He waited a moment, and then followed her out. She knew

he was there, but she kept her attention on the vending machine. He waited impatiently for her to face him.

"What's up, Morosov? Do you need a dollar again?"

He smiled as he remembered his first sight of her and his prediction that she would be trouble.

"No, I just wanted to talk to you about something."

Alarm flashed across her face. "I thought we'd agreed to keep that to ourselves."

"Not *that*. Don't you think it is odd that no one has mentioned anything about what happened with the elevators on Friday?"

"In what way?"

"I would assume the SBLE review the security tapes, so why hasn't someone called Feehan asking what the hell we were up to?"

"I hadn't thought of that."

"We need to tell Feehan what happened." She opened her mouth, and he kept talking. "Not all of it. Just the part about us getting stuck in the elevator."

"Why?"

"Because it doesn't feel right."

"Do you think we were set up?"

"It's possible."

"By whom?"

"That's a great question. But if someone or something managed to get in here and disrupt SBLE security, Feehan needs to know about it."

She met his gaze and he couldn't look away. Without further thought, he reached for her, only to have her step back.

"Don't."

He dropped his hand to his side, his fingers curling into a fist. "I'm not sure if I can stop myself."

"We're at work."

"Then come back to the hotel with me at lunchtime." He couldn't believe he'd just said that. He was *never* the pursuer.

She shook her head and an inhuman growl attempted to work its way out of his chest. Her brown eyes widened.

"I've got to go on a case." She swallowed hard. "Maybe you could come back home with me tonight instead?"

"I'd be honored." He inclined his head. "Now shall we go and tell Feehan about what happened on Friday night?"

"If we must."

He wanted to take her hand, but instead, turned on his heel and went back into the conference room holding the door open for Ella to pass by him. Her denim-clad ass bumped against his groin and he was instantly hard. Thankfully, he was wearing dark pants so he hoped no one would notice.

"There's something Ms. Walsh and I think you should know," Vadim announced.

"You're getting married?" Alexei's smile was a mixture of sweetness and pure malice.

"Yeah, right." Ella snorted. "Last Friday night, Morosov and I were the last people here. When we met at the elevators, I found the stairwell was off-limits thanks to maintenance."

"Wait a minute," Feehan interrupted. "I wasn't told about that."

"Neither was I," Ella added. "Or I would have left earlier. Morosov persuaded me I could face the elevator for a few seconds, so I followed him into the car. Just as the doors opened at the lobby level, the elevator shuddered and fell back down the shaft."

"Holy cow!" Sam whistled. "Did you freak out?"

"I did. Luckily, Morosov kept his head and we managed to climb out of the service hatch, and back up to the lobby."

"We were wondering why no one had mentioned it," Vadim said. "Don't you receive security reports, Mr. Feehan?"

"I do. I saw nothing about any of this." Feehan took off his glasses and stared at Ella and Vadim. "Are you quite sure?"

Ella put her coffee down. "Do I look like the sort of person who would make stuff up about being stuck in an elevator with an irritating Russian?"

Feehan held up a placatory hand. "No, of course not. I wonder if we can review the security tapes?"

"Why don't you do that while I go and sort out this little problem for the Bonetti family on Folsom Street?" Ella picked up her backpack. "The owners think they have a poltergeist. One of the waiters isn't so sure."

Vadim grabbed his jacket. "I'll come with you." She was already moving. "You don't need to do that."

"Yes he does," Feehan raised his voice to her departing back. "You need someone with you at all times."

Ella's answer and gesture was luckily too far away for Feehan to register, although Vadim got the gist of it. He kept after her, taking the elevator as she took the stairs and meeting her in the lobby.

"I'm coming with you."

"All *right*." She glared at him. She seemed even crankier since they'd mated than before. He didn't mind, knowing he was the cause and that it meant he was getting to her. "But don't touch me and don't get in the way, okay?"

It was busy out on the streets and grew even more congested as Ella headed deep into tourist central, at the other end of Market, where the famed trolley buses turned around. The place was noisy with street vendors, bums, and the occasional crazy person. San Francisco always had a nice line of crazy, and it all came out when the sun hit the sidewalks. Ella sidestepped three guys and their bedding huddled in a doorway and ignored a smiling clown jiggling a cup in her face. The smell of onions made her pause and Vadim ran right into her.

"Do you want a hotdog?" Ella asked.

His revolted expression was almost enough to brighten her day. "From a street vendor?"

"Sure. I haven't been sick once." She handed over a five-dollar bill with instructions to put everything on her dog. "Well, not really sick."

Vadim watched in fascinated horror as she chomped on the bun and kept walking. There was one thing you could say about comfort food. It never let you down.

"Where exactly are we going?"

She pointed up the street that ran almost parallel to Market. "There's a diner above one of the big drugstores up here. It's been in the same family for several generations."

"And they think they have a poltergeist?"

"Apparently. I said I'd go and check it out."

"What do you think it is?"

"I won't know until I get there."

"But it's lunchtime. Won't they be too busy to talk?"

"I'm not going to talk right away. I'm going to eat."

She veered off to her left. "Here it is. Right up these stairs."

Once they got above ground level, the space opened up considerably giving the diners a great view of the teeming hordes below the windows. It was decked out in traditional style with Formica topped tables, chrome fittings and red plastic leatherette booths. The place was three-quarters full and the smell of fried food and maple syrup hung thick in the air. She breathed it in appreciatively. A harried looking waiter approached them.

"Two please."

He nodded, picked up two huge plastic covered menus and led them to a small table close to the half-exposed kitchen. There was a lot of yelling going on, but it didn't sound too bad. She'd heard far worse on previous visits, and even seen some hapless waiter chased out of the kitchen by a hail of pots.

"Are you really going to eat here?" Vadim looked around the busy space.

"I'm hungry."

"What about that hotdog you just had?"

"That was just an appetizer."

He looked down at his menu, one eyebrow raised in a way Ella wished she could emulate. "What would you recommend?"

"I'm a big fan of the cheeseburger and sweet potato fries followed by the banana split."

A reluctant smile curved his lush lower lip. "I remember banana splits."

"We could share one if you like."

"That's very tempting." He studied the menu again. "There's definitely some Otherworld magic swirling around in here."

"You feel it too?"

"Hard to miss."

"Let's eat and see if we can get the waiter who called in his suspicions to the SBLE hotline to talk to us. I think he's one of the Bonetti cousins, so he's family."

Another dark-haired waiter appeared and Ella checked out his nametag. "Hey, are you Mark?" She held out her hand. "I'm Ella Walsh from the SBLE. This is my colleague, Vadim Morosov."

Mark briefly shook hands. "Thanks for coming. I talked to my uncle. Despite his initial blustering, he's quite relieved I did something about this."

"That's good to know. How about we eat our lunch and get a feel for the place, and then maybe you can come and tell us what's been going on?"

Mark smiled for the first time. "That's not a problem. It's also on the house. I'll get your food and take my break when you're done. Now what can I get you?" Vadim chose the spinach salad and the banana split.

Despite his disapproving stare, Ella went for the double cheeseburger and fries.

After the server left, he gave her a serious look. "That excuse of yours about eating what you like because you'll die young is no longer valid. You are going to have to start taking care of your body."

"I'll think about it."

"You're still not convinced you're going to live, are you?"

"Well, would you be?" She rested her chin on her fist. "I don't think I'll believe it until way after my twenty-seventh birthday."

"Which is when?"

"In about ten days." She made a face. "My mom left me a message this morning asking me to come and spend next weekend with them to get my presents. She sounded like she was arranging a wake."

"She's probably worried about you."

"I suppose so." She sat back as the waiter put two glasses crammed full with ice and water on the table. "I'm not sure what she wants from me. Why buy me anything if she knows I'm not going to make it? What did she get me? Three wishes from a genie? A burial plot?"

"Maybe she still has hope?"

Ella stared into Vadim's calm blue eyes and thought about how he looked when he was having sex. "You've met her. She's not like that. She always thinks I'm going to fail."

"I understand why your relationship is fraught with difficulties, but she is still your mother."

"The mother who sent me away to school because she was scared of me."

"You told your brother you were drawing Otherworld creatures to the house and that it was probably for the best you were sent away."

"I said that to make *him* feel better. It doesn't mean I actually meant it." His unconvinced expression dared her to continue. "Okay, so I've done therapy. I know as an intelligent adult that me leaving was the best thing for everyone. I still hated it and I have a childish tendency to lash out at my mother."

"At least you acknowledge it."

"Yeah, I'm great like that." Ella looked away and rearranged her silverware. "This is getting far too profound for a lunchtime chat."

He shrugged. "We're linked. We can be as intimate as we like. I won't tell anyone."

She fixed him with her most challenging stare. "How come you know so much about this empath mating thing?"

"Because I had nothing to do all weekend, so I did some research, called a few friends, infiltrated some Fae-Webs..."

"You didn't tell anyone, did you?"

"About us bonding?" He shook his head. "I told you I wouldn't do that yet."

"Apparently, if I agree to the match, we're supposed to get a ton of paperwork from OCOS telling us what to expect."

"Shame we missed that."

She gave him a bright smile. "I don't know. We seem to be managing quite well by ourselves. I hate reading instructions anyway. Oh, look. Food."

She made Vadim try her cheeseburger and he reluctantly agreed that it was rather good. He offered her some of his spinach, but when she pretended to gag he retreated and focused on forking the obnoxious slippery greenery into his mouth. She liked watching him. He was incredibly neat and cut the food up into similar size bundles before eating them.

When the banana split was placed in front of him, he moved it into the center of the table. It was a sight to behold. Three types of ice cream, a whole banana— one half on each side— whipped cream, nuts and cherries on top.

"A classic. It's almost a shame to dig into it, but I'll force myself."

"Be my guest." Vadim gestured at her with his long spoon. "I won't be able to eat all of it."

"Don't worry about that. Desserts are my specialty."

He took a small scoop of the strawberry ice cream and Ella watched his expression change.

"Good?"

He smiled at her and she almost forgot to swallow. "To borrow a phrase from you—that is awesome."

"I think they make their own ice cream."

"You can tell."

It didn't take long for them to finish the whole thing and then Mark reappeared, took away the remaining plates and sat down beside Vadim.

"My uncle wants to talk to you. I hope that's okay?"

"Sure, we can pop into the kitchen after this." Ella pushed her water glass out of the way. "So, what's been happening?"

Mark grimaced. "For the last month or so, every time we open up, the kitchen is a mess. There are broken plates, spilled water, smashed glasses..."

"Do you have a security system?"

"Yeah, that's the kicker. We upgraded it recently so we have cameras and everything."

"And nothing is showing up?"

Mark hesitated. "Well, there is *something*, but it's not so much a person as a green, swirling mist." He attempted a laugh. "That sounds ridiculous, right?"

"Not at all," Ella reassured him. "What do your uncle and aunt think is causing this?"

"They think it's a poltergeist."

"Why's that?"

"Because they recently gave a job washing up to their youngest grandson, my sixteen-year-old cousin Erik."

"And they think Erik is creating the disturbances?"

"Yeah, because he's been in a lot of trouble recently at school: drugs, alcohol, you know the kind of stuff. They gave him the job to help him straighten himself out. He's not taken to the working life real well and they reckon adolescents can cause disturbances in the psychic field." He grinned. "What can I say? My auntie Vita watches a lot of crap TV."

"It makes sense, though. Do you think Erik could be doing it?"

Mark shrugged. "If it *is* him, it's not deliberate."

"What do you think it is?" Vadim asked.

Mark's gaze switched to Vadim. "This is going to sound strange, but when I looked at the footage, I was sure that I could see something *solid* at the center of the mist."

"And what did it look like?"

"Green, short and spiky."

"That's interesting." Vadim looked at Ella, his eyebrow raised. "What do you think, Ms. Walsh?"

Ella stood up. "I think you might be on to something, Mark. I know it's still busy, but can we go into the kitchen now?"

VADIM FOLLOWED Ella and Mark into the surprisingly modern kitchen at the back of the diner. All the surfaces gleamed either white or silver. The staff moved in a blur of speed and efficiency watched over by a small, loud-mouthed man at the pass. It was a kitchen even he would be happy to eat in.

The short, gray-haired man stopped shouting out orders and came toward them, his expression fierce. Mark held up his hand.

"These are the folks from the SBLE, Uncle Roberto." Roberto wiped his hand on his apron and stuck it out. "You are like the

X-Files, yes?" His gaze slid down over Ella's baggy overalls. "Although you are no Scully." Vadim fought a smile.

Ella shook Roberto's hand. "I don't want to get in the way, but can I ask you a couple of questions?"

He nodded.

"Firstly, can I view your security camera data, and secondly, did you recently update your kitchen?"

"Mark will show you the camera tapes, and yes, we did update the kitchen. This building was constructed not long after the last big earthquake in the 1900's. The plumbing and ventilation were no longer up to current Californian health and safety standards. We had no choice." He frowned. "Why, is it important?"

"Sometimes when renovations are made on a building, the inhabitants don't like it."

"The ghosts, you mean?"

"Maybe, but that's not all that might live here." Ella smiled. "Let me check the security data, and then I'll be more certain of what we are dealing with."

Mark took them through into the back office, which smelled deliciously like cinnamon buns, and showed Ella how to work her way through the security camera data. He went back to the front of the house, leaving them alone. Vadim stood behind Ella and watched the screen intently.

"What do you think it is, then?" he finally asked. "I'm not sure, but green, short and spiky doesn't sound like either poltergeist activity or a ghost."

"It sounds like something from Otherworld."

"Yeah." Ella froze the picture. "Do you see that, Morosov? That thin trail of mist rising up from the floor?" He leaned in closer and breathed in the scent of fried onions. He'd never thought it was attractive before...

"Yes. Where is it coming from?"

"Let's back it up a few frames. Look at where the water is pooling on the floor."

He saw it then, the beginning of the mist seeping out in a thin trickle from between the cupboards below the three industrial-sized metal sinks. "It lives under the sink?"

"In the plumbing probably. I should imagine that remodel must have destroyed whatever it calls home. No wonder it's mad. I'll let the film run on a bit longer now, and see if we can actually identify this thing."

"There it is." Vadim pointed at the screen and Ella stilled the footage. "Definitely green and pointy. What do you think it is?"

She leaned back and almost collided with his nose. "I'm thinking some kind of small Fae. We'll have to come back tonight and catch it in the act."

"And what will you tell the Bonettis?"

"The truth."

"Is that wise?"

She regarded him steadily. "I always tell Otherworld victims the truth before I replace the memory. I think they deserve to know."

"Even if they won't remember it?"

"Absolutely." She must have sensed his confusion because she continued. "I think the mind remembers everything, and even if I do my job, there is still a remnant of the truth left in a human's subconscious."

"Like the way every culture has similar myths and fairytales?"

"Exactly, a collective subconscious fear."

He resisted the urge to kiss the top of her head, then stood back to allow her to stand. "What time do we need to be back here tonight?"

"From the security camera log, the culprit tends to appear around 3:00 a.m., so we'd better be in place at midnight." She went over to the door. "I'll okay it with Mr. Bonetti and meet you downstairs, all right?"

He nodded his agreement and waited until she left. Was she finding it as hard to be physically close to him as he was to her? She seemed even pricklier than usual, and keen to get away, but then he was hardly his normal, calm self either. He walked out through the restaurant and down the dark stairs to the street. The noise and heat hit in a dirty, dusty wave and he almost recoiled. He didn't like feeling so on edge. It reminded him of his childhood, when the wrong word could mean death or worse. In order to avoid the vilest excesses of his parents, he'd learned early to avoid antagonizing them, but sometimes that hadn't been enough. Sometimes he had to stand up and face them with all the weapons of his forebears, both magical and physical, at his disposal. And even then that hadn't always saved those he loved... But he'd learned from that and then they'd learned to fear him.

And now here he was, the scourge of Otherworld, afraid of being rejected by a mouthy, tiny blonde who ordered him around and never let him know exactly where he stood with her. Somewhere deep in Otherworld, he guessed someone was laughing.

15

"Ah, there you are Ella, Vadim," Feehan called out to them as they walked past his office. "Have you got a moment?"

She glanced at Vadim but he'd already obediently turned toward Feehan's open door. She'd have to talk to him about that biddable streak of his. It was so not cool and, she now knew, *so* not like him.

Feehan was seated at his desk tapping away at his keyboard. The smell of his tuna sandwiches permeated the air along with the underlying hint of nicotine.

"I have the security footage from last Friday."

"And what does it show?" Ella perched on the side of his desk.

"Nothing."

Feehan rotated his screen to show them a view of the SBLE lobby and then one of the white marble foyer upstairs. He clicked again and showed a frozen image of her and Vadim waiting at the elevator doors, and a later one of them both exiting the building at street level.

"That makes no sense."

"I know. No sign of maintenance, and no evidence that the

elevator didn't behave perfectly." Feehan put down his pen. "Are you certain you were trapped? You don't think it might be some...*empath* issue?"

"Mr. Feehan, I'm no empath," Vadim said. "We were both there, and we both experienced the same thing. And there is one major problem with those pictures."

"What?"

"Ms. Walsh doesn't wait for the elevator. She always uses the stairs."

Feehan nodded slowly. "That's true."

"I suspect someone has gone to a lot of trouble to cover up what happened. I have no idea why, or who would choose to do such a thing," Vadim said.

"Neither do I," Feehan agreed. "But I'll get right on it. What do you think, Ella?"

"It definitely happened. That's all I have to say about it." She rose to her feet. "Are we done?" Ever since she was a kid she'd hated it when she hadn't been believed. It felt odd to have Vadim standing up for her.

"There is one more matter I needed to pass on." Feehan consulted a piece of paper on his desk. "Sam left me a note to tell me that Fay Roberts died just after she graduated from college. He spoke to her parents, and confirmed her death with Otherworld."

"Oh great. That leaves three of us." Ella shoved her hands in her pockets. "I feel like a sitting duck."

"You're the safest of the lot," Feehan said far too cheerfully for her liking. "You are, Ms. Walsh. One of our team will be with you 24/7."

Vadim held the door open for her.

"Thanks." Fear always brought out her most pugnacious side. "I need to do some research on small, green spiky things. I'll be in my office."

As she left she heard Vadim speaking softly to Feehan.

"Don't worry, I'll keep her in my sights. She's just upset you didn't believe her about what happened on Friday."

She almost turned around and went back. Who the hell did Morosov think he was, making excuses for her? Just because it was true didn't mean she wanted her boss to know about it. Had Vadim somehow picked up her earlier thought? This bonding crap could also be a gigantic pain in the ass. No one could be expected to keep her shields up all the time.

She got herself some coffee and stared at the slowly filling cup. But hadn't Mari said something about a mate being able to share the physic burden too? Ella thought she just meant the memories she stole—which was after all, the whole point of the bonding exercise. She hadn't realized Vadim might be able to access *every* thought. It made her far too vulnerable.

She picked up the coffee, jammed a lid on it and went back to her office. There was a light blinking on her phone and she dialed her passcode to receive messages. An unfamiliar voice filled the room.

"Hi, Ella, long time no speak. It's Trini Yamada here!" Ella froze. "I just wanted to touch base with you. I'm staying at the Bay View Hotel on Embarcadero and I was hoping you might want to get together with me to celebrate."

The door to Ella's office flew open and Vadim stood there, his gun out, his expression lethal. She put a shaking finger to her lips as Trini gave a light laugh.

"Thanks so much for inviting me to your birthday party, Ella! It's mine too! Isn't it great!"

There was the sound of whispering and then Trini giggled. "Sure, I'll tell her. The Siren says he can't wait to see you either, so come on over! Bye for now!"

The phone went dead and Ella just stared at Vadim, who jerked his head in the direction of the door. "Let's go."

"She wasn't supposed to be next, Morosov. What the hell is going on?"

Ella checked she had her weapon, and followed Vadim out into the hall. Alexei appeared in the doorway of the conference room and fell in behind them.

"Do we need transport to get there?" Vadim asked as they ran into the lobby.

For a second Ella stared at him. "I…don't know. I don't know where that hotel is."

"Alexei? Can you find it?"

"Yes, it's about a twenty minute walk or I could get us there sooner if I use magic."

"Are you okay with that, Ella?"

She nodded. The next moment both men grabbed her hands, there was a flash of light, and they were outside the neat brown façade of the Bay View Hotel. Ella fought to control the nausea magic always gave her and started up the steps to the hotel.

At the small reception desk, a young man dressed in a smart suit was tapping away at a keyboard. He greeted Ella with a smile.

"Welcome to the Bay View Hotel. Do you have a reservation?"

"No, I've just come by to meet a friend of mine, Trini Yamada. Is she here yet? Can you give me her room number?"

"I'm afraid I can't give you that information, ma'am." Vadim leaned past Ella and smiled charmingly at the receptionist. "Is it possible that Ms. Yamada left a message for Ms. Walsh? She is definitely expecting her."

"I just came on shift. I'll check." The man looked flustered and searched through the various sticky notes that adorned the desk and the computer screen. "Oh, yes, there's something here!" He read the note. "If I could just see some ID, Ms. Walsh, you can go on up." Ella gave him her driver's license and waited another interminable minute before he gave it back to her. "Ms. Yamada is in room 209." He lifted the phone receiver. "I'll call up and let her know you're coming."

"Don't worry about that. We want to surprise her." Alexei leaned across, took the receiver and put it back down. The receptionist didn't say a word, his gaze caught in the Fae's, his will already under Alexei's spell.

Ella was already moving across the lobby, Vadim at her side. He touched her shoulder. "I'll come up the stairs with you."

He pushed the door open and followed her, his weapon drawn, his barriers high. When they emerged onto the second floor, Vadim made her stop.

"Do you want me to go in first?"

"No, he's expecting me. I'd rather you stayed back."

His expression darkened. "I'm not sure if I can do that."

"You have to."

"I know, but something inside me doesn't want to let you out of my sight."

"How sweet." She patted his cheek. "Well suck it up, buttercup. I need to do this alone."

With a terrible sense of déjà vu, she headed down the hallway toward Trini's room. She knew which room it was because of the pounding music that shook the insubstantial hotel door. For a moment, she leaned her hand against the door and tried to concentrate, but she could get no sense of anything apart from the Siren's exultation.

"Do you need me to break in?"

She nodded, then Vadim touched the door handle until the green light flashed over the key card slot. He slowly opened the door and let it swing wide. The ugly blare of the music made it difficult to think, let alone examine the room for danger. She went in with her weapon held in front of her. Not that it would do much good if the Siren was Otherworld, but it might slow him down. The bathroom was to the right of the door and it was empty, the lights over the sink illuminating the empty white space.

Ella moved along the left hand wall, keeping her gun hand

unencumbered until she had a clear view into the main part of the bedroom. There was only one figure there, and it definitely wasn't the Siren. Ella let out her breath and cautiously checked the room again. The windows were shut and, unless the Siren was extremely good at hiding, he wasn't concealed somewhere.

"Bathroom's clear," Vadim called out from behind her.

She walked over to the radio to turn it off. The sudden silence was shocking, revealing the patchiness of her breathing and the loud thump of her heart. When she turned around, she was confronted by the sight of a dark—haired woman sitting bolt upright in the chair, a party hat on her head and a birthday cake on her lap. The candles were still burning, and wax discolored the thick white frosting on the top, which read "Happy Birthday."

Even in death, Trini was still smiling, her grin wide, her brown eyes fixed in eternal approval. An empty bottle of champagne and two glasses sat on the desk along with a box of matches.

"Ms. Walsh, I'm going to call Feehan and the cleanup squad, okay? We need to read this scene before the regular cops get here. Alexei's already got the reception guy's cooperation, and he'll keep it for as long as it is necessary." Vadim paused. "I assume she's dead?"

"Yeah."

"Is there anything else you need to do here?"

"Not really, except catch the sick bastard who thinks this is amusing."

"I wondered about that. You can feel his satisfaction in the air. It's almost alive."

Ella stared at him. Perhaps she wasn't the only one who would be gaining power from their bonding.

"Do you need to touch her?"

She recoiled. "I don't want to, but I have to make sure." She took a reluctant step toward the dead empath and touched her throat. "There's nothing there except his pleasure and her relief." She frowned. "Why don't they struggle? What does he do to them?"

Vadim put his arm around her shoulders. "We can talk about this later. If you are sure she's dead, we need to get out of here."

She shrugged off his attempt to lead her away, and instead turned back to the body.

"Happy birthday, Trini." She carefully blew out the candles. "I'm sorry I didn't get here sooner."

She left then, with Vadim close behind her. There was no sense of the Siren nearby. Had he gotten bored waiting for her, and moved on? Surely not for much longer...he was running out of victims—at least in western USA.

Down in the lobby, Alexei still chatted to the receptionist. He looked up as Vadim and Ella appeared. "Hey guys, I should have called you. I just checked with Adam here, and the person we want isn't staying here after all. The guy *we* want is at the Bay View *Apartments*, not the hotel."

"Oh!" Ella forced a laugh as she approached the receptionist. "I should've checked with my secretary before we left. We're so sorry to have bothered you."

Adam looked confused. "But didn't you want to see Ms. Yamada? I..."

Ella leaned across the desk, took his hand and concentrated on extracting every image he had of the three of them and what they'd asked him. When she'd retrieved the memories she smiled at Adam. "We're so sorry to have bothered you by looking for the wrong person at the wrong hotel. But you're okay about it. It happens so often that you don't even think it's important enough to mention to the authorities."

"Don't even remember you," Adam repeated. "You're not even here."

"That's right." Ella pushed the memory firmly into his head.

"When you look up, everything will be normal and we'll be gone. Okay?"

"Okay."

"Count to one hundred and then open your eyes."

He obediently began counting. Before he reached twenty, Alexei had taken her hand and whisked them all back to SBLE.

ELLA WENT BACK to her office, shut the door and continued to look up information about small green Fae. Around her she could hear her SBLE colleagues dealing with the fallout of another empath murder, but for once, no one came to bother her or ask for her opinion. And what was there to say? Trini had been killed in exactly the same way as the others, her memories removed, her brain emptied of everything that had made her unique. Ella rubbed at her eyes and tried to concentrate on the screen. A knock at the door made her lift her head.

"Come in?"

Vadim appeared. "Are you okay?"

"Why shouldn't I be?"

He leaned against the closed door and studied her. She was pleased to see that for once he looked less than perfect. His tie was askew and the starched collar of his white shirt had wilted in the heat.

"You just had to deal with another murder victim." She opened her mouth and he held up his hand. "Ella, you can say what you like, but I *know* you."

"Biblically, you mean?"

"Biblically, psychically and emotionally." He hesitated. "I know this is hard for you."

"Sure it is, but what good will I do anyone if I make a big deal out of it? Those dead women need me to be strong—to stand up for them."

He inclined his head. "I don't doubt you'll do your best to bring their killer to justice."

"Thanks." Ella let her gaze stray back to her screen. "Was there something in particular you wanted?"

"Just this." He moved so quickly she hardly had time to blink before he hauled her out of her chair and put his arms around her. He kissed her forehead and she elbowed him in the side.

"What are you doing?"

"Holding you." He didn't let her go, just looked down at her. She felt him enfolding her mind.

"Then stop it, you idiot."

"No." A corner of his beautiful mouth kicked up. She narrowed her eyes at him but he still held her.

The desire to rest her head on his shoulder and just let go was almost as overwhelming as it was horrifying. Tears crowded her throat. She shoved her hands between them and pushed at his chest.

"If you make me cry at work, I'll never forgive you." His shields slammed up so fast she winced.

He stepped away. "I apologize, Ms. Walsh. That was the last thing I wanted to do. I assume you'll be putting off the investigation at the Bonettis' for another night?"

She sat down before her knees gave way. "I'm still going. I might take Sam along. He needs to start doing more fieldwork, so you don't have to come."

"I'm damn well coming." Vadim stalked toward the door, his expression icy. "Don't try and skip out on me. I don't want to use our bonded link, but if you try and shut me out, I'll do whatever it takes to keep you safe." He shut the door so hard it rattled the frame.

Ella stared after him. She'd offended him but what had he minded most—being shut out of her next mission, or out of her mind? With a groan, she rubbed her hands over her eyes. Didn't he see that she couldn't cave at work? Did he expect her to cry all over him? She had no experience being in a relationship, especially not one with an OCOS supplied mate who could read at least some of her thoughts without even trying.

She opened her desk drawer and found a bar of chocolate. It looked a little battered, but it would do. When she'd fortified herself sufficiently, she'd go and find Sam and update him on the Bonetti case. Vadim would be accompanying them; she had no doubt about that. A flicker of remorse made the chocolate suddenly tasteless. This mating business was new to Vadim too and he hadn't asked for this. Crap. She probably owed him an apology.

***

VADIM SLAMMED the door of the small conference room and briefly closed his eyes. His flexed his hands. The temptation to blast something into oblivion tingled in his fingertips.

"What's up, Vadim?"

Liz was sitting on Alexei's vacant desk, long legs swinging, coffee cup in her hand.

"Ah, hi, Liz. I didn't realize anyone was in here."

"I saw that." She cocked her head to one side. "Let me guess. Is Ella driving you mad?"

"She…" Vadim hesitated and Liz looked at him expectantly. He reluctantly concluded he could share some of his frustration, even if it was just about work.

"She what?"

Vadim sat down. "I went to see if I could offer her any help and she wouldn't let me near her."

"That sounds like Ella."

"I tried to be sympathetic and respectful but she wouldn't give an inch."

"She's a very private person."

"I *understand* that. I'm the same."

"So how would you take it if someone tried to comfort *you* at work?"

Vadim thought about that. "Not very well."

She clucked her tongue at him as if he were a child. "Then why are you surprised Ella was ticked off?"

"She's always ticked off with me. That wasn't a surprise at all." He contemplated Liz for a long moment. "She's insisting on going out to work the Bonetti case tonight."

Liz finished her coffee and threw the cup neatly into the trash. "That doesn't shock me either. Ella's remedy for avoiding emotional stuff has always been to work and play harder."

"I'm going with her."

Liz's faint smile faded. "You must go with her. In fact, you must stay with her as much as you can."

"Is that an order?"

Liz's Fae-Web shimmered around her and her eyes turned gold. "Yes. You need to face this danger together. Your destinies are linked."

"Not a problem." Vadim hesitated. "Does Alexei know what you know?"

"Not in quite the same way, but he's probably got some idea of the bond between you and Ella. Why?"

Vadim switched on his computer. "No reason."

"What don't you want him to know?"

"I didn't say that."

"He's your friend."

"He's almost one hundred percent Fae. He's no one's *friend*. He was sent here to report to our boss in Russia."

"So he told me." Liz nodded. "But I don't think he's going to have you sent back now. You're far too central to this investigation for that to happen."

"Don't count on it." Vadim clicked on the SBLE website page.

Sam came bounding into the office. "Hey, Liz, Ella's taking me out on a case with her tonight! Isn't that sick?"

"It's great, Sam." Liz smiled enthusiastically at Sam, who blushed. "Just remember to pay attention and don't get in Ella's way."

He made a face. "It's okay. She's already read me the riot act." He paused at the door. "Do you think she's intending to hand over all the cases to me before she…?"

Liz frowned at him. "I have no idea. Just take what you can and be grateful."

Sam gulped. "No offense, Liz."

"None taken, but don't say that to Ella, will you?"

Sam disappeared and Liz grimaced at Vadim. "He's such a kid."

"At least he's honest."

She slid off the desk and headed for the door. "Tell Alexei I was looking for him, will you?"

"I will." Vadim settled down to research the SBLE files for little green men. Ella might not want him there, but he was determined to be as well prepared as he possibly could.

16

"Okay, this is how we're going to proceed." Ella looked at the two men. "The three of us are going to stake out the kitchen. When the creature emerges, I will be the one to engage it. Got that?" Sam and Vadim nodded obediently. "If I am in trouble, please feel free to help out."

"What kind of trouble?" Sam whispered.

"Don't worry, you'll work it out. Remember, the aim is to capture the creature and persuade it to go back to Otherworld, not to kill it."

Sam's face fell. "Why would it want to come back?"

"Did you read the file I sent you? If what I suspect is correct, this creature has been living quite happily in the pipes for almost a hundred years. Now, along come these humans and break up the creature's nest. It's not pleased about that."

Sam nodded. "Got it."

Vadim didn't say anything, but Ella could tell he was listening intently. He'd changed into black jeans and a long sleeved gray T-shirt that blended in with the gloom of the kitchen. The jeans fitted him really nicely. She'd almost salivated when she'd seen his tight, neat denim-clad ass.

For some reason, her eyes had adjusted more quickly than usual to the dark. Sam was the only one of them who was still stumbling around finding his way. Vadim always moved as lightly as a cat and was just as sure-footed. She pointed at a good hiding spot for him. He nodded and disappeared silently from view, a complete professional to his fingertips. After his earlier lapse he'd returned to treating her with a precise courtesy that bordered on uncivil. She wasn't sure if she was pleased or irritated that he had the ability to compartmentalize like that. That was supposed to be her specialty.

She indicated another spot to Sam, and waited until he had subsided rather noisily into the cramped gap between the workstations. She patted his knobbly bare knee, and moved closer to the industrial kitchen sinks where she intended to sit. It was cold in the kitchen, the tang of disinfectant cutting through the lingering smells of cooking oil and grease.

Ella licked her lips and thought longingly about a plate of sweet potato fries sprinkled lavishly with salt and topped with a serving of ranch dressing...

"*I have a protein bar if you need one.*"

She jumped, expecting Vadim to be by her shoulder but he wasn't there. She concentrated hard.

"*Are you talking to me in my head?*"

"*Obviously.*"

"*You can do that?*"

"*What's the problem?*"

"*Is this part of the mating thing?*"

"*It might be easier because of that, but I've always had this ability. Do you want the protein bar?*"

"*No thanks. They suck.*"

"*Okay, then.*"

He disappeared from her thoughts as swiftly as he had arrived. She'd had her shields up, and yet Vadim seemed immune to them. How come he could get into her head so easily when she couldn't get into his? But then, she hadn't really tried, preferring to pretend their relationship was just about sex. She didn't do the emotional stuff. It never worked out well for her. She'd tried to date shapeshifters and Fae who didn't care about her extra abilities, but she'd never been able to get close to any of them. Not that those species were very interested in long-term relationships anyway. The werewolves eventually settled down when they mated, and the Fae would fuck anything without a single qualm. She should be comfortable with just fucking Vadim, but something inside her wanted more... With a sigh, she returned her attention to the kitchen and settled down for a long wait.

After what felt like hours, and probably was, Ella was startled from an uneasy doze by the subtle hint of Otherworld power seeping through the air. A thin trickle of green mist was coming out from the cupboards and she checked her weapon. Suddenly, the door creaked open, and what looked like a small typhoon swirled out into the kitchen making the stacked piles of crockery shudder and the glass tinkle.

Ella concentrated on the center of the storm and made out bony arms and legs that looked like green spiky thorns. When the disturbance came close, she reached out a gloved hand and grabbed hold of whatever it was. With an unearthly shriek, the thing stopped spinning, almost pulling Ella off her feet and into the turmoil. She held on, aware of the rose-like thorns sticking into her skin through the leather glove and the inhuman screeching that rattled around her oversensitive empath's brain like an exploding bomb.

"Stop it." She tightened her grip on the bony arm. "I'm from the SBLE. I have the authority to send you back to Otherworld if you continue to create unnecessary disturbances in the human world."

"What is SBLE?"

The thing stopped spinning and faced Ella. Three green

spikes adorned the top of its head like the diadem on the Statue of Liberty and it had wide-spaced black eyes, no obvious nose and a mouth full of spiked teeth. Its body was composed of sharp multi-jointed green limbs, a small torso and strands of green plantlike hangings that reminded her of vines or ivy. According to her research, a variety of female sprite.

"You might not know about the SBLE, but you know you aren't supposed to cause a disturbance in this world," Ella said.

"They disturbed me!" hissed the sprite. "They destroyed my nest!"

"I understand that, but they didn't do it deliberately."

The sprite showed its teeth. "Humans are worthless!"

"Not all of them." Ella sat more comfortably on the floor, her hand still locked around the sprite's upper arm and her weapon at the ready. Vadim and Sam had come a lot closer. "If you don't like humans, why are you here?"

The sprite looked at her as if she was stupid. "They trapped me. My mother left us younglings in her nest to hunt by the stream, and when we woke up, we were alone, encased inside metal and couldn't get out." It shrugged its bony shoulders. "All my siblings perished. I was too weak to break free, so I made the best of it and stayed in the nest until they destroyed it *again*."

"I'm sorry. The original pipes probably contained iron, which bound you here. The new ones tend to be plastic, so your ability to move around and use your magic has been restored."

"I suppose they did me a favor then, although it doesn't feel like it." Her little mouth turned down at the corners. "I'm sorry about all the mess."

Ella put her gun down. "You can't stay here."

"Do you think I want to?"

"Would you like to go back to Otherworld?"

"Not really. I'd like to live by a creek again, though. Somewhere I can find others of my kind, perhaps a mate."

"*Ms. Walsh, I can find that information for you.*" Vadim's calm voice echoed in Ella's head. *Yes. There are several sprite colonies up in the delta area. We could take her there.*

Ella smiled at the sprite. "We could do that right now."

"Truly?"

"Yeah." Ella looked behind her. "I have a couple of colleagues here who can help with that." She pointed. "That's Sam and the other one is Morosov."

The sprite looked dubiously at Sam and then her eyes widened and she ducked her head.

"I am sorry for looking at you directly, sire. Do not kill me, I beg of you."

Ella frowned at Vadim. "What did you do?"

He held up his hands. "I did nothing. Perhaps the sprite mistakes me for someone else."

"Mayhap you are right, sire, but I beg your pardon, anyway."

She put her ungloved hand on the sprite's shoulder. "There is one more thing I need to do before we can go. I have to erase your memories of this place so that you aren't tempted to return."

"I would not want to come back."

"Unfortunately, female sprites are programmed to return to their original nesting site when they have their own young, and that wouldn't be a good thing."

"You are a soul sucker, then?"

"I'm an empath. I promise I'll just take what I need and not damage you in any other way."

"All right, then. Do your worst."

Ella closed her eyes and concentrated, feeling her way through the young sprite's memories, cherry picking the references to her nest that started even before her birth. She hesitated, unsure of what to put in their place and Vadim's thoughts slid into hers. He sent her images of the delta, of small creeks and inlets, covered bank and concealed nesting holes... It took but a second to feed them to the sprite.

Ella let out her breath and carefully extracted herself from the sprite's mind. "Do you feel all right?"

The sprite blinked. "Yes. I just want to get away from here."

"Just give me a minute to consult with Sam, and then Morosov and I will take you to your new home." Vadim took over her spot and settled to watch the sprite, who wouldn't even look at him. Ella went across to Sam.

"That was really cool," Sam breathed. "It's weird, it didn't exactly speak 'American,' but I could understand it anyway."

"That's because you're an empath."

Sam nodded. "You didn't have to hurt her at all."

"That should always be your aim." Ella felt the beginnings of a terrible headache and was already shaking. "I want you to write up a report of everything you saw tonight so that we can discuss it in detail tomorrow."

"Sure!" Sam stretched. "I'll have it on your desk asap."

"Great." Ella forced a smile. "Go on home now and remember, don't discuss your work with anyone outside the SBLE."

His enthusiastic expression dimmed. "That's the kicker, isn't it? Not being able to share stuff. No wonder we all go nuts."

"It's part of the job, Sam." Ella patted his arm. "I'll see you tomorrow."

"Night, Ella. Night, Vad."

Ella didn't see Vadim's reaction to his new nickname, but it still made her want to smile. She turned to face him and the sprite.

"Do you have enough magic to get us there?"

"Of course."

She didn't have the energy to confront him about the variable estimates of his magical powers tonight, but she sensed a showdown coming. Surely as his mate she should know these things?

"Take my hand, Ms. Walsh. We can do this together. You also have the power now."

Putting the sprite between them, they linked hands, and a moment later, Ella smelled the briny tang of the delta and heard the gentle sound of water and the swish of willow trees. It was still quite dark but the suggestion of dawn lapped at the edges of the blackness making it easier to see.

The sprite inhaled deeply. "This is a good place."

Ella let go of both the sprite's and Vadim's hands. "We'll wait over there until we see that you are okay. If you don't sense anyone, or you don't feel welcome, come and find us, and we'll take you someplace else." The sprite bowed low. "I thank you, soul sucker, and you, sire."

Ella smiled. "Thank you for being so cooperative." They retreated behind a large tree and watched as the sprite approached the bank of the creek. Within moments three other sprites of varying sizes emerged from the murky darkness and began conversing in a strange clicking language that reminded Ella of whale song. All seemed to go well, because within another few seconds the sprite was led toward the nesting holes.

Ella let out her breath. "Looking good. Let's give her a couple more minutes."

"She'll be fine. They have no females left in their particular pack. They will treat her like a queen and vie for her favors."

"Lucky girl." She pulled her hand free of Vadim's. "How do you know all this?"

"I'm part Fae."

"I know that, but what part exactly?"

His smile was meant to distract her and almost succeeded. "Morosov..."

He cupped her chin. "How are you feeling?" His expression darkened. "Your resources are seriously depleted. Why didn't you say something?"

"It's just the way it is." She grimaced. "Every time I take a memory it drains me even more than the last time."

He studied her for a long moment. "I have a solution for that."

"Sex is not the answer to everything, you know."

His mouth hovered a fraction above hers. "In this case, it is. Now kiss me and let me in."

She gave in to the kiss far too easily. It was a guilty relief to lean against his solid strength, slide her fingers into his short hair and be supported. As he kissed her, she felt a visceral tug on her psychic senses—as if she was the one having her memories purged. She bit down on his lip and he recoiled.

"What the hell was that for?"

"What exactly are you doing?"

He stared at her as if she was an idiot. "What I'm supposed to do. Take the memories away so that you don't get overloaded."

"But—"

"Shut up, Ms. Walsh, and let me do my job."

His mouth descended again and she surrendered to his kiss with all the enthusiasm of a heroine in a romance novel. Pathetic, but there was no one there to see, apart from a few sprites who might well be getting up to some mating activities of their own. Vadim deepened the kiss and she responded, unwilling to be the passive partner in their embrace, determined to make him work for it.

With a groan he clamped a hand over her ass and pulled her tight against him until she could feel the hard throb of his denim-encased cock. She wanted to climb him, to fit her sex against his hardness, to have him inside her.

"*Damn it, Ella, slow down.*"

His words reverberated in her mind, but only encouraged her to rub herself against him even more. With a soft curse, he lifted her up, swung her around and placed her back against a tree trunk. She wrapped her legs around his waist and rolled her hips, felt his cock press against her clit, then came hard.

One-handed, he stripped off her overalls and let them fall to the ground. While he was busy doing that, she worked at his belt buckle and zipper to reveal his shaft, which was barely restrained by the waistband of his straining boxers. He took her hand away, and pushed down his jeans and underwear, barely pausing before he shoved his thick length inside her, making her scream and come again.

She tried to control his strokes, but he was too powerful so she sank down on him and just enjoyed the ride, the power of him, his scent, the flex of his tight ass as he drove into her making her climax almost constantly. Magic gathered around them and inside them and when he finally came, she joined him and saw the equivalent of psychic fireworks explode in her mind. She also felt curiously carefree, as if his touch had burned away her burdens, her fears, her...

She opened her eyes to find Vadim holding her up against the tree, his cock still inside her. A quick mental check revealed a lightness of spirit that had evaded her for years. She pushed at his chest and he looked at her.

"What's wrong?"

"Nothing, I just think we should cover up. We're near water, and I don't want my ass covered in mosquito bites."

He didn't move. "What's really wrong?"

She forced herself to meet his gaze. "Nothing. Will you just move, please?"

He pulled out and away from her and she leaned back against the tree, hoping her legs would stop shaking and hold her up. He kept an eye on her as he dressed and then bent down to retrieve her overalls and panties. "Here you go." He hesitated. "Would you like my handkerchief to clean up?"

"Thanks." She took the immaculately laundered cotton square and waited until he turned his back. After she put her clothes on she sauntered over to him.

"Can you get us home?"

"With your help." He took her hand. "But I can only take us to one place."

She'd half expected that. "Then take us both to Tiburon."

He nodded, his expression unreadable in the half light. "When you feel me cast the spell, open your mind to it and imagine that you are adding your power to mine."

"Okay."

Ella shut her eyes and waited. The power of the spell took her by surprise and she wondered why on earth it needed amplifying, but she'd promised to help out, so she took the magic inside herself and added her power. Within the blink of an eye they were outside her front door in Tiburon. For the first time ever, she didn't even feel nauseous. Maybe it was the magical equivalent of not getting sick when driving a car instead of being a passenger.

She found her keys and led the way inside. The message light on her phone was flashing. She hesitated so long that Vadim touched her arm.

"Would you like me to check that for you?"

His question made her feel like a coward. "No, it's okay. It's probably just my mom nagging me about the weekend again."

She wasn't even sure why she was pretending. Vadim probably knew damn well that she was getting leery of picking up any messages at the moment. They all seemed to end in death. She dumped her backpack on the countertop and dialed her messages. Sure enough, it was her mom, her voice loud enough for Vadim to hear every complaining word.

She deleted the message and turned to her silent guest. "I suppose I'll have to go."

"I'll come with you, if you like."

"To do what?"

He shrugged. "Support you?"

Unwanted emotions clawed at her gut. "I don't need anyone

to hold my hand, Morosov. I'm quite used to dealing with my mom."

He stood his ground. "We're not at work now."

"What's that supposed to mean?"

"You told me not to smother you at work, so I'm not doing that. But we are connected now, Ella, and if I want to support you with your family, why can't you just accept it?"

"Because I don't *need* anyone."

He glared at her. "You damn well do."

Anger shoved aside her other more fragile emotions and she embraced it gladly. "I need you for sex, okay? That's all. And as we've already done that tonight, you can sleep on the couch."

She turned around and headed for the bathroom, suddenly eager to wash all traces of him from her body, to eradicate all the erotic images of him fucking her hard and fast against that tree… She slammed the door behind her and turned the shower on full blast. Would he allow his calm, human façade to slip and follow her into the bathroom, fuck her into ecstasy in the shower? Did she want him to?

She studied her face in the gradually steamed up mirror. Her cheeks were flushed, her pupils wide, her hair a straggly mess of half-undone braids and bits of greenery. She had no idea why Vadim would want her anyway, but maybe he had no choice. The mating bond was way more complicated than she had ever realized.

HE STARED at the closed bathroom door and snarled a curse in Fae. Ella Walsh had no idea of his abilities. If he wanted to, he could blow the door down, follow her into the shower and have her obeying his every command. She'd be on her knees, his cock in her mouth, his hands in her hair…she'd be begging him to fuck her forever, until she died from it.

Power roared out of him and the entire house shuddered. With a groan he sat on the couch and covered his face with his hands. What the hell was happening to him? He sounded like Alexei at his most arrogant. God, he hated that about the Fae, that they thought they could just take whatever they wanted, destroy a human's soul purely for their pleasure. Wasn't that why he'd left? Hadn't he wanted to be better than that? This mating bond was affecting him far more seriously than he had anticipated and Ella certainly wasn't making it any easier.

He slowly exhaled as he heard the shower come on. And why should she make it easy? She was not only dealing with the approach of a significant birthday, but with a serial killer who was targeting empaths and closing in on her. The last thing she needed was an overprotective male cluttering up her life. He had to try and remember that, like him, she was used to protecting herself, allowing nobody to get close to her because closeness meant pain.

He got up and went to the closet where the spare bedclothes were kept. She had to *want* to share stuff with him, not have him forcibly demand it. He wanted to laugh. In his relationships, he'd always been the one to withdraw, the one that had been too private, too self-contained, and too elusive.

He punched his pillow, then laid it on top of the neatly tucked sheet. Despite what both Ella and he wanted to believe, mating was obviously a lot more complicated than having sex and sharing a psychic burden. With his mixed heritage it was also potentially dangerous.

The door to the bathroom opened and Ella came out, a towel wrapped around her body and another around her hair. Vadim focused on spreading the light quilt over his makeshift bed.

"I'm going to bed."

He didn't look at her, just nodded and concentrated on the correct placement of the flowery quilt.

"Feel free to use the bathroom."

"Thanks." There, it was all neatly lined up now, just like his emotions, a nice, straight orderly arrangement—except he wanted to follow her into her bed and make love to her all night.

He willed her to leave, but she hovered at the end of the couch.

"It was nice of you to offer to come with me to see my mom," Ella said. Vadim sat down and focused his gaze on her pink toenails. "The only person who ever understood about my family was Laney. I'm used to dealing with them by myself."

He raised his head. "Are you apologizing to me?"

"I suppose I am. It's not your fault that you got forced into this crazy Otherworld arranged mating, is it?" She swallowed hard. "I should be grateful to you for saving me from madness, not shrieking at you every chance I get."

He couldn't look away. Despite everything, there was a core of honesty and decency in Ella that made it hard for him to ignore her, especially when she was like this. The least he could do was try and be honest back—well, as honest as he could be.

"I'm struggling with this myself."

"You are?" She sat on the arm of the couch.

He forced the words out. "I'm part shapeshifter. Those instincts make me want to protect my mate. I forget that you've been doing an excellent job of protecting yourself all your life. I'll do my best to remember that."

"That's very generous of you when I've been behaving like an ungrateful shrew."

He attempted a smile. "I hadn't noticed."

"Liar." She tapped her head. "I know you. I drive you nuts."

He had nothing to say to that and she rose from her perch on the couch.

"I'll see you in the morning, then."

"Good night, Ms. Walsh."

"Night, Morosov."

He waited until he heard her close her bedroom door and then headed for the bathroom, which was its usual mess. While he waited for the shower to heat, he straightened everything up to his, if not to Ella's, satisfaction and stripped off his clothes. Under the punishing heat of the shower he closed his eyes and relived the moments when he'd made love to Ella and taken the burden of her psychic energy into himself. For the first time ever he'd felt as if his Otherworld powers had been used for good. He'd felt like a superhero.

He opened his eyes.

Fuck this.

He'd never stop wanting to protect her. He would lay down his life for her. All he had to do was make sure she never realized the strength of his devotion ever again.

17

"So where were you last night?" Alexei leaned back in his chair to stare at Vadim as he entered their temporary office.

"Where do you think I was?" Vadim took off his jacket and placed it carefully over the back of his chair. Despite the air-conditioning it felt warm in the enclosed space.

Alexei inhaled. "You smell of Ella's shower gel, so my guess would be you were with her."

"Feehan asked me to stay with her."

"How closely?" Alexei's silver gaze narrowed. "You're fucking her, aren't you?"

"Don't be ridiculous." Vadim strengthened his mental barriers. If Liz had picked up on his bonding with Ella in her Fae-Web, Alexei must have too, but he wasn't going to admit that to the devious Fae. "I stayed over at her place after we sorted out a sprite issue. I used her shower this morning."

"Really."

Vadim met Alexei's skeptical gaze head on. "Yes, really. Ask her if you don't believe me. I slept on the couch and it was damned uncomfortable."

"You can't afford to fuck this up, Vadim."

"I know that."

Alexei's Fae-Web streamed out and encircled Vadim. "You are essential to this case."

"I know that too." He resisted the urge to blast the Fae-Web into pieces as it shimmered around him like a fisherman casting a lure. "Do you think I'd do anything to jeopardize my future after the last case?"

"I'm no longer sure."

"Then go and tell tales to Madame Dubinsky. Just remember if she demands my return, this case is ruined and I'm a dead man."

"I'll do what I have to, Vadim."

"Of course you will. You're Fae. You have no conscience at all." He rose from his seat. "Feehan called a meeting at ten. Are you coming?"

Alexei followed him out of the room, his expression petulant, his Fae-Web flashing like a thundercloud. Vadim stood back to let Liz and Ella enter ahead of him and then followed them in. The whiteboard had yet another picture attached to it. This one was a gruesome snap of Trini Yamada in her party hat, her dead eyes fixed on the afterworld.

He hardly listened as Feehan rattled through the details of Trini's short life, her decision to come to San Francisco and the tragic consequences of that choice. Ella doodled flowers on her yellow notepad. Even without trying, he knew it was a front and inside she was grieving for all of her classmates and fellow empaths. She wouldn't allow him to comfort her and he didn't want Alexei picking up any stray communications between them. His Fae colleague was already too suspicious.

"So we have to assume that the Siren isn't murdering his victims in alphabetical order," Feehan concluded.

"I also want you all to know that I've alerted the other empaths who graduated with Ella and sent her twenty-four-hour protection. She's not going to do anything but stay at home until I give her the all-clear."

Ella looked up. "Has anyone contacted the two male empaths yet?"

Sam stuck up his hand. "I did. They are both alive and happily mated."

"Good for them. But just because they are mated doesn't mean they couldn't have killed."

"That's true—" Vadim drew a black box on his legal pad, "—and they do know all of the American victims, which might explain why no one has put up a fight. Can we trace their movements for the past few weeks?"

"I've already got someone on that," Feehan said. "I'll let you know the results as soon as I get them." He looked around the table. "So what else do we have to go on? What are the Fae-Webs telling us?"

Liz looked stricken. "That Ella will be next."

"Oh great, thanks," Ella said.

"The Fae-Web can be wrong, Ms. Walsh." Vadim glared at Alexei and Liz.

"That's right, and the way isn't clear yet. Death is near Ella, but we both feel that she is the key to solving this mystery."

"Over my dead body, right?"

"We'll try and make sure that doesn't happen, Ella." Feehan's smile was strained. "Now, is there anything else?"

Everyone shook their heads.

"Well, let's call it a wrap until tomorrow then." Feehan beckoned to Vadim. "Could I speak to you for a moment, in private?"

Vadim could see no way of avoiding the request and reluctantly followed his superior out of the conference room.

LIZ REACHED over to take Ella's hand.

"I'm so sorry. That came out all wrong."

"It's okay. It's not as if my chances were looking good anyway."

"But to just blurt it out like that!"

Ella squeezed her hand. "It's *okay*, really."

Liz's expression cleared and her Fae-Web glittered brightly. "You feel different."

"Really?" Ella tried to sound disinterested. She was all too aware of Alexei leaning in to overhear their conversation.

"As if you're lighter or something."

Ella winked at her. "I'll tell you all about it later. We can do lunch."

"That would be awesome." Liz moved in closer. "Do you have a new man?"

"I think she does," Alexei said.

Ella turned to meet his gaze. "And how would you know anything?"

"I talked to Vadim this morning."

"About what?"

"I think you know."

She rolled her eyes. "What is this? High school? If you have something to say, just spit it out."

"Vadim stayed over with you last night."

"Yeah, he did."

"He smelled like you this morning."

"That's because even though I tell him it makes him smell like a girl, he uses my shower gel and stuff. What exactly are you getting at?"

"You're dating him."

Ella started laughing. "Dating Morosov? Hell no. I'd rather date you. At least I'd know where I stood."

"There's something going on between you. I see it in my Fae-Web." Alexei's web flowed out and meshed with Liz's. "Yeah, there's definitely something going on. Your fates are linked."

"So everyone keeps telling me."

Alexei's expression darkened. "There's no need to be sarcastic. You have no idea what Vadim Morosov is capable of, do you?"

"No, and I don't want to know. He's a pain in the ass."

"He's dangerous."

"Right." She went to get up and Alexei put out his hand.

"I'm serious. That incident, when the pair of you were stuck in the elevator together last week? That *incident* that no one else knows anything about, including the security cameras?"

"What about it?"

Alexei sat back in his chair, his silver eyes glittering. "Did it occur to you that Vadim might have orchestrated the whole thing?"

"Why on earth would he want to do that?"

"Think about it. He saves you, you're grateful, he gets in your pants."

She tried to ignore the sick feeling in her stomach. "You think he's that desperate? Have you looked at him? *Seriously?*"

"If it makes him look good, he'd do it. Underneath that bland exterior he's as ruthless at getting what he wants as any Fae."

Ella stood up and pushed in her chair. "It's a great theory, but there's a massive flaw in it. I've already asked Morosov to hook up with me, and he turned me down flat."

"I thought you didn't sleep with your colleagues."

"I was drunk. He put me to bed and left me there. I'm glad he did. It would've been awkward otherwise." She glanced over at Liz. "Shall we do lunch?"

Liz rose, as well, ignoring Alexei. "Sure. I'll get us some sandwiches, and we can eat here." She linked arms with Ella and together they walked out.

Over lunch, she managed to keep chatting with Liz, but it was an effort when her mind was dealing with a hundred possible scenarios. She had to assume that Alexei didn't know what had really happened in the elevator or he would have gone for the jugular, not sought information. Would Vadim want to mate with her so badly that he'd arrange such an elaborate stunt? She couldn't see why he'd bother when he was obviously as unprepared for the mating call as she had been.

But what if he wasn't? What possible advantage could mating with her give Vadim? Ella considered his aversion to Otherworld. By allying himself with her was he escaping a more dangerous fate on the other side? Hadn't that letter mentioned that the lucky bonded mate was eligible to live in either world? Another more insidious thought surfaced. What if they weren't really truly mated and Vadim had set the whole thing up simply to get her through the case alive? According to Alexei, Vadim was both ruthless and powerful. Unfortunately she now knew that was true.

Ella picked up her phone and called Liz. "That party you are going to tonight with Doug at the shapeshifters' place? Can I tag along? I'll be safe surrounded by Doug's pack."

Liz squeaked in delight. "Awesome! Come home with me after work and we can get ready together. It'll be fun!"

Ella sat back and contemplated her phone. It would also give her the opportunity to prove whether her mating with Vadim was real or a figment of her imagination.

VADIM NODDED as Feehan went through his list of requirements for Ella's safety again. Unless she was on SBLE property, he had no intention of leaving her unguarded for more than a second. Even if she declined his escort, he would be able to find her through their mated link. She had no idea that he could blast through her shields if he needed to and that he would guard her to the best of his considerable magical ability.

Feehan cleared his throat and shuffled some of the papers on his desk.

"There's one more thing."

Vadim tried to look approachable and willing. "What's that, Mr. Feehan?"

"The head of the SBLE in the U.S., Drew Spencer, is aware of what is happening to the empaths, and is contemplating taking over the case. I'm sure you'll agree that this would not be ideal for either of us or our future careers."

"I'd rather we got to see it through ourselves."

"I agree, but Mr. Spencer doesn't think we are acting fast enough."

"What does he expect us to do? This killer appears and disappears into thin air!"

Feehan turned off his computer. "I spoke with him on the phone this morning. He intends to come down and speak to us all tomorrow."

Vadim fought to control his instant protest. "What good can he do? We had the head of the SBLE in Russia involved and it made no difference."

"I did tell Mr. Spencer about that." Feehan avoided his gaze. "I regret to say he suggested the Russian organization wasn't as capable as ours, and that with our resources we wouldn't have failed."

"What's he offering us—the Navy Seals?"

"I'm not sure exactly what he's offering. All I know is that if all the twenty-seven year-old empaths in America are wiped out, heads will roll."

Vadim sat back. "I can't see Ms. Walsh liking this interference, can you?"

"Not at all. She is very protective of her kind, but if she chooses not to take a mate, her influence will be very short-lived anyway."

Silence fell as he struggled to control his rage at Feehan's offhand comment. No wonder Ella felt her life was dispensable when faced with the ignorance of the SBLE bureaucracy. He got to his feet.

"She's been offered a mate. I hope to God she takes him. No one's life should be considered expendable by the SBLE."

He walked out and wondered where to go next. Alexei wouldn't be pleased to see him and neither would Ella. He noticed Sam strolling along the hallway with a bag of popcorn and headed toward him.

"I thought I could help you with the research on the male empaths."

Sam's face broke into a smile. "That would be cool, Vad. Come into my cubby and pull up a chair."

ELLA PURSED her lips in the mirror and added another layer of bright pink lipstick. She hardly ever bothered with makeup, but tonight was an exception. She wanted to be noticed, to get drunk and maybe even to get laid. Liz had lent her a sleeveless black dress, which came thigh high on the tall blonde, but skimmed Ella's knees. It was made of some stretchy, clingy fabric that stuck to her boobs and tended to ride up. She'd also borrowed a pair of high-heeled sandals that were already making her feet hurt. Ella was satisfied with her appearance. She looked *totally* unlike herself.

Music thumped through the walls of the narrow row house where the party was being held, and even the stairs were full of people. Doug's wolf pack was large, very social and remarkably tolerant of every other kind of magical power including Ella's. She'd already had a beer and been introduced around by Doug to a lot of males who seemed more than happy to see her. Her purse vibrated again and she finally took out her phone and turned it off. It wouldn't deter Vadim for long. He'd have no compunction in ignoring normal avenues of communication and finding her anyway.

She emerged from the bathroom and went down the stairs, wobbling on her high heels toward the kitchen to get herself another beer. Six months ago this would've been her idea of heaven. Good friends, alcohol and plenty of sex if she wanted it. Shapeshifters didn't have the same narrow morals as humans and wouldn't hold a one-night-stand against anyone. Having nothing to live for, she'd been happy to take whatever she could get and enjoyed it.

Big Jim Dresden, the second-in-command of the pack, held out a can of her favorite beer.

"Looking for this, or looking for me?"

She smiled at him. "Can I have both?"

His answering grin showed the sharp points of his canines. "Is that a promise?" He held the beer high over his head. "A kiss if you want the beer."

Ella considered him. He wasn't called Big Jim for nothing. He was at least six-four with hands and feet and, allegedly, other parts of his anatomy to size. She stood on tiptoe and put a hand on his shoulder to balance. He smelled of tobacco and mint. He obligingly bent his head and she allowed her mouth to brush his before kissing him properly. He tasted just fine and had some skills, but she drew back and studied his mouth.

"Can I have my beer now?"

He laughed and handed it over. "That was nice. Want to do it again?"

She held up the beer. "Maybe after I've drunk this, okay?"

He blew her a kiss and she walked over to the window, ostensibly to look outside, but really needing some space. Big Jim was the third guy she'd kissed in the past hour, and none of them had made her feel remotely sexy. She popped the can and drank thirstily. Maybe she needed to be drunk to do this properly. Or maybe, she couldn't do it anymore because none of the males were Vadim Morosov...

She finished the rest of her beer. And what did that prove? That Vadim's magic was strong enough to bind her to him, or that they were truly mated by Otherworld and no one else would do it for her anymore? She turned back to Big Jim, who was still lounging by the refrigerator handing out beer and advice to random partygoers. "Ready for another round, princess?" he asked. "You know the price now, right?"

"I do. Pucker up, baby."

He grinned and bent down to her level. She wrapped a hand around the back of his neck and kissed him slowly until he started to kiss her back, his hand on her ass, drawing her closer. A sudden terrible coldness surrounded her and the hairs on the back of her neck bristled. She wasn't the only one who was affected. Everyone in the small kitchen seemed to freeze into place. Ella slowly released Big Jim and turned around.

Vadim stood by the doorway, immaculate in his dark business suit, his expression cool, his hand fisted at his side.

"Jeez," muttered Big Jim. "Who's that?"

"Oh, that's Morosov. He works with me." She flicked a defiant glance at Vadim. "I didn't know you were planning on coming to this party. You could've tagged along with me and Liz."

"If I'd known that was what you planned, I would've done so." Vadim walked over to her, his blue eyes like ice. No one else moved. "Unfortunately, I was under the mistaken impression that you'd gone home early with a headache."

Big Jim shook his finger at Ella. "Naughty."

She shrugged. "He doesn't own me."

"That's correct but I am supposed to be guarding you." He raised his cool gaze to Big Jim, who immediately held up both his hands and stepped back from Ella. "Any of these males could be a threat to you."

Ella squared up to him. With her high heels she came up to his autocratic nose. "I know these guys. They're Doug's pack. I trust them all."

"So I saw."

She met his gaze and then wished she hadn't. "I'm fine. If you're so worried about my safety that you had to chase me down, you can go and wait in the hallway. I'll find you when I'm ready to leave."

"*Shit*," Big Jim breathed in her ear. "You've got some balls. That is one scary powerful dude."

"I don't think so."

Vadim took hold of her elbow.

The next moment they were alone somewhere in complete darkness. It was still close to the party because she could hear the music. She could smell a faint scent of Big Jim and wondered if they'd ended up in his bedroom at the top of the house.

"Don't play games with me. Take me back, right now."

Vadim didn't say anything but stepped so close that she could feel every furious, vibrating inch of him from head to toe. Something soft touched her cheek and she realized the air was full of swirling black feathers.

"Why did you kiss that male?"

"What is it to you?"

He let out a very controlled breath. "We're mated."

"So you say."

"What the hell is that supposed to mean?"

She pushed away from him, stumbled against the side of a bed and sat on the edge. "Don't get all macho and possessive on me."

"Ms. Walsh, if you had any idea how hard I am trying to stop myself getting 'all macho and possessive on you' right now you'd shut the fuck up."

She glared at him. "There's no need to swear either."

"I apologize." She'd never believed anyone could speak between gritted teeth before, but she believed it now.

"Here's the thing, Morosov. I was conducting an experiment."

"To see how many males you could fuck in one night?"

"There were only three and I only kissed them."

He gave a bark of laughter. "Only three."

She kicked her sandals off and wiggled her tortured toes. "I wanted to see if it felt any different."

"Different to what?"

"Kissing you, of course. It was suggested to me today that you are way more powerful than you let on, which I knew already, and that you might have used your magical powers to convince me that we were mated when we weren't."

"And why would I do that?"

He moved until he was directly in front of her. She could see his expression now and it wasn't very reassuring. "To make sure I got through the case without going nuts and saved your ass."

Magic surged around her and caught at her hair, making it stand on end. She fought a shiver as she remembered how all the big tough shapeshifters downstairs had backed down in Vadim's presence.

"Do you really think that badly of me?"

She forced herself to look at him and found her gaze fixated on his immaculate white shirt. "Obviously not, which is why I, a) didn't storm off in a huff or, b) confront you and instead, c) conducted my experiment at this party."

"And what are the results of your experiment?"

"None of them tasted right."

He leaned in and licked a salacious line along the seam of her lips. "And what about now?"

She inhaled his now familiar scent and lust pooled in her stomach. "Mmm…"

He kissed her again, feather-light touches over her mouth and jaw, her nose, her eyelids. "And now?"

"I think I need to taste you again."

He claimed her mouth in such a way that all thoughts of the other males disappeared, replaced by the ferociousness of his need, his power and her desire for him. He kept kissing her and she slid a hand into his hair and drew him close until he was right where she needed him between her open thighs.

Before she could stop him, he fell to his knees and she felt his teeth nipping her inner thigh. Her panties disappeared and his mouth was on her most intimate parts, sucking her clit, his tongue delving between her folds to push inside her. When he added his fingers to the mix, she writhed against him. He didn't stop, making her climax twice more before crawling up over her body and kissing her.

He snapped his fingers and she was naked, her hands mysteriously bound over her head with his tie. Candles appeared beside the bed, illuminating her flesh.

"That's not fair," she gasped.

He straddled her and ripped off his jacket. "Do you think I care?"

She stared up at him as he yanked off his tie and slowly unbuttoned his shirt. "Make your clothes disappear too. I want to see you."

His smile was lethal. "You can damn well wait."

She tried to pull against her bonds, but they were too strong and she couldn't wiggle out of them either. Were Doug and Liz looking for her? Was anyone worried that she'd been literally magicked away?

Vadim knelt up to continue his leisurely striptease, pushing down his pants and underwear to reveal his already stiff cock. As he palmed himself a bead of moisture gathered at the tip. With a groan, he leaned forward and rubbed his wet thumb against her lips.

"Taste this, too."

She sucked on his thumb until he replaced it with his cock and then she sucked on that until he took control and fucked her mouth, one hand moving between her breasts, pinching and shaping her nipples into hard peaks of need. She used her teeth on him and his breath hissed out. Removing his cock from her mouth he slid it between her breasts, cupping her rounded flesh tightly around him. He groaned her name and came. The sharp scent of the sea and a hint of citrus infused her skin.

"Let me loose now. I want to touch you," Ella demanded.

He took no notice, only knelt between her legs and pushed them wide and over his shoulders before devouring her with his fingers and his mouth again until she screamed his name. Even before she finished coming, he slid his cock back inside her and took her that way, each stroke long and leisurely from tip to root, and then slamming into her, making her beg and scream and forget everything but his taste, his body and his mind claiming hers. So wet now, his clever fingers playing with her clit and the pucker of her ass, marking her as the other men had failed to do, in every way he could. She couldn't escape his thoughts either, and he couldn't control them as well as he controlled his body. She was becoming aware not only of his need for her, but the astounding depth of his magical powers. She bit down hard on his lip.

"You could destroy me."

Vadim went still over her, his cock hard, his heart pounding against hers.

"I couldn't."

"Don't lie."

He kissed her already swollen mouth. "I *couldn't*. I could kill anyone who touched you, though."

"Is that a threat?"

He bit her back. "It just is."

She tried to jerk her head away but he wouldn't let her. "I'm not human. You know that, and I'm now a bonded male. Ask Doug, ask any of those men downstairs what that means and what they would do for their mate. I'm no different."

She stared into his eyes. "So this is you being nice?" He pushed himself deep inside her until she moaned.

"Yes."

"Winning me over with fantastic sex?"

"*Yes.*" He gazed down at her. "I don't think you would enjoy any of the alternatives. Most bonded males would consider me to be within my rights to slaughter the three men you kissed and beat you soundly."

She bared her teeth at him. "Go ahead, if you want me to castrate you with the bread knife."

VADIM REALIZED his black mood was evaporating when he was able to smile at her. "I'm no fool, Ms. Walsh. I'll take what I can get." He released her hands from their bonds. "And I have you right where I want you, under me, wet from my seed and begging."

She opened her mouth—no doubt to argue with him—but he kissed her instead and increased the pace of his thrusts until she was coming all around his shaft. He came with her, fusing his thoughts with hers and making the floor shake with the combined power of their magic.

Reluctantly he rolled away from her and found their clothes. He handed Ella her bra and the sexy black dress she must have borrowed from Liz and placed her shoes neatly in front of her.

"Don't tell me there isn't a shower here." Ella stepped into her shoes.

He raised an eyebrow. "Unfortunately not."

"And you're okay with that, Mr. Clean?"

He stepped into his underwear and pants, dusting the black

feathers off as he dressed. "We'll be home soon. We can shower then."

She narrowed her eyes at him as she struggled into her black bra. "You're up to something."

He continued dressing, zipping her into her dress without a murmur when she ordered him to. Was it petty of him to like the thought of walking her down the stairs, through the rest of the party guests and out the door when she smelled of him? That all the males would know she was his mate and keep away?

Yes, it probably was, and most unlike him, but he was going to make sure it happened.

"Morosov, where are my panties?"

He stopped smiling and studied his indignant colleague, who now stood in front of him, hands on her hips in a stance he knew meant danger.

"I've no idea. Where did you put them?"

"You took them."

"I don't remember that." He tried to look sympathetic. "Does it matter?"

"Not if you can whisk us right out of here and straight home."

"I can't do that."

"Why not?"

"Because this room is warded and we have to let Liz and Doug know you are safe and going home with me."

"Can't you just Fae-interface with Liz or something?" Ella was tapping her foot now, irritation clear on her face. He was enjoying himself.

"No."

"I don't believe you."

He just looked at her and then went over to the door and opened it. "Shall we?"

She clomped down the narrow stairs behind him. Judging

from the noise, the party was still going strong. "They'll know what we've been doing."

"I suppose they might, but Liz can keep it to herself, can't she?" He spotted Liz sitting on one of the couches kissing Doug and pushed his way through to her.

"Liz?"

"Vadim!" She scrambled to untangle herself from Doug, slapping his hand away from her thigh and rearranging the neck of her dress. "I didn't know you were here!"

"I came to collect Ella. Feehan asked me to." He made a face. "I just wanted you to know that we were going now." He waved a vague hand behind him. "Ella's just over there."

Liz tried to look around him at Ella but he made it impossible for her to see much. "Sure! We'll see you in the morning."

Vadim inclined his head. "Good night Liz, Doug."

He sensed Ella was already working her way down to the kitchen and hurried to catch up with her. The same group of guys was hanging around the refrigerator and they went quiet when they saw him. He liked that. He wondered what they had been saying to her, and what she'd said in return. Ignoring the stares, he walked right up to her and took her hand, bent to kiss the luscious curve between her shoulder and neck. He'd marked her there with his teeth. She obviously hadn't noticed yet. "Ready to go, Ms. Walsh?"

He nodded at Big Jim whom he hoped was busy inhaling their bonding scent and getting the correct message.

Ella tried to pull out of his grasp but he held on and followed her out into the street, casting one last meaningful glance over his shoulder at the silent shapeshifters. He didn't think any of them would let Ella kiss them again.

18

Ella went straight into the bathroom, leaving Vadim alone in the kitchen. By the time she got into the shower, he materialized through the locked door and joined her. She was too tired to argue and the sight of him naked and more than willing to have sex with her was far too good to pass up. After they'd washed each other again and she'd forced herself to get out of the cramped shower, she remembered something.

"What's with all the feathers, Morosov?"

He was rinsing his hair and she paused to appreciate the streams of water cascading over his broad shoulders and tight abs.

"What feathers?"

"Don't play dumb with me. The ones that cascaded down over us when you were in a snit." She tried not to smile. "Or should I say, when you were in such a *fowl* mood."

"Funny." He turned his back on her and rubbed vigorously at his hair. "You should go on the stage."

"But what were they? And if you really shapeshift into a chicken or some kind of bird, why wasn't the wolf pack salivating at the thought of eating you up?"

"I have no idea."

Ella wrapped a towel around her waist. "You are impossible."

"So I've been told."

"We're supposed to be mated."

"I thought you didn't believe that was true."

"Oh shut up." Ella flounced out of the bathroom and into the bedroom. She wasn't going to get dressed again. Pink bunny pajamas would do fine. She waited until the shower shut off and dragged a comb through her hair before returning to the kitchen.

Vadim appeared with a towel wrapped around his hips and nothing else. Ella nearly swallowed her tongue. He pointed at a pile of paper on the countertop.

"I picked up your mail."

"Thank you." She didn't bother to ask him how or when he'd managed that. She wasn't talking to him more than was absolutely necessary. To have something to do she pulled the pile toward her and began to sort through, keeping all the take-out menus and chucking the coupons and unsolicited credit card offers in the trash. Her hand stilled over a familiar brown envelope from Otherworld.

"Shall I make some coffee?" Vadim inquired.

She stared at the envelope. "Herbal tea would be better."

"Do you have some?"

"Sure, it's behind the bag of coffee."

"It's out of date."

"It's a bag of dried leaves! It won't kill you." She opened the envelope and studied the single sheet.

"Anything important?"

"Just a reminder to return my letter accepting or declining my OCOS mate."

Vadim put two mugs on the countertop. "You haven't done that yet?"

"Shut *up*! I'll do it when I feel like it."

"But it is already, as you might say, a done deal."

"I know that." She put the letter down. "Why are you so worried?"

He returned his attention to the mugs and filled them with water before putting them in the microwave to heat. "I'm not." His smile was full of sensual satisfaction. "Do you want to take this to bed or have it out here?"

In answer, she pointed at the bedroom. He picked up the two mugs, added the tea bags, and went ahead of her, only to stop short at the door.

"Oh for fuck's sake, Rossa. Not now."

She peered around him and saw the angelic looking blond Fae lounging naked on her bed again.

Rossa nodded at Vadim. "Making progress, I see. She's letting you sleep in here instead of on the couch."

"No, I'm just bringing her tea through so we can talk before we go to bed."

Rossa winked at Ella. "He's such a liar, isn't he? It's no wonder he got into so much trouble in Otherworld." She glanced up at Vadim, whose expression was uncompromisingly blank.

"What exactly did he do?"

The Fae's tone became confiding. "Well—"

"Nothing that concerns you, Ms. Walsh," Vadim interrupted. "Now where do you want your tea?" He glared at Rossa. "Perhaps you might join me in the kitchen so that Ms. Walsh can get some sleep."

"Oh no, that's fine." Ella sank down onto the side of the bed. "You just both carry on. Don't mind me."

"Is there something specific you wanted, Rossa?"

"I have a message for you." Rossa cleared his throat importantly. "If you wish to avoid your fate, you know what to do."

"That's it?"

She looked at Vadim but nothing showed on the surface. She

probed a little deeper and was shocked to sense the fury raging beneath his skin. Even more interesting was that he was letting her feel it. Was it becoming harder for him to shut her out too?

Rossa pouted. "That's what I was told to say. Is there a reply?"

"No." Vadim fixed Rossa with his stare. "Now either leave, or I'll make you."

"You couldn't—"

Before Rossa even finished the sentence, Vadim raised his hand and power flowed through him. Ella found herself adding her own and watched in fascination as Rossa shimmered and then disappeared with a startled yelp.

Vadim smiled. It wasn't pleasant. "Luckily, he's not as powerful in this dimension as he'd like to believe."

Ella got into bed. "Why's that?"

Vadim sipped his tea and sat beside her. His perfectly tucked in towel refused to slip an inch. "Because as you once noted, he's almost completely Fae."

"More than you?"

"Definitely."

"But he's also feathery."

"We share a common ancestor."

"That's right, Colonel Sanders."

He finished his tea, feathers apparently unruffled. "Are you ready to turn the lights out?"

"If you're staying."

He paused to look down at her. "If you're okay with that."

She pulled back the sheets that still bore the imprint of Rossa's luscious naked body. "Hop in."

She'd never been one for pillow talk. It was strange to cuddle up to a man and find that your head fitted nicely into the curve of his shoulder and that the softness of your body aligned with the hardness of his.

"Despite your initial reservations you seem to be taking to

this bonded mate thing quite well—the sex part, I mean." Ella hastened to qualify her comment.

"My earlier reservations matched yours, I think." He hesitated. "It was something of a shock."

"Then why did you put yourself forward to OCOS as a potential mate?"

"I didn't."

Ella opened her eyes and flipped over to stare into his face. "You must have."

"I assure you, I didn't."

"Then how did we end up together?"

"Fate?"

She scowled at him. "I don't believe that for a second."

"Neither do I."

"Then what?"

"I suspect it might have something to do with my visit to Otherworld the other week."

"I remember you were reluctant to go there. Why is that?"

"Because I left."

She poked him in the chest. "Morosov, stop being so damned cryptic."

He sighed. "I left to escape certain malign forces that threatened my existence."

"And going back reignited their interest in you."

"You know the Fae, they like to toy with human emotions."

"Why did you come with us then?"

"Because Alexei was absent, and I couldn't let you go alone."

She sank back down and rested her cheek on his chest. "Oh. Now I feel all responsible."

His quiet chuckle surprised her. "Don't. They would have found me eventually. Rossa has been keeping an eye on me for years."

"Was that what his message was about? That someone wants you to go back to Otherworld permanently?"

"Not exactly." She pinched him hard and he grabbed her hand. "If I go back, I'll probably be executed."

"What did you do?"

She felt him tense beneath her. "It's in the past. I have no intention of talking about it now."

"Why not?"

He kissed her fingers. "If we speak of it, we bring it into the present and Otherworld will know. I'd rather not make things worse."

That made a weird kind of sense and she was too tired to argue anymore.

"Okay, let's go to sleep then."

She sensed Vadim start to relax almost immediately and she didn't disturb him. To be honest, she was amazed he'd taken her into his confidence at all. One of the things she'd learned as an empath was that once a thought was out in the open it definitely took on a life of its own.

ELLA FIRST NOTICED something was up when she spotted Peach the receptionist sitting bolt upright at her post, her hands idle, her expression terrified. Normally Peach would be so busy with her social media and games by now that she barely remembered to look up and check Ella's badge.

"Hey, Peach."

"Ms. Walsh, Mr. Morosov." Peach smiled. "Good *morning!*"

"Are you okay?"

"I'm just *fine*, Ms. Walsh! Can I help you with anything?"

"You can stop scaring me. Is everything okay?"

"Everything is awesome! I love my job!" Peach sang. Ella glanced at Vadim as they approached the elevators.

"Has she been cursed or something?"

"Not that I noticed. Shall we take the stairs?"

They walked down together and entered the main lobby of the SBLE offices. A businesslike hum had replaced the usual peaceful silence and several of Ella's colleagues were walking around purposefully like the folks in TV car ads.

"What's going on?" Ella turned to Vadim.

"I've no idea. Let's see if Alexei knows anything." Vadim held the door open for her and followed her into the smaller conference room. Alexei and Liz huddled together by his desk. "What's up?" Ella demanded.

Liz made an anguished face at her. "Drew Spencer's here!"

"Drew who?" Ella rushed ahead and took Vadim's seat.

"The head of SBLE!"

"What does he want?"

Alexei swung around to look at Vadim. "Didn't you tell her? I thought Feehan took you into his confidence."

"Yes, he took me into his confidence, which in this world means it was a private conversation, Alexei."

"But didn't it concern Ella?" Alexei persisted.

Vadim's gaze rested on her face. "Which is why I didn't tell her anything. She's an adult. She can decide how she wants to deal with this herself."

Ella punched him on the arm. "Thanks, Morosov."

"You're welcome." He paused. "I checked up on Drew Spencer last night. He's about a quarter Fae, so don't expect him to be easy to deal with."

"Wow, the head of the SBLE actually has some Otherworld blood in him? That's great!" Ella said.

Alexei laughed. "Wait until you get to meet him. You might change your mind." He checked his watch. "We're supposed to be in there right now. Shall we go?"

VADIM WAITED until everyone else had taken their seats before sitting opposite the surprisingly young looking head of the American branch of the SBLE. Vadim sensed that in some way he and Drew Spencer were kin, but that wasn't unusual. With his lineage, Vadim was linked to almost all the great Fae houses.

Feehan stood and cleared his throat. "Everyone, I'd like you to meet Mr. Drew Spencer."

Drew Spencer acknowledged their greetings with a brisk nod of his head. His eyes were the watchful opaque black of a shark.

"I'm pleased to meet you all, although I'd rather it was in less trying circumstances." He glanced at Ella. "Ms. Walsh, may I offer you my condolences for the loss of so many of your colleagues, and my assurance that I will do anything in my power to ensure that your life is preserved."

"Gee, thanks." Ella nodded.

Drew swiveled to face the whiteboard. "I've gone through the specifics of this case with Mr. Feehan, and I must admit to having some concerns."

"Which are?" Alexei asked.

"To be brutally honest, your lack of progress worries me."

"What else do you expect us to do, Mr. Spencer?" Vadim asked. "We are dealing with a serial killer who seems to have the ability to appear and murder at will. The only connection between the victims is that they are female and all graduated from Otherworld empath colleges in the same year. We have identified these women, and are now guarding the remaining empaths. We don't intend to let the Siren near them."

Drew studied Vadim, the force of his magic pushing against Vadim's in the equivalent of a psychic handshake. Whatever Spencer felt made him retreat.

"Mr. Morosov, is it not?"

"That's correct."

"The 'expert' from Russia?"

"If that's what you want to call me."

"Isn't that why you were brought on the case?" Drew's quick smile was meant to intimidate. "Unfortunately, your expertise seems to have added nothing so far."

Vadim didn't bother to answer that and continued to look calmly at the man. Feehan shifted uncomfortably in his chair and made no effort to intervene. Vadim remembered his wasn't the only career on the line.

"We've all done our best, Mr. Spencer," Ella said. "No one on this team enjoys seeing empaths die."

"That's very brave of you to say, Ms. Walsh. Personally, if I were you, I think I'd feel let down."

Vadim tensed as Ella stared at Spencer. "I've been let down by way too many people to know when that isn't the case. My colleagues have behaved impeccably."

"But your life is in danger."

She shrugged. "It's going to end soon anyway."

"Only if you don't take an OCOS mate."

"That's hardly relevant, is it?" Ella replied. Vadim wanted to grin at her. "As Morosov said, this particular killer is proving hard to catch."

Spencer steepled his fingers and studied Ella through them. "There is one way we might catch this deviant."

"Let me guess." Ella folded her arms and sat back in her chair. "You want to use me as bait because, hey, I'm not taking an OCOS mate, so I must have a death wish anyway, right?"

"That's not quite what I intended to say, Ms. Walsh, but it is close enough. Would you be willing to offer yourself up as 'bait'?"

"Ms. Walsh, Mr. Spencer, we've already tried that, and you know what happened." Vadim paused. "We ended up with two more dead empaths."

Spencer glared at Vadim. "Seeing as your superiors considered you were at fault in both of those deaths, Mr. Morosov, I suggest you keep out of this."

"I was not found guilty of those accusations, Mr. Spencer."

"That's because you were never charged." Spencer locked gazes with Vadim. "And why was that, I wonder? It might suggest that you have undue influence in high places, which scarcely speaks well for your integrity." Everyone in the room was staring at Vadim with various degrees of consternation. He almost flinched when Ella squeezed his knee under the table.

"You're out of order, Mr. Spencer. Morosov doesn't need to do this shit job, but he does it anyway, and I'd trust him in a heartbeat."

The "so fuck off" that ended that sentence remained unsaid, but somehow reverberated in the air like a challenge.

"I'll think about what you have suggested and discuss it with my team and come to a decision." Ella smiled. "After all, as you said, the choice is mine."

She rose to her feet and nodded at everyone around the table except Spencer.

"Shall we adjourn to the bar on the other side of the street and decide what to do?"

Everyone rose with her, even Feehan, leaving Spencer sitting by himself at the table.

DESPITE HER BRAVE WORDS, Ella was trembling when she finally managed to escape to her office. She'd promised to meet everyone in the bar in fifteen minutes and she intended to honor that promise. But she'd needed a moment alone. Spencer's combative attitude toward Vadim had infuriated her and she'd felt a weird need to protect him. Not that he needed it, but she simply couldn't allow him to be treated like that in front of the rest of the team. They were all at fault, not just him.

There was an internal mail envelope in her tray and needing something to do, she opened it. A photo slid out and she studied it carefully. The printed writing said *Incoming Empath Freshman Class, 2003.* There was nothing else in the envelope. Ella returned her attention to the picture. She picked herself out quite easily. She hadn't changed much—still the same baby face and bad dress sense...

She touched Laney's face and then Christa's, counted the smiling, apprehensive faces. Only eight female empaths and two males had graduated. There were fourteen in the photo. What had happened to the others? She tried to remember...

As if she'd conjured him, Vadim came through her door and shut it behind him. He looked unaffected by Spencer's comments but Ella knew him better now.

"That man is an asshole," Ella said.

"I agree. He seemed determined to get into some pissing contest with me. I have no idea why."

"He's part Fae, right?" Vadim nodded. "None of them seem to like you, do they?"

"You have a point." He took the seat in front of her desk. "It was good of you to stand up for the team. Good of you to stand up for me."

She shrugged. "As I said, the guy is an ass, and we're in this together. Sure, I gave you a hard time when you arrived, but I've gotten used to your ugly face and you're one of us now."

"Thanks." His smile was so beautiful she couldn't look away. He paused. "Don't do what Spencer wants, Ella."

"Play bait?"

"Please, we'll find another way."

Ella stared at him. "Because of what happened with Natasha?"

"No, because of you. I don't think I could let you do it."

"It's not your decision to make."

"We're mated."

"We agreed that it was just about sex."

"No, that's what you wanted."

She wrapped her arms around herself. "You didn't disagree."

"Because I didn't know how I would be affected. I didn't expect it to change me. I thought I was strong enough, secure enough to resist."

"We don't *have* to change," she said quickly.

"I think we already have." Vadim studied her. "Are you afraid?"

"Of what, of you?" She attempted a laugh. "Of course not!"

"Then why would you be willing to sacrifice yourself as SBLE bait? Do you think you are so worthless?"

"I didn't say that."

"*They* say it, Ella. The SBLE has been telling you you're expendable your whole life." He stood up and came toward her, his hand outstretched. "It doesn't have to be like that anymore. You have the ability to live how you want now."

She evaded his touch and he went still. "What's wrong?"

"You're much more powerful than me. You could make me do whatever you want."

"I've already told you I'd never do that." He shook his head. "Don't you trust me at all?"

She found it hard to swallow. "You told me that you were doing this mating thing so that we could finish the case and you'd not get fired."

"I *told* you what you wanted to hear."

"You lied?"

A muscle flexed in his jaw. "You say that with such hope. Is that what you want, Ella? For me to let you down, so that you can continue to believe it's safer not to care about people?"

"You *know* people let you down. We agreed on that!"

"But I didn't know how I'd feel when I bonded with you," he said. "That it wouldn't just be about sex and keeping my pathetic job."

"Just because you've changed, doesn't mean that I have to. Sex was enough for me." God, her voice was trembling. Could she be more pathetic?

"And that's the problem, isn't it?"

"It isn't a problem. I got exactly what I wanted."

"And now you're prepared to throw it all away for the glory of the SBLE?" He hesitated. "Don't you want to live?"

"Why?" She sounded angry now. Angry was good. "With you keeping all your secrets and your power and me an open book you can fuck and control?"

She saw her rage mirrored in his blue eyes and swallowed hard as the floor flexed and rolled as if they were in the midst of an earthquake. He turned away and headed for the door, pausing only to glare at her over his shoulder.

"Everything I have, all my power, all my secrets are yours for the taking, Ella. I can't keep you out. But you didn't want that, did you, didn't want all of me because you've grown so afraid of living that you don't even see a lifeline when it's thrown at you —only another noose."

"That's not fair!"

"Life's not fair, Ella, but hey, why should that bother you? You've already given up."

He slammed out of her office and she stood staring at the door, a bitter taste in her mouth and her thoughts in chaos. She brushed at her face and realized she was crying and that a small black feather was stuck to her cheek. Vadim was wrong. She was just as scared of dying as living.

She put the old photograph in her backpack and blew her nose. She had to go and meet her team and convince them she was willing to act as bait to lure the Siren into their trap. There was no other choice, and if Vadim didn't like it, he knew what he could do.

Go look for another mate.

VADIM STUDIED the half-empty bottle of vodka on the coffee table in front of him and picked up his glass to refill it. Drinking vodka and being Russian might be considered a cliché, but he'd wanted to get drunk fast and his adopted country had provided an excellent way for him to do it. His hotel room was in disarray, his suit lay discarded on the floor and he was sitting on the couch in his boxers.

Ms. Walsh, of course, had ignored his advice to tell Spencer exactly where to put his plan and enthusiastically offered to act as bait for the Siren. Vadim downed his vodka in one and wondered why he was bothering with a glass. Spencer had been delighted and had assured her that no harm would come to her at all.

He borrowed a favorite phrase of Ella's. "Yeah, right."

Vadim hadn't said anything to Spencer but had sat there and let them make plans around him. All his instincts roared that this was a mistake, but who cared about that? Ella didn't, and she was supposed to be his mate. In all other scenarios, as her significant other, he would've at least been asked his opinion. Here it was a secret, and thanks to Spencer, the rest of the team thought he was untrustworthy and worried about being involved in another scandal.

He'd made sure Ella had protection from other members of the team and left work early to hole up in his hotel room. He hadn't intended to start drinking, but his sense of injustice and frustration had demanded an outlet. He couldn't have sex with Ella or blast something to oblivion, so alcohol seemed a good option.

Someone banged on the connecting door between the rooms.

"Vadim? It's me, Alexei."

Vadim concentrated on his vodka. He'd already locked and warded the door so he wasn't worried about Alexei getting in.

"Are you in the shower?"

Vadim ignored the question. When had he become this pathetic version of himself who was afraid for another human being? Had he lived in the human world for too long? In Otherworld, the fate of one individual was considered negligible, but Ella was his *mate*. It seemed she'd roused all his protective human instincts—instincts he'd fought hard to conceal as a child. He rubbed a hand over his face. Did she really believe he was closed off? He'd been more open with her than with any other being in either world since his brother's death. Alexei rattled the door handle one more time and then seemed to give up. Vadim returned to his thoughts and his vodka. Whatever Ella decided, he would do his best to keep her alive despite herself. He was even willing to die for her. If he could die.

He wasn't even sure of that any longer.

ELLA PUT her backpack down on the countertop and let out her breath. The apartment seemed quiet with just her in it. Liz was waiting for the pizza they'd ordered for dinner and would be staying the night. Ella had decided to walk the rest of the way home from the pizza place to get some much-needed air and thinking time. She imagined Vadim's expression if he knew what she'd done. She sure was making some bad horror movie choices for a girl who was the target of a serial killer. Part of her wanted the Siren to find her now, so that she could end it.

It was funny how she always complained about Vadim being over-protective but now that he'd backed off she felt bereft. "It's just lack of sex." She said the words out loud partly to convince herself. "I don't need him."

She took out two plates and found the pizza cutter. The

thing was, it wasn't just sex. She'd come to like and respect him as well. When he hadn't said a word when she'd decided to go along with Drew Spencer's plan she'd almost been disappointed.

She shook her head. "I am so fricking contrary these days."

"Are you talking to me?"

Liz appeared at the door bearing a big cardboard box and Ella decided to put everything else aside and just eat.

Much later, when Liz had fallen asleep on the couch, Ella pulled out the photo of the incoming empaths and studied it more closely. Who had sent it to her and why? She had intended to mention it to the team, but Drew Spencer's presence had upset their normal routine. She counted the smiling faces again. Fourteen potential empaths, four of whom hadn't made it... what had happened to those guys? Why had they failed to graduate and had they been happy about that or not? She frowned. And what happened to an untrained empath anyway? Did they still go nuts at twenty-seven?

She glanced at the clock. It was getting late. The only way she might discover more about the forgotten empaths was to go back to Otherworld, talk to the administrators at the college again and look up the individuals in the Merton records office. What had happened to the information Perry, the college principal, had offered to provide for them? Was he trying to protect someone? His distaste for the killings had seemed quite genuine, but she doubted he was the guy actually doing the checking. Was someone in his office deliberately withholding information?

Her cell phone buzzed and she recognized Vadim's number and hesitated. Did she want to talk to him? If she didn't, would he think she was too afraid?

"Hey."

There was a slight pause before he spoke. "Thanks for picking up."

"Why wouldn't I?"

"I just wanted to check you were okay. Is someone staying with you tonight?"

"Liz is here. We had pizza and she's sleeping on the couch."

"Good." Another pause. "I'll see you at work tomorrow, then."

Ella closed her eyes and gripped the phone hard. He sounded like he didn't give a damn, and even though she'd pushed him away, it hurt. "Morosov, would you come to Otherworld with me in the morning?"

"Why would you want me to do that?"

"There's something I'd like to follow up."

"I thought you'd decided to go with Spencer's plan."

"I have, but I think this might be important."

"What might be?"

She looked at the photo propped up beside her bed. "Four of the incoming empaths in my class didn't graduate."

"So?"

"What happened to them?"

"Why does it matter?"

"Because...I just have this feeling that it does."

"A psychic feeling?"

She heard the skepticism in his voice and found herself bristling. "I'm not Natasha and I'm not going nuts anymore, remember? My intuition is working just fine."

"I wasn't trying to imply..."

"Yes, you were."

He sighed. "Look, why don't you talk this through with the team when you come in tomorrow?"

"Why can't I talk it through with you right now?"

"Because I'm not feeling entirely rational."

"What do you mean?"

"I'm drunk, and I'm missing you."

"Why are you drunk?"

"Why do you think?"

"Because I agreed to Spencer's plan?" She realized she was scowling at the phone. "You've given up on me, then?"

"Ella…" He sounded weary and she felt unaccustomed tears crowd her throat. "Isn't that what you wanted? Me to back off and let you make your own decisions?"

"You know, you're right. I shouldn't have bothered you." She tried to sound brisk and professional. "I'll certainly bring this up at the meeting in the morning and see what everyone else thinks. Night, Morosov, sweet dreams."

"Ella, fuck this. Don't—"

She turned her phone off and took it out into the kitchen to hide in her backpack. He was right. She couldn't jerk him around like that. She'd told him to back off, and he'd done exactly what she'd asked him. Okay, she now thought she might have made a mistake, but she couldn't tell him that. If she survived the Siren, there would be plenty of time to put things right between them.

Plenty of time.

If she survived.

And if Vadim stayed around to find out she'd had a change of heart.

19

"I got this through internal mail yesterday." Ella waved the photograph to get everyone's attention. "Does anyone know anything about it?"

"What is it?" Feehan asked, after a nervous glance at Drew Spencer who had decided to "sit in" on the morning meeting.

"It's a picture of my incoming class at college."

"So what?" Alexei said. He seemed even sulkier than Vadim, which was quite a feat seeing as her erstwhile mate hadn't said a word to her yet and had closed down his shields so she had no clue as to his feelings.

"It shows fourteen of us."

Liz sat up. "But only ten of you graduated, correct?"

"It made me wonder what happened to the others."

She looked around the attentive faces. "Did we ever get that information from Perry at the college, Liz?"

"I thought we did." Liz turned to Sam. "Didn't I give it to you?"

"Oh shit." Sam's face turned red and he opened his file and began rummaging through it. "I have it here somewhere. I forgot to pass it on to Ella and the rest of you guys."

Ella held out her hand. "Can I see it now?"

Sam found the letter and passed it across. "I'm sorry, Ella. I suck."

"It's okay. It might be nothing."

Drew Spencer cleared his throat. "Ms. Walsh, if we're going to trap the Siren anyway, is this really necessary?"

Ella met his irritated gaze. "Before I offer myself up as the ultimate sacrifice, I believe we should investigate every available avenue, don't you?"

His eyes narrowed. "Why? Don't you think the entire resources of the SBLE can keep you safe?"

"They haven't done a very good job with their empaths so far, have they?"

Magical power gathered around Spencer's head and Ella instinctively raised her shields. Since bonding with Vadim they had improved tremendously.

"You can hardly blame the whole of the SBLE for your own team's incompetence."

"We've had this conversation before, Mr. Spencer. I don't think my team is incompetent. I *think* the upper echelons of the SBLE should be addressing the way it deals with empaths, not criticizing those of us who work in the field." She took a deep breath. "I sense something is wrong here. I *know* it."

Spencer smiled and sat back in his seat. "Ms. Walsh, you are under a lot of strain, we all realize that. I'm sure even Mr. Morosov would agree that an empath under stress—even through no fault of their own—can ruin an investigation." His patronizing tone was grating. "Perhaps you might consider stepping back and reassessing your input into this matter."

"Are you taking me off the case?"

He smiled again and she wanted to leap across the table and scratch out his eyes. "How about you concentrate on our plan to trap the Siren and forget about all these wild goose chases of yours? We wouldn't want you to overtax yourself, especially with your twenty-seventh birthday coming up."

Beside her Vadim shifted minutely in his seat as if preparing to come to her defense. Should she blow the idea that her physic abilities were compromised right out of the water, or was it better to keep quiet? Perhaps it was easier to pretend to agree and do things her preferred way—behind the authorities' back.

She gave Spencer her best team-building smile. "Fine, whatever. I'll think about it."

As Feehan concluded the meeting, she placed the photo on top of the letter Sam had passed her and slid them into her backpack. No one looked at her when she was the first to rise and head out. Were they worried that she was losing it too, or would they stand by her? Between Morosov's crazy Natasha and Spencer's insinuations, it was no wonder no one trusted an empath. In the quiet of her office she checked the list of names against the photo, matching them to the young faces. Two of the males and two of the females had failed to complete the course. She remembered two of them quite clearly now, one man and one woman who had bailed at the end of year two because they'd fallen in love. They should be relatively easy to trace. She looked up his last name and found them, both still alive and living in New Zealand keeping sheep.

She couldn't help but smile as she fired up an image of the couple in matching knitted sweaters on top of a craggy snow-covered peak. Perhaps marrying another empath kept you sane after all. The college definitely didn't encourage it. Ella had always wondered if they said that because they wanted empaths to marry outsiders and spread the load. It didn't matter now. They looked happy.

Two names left. Anna Wheeler and Geoffrey White. Ella studied their faces on the photograph. They both looked quite normal but she had a sense that she'd seen one or the other of them more recently...

Someone knocked on her door and she hid the photo and list in her desk. Liz poked her head around the door.

"You okay?"

"I'm fine."

Liz came to perch on the side of Ella's desk. "That man is an idiot."

"Drew Spencer?"

"Who else? I just wanted you to know that the rest of us have complete confidence in you, okay?"

"Thanks."

Liz shook her finger at Ella. "Why didn't you tell him the truth?"

"About what?"

"I *saw* you with Vadim at the party, Ella. If you're not mated to the guy, I'm resigning my right to operate a Fae-Web."

"*Shit.*" Ella stared at Liz. "Who else knows?"

"Only Doug, Big Jim and the entire wolf pack. Vadim did everything but bare his teeth at them before you both left."

"What about Alexei?"

Liz bit her lip. "I've been trying to keep it from him and my Fae-Web but it's becoming increasingly difficult. I don't think Alexei is contributing much to this investigation at all. He seems more intent on tripping Vadim up than anything else."

"Morosov said that Alexei had been sent to spy on him and bring him down."

"He's right."

They regarded each other glumly for a moment. "If you accept I'm not going nuts because I'm mated, can you also accept this sense I have that the empaths who didn't graduate are important?"

"Sure."

Ella frowned. "I also feel like I've met one of them again recently." She retrieved Perry's letter and showed it to Liz. "Two of these people eloped and got married, so it only leaves two."

"One male and one female. We've always assumed the Siren is male. Hang on a minute." Liz's finger remained on the letter. "Anna Wheeler works at the empath college. I spoke to her when I chased up the information last week."

Ella met Liz's gaze. "I'm going to have to return to Otherworld, aren't I? I just *know* the solution lies there."

"Not by yourself."

"Liz, I can't ask Feehan. He'll tell Spencer and he's already told me to back off and await my fate."

"Vadim?"

"I don't think I can do that to him, Liz."

"He's your mate. He'll want to be by your side."

"Not in Otherworld, he won't. I did kind of ask him already, and he didn't exactly sound keen. Don't you remember what happened last time? He barely got out alive and ended up mated to me. I can't do that to him." There was one thing she could do for him while she was in Otherworld. Something that might convince Vadim she was taking the mating business seriously. Liz uncrossed her legs and slid off the table. "I'll come with you, but we have to let someone know where we are."

"Cool, let's go and tell Sam." Hopefully he'd forget to mention it to anyone.

"The portal on Embarcadero is still open." Liz put away her phone.

"That's useful." Ella picked up her backpack and shoved the photo and letter inside. "Hopefully we'll be back before anyone notices we've even gone."

"I wish." Liz glanced up at the sky as they exited the building. "I told Sam that if we weren't back in two hours, he should tell Vadim and Doug where we are, okay?"

"Sounds like a plan." Ella concentrated on avoiding another speeding passerby. "Why is it so busy today?"

"It's Friday. Everyone's either out for a long lunch, or skipping off home early."

"Oh God, I promised to visit my mom tomorrow. She has a birthday surprise for me."

"Lucky you."

"Funny, Liz."

"No, I mean it. You can give her the good news about you and Vadim. She'll be thrilled."

"Do you think so?"

"Ella, in her own peculiar way she loves you."

Ella didn't answer, just pretended she needed all her resources to get across the street. The baseball park loomed up ahead of them and they turned toward the bay and the portal.

As Ella checked for the portal, Liz nudged her in the ribs. "Ooh, I meant to ask how you and Vadim ended up mated."

"It's a long story."

"But it's a bit weird isn't it? Him being right here and not needing to come and find you?"

"Weird doesn't even begin to describe it, seeing as Morosov says he wasn't even on the OCOS list."

"What?"

"I know. He thinks it might have something to do with his visit to Otherworld with us."

"Someone set him up? That's typical Fae." Liz made a face. "The poor guy. Someone in Otherworld must really hate him."

"Yeah, sticking him with me."

"That's not what I meant." Liz shivered and Ella glanced at her.

"What's wrong?"

"I don't know. Something just set off all my warning instincts." Liz looked around. "Did you feel it?"

"Nope." Ella pressed the brick wall and the entrance to the portal appeared. "Let's go." She focused her attention on the green light on the ground and then closed her eyes. Sometimes she wished the portals didn't resemble elevators, but she had no other option. "Merton records office, please."

The light blinked and threw them forward to wherever Otherworld was or wasn't. Liz screamed and then everything stopped moving and she frantically pushed against the side of the portal, falling into the street outside the records office.

"Liz?" Ella looked around but there was no sign of her friend. "Where are you?"

The first stirring of unease settled in her gut. She'd promised Liz she wouldn't go to Otherworld alone, and yet she'd done it anyway. She hoped Liz was okay, and not trapped somewhere between the two worlds as a portal relocated itself. It happened occasionally, and didn't result in many deaths... Ella looked around the deserted street and then set off at a run for the college. Miss Vera might not like her, but she was incredibly efficient, and would know how to alert the authorities that one of the portals had malfunctioned.

By the time she arrived at the college, she was panting and her hair was coming out of its already untidy braids. Miss Vera glanced up from her typewriter, her mouth settling into a thin line.

"What have you done now, Miss Walsh?"

Ella immediately felt like a guilty teen. "The portal I arrived in didn't release my colleague, Liz Smith. Is there someone we could call to check that she is okay?"

"Miss Smith is the lady who came with you before?"

"Yes." Ella nodded. "She seemed nice."

"She is."

"She isn't an empath, though."

"No, she's a Fae-Web specialist."

"Part Fae, then?" Miss Vera picked up the phone. "Yes." Ella let her gaze scan the office and tried to see if she recognized anyone. She was reluctant to drop her guard and use her psychic abilities when there were so many empaths around.

Miss Vera put her finger to her lips and focused her attention on the phone. "Maintenance? This is Miss Vera from the

Empath College. Yes, how are you, Claude? I'm very well." She nodded. "The portal outside the college? Has it moved?"

Thanks to Vadim's superior genes, Ella's breathing evened out far more quickly than usual. She eyed Miss Vera's desk. If she sat on the corner edge, would she be breaking some kind of unwritten rule? Did she even care anymore? Reluctantly she decided to keep standing. She needed Miss V on her side at the moment.

Miss Vera covered the mouthpiece and looked up at Ella. "The one at your end moved. Your friend is alive and has ended up in Netherfield."

"Will she be able to get back here?" Ella asked. Miss Vera consulted Claude. "Eventually."

"Thank you." Ella smiled. "I really appreciate it."

Miss Vera put the phone down and studied Ella who wore a short black stretchy skirt, blue leggings and a purple top with silver bling on it. She shook her head. "You should smile more. It suits you."

"Thanks."

"Although you really should do something about your appearance. You can't look like an eighteen-year-old college student forever."

Ella nodded. "You have a point, Miss Vera. Now, could you help me with something else? Is Anna Wheeler in today?"

"I think so." Miss Vera turned to survey the office. "She's over there in the corner."

Ella managed another smile. "I need to touch base with her about something. Is it okay if I just go and speak to her?"

Miss Vera nodded graciously and Ella was allowed into the inner sanctum of the office. It was strange to be in a place that had no computers sitting on the desks, only typewriters. The internet didn't work well with Otherworld and humans who visited or lived there just had to deal with it.

Ella approached the young dark-haired woman who was reading something at her desk. "Anna?"

Anna looked up and smiled. "Ella Walsh? You haven't changed a bit."

"So Miss Vera was telling me. Long time, no see." Ella gestured at the empty chair. "May I talk to you for a minute?"

"Certainly." Anna put a bookmark in her book and closed it. "What can I do for you?"

"This might sound crazy, but why didn't you graduate from college?"

"So much for small talk." Anna shuddered, her hands clenched together on her lap. "I try not to think about it."

"I wouldn't ask, but I work for the SBLE now. It might be a matter of life and death. Almost all the empaths from our year at college are dead."

"That's quite common for empaths at our age."

"I know, but this is way beyond the norm."

"And what does it have to do with me?" Anna asked. "You've probably already noticed I'm no longer an empath."

"I noticed, but what I need to understand is *why*." Anna looked away and Ella tried again. "I don't want to cause you pain, but I really need to know."

"Something happened to me in the first year of college. I lost my abilities."

"Did you tangle with the Fae?"

"Oh no, I went to a party, got drunk and when I woke up, I was in an Otherworld hospital in terrible pain."

"Do you remember anything else?"

"Only that they had to operate to relieve pressure on my brain. Someone had tried to destroy my hippocampus. Luckily for me they made a real botch job of it."

"Oh my God." Ella almost stopped breathing. "Did they ever find out who did it?"

"How could they? I was at a party with about forty other

empaths. The doctors suggested that maybe some kind of Fae had literally decided to mess with my head, but they never caught anyone."

"That's terrible." Ella reached out for Anna's hand.

"I thought so at the time, but over the years I've changed my mind. Working here I've seen so many empaths die young or go insane. I've been spared that at least." She squeezed Ella's fingers. "Really, I mean it. I'm married to a really nice Fae male, we have two kids and I'm happy here."

Ella used her abilities to search Anna's mind, but found nothing but truth in her words.

"Thank you for your time."

"Have I helped you at all?"

"Yes, you have." Ella rose. "If Liz Smith from the SBLE turns up, would you do me an enormous favor and tell her what you told me? It's very important to our investigation."

Anna stood too. "I'm glad to have helped."

"And I'm glad I met you again." Ella smiled. "There is only one more member of our incoming class I need to track down. Tell Liz I'll be at the Merton record office."

VADIM STARED at his cup of black coffee and took another three painkillers. He could magic himself up a potion and get rid of his hangover, but he almost preferred to suffer. It made him feel more human, something that had begun to escape him again when Ella Walsh took over his life. He wasn't proud of what he'd said to her the previous day, but she needed to know the truth. He was *mated* to her. He needed her whether he liked it or not. What he couldn't understand was why she refused to believe it too.

He took another gulp of coffee and shuddered at the bitter taste. She had no idea how damned hard he had to work to stay out of her way, and to conceal his natural desire to protect her from *everything*. Females of his line were considered so precious that they spent most of their lives in seclusion—unless they developed a taste for power when all hell broke loose. He had no idea how they'd react to Ella, either kill her or love her, he wasn't sure, but there wouldn't be anything weak about the response.

"Hey."

Vadim looked up at Alexei, who had started to adopt the more casual dress of those around them and today wore khakis and an open-neck blue shirt.

"Good morning."

"Drinking alone isn't good for you."

Vadim held up his mug. "You want to share?"

"I'm not talking about now. I'm talking about last night."

"Spying on me again?"

Alexei frowned. "It's my job. You know that."

"Hopefully it will soon be over, and you can return to your lover and whisper sweet nothings in her ear about me."

"What makes you think Madame and I are lovers?" Vadim just stared at Alexei who eventually shrugged. "So what if we are?"

"Doesn't that compromise your objectivity in this case?"

"Why should that bother you? You lost your objectivity the minute you fucked Ella Walsh."

Vadim stared at Alexei. "Whatever you think you know is probably incorrect. I suggest you don't pass it on to Madame. She won't thank you."

"I know the truth. You're so desperate not to fail again that you'd do anything to keep Ella Walsh happy and she's been dying to get into your pants since you got here."

"My reasons are my own. Keep your remarks about Ms. Walsh out of it."

Alexei shook his head. "You're hosed, Vadim, whatever way

you look at it. What's wrong with you? Did you think you could fuck Ella before she goes nuts and no one would know or care? Madame Dubinsky cares and she won't like the fact that you probably used your magical power to enthrall Ella."

Vadim found himself smiling. "That's right. Ms. Walsh is so easy to overpower."

"Empaths of her age are notoriously easy." Alexei closed the door and came back to sit on the edge of Vadim's desk. "I have to report back to Madame about you. She has me over a barrel."

"And do you like it?"

"She says if I don't complete my job here to her satisfaction, she will expose our relationship."

"But won't that hurt her?"

"Not the way she intends to spin it." Alexei shrugged. "Let's just say I come out of it looking like a psychotic, deranged blackmailer and she a pure white dove." He hesitated. "I haven't told her about your physical relationship with Ella yet."

Vadim searched Alexei's gaze and then skimmed his mind. Since mating with Ella he was getting far better at sensing the subtle nuances of the flow of people's emotion.

"I appreciate that."

"Depending on how Drew Spencer's plan goes, I might not have to."

"You mean if Ms. Walsh dies?"

"It seems likely, doesn't it? The good thing for you is that if Spencer's plan doesn't work, the blame will be on him and not you."

"And Ms. Walsh will be dead."

Alexei waved a casual hand. "Collateral damage, my friend."

Vadim looked down at his coffee and concentrated on not annihilating his old associate. It was surprisingly hard. He thought about Ella instead. She'd asked him to go to Other-world with her and immediately retracted her request when he'd seemed reluctant. Why was he afraid to go to Otherworld now? What else could go wrong? He'd already been punished. He pushed back his chair.

"Have you seen Ms. Walsh since the meeting?"

"She was in her office with Liz for a while. I have no idea whether they are still there."

He had a bad feeling he knew the answer to that. Her helpful attitude toward Spencer in the meeting hadn't fooled him at all. She was up to something.

"I'll go and check."

Would Ella see his offer to come with her to Otherworld as him trying to overprotect her, or as a symbol of his desire to protect her over himself? Would she even see the difference? The only way to know would be to ask. He knocked on her office door and then knocked again. He opened the door and looked inside. There was no sign of her or Liz.

Trying to look casual, he checked Liz's cubicle and then wandered out into the main office. He couldn't sense Ella anywhere. His gut tightened as he considered what that meant and he kept walking until he reached the main lobby.

"Peach, have you seen Liz or Ms. Walsh go by?"

"Good morning, Mr. Morosov. Yes I have. They left about half an hour ago."

"I don't suppose they mentioned where they were going, did they?"

"They didn't, but I did notice Ella had her cell out and was checking for portals."

Damn. She'd gone without him. Of *course* she had. "Thanks, that's very helpful."

"You're welcome, Mr. Morosov. Do you want me to tell you when they come back?"

"That would be great." He smiled at her and she turned a delicious shade of pink. Just as he was about to call the elevator to go down to the SBLE floors, Doug Smith came in through the revolving doors. Vadim froze, his finger poised over the button.

"Doug? What's wrong?"

Doug ran a hand through his already disordered hair. "Hey, Vad. Something's up with Liz. I feel it in my gut."

"As far as I know she's out with Ms. Walsh. Did she tell you where they were going?"

"Nope. I just know something's wrong." He shivered. "I felt her scream."

"Peach thought they might be going to Otherworld." Doug raised his gaze to Vadim's. His eyes looked more wolf than human. "Can we find out? I need to get to her."

"We can certainly try." Vadim hurried Doug into the elevator and followed him in, his mind working furiously. When they reached their level, he went straight to his own office.

"Alexei, you know Doug. Can you locate Liz? Doug thinks she's in trouble."

"I'll do my best." Alexei's Fae-Web surrounded him. "She's… unclear."

"What the hell does that mean?" Doug snarled. "She's neither here nor quite in Otherworld." Alexei frowned at Vadim. "How weird is that? She's not dead though." He held up his hand. "Hold on, I'm getting a sense of portal disruption. Did the one by the bay move or something?"

"Hopefully not when Liz was in it," Vadim muttered. He set himself to locating the portals. "Yes, it's definitely moved. It's closer now, by the clock tower at the Ferry building." He looked at Doug. "What do you want to do?"

"It depends what has happened to her. Is she hurt?"

"I don't know. As Alexei said, she is alive. Do you want to come with me and find out?"

Alexei stared at Vadim. "You're going to Otherworld?"

"I have no choice. Liz wasn't the only one on the way to Otherworld. I'm getting no sense of Ms. Walsh either."

ELLA WALKED into the public office of the Merton records office and found that nothing had changed. There was no one around, the clock on the counter continued to tick away the seconds, and the sense of being in another century deepened. She put her backpack on the countertop and fished for the OCOS form she'd completed that morning. She put it in the wire IN tray and then turned her attention to writing out a request form. As she thought how to pose her question, she bit the end of the pencil. What did she need to know about Geoffrey White? She decided to keep it simple and just ask for current information as to his address and occupation. Was he the empath who had damaged Anna Wheeler at that party? Had the college discovered his identity and gotten rid of him or had he left? If he was the man calling himself the Siren, she needed to get answers as quickly as possible.

She finished writing her note and read it through before placing it on top of her OCOS letter. According to the clock, there was another fifteen minutes before someone would be by to pick up the information. Ella picked up the silver bell that set next to it. Engraved around the outside of the bell were the words, 'For EMERGENCIES only.'

This was a fucking emergency.

She rang the bell and the sweet sound echoed through the joyless room. No one came and Ella considered leaping over the countertop, running to the door at the back and doing some good old-fashioned hollering. She picked up her backpack and dumped it on the nearest chair.

"Ms. Walsh, where are you?"

At the sound of Vadim's voice, she almost dropped her backpack.

"I'm at the records office in Otherworld. How the hell are you talking to me here?"

"I'm on my way. Is Liz with you?"

"No, the portal shifted when we were in it. Liz ended up about twenty miles away in a place called Netherfield. She's going to join me here as soon as she can." From the corner of her eye she saw the door at the back of the office start to open. *"I've got to go. The guy's coming to pick up the paperwork."*

"What paperwork? Ella, listen to me, don't do anything until I get there. Sit tight, talk to no one."

"Yeah right, like I'm going to be attacked by a mild-mannered civil servant."

"Fuck it, Ella, listen to me, I..."

She frowned as she caught a hint of fear in his voice. *"What's wrong, Morosov, what..."*

It was the same nondescript guy who'd picked up the paperwork before. Ella nodded at him. "Thanks, could you make it snappy? I'm in a bit of a hurry."

He stared at her for a long moment and then reset the clock, scooped up the paperwork and left her alone again. She slumped back in her chair, drumming her fingers on the wooden desk in front of her.

"Morosov?"

Her thought echoed weirdly inside her own head and bounced back. Where had Vadim gone? Had someone detected their communication and shut them down? Considering his reluctance to enter Otherworld it wasn't surprising. But why had Vadim come after her? And why was he so uncharacteristically afraid?

"Morosov."

Again, nothing. She rubbed her forehead as a headache threatened. It felt as if there was a thunderstorm about to break inside her. She needed to get out of this place and back to work. She glanced impatiently at the clock. Where the hell *was* the clerk?

The door at the back of the office opened and Ella waited as the guy came toward the counter. Outside, real thunder boomed followed by the gentle patter of rain on the closed, shuttered windows.

"Miss Walsh?"

Startled, Ella stood up. "Yes?"

"Would you mind coming through to my office?"

"Why?"

"There is some paperwork you might wish to see."

"Can't you give it to me here?"

"Unfortunately not. I'm not even supposed to let you see these items, but I'm trying to be helpful." He lowered his voice. "It concerns Geoffrey White."

Ella left her backpack on the seat and allowed the man to usher her through the silent office and out into the hallway beyond. There were at least twenty matching oak doors all currently closed, except for one right at the end of the hall. Despite the booming thunder, the pressure in Ella's head hadn't receded at all. In fact, the farther she went down the corridor, the worse it got. Somewhere in the back of her mind she was aware of Vadim trying to reach her. Somehow it didn't seem to matter.

She smiled at her silent companion. "I appreciate your help."

He shrugged and she noted how perfectly ironed his shirt was. Vadim would approve. She frowned as she tried to picture him and found it increasingly difficult. She had to concentrate; there was a killer at large.

"Please take a seat, Miss Walsh."

Ella sat in the proffered chair and rested her linked hands in her lap. There was something about the man that made her feel relaxed—as if she didn't have to worry about Morosov, or the Siren, or anything really... He took off his glasses and she realized he was way younger than she had thought. His gray eyes were kind and crinkled at the corners. "Firstly, may I congratulate you on turning in your OCOS paperwork? I'm sure you are looking forward to meeting your mate."

"Yes, I am." Ella nodded. He didn't need to know that she'd done it as a show of faith so Vadim would know she was taking their relationship seriously—well, as seriously as she could take anything.

"I know it is always a struggle for an empath to decide what path to take—to commit to a stranger, or to allow nature to take its course and send you plummeting into madness."

"I wasn't going to do it," Ella found herself saying. "I was convinced I'd rather go nuts."

He sat forward. "Really? What changed your mind?"

"Fear, I suppose. Fear of going mad and somehow damaging those I work with, or those I love."

He nodded sympathetically. "I can understand that. Being an empath is a heavy burden." He hesitated. "But isn't there another way?"

"What do you mean?"

"I heard you were investigating a serial killer called the Siren."

Somewhere faintly in the back of her head warning bells sounded and she sensed Vadim shouting at her. She blinked and refocused her gaze on the tranquil face of the man in front of her. When she stared at him, all her anxiety slipped away and she felt calm and sure, and, yeah…almost happy.

"Yes, I am. What of it?"

He smiled and she found herself smiling back. "I heard he offers empaths another way out of their dilemma."

"What do you mean?"

"He relieves them of their pain and sets them free."

Ella considered that. "But they die."

"They die at peace, though, don't they?"

"I suppose so." She found herself nodding. "It's hard being an empath."

"I know. All that psychic burden, all that *knowledge* bringing you down. You can see why none of the empaths struggled at the end." He sat forward. "Didn't you sense that? That they were happy to die?"

She stared at him. "I'm...not sure. How come you know so much about this?"

He ignored her question and brought his chair around to sit beside her. "Don't you feel that, right now? That the burden is crushing you, that you can't go on?"

God, she wanted to agree with him. A single tear ran down her cheek. He reached forward and gently wiped it away.

"You've been under so much stress, haven't you? You've been so alone. Your family doesn't understand you, your colleagues fear you, and madness is approaching. No wonder you panicked and chose to take an OCOS mate."

She found herself nodding again as more tears spilled. He gave her his ironed cotton handkerchief.

"It's all right. I understand what you are going through, I really do." He grasped her left hand and she shuddered as his power rolled over her and through her. "Just let it go. I'll make sure that everything is all right for you."

VADIM POINTED Doug toward Netherfield Hospital. "Liz is in there. She's fine, but a bit confused. Go and see if they'll let you take her home."

"Thanks, dude." Doug slapped him on the back. "Are you sure you don't want me to come with you?"

"No, you go take care of Liz. I'll manage."

Doug headed up the steps and Vadim turned back toward the main road. Ella was definitely in Otherworld but she'd stopped communicating with him. He wasn't sure if she just didn't want to talk, or if she was being prevented. It didn't make any difference. He was going to find her and God help anyone who had harmed her. Otherworld always put him in the mood to kill.

He didn't have time to be careful anymore, and he was twenty human miles from the records office where Ella was. He closed his eyes and materialized on the cobbled street outside the building. Rossa sat on the steps shivering in a thin gold cloak and green hose that clung to his muscular thighs.

"I was wondering when you'd get here."

Vadim jerked his head at the records office. "Is she in there?"

"Your female?"

"No, the Queen of the Fae."

Rossa went pale. "Don't even joke about her. Of course I meant your woman. She went in about half an hour ago, and she hasn't come out yet."

Vadim walked around to the side door and tried it. "It's locked."

"That's because the place is shut for the day."

"Not if Ella is still inside." Vadim lowered his shields an inch and frowned. "There's a lot of magic around. It's trying to keep me out."

Rossa gave a crack of laughter. "Keep *you* out? They must be insane."

"Unfortunately I think they might be." Vadim nodded at Rossa. "Can you stay here and make sure no one else comes in?"

"I'm not risking my life for you or anything." Rossa ambled back around to the front of the building. "But I'll wait. This could be seriously amusing."

Vadim ignored his half-sibling and concentrated his formidable talents on the task in front of him. He could only hope the abilities he'd buried so successfully in order to function as human were still there beneath his skin and his shields. He lifted his hand and power danced like lightning at the end of his fingertips. Ah yes, he still had it. Now he just had to hope it was enough to deal with whatever was behind that door.

ELLA REALIZED she was still holding the man's hand and that she was surrounded by a curious sense of warmth and complete understanding. His mind enfolded hers, stroking her psyche, making her want to lean against him and...

"Ella Walsh, fucking pay attention!"

Who was that roaring at her in her head? She stiffened and the warm glow around her dissipated a little. She snatched back her hand.

"Did you say something?"

"Only that you can confide in me, Miss Walsh."

"But, I didn't come here to do that, did I? I came to—to give back my OCOS form and to find out what happened to Geoffrey White. Oh God, you're Geoffrey White, aren't you?"

He looked pleased. "Do you remember me at all? Unfortunately my time at college was cut short."

"When you stole Anna's empath powers."

"I didn't steal them. She let me in her head and I realized I had special abilities far beyond most mortals' understanding."

"You almost destroyed her."

"I was still learning my craft. Eventually I perfected my technique."

"Your technique to do what? Murder other empaths?" A stab of pain lanced through her head and he reclaimed her hand.

"That wasn't nice, Miss Walsh." His thoughts poured over her, soothing the hurt. "We were talking about your psychic burden, about how you could lay it down and be free."

She wanted to nod, to agree with him, but something nagged at her, *someone who wouldn't shut the fuck up in her head...*

"It's okay. I don't need to lay down my burden. I just remembered. I have a mate."

"You have a *potential* mate. I know. I'm the one who sends out the paperwork." Her companion's smile was beautiful.

"Of course you do." She found herself agreeing again. God, it was so hard not to simply relinquish control and let him in. "You know everyone, don't you? You met us all at college."

"Luckily for you, I did. It makes my life's work so much easier."

"Your life's work being…?"

"Bringing an empath peace at the end of her life." He touched her knee. "You know what I do. You've seen the results."

Laney.

Vadim was closer, she could feel him now, but he was different, stronger, more powerful, more *Other*. She had to fight, had to make sense of all this.

"You *murder* empaths."

"No, I offer empaths an alternate way to leave this life with dignity and with their souls intact." A flare of anger resonated through his happiness. Ella wasn't sure if she was pleased about that or scared. She sensed he could hurt her very badly.

"Why are you trying to resist me, Miss Walsh? I'm offering you peace."

"At a price." Damn, creating an individual thought was like wading waist-high through molasses. She tried to cling to the chaos of Vadim shouting at her, telling her to let him in. *Let him in where?* "What do you gain out of it?"

A small frown marred his brow. "I only take what is offered freely."

"I know that, but what do you do with it?" His expression gentled. "I use it for good."

"Your own good?"

"Taking your pain is a gift to me. It enables me to increase my powers and help others. Eventually there will be no more empaths left—just me—and then Otherworld and the humans who tossed me aside as some kind of freak will come crawling back and beg for my help."

Okay, even in her currently deluded state she knew this guy was seriously nuts.

There was a crashing sound and Vadim appeared in the now smashed doorway. He seemed to be speaking, but Ella couldn't understand what he was saying. He also looked murderous. She unconsciously shifted closer to the Siren, or Geoffrey or the desk nerd, whatever he was called.

He stroked her arm. "It's all right. You don't have to take any notice of him. Do you have your gun on you?" She nodded and brought it out. The Siren smiled and Vadim went still, although she suspected he was still shouting at her in some realm. He loved shouting at her almost as much as he enjoyed being cryptic and mysterious. She imagined him moving over her, the taste of his skin, his sweat, his come...

"I can see that you are conflicted, Miss Walsh." The Siren's compassion washed over her and she shivered. "If you want him to go away, you can just shoot him." Ella nodded and slowly stood up, the gun pointed at Vadim. If he just stopped shouting at her it would be so nice, so quiet, so *peaceful...*

"Ella, don't you damn well give up on me!" The power of Vadim, his rage entranced her and she held still. *"Turn that gun around and shoot him. He's trying to kill you."*

She rolled her eyes. "No, Morosov, you idiot, he's trying to make me shoot *you*."

Vadim's hand shot out and she could've sworn she saw sparks. Puzzled she turned to look at the Siren who was trying to hide behind her.

"Ouch!" Ella squeaked as one of the sparks hit her shoulder. "That hurt!"

"Then get out of the damned way, and let me kill him!"

She heard that real time and turned helplessly toward the

Siren. "I can't get him out of my head. I'm sorry. He'll never let me seek peace."

The Siren gripped her hand and she almost staggered beneath the force of his rising power. "That's *impossible*."

"He's my mate. I can't help it." Vadim's magic surged through her like a tidal wave, displacing the Siren's hold. It felt like a nuclear war was being fought inside her head. The gun wavered in her hand. "Stop it. I can't kill my mate and be happy forever-more. I just *can't*."

Vadim smiled at the Siren. "Are you listening? You can't have her. She's already mine."

"No!"

Pain splintered across Ella's skull and she closed her eyes.

"That can't be correct. You're not the right male for her," the Siren shouted, his features distorted with rage. "She *needs* me. She only just turned the consent form in. I defeated *you* in Russia! You weren't chosen for her. You aren't worthy!"

Vadim looked at Ella. "You turned in the form?"

She could barely manage a nod. "Morosov, he says he can give me peace, take away my burdens..."

"By killing you? By stealing everything that makes you special? Fuck that, Ella. We can do so much better together."

She managed to look into his eyes. They glowed like blue sapphires. He looked all Fae, his power flowing over her, pushing at the Siren's hold. Punching holes in her certainties, reminding her why she wanted to live and love and...

She turned the gun toward the Siren. "I want to kill you so badly right now."

Vadim cleared this throat. "So do I, but don't you think we should bring him to justice?"

"Why?" She stepped back until she was against Vadim's chest. "You promised me vengeance, remember?" He kissed the top of her head. "After the trial we can turn him over to the

Otherworld prison system. Trust me, they'll make him suffer for the rest of his life."

"Never!"

The Siren leapt toward Ella, his hands raised to her throat, his power arching inside her like an electrical storm. Even as she fired her gun, Vadim was quicker. Magic roared through him and the Siren was lifted in the air and slammed against the opposite wall. He landed in a tangle of limbs; his neck broken, his gray eyes wide open and tinged with shock. Blood dripped from his shoulder where Ella's bullet had lodged.

Vadim drew Ella close. "If I act now, I can bring him back to life in a different form and we can kill him again."

She shuddered. "No, once was quite enough, thanks."

"Are you sure?"

She punched him in the chest. "Stop showing off." He bent to kiss her mouth, kissed her again until she stopped shivering and returned the kiss. After a long while, she drew away from him. "We should call this in."

"We should." He headed for the door, still holding her hand. "Why the hell did you let him take you into his office like that?"

"Because I didn't realize who he was at that point." She glared at him. "He seemed so *nice*. I understand exactly how he got all those empaths to trust him now. As some weird kind of empath himself he understood and sounded as if he genuinely wanted what was best for them." She put her gun away. "Dammit, the man almost had me convinced."

Vadim took his cell phone out of his pocket. "What stopped you?"

She made a face. "You did."

His smile was slow in coming but incredibly self-satisfied. "I knew it."

"He wasn't expecting us to be fully mated. He couldn't gain total control of my mind because I'd already found someone to take on my psychic burden." Ella looked around the main office.

"No wonder he knew who to pick next. He knew everything about us."

"I'm sure there'll be a full investigation as to how he ended up working in here." Vadim pressed a few keys. "I wonder why he waited until the empaths chose a mate?"

"Either because he knew they wouldn't be going mad by themselves or because he wanted them to feel saved and relaxed when he came to call." Ella grimaced. "It depends whether you believe he genuinely wanted the best for empaths, or simply hated us and wanted more power."

"As I said, that will all come out in the investigation. Personally I think he was in it for the power and control. But I might be biased because he just tried to make you shoot me." He propelled her toward the door. "Let's get out of here before anything else happens."

"But won't they want to..." Ella stopped talking as she noticed the small gathering out by the main road.

"Oh hell," muttered Vadim.

He took her hand and walked into the center of the crowd. Sitting in the midst of a group of Fae was the most beautiful woman Ella had ever seen.

"Has she got anything to do with your reluctance to return to Otherworld?" Ella whispered.

"Yes."

"Are you engaged to her?"

"It's much worse than that."

"She's your wife?"

Vadim's laugh was short. "No, she's my grandmother."

"No way. She doesn't look old enough."

"That's because she's Fae."

"Morosov, she's wearing a crown." Ella smiled at the woman who had dark hair and blue eyes just like Vadim. She didn't smile back. "Are we going to say hello?"

"Unless we want to die a slow and painful death, I suppose

we have to." Vadim kept hold of Ella's hand and inclined his head a regal inch.

"Grandmother, may I introduce Miss Ella Walsh?"

"I know who she is, Cygnet."

"Then you'll know we are mated."

The Fae waved an impatient bejeweled hand. "Naturally. I am the one who arranged it."

Ella opened her mouth, but Vadim squeezed her fingers even more tightly in a clear signal for her to shut up.

"I wondered if that had anything to do with you." He bowed. "As you can see, you might have forced my temporary return to Otherworld, but not my compliance."

"You wish to stay bonded to this *human*? If you hadn't interfered that maniac would have killed her for you."

"I will never willingly give her up." Vadim smiled. "You have done me a great favor, Grandmother. I can now live legally in the human realm with my mate." He bowed again. "We have to get back to work now. It was a pleasure seeing you again. Take care."

Ella gulped as a roaring sound filled her ears and she found herself outside the SBLE building on Market still holding Vadim's hand.

"You don't need to use the portals?"

"Obviously not." Vadim dusted down his suit and headed toward the main lobby. "Are you coming? We need to get a special unit down to the Merton office immediately."

"Wait a minute. Did you just tell your grandmother that you mated with me so that you could live permanently on the human side?"

"It is one of the advantages a bonded male gets for mating with an empath."

"So I'm like your fricking psychic green card?" Ella scowled at him. "You're way more than fifty percent Fae, aren't you?"

He shrugged. "It depends on which version of my ancestry you believe."

"Bullshit! She tied you to me so that you'd come running back to Otherworld begging her to release you from our bond."

"I'm quite sure that was her original idea. But, as I said, she miscalculated."

Ella simply stared at him and wondered whether he could see the steam coming out of her ears. He was the most infuriating man she'd ever met.

"Why did your grandmother call you signet?"

"It's just a pet name."

She stamped her foot. "Dammit, Morosov, you aren't going to tell me anything, are you?"

He swung around and wrapped his hand around the back of her neck, yanking her hard against him. "I'll tell you this. We're mated. I'm staying and you're just going to have to suck it up and deal with it, soul sucker." He kissed her and then stepped away. "Got that, Ms. Walsh?"

He had already walked into the lobby and headed for the elevators before she deigned to follow him.

"Signet," she murmured. "Just a pet name. Pah."

A lone black feather floated toward her and she started to smile. "Silly me. Not *signet*. Cygnet. Baby swan."

A delightful vision of the future unrolled in front of her. How many references to Hans Christian Andersen, ballet and Natalie Portman's fingernails would she be able to get into their conversations before Vadim finally lost it?

There would be a ton of paperwork to fill out, but for once she was happy to do it. Laney and the rest of the empaths had been avenged. She found herself smiling at the thought of taking Vadim to see her mother over the weekend and maybe suggesting their future offspring might be able to fly... There was no point in letting Morosov think he had the upper hand quite yet. He might have declared his intentions, but she certainly hadn't declared hers.

She waved at Peach and waited for the elevator to return. She'd gotten over her fear of them. Life had suddenly become so much more *fun*.

DEAR READER,

If you enjoyed this book, please consider leaving a review at your favorite retailer.

If you want to read more of my books, please check out my website and consider joining my newsletter for the fastest updates and early contests to win new books.

katepearce.com/newsletter

Thank you for reading!
Kate Pearce

NEXT UP FOR ELLA AND VADIM...

Prologue

San Francisco

Brad Dailey woke to sunlight streaming through open blinds and wondered where the hell he was. The last thing he remembered was a bar in the city, being dumped by his chick and ending up talking to the bartender and the only other guy left in the place. Nice guys who'd drunk with him until he couldn't remember the girl's name, let alone why he'd liked her in the first place.

Her loss.

He swallowed, and his tongue stuck to the roof of his mouth like spit to an envelope. What the fuck had he ended up drinking? He was going to have the hangover from hell, and he was due in class at ten. He grabbed his cell phone and squinted at the numbers. It was already nine thirty. Even if he busted a gut, he'd never get there in time.

But he had to go. Dr. Blinz was a bastard. He'd be chucked out of the class if he didn't show up again, and his parents would kill him. With superhuman effort, he rolled out of bed and staggered toward the bathroom. First, he needed to pee real bad. That accomplished, he turned on the faucets and faced his reflection in the mirror.

And screamed.

CHAPTER 1

"What do you mean, I can't spend the night?"

Ignoring the interested glances of the other passengers on the packed Blue & Gold ferry to Tiburon, Ella glared right back at Vadim.

"You can't."

"Why not?"

"Because you haven't asked nicely, and I don't like being taken for granted. We might be stuck together for life, but it doesn't mean you own me or anything." She walked away from him and looked back at the city. The incoming fog crawling in under the Golden Gate Bridge was slowly swallowing up the gray, square lines and glinting glass buildings.

"Then why didn't you say something when I got on this damn boat with you?"

He was right behind her again. His voice was quiet, but fury emanated from every pore. He wore a long dark coat and blue cashmere scarf that screamed Italian designer. Tendrils of his black hair danced coyly in the breeze, caressing his awesome cheekbones. He might look like a model in the middle of a photo shoot, but he was much more than a pretty face.

She shrugged. "I don't know where you're living. I assumed you must have moved over here."

"I haven't moved anywhere. When the hell did I have time to

do that? Alexei left for Russia this evening. I paid off his extortionate bill, but kept my room on."

"Well, that's lucky. You can stay on the ferry and go right back again."

"You know damn well that this is the last one tonight."

She swiveled to face him, her arms crossed over her chest. "Then you know what you can do, don't you?"

"What's that, Ms. Walsh?" He moved so close that she could see into his dark blue eyes. So much bluer than the murky waters of the bay, and so much more dangerous too… His gaze flashed black, and her pulse jumped in her throat.

"You can use magic, Morosov, and fly away home."

"Yes, I can." He slowly let out his breath. "What I don't understand is what the hell is wrong with you. You've been treating me like dirt all day."

"What's new?" He didn't lighten up, and she looked away from his intense gaze. "I just need an evening to myself, that's all."

Silence greeted her remark. She concentrated on maintaining her mental shields, even though if he really wanted to get through them, he could do it with ease.

"You nearly died yesterday."

"So?"

"We've spent the last twenty-four hours being debriefed by the SBLE authorities, and now I want to sleep for a hundred years. With you."

"It's not just your decision, is it?" She hunched a shoulder at him. "Oh, for God's sake, Morosov, don't get all primitive and possessive. I really can't handle it at the moment."

"You can't handle it, period. That's why you don't want me here. You're scared."

"And you aren't?"

"At least I'm trying to deal with it."

"Well, good for you."

The ferry slowed and shuddered against the pull of the tide as, engines churning, it turned clumsily toward the dock. Seagulls flew off the sea wall to encircle the craft, looking for rich pickings from the tourists.

Ella pushed past Vadim and walked over to the stairs that led to the lower deck. She stomped down them and joined the line of passengers ready to exit the boat the moment it docked. She felt rather than saw him fall in behind her.

"Go *away*, Morosov."

"I'm just getting off the ferry."

"And then what will you do? Sit on the beach all night?"

"If I have to."

The older woman in the line in front of Ella turned around. "Is he annoying you, dear? Do you want me to call the cops?" Her gaze drifted up to Vadim's. "Wow, he's really cute. Are you sure you don't want him, because I'd take him off your hands in a second."

"Be my guest." Ella smiled at the woman. "He's almost house-trained."

"Ms. Walsh."

There was a definite note of warning in Vadim's tone, but when had that ever stopped her? She turned her attention to the deckhand who was opening the gate and shuffled forward with the rest of the weary commuters. The salty air hit her like a shot of tequila, and she breathed it in. After twenty-four hours stuck at the Supernatural Branch of Law Enforcement, she'd wanted to scream. Only the thought that her testimony would put on record who had been killing empaths had made her stay and endure the endless, repetitive questions from a bunch of morons who should know better.

"*Agreed.*"

Vadim's voice echoed in her head. Damn, she must be tired if she couldn't keep him out at this stage of the evening. She stumbled on the uneven deck, and he attempted to catch her elbow. She jerked away and almost fell again.

"Ella, let me help you. You're weaving around like a drunk."

"I'm fine. Go away."

He took hold of her arm and spun her around to face him. "I'm not going anywhere. I'm taking you home, where we will go to sleep. If you want to continue this discussion in the morning, when we're both refreshed, I'll be more than willing to do so." He paused. "Are you *mimicking* me?"

"I can't help it. You get so polite and Russian when you're pissed with me."

He let go of her and looked down at the ground. "I can't do this right now. Can we just go home?"

Without giving him a direct answer, she set off along the coastal path and up the hill, toward her basement apartment. Things really were bad if they didn't have the energy to fight with each other. He followed her silently, his breathing even, his presence a comfort she refused to acknowledge.

She still couldn't deal with the fact that she was a) alive and b) mated to an enigma. She'd confidently expected to go nuts in a week, when she turned twenty-seven. It happened to empaths. She'd assumed it would happen to her and had lived her whole life accordingly. But in a strange twist of fate, she'd ended up with Mr. "I'm not quite human" GQ.

She snorted. Strike that. He wasn't human at all. He was Fae fucking royalty.

"What's wrong?"

She'd stopped walking and was breathing hard through her nose.

"Nothing!"

Perhaps it was a good idea to let him spend the night. When she'd rested, she'd make sure to interrogate him thoroughly about his family in Otherworld before she let him eat or have sex with her ever again.

Not that she needed to have sex with him like she needed her next breath.

"Do you want a push up the hill?"

"I'm fine, thank you." She kept walking, her gaze fixed on the looming Victorian house with its white railings, steep steps and gabled roofline.

"I'll get the door."

He disappeared ahead of her. Could she do that now? Use magic to get stuff done? She hadn't actually asked Vadim how much of his power she could control and manipulate, now that they were bonded. She'd tried not to ask him anything at all.

By the time she reached the front door, he'd turned on the lights, started a fire in the grate and put the coffee on. Her mail was stacked on the countertop, and he was already in the bathroom sloshing water around. Not that she minded. He would always leave the place cleaner than when he'd entered it. It was one of his more endearing, yet annoying, habits.

Wearily, she stripped off her coat and hat and threw them toward the back of the couch. All she wanted was a shower and her bed and two days to sleep.

A blast of fragrant steam billowed out of the bathroom, and Vadim came out. He picked up her coat and put it over his arm.

"The shower's on. You go ahead. Do you want me to bring you some coffee or anything to eat?"

Ella just stared at him until he took her by the hand and gently pushed her into the bathroom. By the time she opened her mouth to reply, he'd closed the door behind him, leaving her alone. She took off her clothes and got into the shower, sighing as the hot water streamed over her. It took all her remaining energy to lift her arms long enough to shampoo her hair.

When she finally rinsed out the conditioner and could see again, a mug of herbal tea stood on the ledge next to her. Had Vadim come in while she was showering, or was he no longer hiding the extent of his abilities? She guessed the latter. After sipping the tea, she stepped out onto the fluffy mat and found two warm towels and her favorite pink bunny pajamas awaiting her.

Damn, the man was good.

She dressed and didn't bother to dry her hair, just wrapped it up in the towel and went back into the kitchen. He was standing at the kitchen counter, drinking coffee and watching something in the toaster. He'd taken off his coat, jacket and tie and rolled up his shirtsleeves.

"Are you sure you don't want something to eat?"

"No, thanks. I think I'll head straight to bed."

He looked up. "Good night, Ella."

"'Night, Morosov."

When she closed her bedroom door, she realized he'd put the bedside lamp on and turned on her heated blankie. With a sigh, she threw herself into bed and wrapped the warmed quilt around her. *Bliss.*

Twenty minutes later she opened one eye and listened intently to the silence around her. Where was Vadim? She couldn't sleep without knowing what he was doing.

She got out of bed and opened the door a crack. The scent of toasted bread floated over her, but the kitchen was in darkness and so was the bathroom. Had he really gone? A feeling not unlike terror clutched at her heart. She opened the door wider and stepped into the hallway.

"Morosov?"

A slight sound made her peer into the gloom. Was that a hint of white on the couch?

"Ouch!" She recoiled as her knee collided with the chair arm.

"Ella, are you all right?"

She fumbled her way to the seat, still holding her knee, and sat down. "You're sleeping on the couch?"

"Where else would I sleep?" His voice was low and husky. "It's better than the beach."

She touched his leg. "I thought you'd gone."

"Do you want me to?"

"No."

His fingers curled around hers, and he brought her hand to his mouth and kissed it. "Then go back to bed."

"Okay." He let go of her and she slowly stood up. "See you in the morning, then."

"I'll be here."

"Good to know." She went back to bed and slid between the sheets. With an exhausted sigh, she closed her eyes.

"You don't need to come and find me. You'll know if I've really gone."

"How?"

"You won't sense me in your head."

"That would be a blessing."

She waited but he didn't reply, and she gradually relaxed again. She might not have come to terms with him, or anything in her life yet, but she was glad he was there.

In her head.

In her heart?

With a groan, she rolled over and went to sleep.

"Coffee?"

Vadim held up the half-empty pot as Ella came out of the bathroom. She stared at him as if he were speaking Russian and briefly closed her eyes. Her blond hair was standing on end as if she'd stuck her finger in an electrical outlet He wouldn't put it past her. Concealing a smile, he found one of the mugs he'd just rewashed, filled it with coffee and put it on the countertop next to her.

"Do you want me to toast you a bagel?"

She clambered up onto the kitchen stool and nodded, both

hands wrapped around her mug of coffee as she inhaled the rising steam. He sliced the bagel, put it in the toaster and went to the refrigerator to get the cream cheese.

"I went out for a run earlier, so I got some supplies."

She sipped at her coffee, and her shoulders slowly came down from around her ears. It had been a stressful couple of days. "Thanks."

"You're welcome." He turned away and studied the newspaper until the bagel was toasted. "Did you sleep well?"

"I think so. I don't remember dreaming or anything."

"That's good." He'd had enough nightmares for both of them. He was surprised he hadn't woken her. "I'm not planning on going into the office today. How about you?"

"Hold it. Stop with the casual small talk." She pointed her knife at him. "Why aren't you on that plane going back to Russia with Alexei?"

"Because the SBLE decided I should stay here."

"Why?"

He shrugged. "I have no idea."

"They don't know about...us, do they?"

"I should imagine they'll work it out fairly quickly when you don't start going insane on your birthday."

"Oh, damn. I'd forgotten about that. Maybe I could pretend to go nuts?"

"And lose the job you love so much?" Ignoring her impression of sticking her fingers down her throat, he stuck another bagel in the toaster. "And remember, they won't necessarily know *whom* you're mated to, just that you are mated."

"But won't everyone wonder why you're still here?"

"The last I heard, everyone was hoping I'd stay because I'm the only partner you've ever worked with that you respect."

She stuck out her tongue at him. He handed her another bagel.

"So you're planning on staying, then?"

Despite the casual nature of her question, he heard the serious intent behind it.

"I thought I'd made that quite clear."

"Are you afraid I'll go nuts if you don't?"

He smiled down at his coffee. "No, I'm afraid I'll go nuts. I don't think I would function very well if I couldn't be with you."

She slammed her mug down on the countertop. "Morosov, don't *say* things like that. You're supposed to be running away from me, not offering yourself up for more punishment."

"It's just the way it is."

"I don't like it." She bit into her bagel and crumbs flew everywhere. He resisted the urge to fetch a dustpan and brush and gather them up. Maybe it would be better to wait until she finished...

"I can't change my nature, Ella."

"As to that." She swiveled on her seat so that she could face him. "What exactly are you? I know you're a swan shifter and some kind of Fae royalty. Is there anything else you'd like to tell me?"

"Don't you think that's enough to be getting along with?" He darn well hoped so. He had no intention of telling her the rest unless he was in mortal peril. "I'm sure you have questions."

She held out her coffee mug. "Fill this up first, and then we'll talk."

He studied her bunny pajamas and tatty white robe. "Don't you want to get dressed first?"

"Why? We're not going anywhere, are we?" She slid off the stool and headed for the couch.

Vadim waited until her back was turned and swiftly cleaned up the crumbs, put her plate in the sink and wiped off the surfaces. Picking up his own cup of coffee, he joined her on the couch. She'd kicked off her slippers. Her toenails were bright pink with orange sparkles. He wanted to kiss them...

He was in deep shit.

"So tell me about the shape-shifting first."

He forced his gaze back up to her face. "One of my... grandfathers is the current swan king. I get the ability from him."

"It's not much use is it? What can a swan actually do? Peck someone to death?"

"They can do much more than that."

"Yeah?" She tucked her feet up under her. "I hear they're really good at ballet and telling fairy tales, as well."

He took a long, slow breath and let it out through his nose. "Are you just going to mock, or are you actually interested in learning about the abilities you've acquired?"

"You have no sense of humor, Morosov."

"I believe you have enough for both of us." He stopped talking and just stared at her.

She sighed. "I suppose you can fly, right? That's quite useful. Can I do that?" By mating with him, she'd acquired his Other-world powers, and he'd stabilized her empath abilities. In fact, she'd come out of the deal really well. Maybe she should be more grateful.

"If you practice."

"Do I have to shape-shift?" She leaned forward. "*Can* I shape-shift?"

"I'm not sure. With my other powers, I can just grow wings and fly. I should imagine you'd be able to do that too."

"That's kind of cool." She picked up the cushion next to her. "And if you shed, I'll never have to worry about stuffing my cushions again."

He sipped his coffee. "How long are you going to keep this up?"

"The jokes?"

He inclined his head a frigid inch.

"For as long as I can think of them."

"Fine. Do you have any other questions for me?"

"I sure do, buster, don't think I'm that easy. Why didn't you mention that your grandmother is the queen of the Fae?"

"She's one of the queens. There are several warring factions in Otherworld."

"I know that, but I asked around the office yesterday, and she's considered the most powerful one at the moment."

"I didn't mention it, because it never came up."

"Bullshit. You didn't mention it, because you hate being associated with anything from Otherworld."

"Maybe that, as well." He was willing to concede the point if it kept her from inquiring further. "And as I told you before, the more I talk about my Otherworld connections, the more likely they are to become aware of me."

"Because you've been trying to hide out here and pass as human."

"Obviously not very successfully."

"You were doing pretty well, until I dragged you back there."

"Trust me, I'd love to blame you, but Rossa already knew I was here and was keeping an eye on me. It was just a matter of time before my grandmother found a way to try and force me back there."

"Why does she want you back?"

"Because I performed certain tasks for her and the Fae."

"Magical ones?"

"Usually."

"But what good is a shape-shifting swan?"

"You'd be surprised." She'd be horrified, but he definitely wasn't going to get into that. He stood up and held out his mug. "I'm getting more coffee. Do you want some?"

"No thanks." She handed him her empty mug. "Stick it in the sink. I'll use it later."

With an inward shudder, he put her mug in the dishwasher and refilled his own. "You're still a bit low on food. Do you want to go to the supermarket?"

She stretched her arms over her head and yawned until her jaw cracked. "I suppose I should."

His cell phone went off, and a second later he heard hers ring too. She wandered into the bedroom to get it as he answered his.

"Mr. Feehan."

"Vadim. We have a situation here. Can you liaise with Ella and meet her at San Francisco General? There's a man there I want you both to see."

"I'll do that, Mr. Feehan. We'll see you there as soon as we can."

He looked up to see Ella in the doorway of her bedroom, phone clamped to her ear. "It's Feehan. He left a message. He wants us to meet him at the hospital." She pouted. "So much for our day off."

Vadim shut his cell phone and put it back in his pocket. "How soon can you be ready to go?"

"Give me five minutes." She checked her cell. "There's a ferry leaving at ten, if we hurry. Where did you put my coat?"

"In the closet with mine."

She turned a slow circle. "Which closet?"

"The one by the front door, where you are supposed to hang things."

"Really?" She wandered over to it and opened it. "I always wondered what it was for."

She tossed him his coat and suit jacket and retrieved her own. "I'll just be a minute."

In less than ten, they were walking down the hill toward the ferry, which had just docked. A stream of tourists poured from the gangplank, their eager faces scanning the small town and exclaiming at the views back across the bay. Getting through them made Vadim feel like a lone salmon fighting to swim upstream against the current.

They made it just in time and headed for the top desk. He

would never tire of the view or the experience of approaching a great city by water. It was the first place he'd ever considered putting down roots. He glanced down at Ella in her blue and orange knitted hat, denim jacket and pink ripped jeans. But maybe it wasn't the place. Maybe it was her. His grandmother might have meddled in his life simply to force him back to Otherworld, but she'd started a whole chain of events he didn't even dare contemplate. He had no doubt that less benign forces would soon be on his tail, demanding his return. But now he had a mate to fight for and a reason to live.

He slowly shook his head. He was not going back willingly. They'd have to come and get him, and even in this realm, his powers still trumped most of theirs. With one snap of his fingers he could annihilate the entire city that lay before him. He smiled as they approached the pier. Let them come. He'd be more than ready.

End of Sample
To continue reading, be sure to pick up *Death Bringer* at your favorite retailer.

ALSO BY KATE PEARCE

FOR A FULL LIST PLEASE GO TO KATEPEARCE.COM/BOOKS

The Diable Delamere Series
Historical Romance
Completed Series

Regency dukes, disinherited aristocrats and a plot to assassinate the Prince Regent create plenty of problems for all the heroes and heroines as they struggle to trust each other in an ever-changing game of love, deceit and treachery.

.

The Millcastle Series
Historical Romance

On the cusp of the industrial revolution in the northern town of Millcastle the old and the new clash both in matters of business and of the heart. Can love flourish among the rush to make a profit?

.

The Harcourt Twins Duology
Historical Erotic Romance
Completed Series

Identical twins Gideon and Gervase Harcourt share more than a birthday and an insatiable interest in sex. They also believe in sharing their sexual expertise with the women they lust after in whatever combination is required. But when two very different women enter their lives will they be able to reconcile their complicated needs with their desire to fall in love?

.

The House of Pleasure Series

Historical Erotic Romance

Completed Series

Enter a Regency house of pleasure where nothing is forbidden and every sexual desire you have ever imagined can come true...

.

The Sinners Club Series

Historical Erotic Romance

Completed Series

When intrigue collides with heated passion behind the closed doors of the Sinners Club there is nowhere left to hide.

.

The Morgan Ranch Series

Contemporary Western Romance

Completed Series

A Northern Californian ranching family torn apart by tragedy reluctantly return home to discover not everything was as they thought it was, and that love, and forgiveness can sometimes go hand in hand.

.

The Millers of Morgan Valley Series

Contemporary Western Romance

Completed Series

When the mother you haven't seen for twenty years asks to visit your family ranch and set the record straight, how will her ex and six adult children react? The loves and sometimes messy lives of a ranching family.

·

The Three Cowboys Series
Contemporary Western Romance

The Three Cowboys series centers on three retired Marines living on a ranch in Northern California coming to terms in their own different ways with their experience in combat. From grumpy Noah and an unexpected baby to unruffled Luke who hides things almost too well, and the prickly puzzle of Max, each man will find the perfect woman to bring them to their knees—but not without navigating a lot of bumps in the rocky road to true love along the way.

·

The Turner Brothers Series
Contemporary Erotic Western Romance
Completed Series

As the oldest sibling in a spectacularly dysfunctional family, Grayson Turner has made it his life's mission not only to distance himself from his famous father, but to connect with the half-siblings his father's multiple marriages scattered across the country. Getting to know his siblings and creating trust between them hasn't been easy, but Grayson is determined to succeed because he, Jay and Dakota all deserve a happy ending with the women they love.

·

The Obsidian Series
Sci-Fi Romance

Join a renegade band of telepaths roaming the galaxy to protect and rescue their race from the evil empire intent on destroying them.

The Planet Valhalla Series
Sci-Fi Erotic Romance
Completed Series

A human female crash lands on a planet full of men descended from the Vikings, one of whom is the King who claims her as his mate— what could possibly go wrong? A sexy romp through the stars with excessive sex, a touch of humor and some very satisfied women...

The Triad Series
Sci-Fi Erotic Romance
Completed Series

Welcome to an imaginary world where civilizations clash against the new and unknown, where telepaths are revered and reviled, and where your destiny can be preordained by a living oracle. Add in a group of super-soldier telepaths rescued from Earth, and forming sexual triads for life becomes even more complex and life changing.

The Kate Pearce Paranormal Romance Series
Paranormal Historical Romance

A collection of lighthearted historical paranormal novellas centered in a mystical faerie-ridden village in Cornwall. If you enjoy love at first sight, mistaken identity, ghostly and mystical advice, and fated lovers then you're in for a treat!

The Soul Justice Series

Paranormal Urban Fantasy Romance

Completed Series

The *Soul Justice* series by Kate Pearce is a paranormal urban fantasy romance set in a world where supernatural law enforcement agents uphold the balance between the realms.

·

The Kurland St. Mary Mysteries Series

Historical Mystery

Writing as Catherine Lloyd

Completed Series

Join wounded cavalry hero Major Sir Robert Kurland and Lucy Harrington, the rector's eldest daughter, as they solve crimes in their quiet little village and gradually learn to appreciate each other.

·

The Miss Morton Mystery Series

Historical Mystery

Writing as Catherine Lloyd

Miss Morton, the daughter of a disgraced peer, is forced to seek employment and navigate her way through a society that no longer wishes to acknowledge her existence. But with her no-nonsense employer at her side, Caroline discovers her rebellious nature and that family and friends can be found in the most unlikely of situations— even while investigating the occasional murder.

ABOUT KATE PEARCE

New York Times and *USA Today* bestselling author Kate Pearce was born in England in the middle of a large family of girls and quickly found that her imagination was far more interesting than real life. After acquiring a degree in history and barely escaping from the British Civil Service alive, she moved to California and then to Hawaii with her kids and her husband and set about reinventing herself as a romance writer.

She is known for both her unconventional heroes and her joy at subverting romance clichés. In her spare time she self publishes science fiction erotic romance, historical romance, and whatever else she can imagine. You can find Kate at katepearce.com.

🅐 amazon.com/author/katepearce

🅖 goodreads.com/katepearce

🆱🅱 bookbub.com/authors/kate-pearce

🅕 facebook.com/KatePearceAuthor

𝕏 x.com/kate4queen

www.ingramcontent.com/pod-product-compliance
Lightning Source LLC
Chambersburg PA
CBHW020332180626
46812CB00001B/158

* 9 7 8 1 9 5 7 7 2 7 0 5 9 *